About the author

Complications are the last thing surgeons want to encounter when they operate on their patients and they make every effort to avoid them. After many years evaluating such cases for Quality Assurance, Dr. Herbert Perry, a surgeon with over fifty years of experience, wondered if it would be possible to develop a plausible account of a surgeon who does just the opposite knowing it might be impossible to judge complications that are otherwise indistinguishable from ones that occur during well-intentioned surgical procedures. *Paper Drapes, Paper Gowns* is that account.

This is a work of fiction. Names, characters, businesses, places, events and incidents are either the products of the author's imagination or used in a fictitious manner. Any resemblance to actual persons, living or dead, or actual events is purely coincidental.

PAPER DRAPES, PAPER GOWNS

PAPER DRAPES, PAPER GOWNS

HERBERT S. PERRY, M.D.

Vanguard Press

VANGUARD PAPERBACK

© Copyright 2023
Herbert S. Perry, M.D.

The right of Herbert S. Perry, M.D. to be identified as author of this work has been asserted by him in accordance with the Copyright, Designs and Patents Act 1988.

All Rights Reserved

No reproduction, copy or transmission of this publication may be made without written permission.
No paragraph of this publication may be reproduced, copied or transmitted save with the written permission of the publisher, or in accordance with the provisions of the Copyright Act 1956 (as amended).

Any person who commits any unauthorised act in relation to this publication may be liable to criminal prosecution and civil claims for damages.

A CIP catalogue record for this title is available from the British Library.

ISBN 978 1 80016 474 1

Vanguard Press is an imprint of
Pegasus Elliot Mackenzie Publishers Ltd.
www.pegasuspublishers.com

First Published in 2023

Vanguard Press
Sheraton House Castle Park
Cambridge England

Printed & Bound in Great Britain

To all those who chose medicine and worked very hard to maintain the highest ethical and technical standards.

I

Phil Berger stepped out of the elevator and walked towards the OR suite. He glanced quickly into the waiting area where friends and family members gathered while the patients were undergoing surgery. This was not the preferred route for most surgeons, but Phil thought it was a reasonable courtesy. Also, he avoided slighting anyone he knew, and later being chided by them even though that was most often meant in jest.

At first, he did not recognize anyone but then he spotted Ann Hartway leafing through a magazine. He'd seen her husband, Jack, in his office about six months earlier for a vascular problem. He started towards the operating room but then thought the better of it and stepped back into the waiting area.

"Hello, Ann. What brings you here?"

"Oh, hi Phil. Jack's inside, having his leg worked on." She got up from her chair and walked over to him. "I don't want to shout across the room," she said in a lower tone. "It's that same problem he had when he saw you last year. It doesn't seem to have gotten worse, but he's been more concerned about his diabetes and I think he was getting impatient. He really wanted to come back to you, but he felt you still wouldn't want to do anything. Someone recommended Dr. Stallings. I'd seen him myself, years ago. The way he explained things, Jack decided to have the surgery." She waited for his response.

"Well, I'm sorry he didn't come back to see me. We could have discussed it further. In any case, I'm sure Dr. Stallings feels he's doing the right thing." It seemed appropriate to offer his reassurance although it made him uncomfortable. "What is he planning to do?"

"A bypass."

"That's certainly one option. Well, Jack should do fine. I'll stop in to say hello in a few days when he's feeling better. I just got back from vacation, so I really don't know what's been going on for the past week. I'll talk to you again, Ann. Good luck."

He continued down the corridor scarcely paying attention to anyone. Should he have given more thought to surgery in Jack Hartway's case? He hoped Ann wouldn't notice that he was disturbed. It wasn't just a matter of losing a case to another surgeon. Now there was the question of being too conservative. No matter how convinced he was that his original decision not to operate was correct, all it ever took to start a lot of soul-searching and self-doubt was for another surgeon to offer a totally different recommendation and the patient to accept it.

Phil Berger was not looking forward to a particularly pleasant day.

After he had gotten into his scrub suit, he put on the disposable paper shoe covers, cap, and mask the hospital had recently began using and entered the operating room where his patient was waiting. The other members of his team were already there awaiting his arrival.

"Could you say hello to your patient, Dr. Berger, so that I may put him to sleep, and have you proceed with your operation? You are back from vacation now, aren't you?" George Bigelow, the anesthesiologist, couldn't resist the comment. Phil recognized the teasing in his tone but felt too distressed to respond. He addressed only the patient.

"Hi, Mr. Schaeffer. Sorry I'm late. We'll have that hernia fixed very shortly. I'll call Mrs. Schaeffer as soon as we're finished. You've met Dr. Rogoff, I hope?" He pointed to Valentin Rogoff who was already completely scrubbed and gowned, sitting on a stool.

"Dr. Rogoff will be assisting me." With that last remark, a cavernous yawn heralded the effect of the sodium pentothal administered even as Phil continued to talk to his patient.

"Impeccable timing, George," he said.

"You too, Phil. Now will you get on with this goddamn case. You've had us all waiting for over twenty minutes."

The repair proceeded very quickly. Both surgeons had worked together sufficiently often to complement each other well. Valentin Rogoff sensed Phil's displeasure and, aside from the usual inquiries about his vacation, made no other effort to maintain a conversation. It was Phil who finally brought up the subject of the operation going on two doors down from their room.

"Were things pretty busy while I was gone, Rogie?" he asked. "The usual."

"I haven't completely finished rounds or been to the office yet, so I don't know what catastrophes are waiting for me. I've already found one of my patients under the knife, so to speak, with one of our colleagues."

"Oh, yes. Who's that?"

"Jack Hartway. I guess Stanley Stallings is doing a femoro-popliteal bypass on him right now."

"Are you implying something improper is going on?" Dr. Rogoff's eyebrows arched, and his sarcasm was obvious. "I could never believe that, you know. I hope you are not about to impugn the most sacred and inviolate rule of our profession's code of ethics, that one surgeon might try to lure away another surgeon's patient. I've never heard of this happening."

"You're very funny, Rogie, but it wasn't one of those. I'd seen this fellow, months earlier for some mild claudication and I didn't think anything should be done then but now Stanley has me wondering. He had some reduced Doppler pressures but otherwise his circulation seemed pretty reasonable. He would get symptoms only while playing tennis and then it was just some mild cramping. I can't even remember which leg it was. It didn't seem like much of a history, and I didn't think it was time to do an arteriogram."

"Well, that's a judgment thing," Dr. Rogoff replied. "Maybe the patient pushed Stanley a bit. Of course, it doesn't take much pushing to get Stanley into the operating room."

"I don't know, Rogie, unless his symptoms had really worsened. I can't help wondering if I should have been more aggressive. I must admit this whole thing really bothers me."

"I thought you had something on your mind this morning. Anyway, you will have answers in a few days. If the patient gets a good result and is much happier afterwards, then perhaps you should have acted differently. If he doesn't, then perhaps you were right, and Stanley is wrong. And of course, the patient then has a much bigger problem. In any event, your patient, Mr. Schaeffer, should be very happy. That was a very nice job. You won't need me to close the skin, will you?"

"Oh, no. Thank you very much, Rogie. I can finish the rest." Despite his preoccupation Phil had all but completed the repair except for the skin closure. Fortunately, the case had been quite straightforward.

"Thanks again, Rogie," he said as Dr. Rogoff left the room. In two or three days he'd op into Jack Hartway's room just to let him know he wasn't annoyed. Under the circumstances he felt that would be the proper thing to do.

He finished applying the dressing. "Thank you very much, everyone," he called to the others, realizing he had largely ignored them during the case. Perhaps he shouldn't have discussed his concerns so openly in their presence but then again, these were comments they had certainly heard before.

"You're welcome, Dr. Berger. Have a nice day."

Although he realized it would be difficult, he thought he would at least try.

Over the next few days, Phil found himself thinking less about Jack Hartway than he thought he would. The pace had picked up considerably as he tried to clear up matters left over from his vacation as well as new patients scheduled for that week. In very short order it had once again become a matter of too many things to do and too little time in which to get them done. Late Thursday afternoon, three days after the surgery on Mr. Schaeffer and Jack Hartway, he was called to the emergency room to see a thirteen-year-old boy with right lower quant pain and probable early appendicitis.

As soon as he was certain of the diagnosis, he called the operating room to schedule the case for that evening.

"We have another case scheduled before we can let you do your appendix, Dr. Berger," the evening OR nurse replied over the phone. "Dr. Stallings is bringing back the femoro-popliteal he did on Monday. He's going to try Fogarty catheters first, but he said he'll probably have to do an arteriogram and may even have to redo the graft. You know how long that can take. Should I get another team in?"

Phil hadn't expected this and for an instant was too stunned to reply. He had really thought Dr. Stallings would get an excellent result and it would look as though Phil was the one to have misjudged Jack Hartway's complaint. He felt bad for the patient, but, at the same time, also an undeniable sense of relief.

He heard himself answering, "No, the patient had lunch. We can wait."

"That's good. The other girls wouldn't be too happy coming in now. What's the patient's name and what floor is he going to?"

Phil gave her the information and then tried to sort out his thoughts. He had felt very defensive at first, convinced he had probably made an incorrect judgment, but now he felt vindicated, just as if he had been on trial since Monday. And Stanley Stallings was no longer someone who had simply upstaged him. He was the guilty one now, not just of poor judgment but more seriously, of some sort of error in management leading to a very significant complication. In his mind Phil Berger committed himself to a virtual inquisition of Stanley Stallings if Jack Hartway did poorly. In no way would he let this case be explained away like so many others, with vague half-answers and inaccurate recollections. Stanley Stallings was going to have to describe this one, just the way it really happened. Phil decided to go home and wait for the OR to call. The surgery on Jack Hartway might take a very long time.

The telephone rang at ten p.m. and Phil picked it up on the first ring. The OR would be ready for him in forty-five minutes. That meant the surgery on Jack Hartway had taken at least five hours and probably longer. That had ominous implications for a second attempt on a vascular case. He knew it wouldn't be long before he would have all the details.

He got to the hospital in time to have a short conversation with the patient's parents outside the operating room and to reassure them. He quickly changed into a scrub suit, put on the cap, mask and shoe covers and had a very brief chat with the patient. He was a pleasant, well-behaved thirteen-year-old boy who didn't seem the least bit apprehensive. For a moment he reflected on how the young boy would probably be a very good patient postoperatively, taking pretty much everything in his stride. He thought he'd probably go home in two to three days.

"How'd the other case go?" he tried to ask casually as he was being helped into his gown. He double-checked to be certain his patient was asleep.

"Terribly," answered Betty Strong, the circulating nurse. "How do most of these cases go when you have to bring them back? He'll probably lose his leg."

This was much worse than he had imagined.

"It's that bad?"

"It's that bad. Dr. Stallings is afraid the patient won't consent to an amputation. That's probably what we should have done tonight."

"You mean the leg is gangrenous already?"

"No, but it's cold and blue from the calf down and it wasn't any better after we finished tonight."

"That's just awful. I know the patient. What does Dr. Stallings think went wrong?"

"He thinks the patient's saphenous vein was too small. He thinks now he should have used an artificial graft. He put in a Gore-Tex tonight after the Fogarty catheters didn't work but he thinks there's already too many vessels clotted in the leg. The arteriogram didn't look good."

"He's also diabetic," Dr. Mary Chen, the anesthesiologist, added. "I hope there was a good reason for doing him in the first place. It's terrible to see a thing like this. He's only forty-five."

Phil took a deep breath. "Well, I don't know what else to say. Anyway, let's get going with this little guy." He motioned for a prep stick. "There shouldn't be any complications here and I told the parents we'd be out in forty-five minutes."

He began the appendectomy.

Jack Hartway continued to deteriorate over the next few days. Although Phil did not feel he could visit him under the present circumstances, he did hear enough through conversations around the hospital that the situation was very bad and yet the patient continued to refuse amputation. Several days later he ran into Ann Hartway while she was visiting. She was about to enter the elevator on the first floor of the Humboldt Pavilion when she saw him approaching and stepped back so that he could catch up. Phil hesitated and then started towards her, trying to decide what he should say.

"I'm sorry Jack is having such a tough time, Ann. I purposely haven't been in to see him because I didn't think my presence would be of any help. I've heard from enough of the people involved that there are some very serious problems."

"Thank you, Phil. I understand. It would be awkward. I just don't know what's going to happen at this point. They want to take his leg off and Jack just outright refuses."

"Is it gangrenous now? I couldn't be sure from what I've been hearing." Phil asked the question even though he had been told two days ago there was gangrene to the mid-calf level.

"The lower leg is black. I've seen it myself. Even he's seen it, but he refuses to accept it. He says it will be all right."

"Doesn't he realize what will happen to him if he doesn't have an amputation?"

"It's been explained to him a hundred times. He says it's going to heal. There's nothing anyone can do while he's like this. In every other way his mind seems clear. He's been on the phone with his office every day, even today."

Phil suddenly became aware of their visibility, discussing Jack's condition right next to the busiest elevators in the hospital. People were passing by undoubtedly catching portions of their conversation. He noticed one after another staring intently and guided Ann Hartway to a less crowded part of the lobby.

"I didn't realize the situation was so difficult, Ann. I'm really very sorry. How about your daughters? How have they been handling it?"

"That's probably the worst part. They're crying all the time. They can't even visit him now, they're so upset."

"They're how old now, Ann?"

"Thirteen and eleven."

"Doesn't Jack realize what may happen to them—that they can lose their father? Hasn't that been explained to him?"

"Everything's been explained to him. I've even spoken with the hospital's lawyers, and they say nothing can be done while he's in control of his senses."

"What about a court order?"

"Dr. Stallings would like to avoid that. He feels Jack will accept the amputation much better in the long run if he is the one to agree to it. His brother is flying in from Chicago this evening and will try to talk to him. If he can't get him to agree, maybe we'll have to do the other. I just don't know." She looked distraught. "I'm so afraid, Phil. Jack hasn't always been the easiest person to live with and after this, I know it's going to get worse. He'll know I allowed the amputation and he'll always blame me. That's probably what will happen. The lawyers said that as soon as it's obvious that he's so sick that he's no longer responsible for himself, then I'll be able to give permission for the surgery and they'll do the amputation."

"You have to worry about time, Ann. You don't want it to be too late."

"I know, Phil. I can see that Jack's eyes and skin are yellow and they're also worried about how much urine he's making. I've been warned that these could be serious problems. You tried to tell us last year that this could happen, didn't you, Phil?"

"The operation could have gone well, Ann. I only felt if the operation were to be done, it should be done for a good enough reason. I didn't think the reason was good enough then, but maybe things changed. I'm in no position to say anything else. I only hope Jack gets through this in the best way possible, and I really mean that."

"Thank you, Phil. I know you do. And you have made me feel a little better." She placed her hand on his arm and very slowly drew it away.

Both knew there was nothing further to be said and Phil watched Ann walk away and then disappear into the next elevator. He stood there for a moment thinking about what he had said to her. He had been sincere. He was concerned and had tried to console her and knew she appreciated this. This pleased him and he was glad they had finally been able to talk while Jack Hartway was still in the hospital. But there was one thing that bothered him then and still bothered him now. He just couldn't believe there was any way that Jack Hartway could have needed that operation. He would wait, though, for the next surgical staff conference, to have Dr. Stallings try to convince him otherwise. He knew the case would have to be presented. He just didn't know if it would be as a complication, or as a mortality

II

Jack Hartway died exactly two weeks to the day on which his wife and Phil Berger had spoken at the elevator. His brother had arrived from Chicago that same day and after an initially warm, loving exchange of concern for one another, their meeting gradually deteriorated into a very angry, although subdued, exchange of pleadings, refusals, threats, and then, insults. The brother finally left, totally frustrated, confused, and not in any way able to understand his own brother's decision not to allow the amputation. Two days later, Jack Hartway lapsed into a coma and Ann Hartway signed the consent for surgery. The surgery was performed promptly by Stanley Stallings but by that time there was irreversible failure of both the liver and the kidneys. The patient was kept alive for one week with dialysis although everyone knew the situation was hopeless, and at the end of that time it was discontinued. He never regained consciousness before his death. His condition had deteriorated so, through sepsis and multiple organ failure, that not even his corneas were considered for donation and implantation elsewhere.

Since he had anticipated Jack Hartway's death, from the time he had become comatose, Phil Berger's reaction to it was very reserved. He purposely avoided any comment and found an excuse to leave if it were mentioned in conversations with his colleagues. There would be only one place appropriate for his comments and that would be at the next surgical conference, after Stanley Stallings had made his presentation.

The meeting took, place, as was the weekly custom, at twelve thirty p.m. the following Friday. Phil arrived several minutes early and found an unusually large number of staff members already present. At this time of the year, July and August, there were many new people on the hospital staff, both physicians and nurses. First-year residents had started their training on July 1 and most of the recent nursing school graduates had been on staff an even shorter period of time. The surgical conferences were geared more to the house staff during the summer months, for the purpose of indoctrination and training. Phil noticed that the first case to be presented was a multiple trauma patient. This was quite expected as it had become rather a tradition to introduce the new residents to the management of multiple trauma, early in their first year at Middle Valley General Hospital. The hospital was located in an area of considerable industrial development and also at the convergence of several major highways. Therefore, it was the main receiving station for a great deal of trauma and the residents would be expected to become quite proficient with the initial management of these cases.

Phil was somewhat familiar with the first case. A twenty-nine-year-old postal worker was driving home rather late one night and had forgotten to keep his eyes on the road. He apparently must have remembered to look up just as his car was about to go under the rear end of a slow-moving flat-bed trailer and he managed to throw his head back far enough to avoid decapitation but not enough to prevent his face from winding up in the back seat. He sustained multiple fractures of all four of his extremities as well as his pelvis and the reconstruction of his face was a tour de force for the plastic surgeons. Phil had heard about the case from Gary Barlow, his closest friend on the surgical staff and the general surgeon who had initially attended the patient — he would be presenting the case. And whereas this type of clinical presentation could most often be extremely boring, Gary Barlow had just enough of an unpredictable and outrageous sense of humor to make his presentation, if not enlightening, at least amusing and off-beat. In addition, he had a passionate disdain for anything that even suggested traditional medical protocol.

Malcolm Mueller, Middle Valley's chief of surgery for the past nine years, made his customary opening comments at the start of the meeting, particularly thanking all those present for attending, even though it was mandatory for house staff and all members of the surgery department. He quickly turned the meeting over to Gary Barlow who wasted no time in drawing on the similarities between the injuries suffered by the patient and the many combat injuries he saw as a surgeon with the US Army in Vietnam. His experience there made him the acknowledged expert in trauma at Middle Valley although any reference to this exposure was always regarded as grandstanding by his colleagues. It did, however, impress the house staff and his patients.

His narration continued in a most uncharacteristic bland manner. At one point he did comment that, except for an initial tracheostomy, there had been very little else for him to do other than watch the fluid and electrolytes while the other specialists — the orthopedists and plastic surgeons in particular — had a field day. In every other instance of this sort the least he could have expected, he ventured, would have been a ruptured spleen but even this failed to materialize after four days of observation. This brought a smattering of laughter from the audience, but it was restrained and certainly not up to the level of his previous presentations. Perhaps since his role in this case had become one of coordinating the efforts of all those who were involved in the patient's care, it was just this level of involvement that was responsible for his very colorless and indifferent presentation. Certainly, it did nothing to alter Phil Berger's mood prior to the next presentation, which would be that of Stanley Stallings.

The first case was concluded by each of the surgical specialists summarizing his or her management of the patient's specific injuries. Since x-ray studies were pertinent to each one's presentation and each of these was described in detail, the case seemed to drag on interminably. However, because of its excessive length the usual question-and-answer period was deferred, and Stanley Stallings began placing Jack Hartway's arteriogram on the x-ray view box. Dr. Mueller's introductory remarks were very brief and referred only to the next case having had a very unexpected result and that it represented some unusual aspects in the management of complications following vascular surgery.

Phil was not interested in the entire description of Jack Hartway's case. His main concern was whether or not Stanley Stallings would try to make Jack Hartway's symptoms seem worse than they were, thus making the surgery seem justified at the time. He also had to see how much disease was demonstrated by the arteriograms. He had not seen them previously. He listened carefully as Stanley Stallings proceeded in the customary fashion, first stating the patient's chief complaint, and then describing additional pertinent history. This enabled the audience to further appreciate the degree of disability imposed upon the patient by the vascular insufficiency. Surprisingly, his description of these symptoms did not differ very much from Phil's recollection of the history he had obtained. Dr. Stallings made frequent references to the patient's repeated insistence that something be done to correct the problem, which the patient felt was getting worse. Indeed, his own initial recommendation had been to defer surgery, but after hearing that the patient had already been to one surgeon who would not operate and was determined to find one who would, he decided to order an arteriogram; particularly after Doppler studies had shown a significant op in pressure in the lower leg. At this point he went to the view box and began to describe the arteriogram. An area of significant narrowing was clearly evident in the superficial femoral artery in the right lower thigh. Except for some minimal irregularity of the artery in other areas, the remainder of the vessels were quite satisfactory, and it should have been expected that the patient would obtain a good result from the surgery. He went on to describe the operative procedure and why he felt it failed. Of course, the patient's death was a needless tragedy and one that could have easily been prevented if only the patient had consented to an amputation. A discussion then followed on the medico-legal aspects of the patient's refusal to permit amputation and it was generally agreed that the surgeon was powerless to act as long as the patient seemed to be in control of his faculties. There was even further support for Dr. Stallings' course of action when he made it known that Jack Hartway had threatened him with a malpractice action if he did perform the amputation.

Phil had not expected Jack Hartway's case to be presented quite this way. He had thought it would be obvious that his surgery was inappropriate but now it seemed it was more a matter of individual judgment. The arteriogram in particular lent a great deal of credence to the patient's symptoms and certainly its appearance would have made one expect a good surgical result.

Nevertheless, Phil felt more discretion was warranted and when questions were asked from the audience, he raised his hand and was the first person called upon by Dr. Stallings.

"Dr. Berger, you have a question?"

"Yes, Stanley. Thank you. First, I'd like to get some clarification. For years it seemed to be an established policy in this department that vascular reconstructions would only be done for limb salvage. More recently this has been extended to cases of intractable pain and severe disability because of claudication. Now I know each case has to be individualized but in view of the potentially disastrous complications that can occur, and do occur, in these cases, don't you think surgery should be reserved only for those cases where there is absolute necessity for it? After all, this patient was not in any danger of losing his leg, but now as a result of the surgery, he's lost his life, and I really don't think we can blame his reluctance to accept amputation for his death. I can certainly appreciate the findings in this case and can understand why surgery must be considered, but I can't help but feel that it should be reserved for more advanced cases, particularly when a failure is going to mean an amputation, at the very least. I would also like to know if you considered using a balloon catheter to dilate the vessel since this procedure has less risk and might be appropriate for the type of stenosis we see here?"

Dr. Stallings thought for a moment. "I think I'll answer the last part of your question first. That may be easier. I personally do not think balloon angioplasty gives as good long-term results and serious complications have been reported with its use. As I mentioned earlier, and most of you seemed to agree, the appearance of the arteriogram certainly seemed to suggest that a bypass would be successful. I had no—"

"I'm not so concerned with the operative procedure, Stan, as I am with its timing."

The intensity in Phil's voice could not be ignored as he cut Dr. Stallings short. "I would think if his symptoms flared up only after playing one or two sets of tennis, which is a stop-and-go sport, that's really not an adequate indication for an operation with this much potential for serious complications. He was never bothered at other times, as you yourself said. I don't think it makes any difference how avid a tennis player the patient is. If he made a living at it, that would be a different situation."

"I think his symptoms were considerably worse than the way you've described them," Dr. Stallings replied. "The patient did mention to me that he had seen you earlier for the same problem and you advised against surgery, but his symptoms were not as bad then. I'm certain I would have made the same recommendation, but his claudication had become worse since then."

Phil was annoyed that Dr. Stallings had revealed his previous contact with the patient. He did not want his comments to appear as if they might be motivated by something other than pure surgical curiosity. He tried not to notice if his colleagues, who had been listening quite intently to the discussion, were visibly upset by the remark. He was most anxious to avoid any comments that might suggest that this was a personal matter between the two surgeons. Dr. Stallings continued.

"Even at that time, I didn't think surgery was indicated until I saw the arteriograms. I still feel the decision to operate was correct. I had no way of foreseeing the difficulty I would have in using the patient's vein for the graft or the final result. The best results, of course, are obtained with the patient's own vein, but in this case some other material would have been a better choice. Also, I should add had I known the patient would not agree to an amputation if the procedure failed and amputation became necessary, then I never would have done the surgery at the outset. I strongly agree with Dr. Berger that these conditions and procedures are fraught with all kinds of difficulties and should be done only after the most careful consideration." He paused for any further comments or new questions but both Phil and the audience seemed to have had enough and it was then left to Malcolm Mueller to make his comments about the case.

"I was particularly interested in having Stanley present this case because of the very unusual medico-legal aspects, which, I'm afraid, had very disastrous consequences for the patient. I'm also glad the discussion brought out a question I might have had, that being the timing of the procedure. I think it is very beneficial for the house staff to become aware that there are often valid reasons for differing opinions and often no one can be sure who is correct. It is unfair, in retrospect, to use the often referred to 'retrospectroscope,' to decide what should have been the proper approach. These are matters of individual judgment and as long as they do not deviate too far from accepted standards of practice, quite differing courses of treatment can have merit. Could we have the presentation of the next case now, please?"

Phil did not pay too much attention to the last two presentations. His mind was too preoccupied with trying to get a clearer perspective of Jack Hartway's case. He had to admit, after having heard Stanley's reasoning, that it was probably just a legitimate difference in attitude towards this type of case. He was even somewhat pleased with himself that he hadn't been more vocal about his feelings before the presentation and thereby avoided giving the impression that there was more to his sentiments about Dr. Stallings than just an occasional professional disagreement.

As he walked down the hall after the conference had finished, he suddenly felt a hand on his shoulder. He turned and saw Dr. Valentin Rogoff.

"Did you enjoy your day in court, counselor? That was your friend Stanley presented, wasn't it?"

"That was him," Phil said. "I listened to that presentation and I'm trying to be fair, but somehow I still have the thought we may have been had."

"It probably wouldn't be the first time."

"I guess. These conferences can really be aggravating at times."

"I think I know what you mean. It certainly would be nice to know what he's really thinking with some of his cases."

"You get that feeling, too? I always thought I was the only one."

Rogie laughed. "The man is one of a kind, a master of subterfuge, and that's the problem. I think a few of us know it, but what can you do? He can talk himself out of anything, and he always does. End of story, just like this case."

Phil looked at Rogie. "I'm glad to hear you say that. He just about had me believing it this time. Damn!"

Just then they became aware of rapidly approaching footsteps, faint at first but becoming much louder as they drew close. Taken aback somewhat, they glanced at each other just as the gangling figure of Dr. Stallings rushed past. Then just as abruptly, Dr. Stallings' pace slowed, and he looked back.

"Sorry I have to run like this but they're waiting for me upstairs. It's a terrible shame about that patient, Phil. I really expected a much better result. I know you had a personal interest in the case, but you can't feel any worse than I do." His tone became supplicating as he stood, arms out, palms up. Phil winced but Stallings didn't appear to notice.

"Then to have him refuse an amputation. Who could ever have expected that?" Dr. Stallings shook his head. "This whole thing has devastated me. Treating vascular problems can be bad enough, but then not to be able to treat the complication." His voice shuddered. "I really do have to get upstairs."

Phil was able to catch his expression for only a split second before he briskly resumed his pace leaving the two behind. He did seem upset.

There was a brief silence. Phil looked at Rogie.

"Well, what did you think of all that?"

"I really don't know. I know what I said before but maybe we're too hard on the guy sometimes. Maybe it was an honest effort, and it just didn't work out. How can you ever really know with him?"

"That's your answer. OK, I follow you. Either way you have to take your hat off to him. He's either very compassionate and concerned or we've just witnessed one of the greatest performances we'll ever see. To put it the best way I can, he wins again."

Rogie nodded and thought for a moment. "There's one other thing that should be mentioned." He spoke very deliberately. "You can be awfully annoying at times, Phil."

He couldn't hide the smirk on his face and they both laughed. But there may have been more truth in what was said than either was willing to admit.

III

The next two months were uneventful and gratifyingly pleasant for Phil Berger. He was quite busy; his cases were going well, and collections were exceptionally satisfactory. He managed to make his quarterly malpractice premium payment, which was over $10,000, without having to borrow the money and twice got into the city for dinner and shows with his wife, Maralyn. His two daughters were well into their respective new school years, achieving very high grades. In fact, if he were having any problems and if the problems were with any particular doctor, it wasn't Stanley Stallings but rather with the irrepressible Dr. Gary Barlow.

On one particular Monday morning he came into Phil's operating room just as a ligation and stripping of varicose veins was to begin. Phil was prepping the patient's leg, which was being held in the air by the circulating nurse Betty Stieve.

"What's the matter, Phil? You don't ask your buddies for help on your cases anymore?"

"How are you, Gary? I'm just trying to give the resident some experience tying knots. Anyway, I know you have a case scheduled in the next room."

"Yup, just a breast biopsy. Not a big vascular case like you're doing. Actually, I came in here to ask if you want to go out to Las Vegas with me in November for a workshop on colonoscopy. It's 3½ days and 24 continuing medical education credits. I'm gonna need 'em by the end of the year. I just found out they disallowed all my Wednesday afternoon tennis matches even though I always played against doctors."

That produced some snickering and polite laughter but apparently that was not enough for Gary Barlow.

"Oops, just a second, Phil. I think I see a pretty serious problem."

Phil quickly stopped the prepping and stepped back from the table looking for something that may have been contaminated.

"Just look at this," Gary said as he walked to the tape rack, took a roll of three-inch tape and walked back to Betty Stieve's side. While holding up the patient's leg, Betty's OR top had risen to her waist exposing an opening on the side of her scrub pants and an unusually wide expanse of skin right down to the top of her bikini panties. Gary began tearing strips of three-inch tape and pressing them against the area. The nurse, of course, tried to wriggle away. Since she had to hold the leg and not allow it to become contaminated, there wasn't much she could do and eventually, she had to hold her ground. Betty began to giggle and whether encouraged by this or not, Gary very matter-of-factly continued to cover the area with tape.

"Just trying to prevent an ugly scene, Betty. No telling what can happen in here with that kind of provocation." He looked up. "Need more tape, someone."

"Remember, I can still get back at you, Gary. Just wait until the next time I have to tie your gown."

"C'mon, Betty, I'm doing you a favor. I don't think you would have anything to worry about from Dr. Berger, but I wouldn't trust any of the others. Unfortunately, I've had to listen to some of the comments made in the doctors' dressing room and believe me, you would be shocked. I hate to tell you, but your name is mentioned an awful lot."

By now, all the OR people were laughing, and all activity had stopped. Even Phil was laughing. Gary went on as usual, talking nonstop, methodically tearing additional strips of tape.

"You're very lucky I was the one that spotted this. Fortunately, I've had very extensive training in the military to avoid being affected by this. You know, this was a very common ploy by the enemy, to have our men enticed by very comely members, female of course, from their side. In all my time in Vietnam I never gave in. Two of my decorations, I think, are for that. I guess that's the reason they made me chairman of the hospital's morals committee."

"We have a morals committee?" a nurse asked.

"Oh yes. We just don't publicize it very much. Most of our work is done undercover."

"That does it," Phil said at last. "You're holding us up, Gary. Will you get out of here. You're not letting us get anything done."

"OK You haven't finished rounds yet, have you, Phil?"

"No."

"Would you page me when you're on the floor? I want to talk to you further about that colonoscopy thing." He then turned to Betty Stieve. "I know how grateful you must feel, Betty, but it really isn't necessary to thank me. This is something I do not because I have to, but because I want to." And with a bit of a flourish, Gary made his exit.

"He's getting worse," Betty Stieve said, and everyone laughed.

Phil was well into the last part of his rounds before he remembered that Gary had wanted to see him. He stopped at the nursing station on 3 Central and asked if anyone had seen Dr. Barlow and was told he was in Room 320 changing a dressing. He walked to the room and waited in the doorway for Gary to finish. The curtain was awn around the patient's bed and he could hear Gary speaking.

"Could you just reach over and hold this too, please? ...Thank you... Just another second... I want to be sure we have enough tape on this spot, so she won't pull this dressing off again. Thank you, Miss Rogers. By the way, Miss Rogers, I don't want to upset you, but I have to tell you something. All during this dressing change I couldn't avoid looking down the top of your blouse." Phil heard a muffled gasp. "You really should be more careful. That can be very dangerous for the patient if you're helping someone carry out a more complicated procedure. Fortunately, I've received extensive training in the past, particularly in the military, so this hasn't been a problem for me. However, I must tell you that many of my colleagues are extremely vulnerable to even the slightest enticement and I would just hate to see you get involved in some ugly incident. Look, you don't have to say anything. This will just be our little secret."

The curtain was abruptly drawn back from around the bed. Phil tried to step away from the door. He did not want to embarrass the nurse, but they both saw him.

"Hey, Phil. Just the man I wanted to see. Come with me while I wash my hands." Gary walked past Phil; Miss Rogers now totally forgotten. Phil joined him in the utility room.

"Gary, how could you let the patient hear you talk to the nurse like that?"

Gary laughed. "That's the eighty-nine-year-old gangrenous gallbladder you helped me with last week. They lost her hearing aid when she was transferred from the ICU, but she couldn't hear anything even when she had it. I didn't realize anyone else could hear me, though. I was just trying to be helpful."

"Helpful?"

"Sure, Phil. I've been doing it since my residency. This time of the year there are all sorts of new graduate nurses on staff. They're so inexperienced. Someone has to offer them warmth and compassion. Maybe I just saved her from some awful fate. Come on, now. Don't look at me like I'm nuts. You know I can't do it your way. There are times when I just have to have some fun with this crap. You understand that, don't you?"

"Yes, maybe I do understand that."

"Good. Now come with me while I put a note in this woman's chart. I promise I'll behave, unless of course, something too good to pass up comes along."

Phil followed Gary to the nurses' station and waited as Gary made his entry in the chart. One of the first-year residents sat nearby with a Physicians' Desk Reference and appeared perplexed. He looked up at Phil.

"Excuse me, sir, but this doesn't seem right. I'm treating a patient with pinworms and my preceptor says one dose of oral medication is all that's required. He's going home today, and I have to write the prescription but I've never seen a prescription for just one tablet before. Does that seem right to you?"

"Gee, I'm sorry," Phil said. "I can't recall ever having to treat pinworms so I just wouldn't know."

"Just a moment, I can help you with that one," Gary said. "Your preceptor's right. You just need one pill, but you have to get it in the worm's mouth."

Everyone within earshot cracked up and Gary, sensing further opportunity, went on.

"Doctor, when you don't have an answer like that, you're supposed to look it up. That's why we have a medical library.

"I don't suppose you know the mechanism of action for this drug either?"

"No sir, I'm sorry I don't."

"I didn't think you did. Well, since this is supposed to be a teaching institution, I'll tell you. You see, the pill is larger than the worm and it gets stuck right here." He pointed to his throat. "The worm chokes to death. That's also the reason you need only one pill. It never gets into the worm's intestinal tract so it can be reused. All you do is retrieve the pill, grab your next pinworm, and shove the pill into the little sucker's throat. Keep doin' that until you get 'em all. If you want the reference, it's in last month's volume of the Russian Journal of Parasitology. It's my favorite read."

Everyone was in hysterics, doctors, nurses, ward clerk, even some visitors who were standing close enough to overhear Gary. It was late and even though he was still laughing, Phil had heard enough of Gary for one day and started to leave.

"Where you goin'?"

"To the office and then home."

"I thought we were going to talk. What about that course?"

"I don't think so, Gary. Maralyn and I were planning to go away around Thanksgiving, and I can't take off twice in the same month. Maybe after the first of the year if there's something pretty good."

"Twenty-four credits and Las Vegas. You ought to keep thinking about it. One other thing, Phil. I may have a left colon to do Thursday. Could you help me?"

"Sure, I'll check the schedule."

"Thanks. See you tomorrow."

Gary had already begun draping the patient on Thursday morning when Phil began to scrub. By the time Phil stepped to the table, gowned and gloved, Gary was well into opening the abdomen. He was being helped by a first-year resident who then relinquished his position to Phil and went around to the other side where he'd be in a better position to hold the retractors.

"Where would you like me, Dr. Barlow?" the scrub nurse asked.

Gary looked up at Phil and winked. "Right here next to me would be fine." He indicated his left side.

"Won't it be too crowded? I have to bring both of my instrument tables over to that side."

"I know it will be crowded and I know we'll probably have to spend the next couple of hours with our bodies squeezed together. I hate to keep going through this but if that's what it will take to get this poor creature through this delicate procedure, then I'll make the sacrifice. In case you find yourself getting aroused because of this, feel free to rub against me or relieve yourself in any other manner you find necessary." He sighed. "Don't worry about my reaction. I've had very extensive previous training, particularly in the military. I can assure you I will in no way be affected by this and the procedure will continue to be performed most expeditiously. I hope we're clear on this." He then turned to Stu Baldwin, the resident who was holding the retractors. "There's one understanding you and I absolutely must have. In no way are you to assume that any of the remarks I just made might have, even remotely, been directed towards you. In other words, one false move and that retractor you're holding could become a permanent part of your anatomy."

Phil looked at the resident. "Have you ever scrubbed with Dr. Barlow before?"

"No, sir."

"You have scrubbed with some of our other surgeons, though?"

"Yes, I have."

"Thank goodness. It would have been awful if this were your first operating room exposure and you wound up emotionally scarred for the rest of your professional life."

"Hold on!" Gary said. "Why is everyone concerned about Dr. Baldwin? I'm much more concerned about the enormous sexual energy that is building up in Mary here."

"I wouldn't worry, Dr. Barlow." The nurse was laughing. "I haven't really noticed anything yet. Do you think you will want the staples for the anastomosis?"

"A nice ploy, Mary, changing the subject, but I'm afraid it won't work. I remember another scrub nurse who always tried to do the same thing, ignore the situation. She finally exploded into a sexual frenzy during a case. Most of us were lucky enough to get out of the room in one piece but the resident was just a step too slow. Tore 'em up real bad.

He was in the ICU for three weeks before they would let any of us see him. The plastic surgeons tried to put everything back. That was after the urologists kinda gave up. There's a lesson in there somewhere for you, Mary, and you too, Dr. Baldwin."

"We would still like to know if you want the staples, Gary? We'd like to move along, if that's not a problem."

"Sure, Phil. Might as well. They worry me, though."

"Why is that?" Phil suddenly closed his eyes. "Oh God, you're going to start again, aren't you?"

"If you haven't figured it out by now and you don't want me to say anything, I'll keep quiet."

"That'll be the day," the circulating nurse said.

"You use them more than anyone else around here and you're always saying how they do a much better job than sewing by hand."

"True. There's no question about it, but that's not the problem. Everyone says they're a major advance in surgery, but don't you realize it's all part of the plot. You see what's happening today? Nurses are getting more authority, pharmacists want to write prescriptions, chiropractors are taking all kinds of x-rays. Everyone is trying to take more and more away from us and what do you think will happen with all these staplers? Some tool manufacturer is going to get hold of them and start turning them out for home use. Just mark my words. One of these days you're going to see them advertised on television. Want me to tell you what'll happen next?"

A loud "No!" resounded in unison.

Gary took it in his stride. "You wait and see. Anyone who's got a flat surface at home and is too cheap to see a doctor is gonna take a lot of work away from us." He looked at everyone at the OR table. "I'll betcha it happens."

All the while he and Phil had been mobilizing the tumor and at this point Gary divided the bowel at the proximal and distal ends and as he passed the specimen from the surgical field, he reflected further. "Somehow even with this, we're not doing things right."

"What do you mean?" Phil asked.

"I mean our results aren't that much better today than they were fifty years ago."

"That's not true. Chemotherapy alone has made a big difference."

"Sometimes, but that's just it. Basic surgical technique hasn't changed, and I really think we're missing the boat."

"You think we should be doing this sort of thing differently?"

"Yes."

"Are you serious now, Gary, or is this another one of your jokes?" Gary looked up at Phil but didn't say anything more.

"OK How should we be doing this case?"

"Well," Gary said, "look at the clock. What time is it? Almost 10 A.M., right? What do you think this lady's cancer cells have been doing for the past few hours, just sit ting around waiting for us to get our act together? Hell, no! Those little mothers have probably been scurrying around since the crack of dawn looking for all kinds of new locations to set up housekeeping and as soon as we make our move on the primary, word gets out to them and presto, metastases."

Gary handed back the stapling instruments. He carefully inspected the anastomosis.

"What we should be doing is to go after these tumors at night when all those com-muting cancer cells are back at the ranch. This way we can have 'em all in one place and the cure rate's gotta go way up. We can even do these cases like military operations. Use the element of surprise. Get the patients to sign the op permit routinely as soon as they're admitted, not just before surgery. You gotta avoid any tip-offs. Then let 'em sit around for a while after the work-up's completed. That throws their timing off. You might even say that you think surgery might not be necessary. What you want to do is get these tumors feeling overconfident. Then they get sloppy. Next you pick some night when they least expect it to take 'em to the OR. Muffle the wheels of the gurney and no talking. Instruments are blackened to cut down on glare and lights are kept low until the final assault. Maybe if this catches on we could get little decorations for our scrub suits for each five-year cure."

"If this catches on, your little decorations may just have to be put on a little old strait jacket. Forget the scrub suit. That's what you're going to be wearing at the rate you're going.

"Gee, I wouldn't have expected that from you, Phil. I might have from the older guys, but I would have figured us younger guys would be more receptive to new ideas. Well, I see where I'm just gonna have to blaze new paths by myself. It's gonna be lonely up there on the frontier of medical progress. Just me. No one else. Not even my best buddy. But I have my faith."

"And the courage of your convictions." "Thanks, Phil. How could I forget."

"And of course, as you have so often reminded us in the past, your heart is pure and all you ever think of is good thoughts."

"Yes, but you're starting to embarrass me now, Phil. You know how often I've asked you to ignore all that and try treating me just like any one of the other guys."

"Of course, Gary, but it's so difficult, especially with the aura that's surrounding you right now. You'll have to forgive me. All I expected to do today was help you with a case. I did not expect to undergo such a profound experience."

"Well, at least that shows you're able to appreciate a truly great surgical mind. How about you, Dr. Baldwin, did you think this was profound?"

"Oh, very profound, Sir. I, too, am very impressed."

"Very good, Dr. Baldwin. You see, Phil, he can appreciate a higher intellect and he hasn't been a doctor anywhere near as long as you have."

"Anywhere near as long? Now you're corrupting him grammatically as well as surgically." Phil turned to the assistant. "Dr. Baldwin, who was it who thought having you scrub here today would be a worthwhile educational experience for you? I would really like to leave now that we have the anastomosis done, but I'm really afraid to leave you alone with Dr. Barlow."

"That's all right, Dr. Berger. I know where he's coming from. I really did enjoy this case. That was the first time I saw the staples used and I really can't understand why they aren't used all the time. Most of the other surgeons I've assisted haven't been too interested in teaching or have been awfully serious. This was much more fun."

"You consider this teaching?"

"Wait a second, Phil," Gary said. "Let's be fair. We got the job done. The case went well, and everyone had a good time. What more could you ask? The only thing I'm unhappy with is that I didn't get even the slightest indication of sexual arousal from you-know-who. Obviously, nothing else is going to happen so if you want to leave now, Phil, that's OK. We can get along. As you can see, I'm in teaching mode now. Thanks very much for your help."

"That's OK, Gary. You did a very nice job. Glad to help anytime, really."

"Gee, I'm glad you said that Phil. Now that we're friends again, I just know we're going to have a great time together in Las Vegas."

"No, Gary." Phil didn't even look back as he left the operating room. "No Las Vegas."

He made sure his voice carried.

Phil had almost completely forgotten about Jack Hartway and Stanley Stallings. Previously he would pay attention to the operating schedule and make note of the cases scheduled for Dr. Stallings. He would occasionally ask the OR staff how his cases had gone trying to get some idea of his patient selection. After the surgical conference, however, he no longer felt any urge to do this. He had neither seen Ann Hartway nor heard anything about her other than someone having mentioned that both her daughters were now going to a private school quite some distance from home. Then, on a Thursday afternoon in early October, while on an errand for his wife at the local shopping center, the two met unexpectedly. Ann was on her way into the bakery just as Phil was leaving.

"Hello, Ann."

"Oh, Phil. I'm so glad to see you."

"You look very well, Ann. I want to apologize for not having gotten in touch with you before this. You know how badly I felt about Jack's death."

"Yes, I know, Phil, but things have really turned out for the best."

It was an odd reply. Phil took it to mean she had found herself able to cope unexpectedly well with Jack's death.

"I'm glad you're doing well, Ann."

"I really am, Phil. As I said, this really has been for the best. Or at least it was, for a while."

Phil was struck by that same response. It couldn't be ignored a second time. "I'm not quite sure I understand you, Ann."

Ann was quick to reply. "I've been meaning to call you for some time now, Phil. I really have wanted to talk to you. Is there any chance we might be able to get together soon? It wouldn't take very long."

Phil felt uneasy. The only thing he could come up with was that Ann Hartway might be considering malpractice action against Stanley Stallings. He thought it best if he could resolve whatever she had on her mind as quickly as possible. Then at least, he wouldn't have his curiosity nagging him.

"I'm going to my office to check my mail. I have some time now and if this is convenient for you, perhaps this might be the best time."

"Oh, this would be perfect, Phil. I'll just follow you."

The office was just a short distance away, and after they arrived Phil escorted Ann into the building and up to his suite. She made herself comfortable as Phil leafed through his mail. Neither spoke at first. Phil sat back in his chair and looked at her. There was further hesitation.

"Ann?"

"I'm sorry, Phil. I thought I knew just how I was going to say this, but I'm finding it very difficult now. Let me just say that the whole situation with Jack is not what you think. I'm not going to make any excuses for myself. For weeks now, I've been trying to find some way to get to see you. Someone like you has to know what happened.

Afterwards, you can tell me whatever you think, of me, Dr. Stallings, anything. Right now, I just need you to listen to me."

Completely bewildered, Phil sat motionless, his face devoid of expression.

"The first thing you must know, I'm not sorry Jack is gone." She held up her hand as if to stay an expected reaction, but Phil appeared to have been rendered incapable even of that.

"Jack was very hard to live with, even when he was feeling well. This last year, though, was worse than anything I could ever have imagined. His illness, whether or not it was ever that bad, just devastated our relationship. He had diabetes and he knew what that could do. I know he was depressed because he was only forty-five but any time I tried to help him, he'd only become angrier with me. He could be very abusive. Once, I tried to bring up the subject of a psychiatrist or counseling and for a moment, I thought he was going to hit me. There were some pretty violent outbursts."

Ann's lips quivered but she maintained her composure.

"I suppose I could have left him, and I thought about that pretty often but I had my reasons why I wouldn't do that. Anyway, something had to be done and when you said he didn't need surgery at that time, I knew he wasn't going to be satisfied until he found a surgeon who would operate. I certainly wasn't going to stand in Dr. Stallings' way. What you're going to find hard to believe, though, is that Jack's death wasn't just the result of a bunch of complications that just seemed to happen. Stallings made them happen. As a surgeon, I would think you would know better than anyone else just how he managed to do that. And he did do it. We had an understanding."

This time Phil did react, suddenly sitting forward in his chair. "Say that again!"

"We had an understanding. Dr. Stallings wasn't going to let Jack leave the hospital."

Phil was dumbfounded, his expression incredulous. "What are you trying to tell me?"

Ann remained calm. "Dr. Stallings was going to see to it that Jack had a problem and that he wouldn't get over it. He left no question in my mind that that was what he was going to do. I don't know how he did it, but I think the result speaks for itself. I realize if you are going to believe me, you're going to have to find out how it was done. That's one of the reasons I had to speak to you. You're a surgeon. You would know."

Phil shook his head. His mind was racing. He had known Ann Hartway reasonably well for a number of years. There had never been any reason to think that she might be unstable. He hesitated.

"Ann, there's just no way I can believe what you're saying. You may believe it, but there are just too many reasons why I can't. I know what goes on in the hospital, in the operating rooms. Complications happen. Nobody tries to create them. We don't have to. They happen and sometimes the results are bad. I have to be honest. I think you're feeling some guilt and maybe you're just trying to punish yourself."

Ann smiled. "Punished? Far from it." She hesitated briefly. "Well, maybe now. I don't know. Anyway, I really can't expect you to react any differently right now. It took me quite a while before I was sure just what was going on. If you let me tell you what was said in Dr. Stallings' office, I think it may change your mind." She did not wait for Phil's response but went on.

"The first time we went to his office, he said pretty much the same thing as you, that Jack's condition wasn't really that bad and that he didn't think surgery would be required at the time. Jack was still in the examining room getting dressed and Dr. Stallings had come out to talk to me. I happened to mention that you had said the same thing six months before, but that Jack had never stopped complaining about the pain and really seemed determined to have something done."

Ann stopped at that point and looked away. She took a deep breath and then continued.

"He told me about the risk of complications and how that had to be weighed against the amount of improvement Jack could expect. He didn't think Jack was that limited, but when Jack came out, he made it clear to Dr. Stallings that he would not accept any limitation on his activities whatsoever. So Dr. Stallings arranged to have some Doppler studies done on his legs. We had to come back after Dr. Stallings had gotten the results and he said he was surprised that the pressures in the right leg were lower than he would have expected. He still didn't think they were very bad but recommended an arteriogram to settle the question. I remember clearly, once Jack started having the tests, he continued to play tennis just as much as before, but I hardly ever heard him complain. That made me wonder about him and I guess I just became that much more disgusted with this whole thing."

She paused again, closing her eyes for a moment.

"Anyway, Jack had the arteriogram and again, Dr. Stallings wasn't sure if surgery was really necessary. He did say there was a method for relieving the obstruction by using a thin tube and a balloon and if it was decided that something should be done, this was probably the way to go. It was safer and easier. I'm sure you know what he was talking about."

Phil was listening very carefully. The significance of that last statement had not eluded him.

"Anyway, I remember being in Dr. Stallings' office again while Jack was in the examining, and he came out to talk to me and he was still undecided. I told him, very firmly, 'just do something.' I had had it. He started in about the possibility of complications again and I just cut him off. I told him I didn't care what could happen. Anything was better than this. This operation wasn't for Jack anymore. It was for me. He just stood there and looked at me. I had no idea what he was thinking. Jack came out and Dr. Stallings said he would go ahead with the surgery, just like that."

"He didn't say anything more about a balloon dilatation?"

"You mean the balloon thing? No. Wait, yes! He did say he would do a bypass because that would stay open longer and he knew Jack would want the best thing for the long term. Jack was ecstatic. He even started being nice to me. Took me to dinner that evening, first time in months. Jack needed a few weeks to clear up some business matters, so the surgery wasn't scheduled just then."

Phil rubbed his face. He looked very disturbed. "You OK?"

"Yeah, OK." He put his hands down. Ann sat forward. "You're sure?"

"Yes."

She sat back.

"I'd like to continue. I got a call from Dr. Stallings a couple of days later. He had discussed Jack's case with another surgeon and apparently that surgeon didn't think the surgery should be done. Dr. Stallings was having second thoughts and he wanted to discuss it with me. He didn't want to see Jack. He asked me to come to his office."

"Without Jack? That would seem rather peculiar, wouldn't it?"

"At the time I just thought he knew how much this would upset Jack, so he wanted to talk to me first. I was pretty upset myself. It couldn't have been more than twenty minutes before I was in his office. I was very angry, but I didn't want to overreact. I remember the conversation so well because I've gone over it in my own mind so many times since then. We were in his office, just the two of us. I remember he made a point of having the door completely closed. The first thing he said was that he understood how difficult this situation had become for Jack and me. I had made that infinitely clear to him. He said he really wanted to help but he was in a very difficult position. This was a pretty big procedure, and he could be in for considerable criticism if it didn't go well. He could still go ahead with the surgery but only if he felt I really understood this." Ann stopped again and put a hand to her throat. "Phil, I'm very dry. Could I have some water?"

"I'm sorry. We may have diet soda. Is that OK?"

"Yes, fine."

Phil returned with a full glass and Ann drank about half. She gave a fleeting smile and thanked him.

"I still wasn't clear what he was leading up to but for what seemed like the hundredth time, I said yes, I do understand. He said he'd speak with Jack again, but I don't think he ever did. Then he said that I had never seemed concerned or had gotten upset any time he had mentioned that there could be complications and it was important for him to know just how I felt about that. I just sat there thinking to myself how much clearer could I possibly make it to this man. All I wanted him to do was just get the goddamn thing over with. Then he said it seemed to him that it wouldn't bother me that much if Jack did have some problems after the surgery, that I could handle it either way, that maybe, I even had a particular preference. Well, needless to say, I did not find that remark insulting or offensive. Instead, I began to realize he knew just what I had been thinking, that my life would be so much better without Jack. Of course, I never did make much effort to conceal those feelings."

Ann took several more sips from the glass. She looked at it, slowly swirling what was left.

"Anyway, I found myself agreeing with him. I remember telling him he was right, that I could accept anything, that things were so bad I didn't really care. I think that satisfied him. He said he felt better and that he would schedule the surgery now that we had an understanding. He said his fee would have to be higher than his usual charge because of the personal risk he was taking, and we'd have to discuss that soon. I told him that would not be a problem. All he said then was that

He liked me and would do everything possible to help me. He never even talked about Jack, and he was the one having the operation." Ann shrugged. "He said we'd talk again soon. I left his office in a daze. I kept going over his words, over and over again. I couldn't believe it at first. Then I gradually began to realize there was nothing else to think. He was actually going to kill Jack."

Phil continued to stare at Ann. There was no reaction at first. Finally, he asked, "Did you talk with him again?"

"Oh, yes. I got a couple more calls to the office. We went over how I was feeling, if I was still feeling the same, that I shouldn't worry, that he was going to take care of everything. I think he really needed the pep talks, not me. He did finally bring up the fee. He wanted thirty thousand dollars."

"Thirty thousand!"

"Thirty thousand. He said I knew what he was going to do, and it would be worth every penny to me. I must have agreed. I paid him." Ann looked blankly at Phil. "And he also got the insurance money. That was almost ten thousand dollars, for the two operations."

Ann said nothing more. "Is that it?"

"Isn't that enough?"

Phil sank back in his chair and shook his head. "Ann, no one, including myself, could ever believe this. There is no way what happened to Jack could have been planned. Do you mean to tell me Stanley Stallings knew Jack's leg would become gangrenous and that he would refuse an amputation? That's absurd. He did a vascular reconstruction and had a complication. That happens. I've heard enough about the case to know he didn't do anything unethical. He even took Jack back to the operating room a second time to try to correct the problem. If there was anything he could have done differently, it might have been to choose a different graft material, but that's just a matter of judgment."

"Couldn't he have done that on purpose? Isn't that what started Jack's problems?"

"Then that would mean any surgeon who has a complication could be accused of the same thing and you know that simply can't be true. No, Ann, you may think this, but I don't know how anyone else would."

"I know what I've told you is true."

"I'm sure you do, but you also have to realize what everyone else is going to think." Phil's tone became softer, more reassuring. "Everyone feels badly about Jack's case. I don't think there's anyone who isn't going to feel some guilt about the way things turned out, but maybe you're feeling much more responsibility for that than you should. I can certainly understand that you might want to reproach yourself and possibly some others for what has happened, but this seems to have gone far beyond that. I don't think you're being fair to yourself, and I would also be concerned that this may be affecting you more than you realize."

Ann listened quietly with only a brief, wry smile betraying her thoughts. "I guess I should have expected this. You think I'm losing my senses, don't you? You're really missing the point. You have someone on staff at your hospital who is capable of doing some terrible things. I should think you wouldn't want to let him do anything like this again."

Phil held up his hand to stop Ann from going any further.

"Just a second. You're getting me confused. You led this person on and now you say you want him stopped?"

"No! He led *me* on, but that doesn't really matter. I understood what was happening and I don't regret it for one moment. You have to have known Jack the way I knew him. I've accepted what I've done, and I have very little trouble living with it." Then her expression changed. Suddenly, she looked very troubled. "No, that's not true. Something is wrong now."

"What do you mean?"

"I don't know. I have complete freedom. I was very happy at first. It's not that way now. Why?"

"People handle their losses differently. I don't know why you have these ideas about Jack's death. Maybe they're not as clear as you think. Maybe you've just begun to realize that, and that's what's troubling you."

Ann shook her head. "No, it's not that. It's something else, and lately it's been tearing at me. The part about Jack's death is true. Maybe I'm guilty of selfish or distorted thinking but now I feel whatever may have been good for me, shouldn't be an available solution for everyone else. Maybe that has something to do with it."

"That's quite an admission. You're apparently the only one who's ever had a bad enough problem who was justified in having had it handled this way. Assuming what you say is true, you now want me to believe that no one else' problems would qualify."

Ann immediately straightened herself. "That's meant as sarcasm, isn't it, Phil? Then I'm afraid I may have antagonized you and I really don't want to do that. Maybe I've said all that I should at this point.

Perhaps you'll give what I've said some thought and we can talk again later. I really want you to understand."

"But I don't understand! And I don't know how you could expect me or anyone else to understand. It just doesn't make sense, Ann. If your marriage was so terrible, why didn't you just get a divorce? Anyone else who hears this is certainly going to ask that."

"You really think Jack would simply have given me a divorce after what I've told you? That man would have had a vendetta against me for the rest of my life. Every moment would have been a living hell for me, and for the girls. He would have drained every drop of blood from me before it would have been over and even then, he wouldn't have stopped until he completely destroyed me. He was a bastard. Even though I know he didn't love me, he never would have accepted a divorce. It would have meant giving up control and that was something he'd never do."

Ann's eyes moistened and she looked away for a moment.

"I never had any idea that this could happen. I did think at times that the perfect solution for me would be a bad accident or a massive heart attack. Could you ever imagine that a woman would be envious of another woman who lost her husband that way? That was me. When this thing happened with Dr. Stallings and I finally realized what he intended to do, I was delirious. I would have given him the moon. He was going to give me the one solution to all my problems. I didn't know how he was going to do it, but I believed him. And he did."

For just a brief instant, Phil thought there might be some credibility. But then, just as quickly, he decided it was only because of Ann's persistence.

"I can't understand why you would want to admit all this to me now. If everything has become so much better for you, why would you want to risk being made an accessory or accomplice to a very serious crime? I would imagine if you've gotten away with the perfect crime, and you've made it sound that way, you'd want to keep quiet about it."

"I guess you could call it my distorted sense of justice. I think I will always feel justice was served in my particular case, but I don't want to think it could happen again to someone else, and with Dr. Stallings still out there practicing, I'm afraid that's always going to be possible. He's a very clever man. He knows how to get at your deepest thoughts and if it's to his advantage, he will exploit them, no matter what the cost may be. And I think there are probably a lot of people who would like to meet Dr. Stallings once they know what kind of service he provides. I think it's that kind of society that we live in. I may not be the best person to sound morally righteous, but I just don't think this should ever happen again. I think you should be able to do something about that, knowing what I've told you, but you'll have to do it without involving me. I have no intention of allowing myself to be implicated. I've never told this to anyone else and I don't intend to."

Phil pushed himself back from his desk. "Well, I don't know what you expect me to do. Obviously, I'm having a great deal of difficulty believing this and that should make it equally obvious that I don't know if there's anything I should do. If I thought there could be some truth to this, I suppose I'd have to consider going to the police, but you can't be involved, so how am I to tell them what allegedly happened? You've obviously given this a great deal of thought. What do you suggest?"

"Oh, no! I certainly wouldn't go to the police. I don't want him punished. He helped me. I just don't ever want this to happen again. I'm not judging him. I don't know if he's immoral, amoral, or just plain evil. I do know he's avaricious but that's not really my concern. Most people are. I just think that someone should watch him very carefully at the hospital and prevent him from doing this again."

"You really think he's capable of that?"

"I'm sure he is and the more times he does it, the greater the chances are that he'll be caught and then, I'm afraid, everything will come out."

Phil leaned forward in his chair, and for the first time, he smiled.

"So that's it. You're afraid one of these days he'll be caught, and then you'll be caught. So that's the reason for all this. You really do think he's responsible for Jack's death. At least some of this is beginning to make some sense."

"Of course. There are other reasons, but now is not the time. I've told you I have no intention of being anyone's accomplice. Maybe what he's done is more obvious than you think. Maybe someone else can prove it. I've become very worried about that. Then again, I would also think that you wouldn't want to tolerate something like this in your profession. I think we would both stand to gain from this."

"I'm not sure I would quite put it that way, but I do understand what you're saying. So, you want me to watch what he does at the hospital. You really think he would try something again?"

"I know he would, and he probably already has. I know what you're thinking so I probably shouldn't tell you this now, but did you know Frank Spalding?"

"I know the name, but I don't think we ever met."

"You know he's dead, don't you?"

"Yes."

"Then you know he died after Dr. Stallings operated on him?"

"Yes, he was presented at one of our conferences a few weeks ago. I remember there was a little controversy, but I don't recall anyone taking any real exception to his management. I must admit I don't remember too much about the case. I recall he had bad lungs and that had some people questioning the surgery, but in general everyone did agree his condition justified the risk." Phil looked intently at Ann. "Is there something I should know about that case?"

"I think so. Sally Prescott is his daughter and she and I used to be very close. We kept very few secrets from each other, and she knew how unhappy I was, and why. And I knew her husband hadn't been doing that well in business and that she'd inherit an awful lot of property when her father died. He probably owned half the stores in the village. He was also very sick and even though he hadn't been expected to last this long, he still managed to keep going. I knew her husband had gotten into some very serious financial difficulty recently and when Jack died, it was pretty easy for her to see what a difference that made with my financial situation. That's something else I should have mentioned when you asked about a divorce. Moneywise, there's no comparison, and I must admit I knew that. Anyway, I remember she was very curious about Dr. Stallings. She kept wanting to know what kind of a person he was. Actually, I kept telling her if I had a surgical problem, I would go to you. I didn't realize then what she probably had on her mind. Regardless, Frank Spalding's dead now and Sally hasn't talked to me since the funeral. Would you call that a coincidence?"

Phil apparently had heard enough. He got up from his chair.

"Ann, I think this is getting to be a little too much for one afternoon. I think you're going to have to ask yourself if there isn't some guilt and paranoia that's making you feel this way. I know that's not what you want to hear, but I'm sure you would want me to be honest with you."

Ann looked resigned and did not answer.

"But I will look into this, in whatever way I can. I can't promise you what that will be, but I will go over these cases and let you know what I think. I just hope if someone catches me with these charts, they don't ask why I have them."

Ann sighed. "Look, Phil, if this is going to make you so uncomfortable, why don't we just forget it. I don't want you to patronize me. I'm not going to repeat what I've already told you. I had a lot of reservations about this. I knew I might be making a very big mistake."

"No, I'm curious. It won't be so difficult to look over the charts but if I don't find anything questionable, I want you to promise that you'll think about some form of counselling. I want to do what I can. I'm in no position to say that you have a problem dealing with Jack's death and some of the other things that have gone on, but I would ask that you be open to that possibility."

"Fair enough. I'll go along with that for now. I will say you drive a hard bargain, but I trust you and I know you will be fair and do what's right. Will you call me when you know something?"

She rose and extended her hand, which Phil grasped reassuringly. "You know I will." There was warmth in his tone and for a moment Ann looked at him.

"On second thought," she said, "it may not be such a good idea to discuss this over the phone. That's too much of a risk. It would probably be much better if you came over to my place. Just call first to make sure I'm home."

Ann aped her coat over her arm and started for the door.

"You don't have to go downstairs with me, Phil. I can leave by myself. You may have some work you want to do." Then she paused. "It took a lot for me to come here. No one else knows any of this. I hope I've done the right thing." With that, she turned and walked out of the office.

Phil heard the outer door close and went back to his chair. He didn't know where his thoughts should begin. All at once he tried to recall everything that Ann had said. His mind searched for whatever was most credible but what he did remember more often only added to the absurdity of it all. Still, he knew he was faced with questions that he eventually would have to resolve. There was no question that everything he had heard had been very well contrived, but by whom? His immediate thought was that it had to be the distortions within Ann's mind, but as he continued to sort through all this, he began to think more and more about Dr. Stallings. He remembered how he had so persuasively dispelled Phil's initial concerns about Jack Hartway's surgery.

He thought back to how he had at first been so distrustful of Dr. Stallings but later came to think that perhaps his decision was sufficiently reasonable. He did not want to think it possible, but could this have been a deception, and could Dr. Stallings have carried it out, as Ann Hartway alleged? Could Phil and the others have been so duped and manipulated that an act of this sort could occur without anyone being aware? Again, he thought long and hard, and again he just did not think it could be. But there was one thing that he could do to possibly clarify the matter. Tomorrow morning, he would go to the record room at the hospital and pull Frank Spalding's chart. He knew much of the information that he would find had to be supplied by Dr. Stallings and that it might have been exaggerated or made self-serving to justify the patient's treatment, but certain other data would also have to be in the record and that could not be altered. If there had been the proper indications and if the patient had been a reasonable surgical risk, then it was unlikely Dr. Stallings had acted improperly and any suspicions could probably be laid to rest right then and there. If, however, the opposite was true, then only God might know what he should do next. Hopefully, he would know by tomorrow if Frank Spalding had really needed surgery and if there had been a reasonable chance for his survival.

Phil arrived home late for dinner but that was not unusual. Maralyn met him at the door with an affectionate kiss and led him into the kitchen where she immediately began to rewarm the food she had prepared. He watched as she went about resetting the table and the oft-repeated routine had a calming and reassuring effect on him, particularly after the afternoon's session with Ann Hartway. He felt even more fortunate to have had Maralyn's love and support all the years they had been married. They had been introduced by mutual friends almost twenty years ago and it was an attraction that grew from that very first day. Impressed by her intelligence and wit, he was also drawn to her physically although this had never been an important priority in his previous relationships with women. Tall, with a well-proportioned, athletic figure, she had very pretty features, which were often emphasized by the understated way she dressed and an apparent reluctance to use make-up. And in almost twenty years, none of this had changed. He again thought how fortunate he was and perhaps Maralyn had some sense of what he was thinking because she looked over at him several times and smiled. It gave Phil a relaxing feeling of warmth. This was short-lived, however, and inevitably his thoughts turned back to Ann Hartway. He was surprised to find himself at first making a physical comparison between the two women. Whereas they were both of approximately the same height, Ann was the darker of the two with fuller, more exotic features and a much more ample figure. Her appearance often generated comments, all complimentary, and it was said that she had danced professionally for several years before her marriage. He and Maralyn had known Ann and her husband reasonably well as casual friends but not to the degree one would have thought after today's conversation. Those revelations were again starting to turn in his mind and Phil was becoming irritable and finally could no longer contain his thoughts.

"Have you seen or spoken to Ann Hartway recently?"

Maralyn reacted with surprise. "That's a strange question. No. Why do you ask?"

"Because I saw her in my office today and the whole thing was very bizarre. Has anyone ever said how she seemed to be taking Jack's death?"

"No, but I would think pretty well. She seemed OK whenever I saw her at school with the girls, but now they're going away to school. I haven't called her, if that's what you mean. Why do you say bizarre? Is she sick?"

"No, but she may be feeling some guilt over his death."

"Well, I do know she was sorry Jack didn't stay with you. Maybe she thinks this wouldn't have happened if you were still taking care of him."

"Really?" Phil had to smile. "I don't think I got that impression today."

Maralyn shook her head. "Well, I wasn't there, but you know how she feels about you. She never stopped raving about you after you took out Melissa's appendix. I told you. Don't you remember that I said you might have made too much of an impression? There were a few times that I thought she overdid this thing about how wonderful you are and how much she really liked you. Now I really would like to know what went on today."

"Nothing like that, if that's what you're thinking. It was just some strange things she said about Jack's surgery. You don't know if she's ever had any emotional problems, do you? I don't want you discussing this with anyone else, but some of the things she said make me wonder if she's really that well."

Maralyn looked puzzled. "I think she's OK. No one's ever said anything. You realize you're making this very mysterious, don't you? What was her point in seeing you?"

"She wants me to look into some things about Jack's surgery."

"Do you think she wants to sue?"

"No, that's what I thought at first too, but I can assure you that's the last thing she wants to do. She just has some really strange ideas about what may have happened to Jack, and I agreed to see if there's any sort of evidence for that. I know it sounds crazy, but I didn't know what else to tell her. It isn't even worth discussing any more. Could we eat? I'm really hungry now."

Maralyn brought the food to the table and they both sat down. She clearly understood there wouldn't be any further mention of Ann Hartway. Phil placed his hand on her arm.

"Thanks for listening."

Maralyn smiled.

Phil knew he'd have trouble falling asleep that night. Later, he told Maralyn she probably shouldn't wait for him and to go upstairs whenever she was ready. He would read for a while, hoping that would make him tired. That wasn't unusual and Maralyn left him in his study with the newspaper and several journals. They spoke briefly several times and then she went to bed just before eleven. Phil had trouble concentrating but never became drowsy.

His thoughts were rambling when his beeper suddenly went off at eleven thirty. He flicked on its screen. The message read, "Emergency. Call Mrs. Hartway. 578-3044. ASAP."

He almost knocked over the lamp as he reached for the phone. The call was answered on the second ring.

"Ann! What's wrong?"

"Phil. I'm OK now. I'm sorry." She was crying. "Ann! What happened?"

"It's OK, Phil. I took some sleeping pills, but I think I'm all right."

Phil immediately felt his heart pounding. His forehead and hands began to sweat. His face was flushed.

"Ann, I'll get an ambulance. I'll be right over."

"No, it's not that. I'm better now."

"You didn't try…"

"No! I've been taking them. I just thought I'd need more tonight. I lost count."

"How many did you take?"

"I wanted to take an extra one but then I couldn't remember. I took another one, or maybe two. Altogether, it might have been four or five."

"How do you feel?"

"Better." She had stopped crying. "I got so scared when I realized it. It made me throw up. I couldn't stop. My stomach hurts so much now."

Phil took several deep breaths trying to slow his rapid heartbeat. He felt some relief.

"It wasn't that many. You probably got rid of it. That's good."

"I panicked, Phil. That's why I called you. I'm also taking Mellaril. I thought the two of them might be bad."

"You're taking Mellaril? When did you start taking that? You're right. That is pretty strong stuff."

"I needed it while Jack was alive. That's the only thing that helped me. I stopped after he died but I just started taking it again."

"Who gave it to you?" There wasn't any answer. "Ann!"

"I'm sorry. I had to catch my breath." There was a pause. "I had to see someone for a while. He was treating me."

"That's something else we have to think about. I didn't know this. I'm glad you told me. The safest thing would be to have yourself observed. When did you take the pills?"

"A half-hour ago."

"You won't go to the emergency room?"

"No."

"I could come over."

"I don't want you to do that. It's a mess here. I am, too. I'm sure I'll be all right. I just had to speak with someone."

"You're sure you're OK?"

"Yes."

"I'll tell you what. I'll call back in a half-hour. You absolutely had better pick up the phone. Otherwise, the police are going to be breaking down your door. I won't wait to call them."

"I understand. I'm sure I'll be all right."

"I'm sure, too. Otherwise, I would have sent them by now, regardless of what you say. I'll call you. Thirty minutes."

"I'll pick up. I promise. Thank you so very much, Phil. I don't know what I would have done without you. I'm so sorry I had to bother you."

"Remember, thirty minutes. Bye, Ann."

If Phil had been having trouble easing his mind earlier, it was nothing in comparison to what he was thinking now. Regardless of how Ann explained it, she had taken an overdose of sleeping pills and someone had also ordered Mellaril for her. Phil's knowledge of psychiatry was limited but he did know Mellaril was often used for psychotic disorders. He couldn't have been more confused now. The better part of the half-hour was spent staring at the telephone.

Ann answered her phone on the first ring.

"Phil? How was that? I've been carrying the portable the whole time?"

"Not taking any chances, right?"

"Right. I don't want the neighbors wondering why the police are here at twelve thirty in the morning."

"You sound fine now."

"I'm OK I'm just still wondering if I did the right thing. That's what probably started this whole thing tonight."

"What was that? I don't understand."

"Telling you what happened to Jack. I thought I wanted to. Now, I think it could be a big mistake. I just don't know what to think any more."

"Well, don't worry about that now. Why don't you wait until I look over the charts in the morning? Then we'll both have a better idea."

"You'll call me?"

"I'll talk to you in the morning. You're not going to take any more pills, are you?"

"Not unless I have to. Certainly not now."

"You'll be able to sleep?"

"No, but I'm used to it. I probably ruined your night, too."

"You might have before, but you sound a lot better now. I'll probably get some sleep. Why don't you try? I'll talk to you later."

"I will. Bye, Phil."

He put down the phone. He wasn't worried about her now, but he still had no idea what to make of all this. Several minutes passed. He gave up trying to read, turned off the lights and started up the stairs. It couldn't be put from his mind but perhaps if he tried, he'd fall asleep. He slipped into bed quietly beside Maralyn. It was a long time before his eyes closed.

Phil arrived at the hospital very early the next morning. He planned to make the record room his first stop but as he made his way through the basement corridors, the day's first call came through on his beeper. It was from Ann Hartway and he immediately detoured to the nearest phone.

"Hello?"

"Hello, Ann. It's Phil. Is everything OK?"

"Phil, I'm so glad it's you. I wasn't sure you'd be able to get back to me so quickly. Thanks for calling right back."

"I thought it might be important. You're feeling better this morning?"

"I'm afraid I'm getting to be a real nuisance."

"No."

"I know I shouldn't have called. It's just that I'm still so worried. I'm not sure that I'm doing the right thing. I wanted to speak with you before you did anything."

"I'm just going to look at that one chart. I'm not even going to look at any others. I don't think I have to. Why are you having a problem with this?"

"I don't know. I don't think now I should have said anything to you. I didn't sleep at all last night. I told you why I was concerned. I thought I'd feel better after I spoke to you, but I'm even more worried now."

"Why?"

"I've been trying to explain it to myself, and I can't, so how can I explain it to you? It's just something that I don't think will work out. I was hoping some good would come of it, but now I think I'm just going to cause trouble for myself. I'm very confused right now."

"I'm just going to look into that matter we talked about. That's all I'm going to do."

"You're not going to talk with anyone?"

"No. How can I? I wouldn't know what to say."

"I wish I knew what I should do?" There was a pause. "I guess what you're going to do will be all right. I don't want to talk any more about this over the phone. Will you get back to me as soon as you can?"

"It's going to be the weekend and I'm planning to be with the family. It may be difficult. I'll certainly get back to you the beginning of the week."

"That'll be OK I don't want to pressure you. Just be patient with me, please. All of a sudden, I'm having a very difficult time with this. I think I know why but then there are times when I'm not so sure. I'm afraid I may have panicked again."

"If it happens, Ann, just call me. I still think you're overreacting. As I told you before, I can't imagine there's anything to this. Let me look things over and see what I can find out. OK?"

"OK, I guess. You'll get back to me?"

"As soon as I can."

"I just hope I don't regret this."

"You won't, I promise. Do you feel better now?"

"A little. I'll see how it goes over the weekend. I'd like to say I'm not like this most of the time. I'm afraid that hasn't been the case lately."

"Well, call me if you have to."

"Thanks, Phil. Bye."

"Bye, Ann."

Phil continued to the record room. He was determined to remain focused and not let Ann's phone call or anything else distract him. Frank Spalding's chart was quickly gotten for him by one of the record room staff, and he took it to a nearby cubicle where he would not be disturbed. He ignored the summary that he found in the front of the chart since it would be too sketchy. He read through the history and physical exam, which Dr. Stallings had chosen to have transcribed rather than write out in his own hand. It was very neat, not only because it was typewritten but also because it contained all the essentials for a classical history of a symptomatic hiatus hernia with reflux and spasm. If the record were to be believed, Frank Spalding continued to have a burning substernal pain and belching for the past fifteen years and more recently, vomiting and weight loss. This was in spite of the most intensive medical treatment for this particular condition. Now, after all else had failed and with the utmost reluctance, surgery was finally to be carried out.

As he read further, Phil tried to remain objective. Whatever surgery was to be performed on Frank Spalding; he expected the surgeon to make a very convincing case for its need. Even if the patient had not complained of some symptoms, it would not necessarily be improper if the surgeon added them to his description of the patient's illness. After all, it just might be that the patient wasn't sufficiently intuitive to have recognized these symptoms that were there all along. If Phil was going to find serious fault with Frank Spalding's management, it would have to be either by establishing that he was too great a risk for the surgery or that the results of his diagnostic studies did not bear out the severity of his symptoms. He looked for the pre-operative medical consultation. At seventy-four years of age the patient certainly would have required medical clearance by an internist before surgery could be undertaken. He found the note and read slowly since the consultant's findings and opinion were assumed to be impartial and would be crucial.

As he read, Phil began to sense a rather different picture of Frank Spalding's general medical condition. Indeed, the consultant had also elicited the same gastrointestinal symptoms as noted by Dr. Stallings, but clearly was more concerned about his cardiopulmonary status, which was only briefly alluded to by the surgeon. The patient had significant coronary artery disease with frequent episodes of angina for which he took nitroglycerine, and he was also on digoxin and a mild diuretic. In addition, whereas the surgeon had described the patient as no longer smoking, the consultant pointed out that this was only within the past five years and for forty-five years before that, he smoked between two and three packs of cigarettes a day. Although pulmonary function studies had not been done, a chest x-ray clearly showed emphysematous lung changes.

It was the medical consultant's opinion that Frank Spalding was obviously a significant surgical risk. He pointed out that the current trend has been to rely much more on medical measures to treat hiatus hernia and that surgery is being used much less frequently at the present time. The latter should really be reserved only for those cases refractory to medical treatment and having significant complications. He concluded that the patient probably required surgery, but only if all appropriate medical measures had been thoroughly tried and failed and there were advanced pathological changes seen within the esophagus on endoscopy.

The latter bothered Phil a great deal. If the consultant relied heavily on these findings, it was an examination the surgeon most probably performed and described himself. He looked further through the chart. The examination had been carried out shortly after the patient's admission to the hospital by Dr. Stallings who described a very congested, hemorrhagic esophageal lining with a stricture at the junction with the stomach. Surprisingly, biopsies had not been taken so the tissue changes could not be confirmed. The severity of the stricture was also questionable since the gastroscope did pass into the stomach, although 'with difficulty'.

Phil sat back to think over what he had just read. Again, his intention was to remain totally objective. Suddenly, he bent forward and began leafing quickly through the chart. He stopped when he came upon an out-patient x-ray report. It was an esophagram and upper GI series performed two weeks before Frank Spalding was admitted to the hospital. Phil was looking for corroboration of the advanced changes noted by Stanley Stallings on esophagoscopy, but the x-ray report cited only a moderate-sized hiatus hernia with minimal spasm at the gastroesophageal junction. Some reflux of barium into the esophagus was seen on fluoroscopy to support the diagnosis but there was no mention of a stricture or of dilatation of the esophagus as one might expect. Phil would have to review the films himself but thus far he did not feel that the findings were sufficiently consistent to justify subjecting a seventy-four-year-old patient with significant medical problems to an operation to correct a hiatus hernia. If that decision had been made, perhaps he should consider the possibility that it was for some reason other than Frank Spalding's well-being.

He had not hoped for this. He had preferred that he would find the indications for Frank Spalding's surgery to be clear-cut and that he could tell Ann Hartway her assertions were not supported by the clinical evidence. Now he was not sure what he would tell her.

He started to return the chart to one of the record room personnel when he remembered that he didn't know how Frank Spalding had died. He had been so preoccupied with everything leading up to the surgery that he forgot to read that part of the hospital record concerned with the patient's post-operative course. Just from what he had read so far, he could have assumed the patient might have had significant respiratory difficulties post-operatively and could have died either from pneumonia or an acute myocardial infarction. And just as he had assumed, reading further, he found that Frank Spalding had indeed encountered respiratory difficulties after surgery. They were unable to remove his endotracheal tube and eventually a tracheostomy had to be performed. Pneumonia did develop and on the eleventh post-operative day he suffered a sudden drop in blood pressure. An electrocardiogram at that time showed an acute myocardial infarction and he expired six hours later. Phil suddenly realized just how neat and predictable it all could be.

This time he did return the chart. He still had to look at the GI series, but remembering Jack Hartway's arteriogram, he did not expect this to make any difference. Even if he had disturbing questions about Ann, all he could think was that perhaps, just perhaps, there might be a much more serious problem with Stanley Stallings.

IV

Earlier in the week Phil had begun looking forward to a quiet, relaxing weekend at home. He wasn't on call and other than his usual daily rounds, he thought he could forget about his practice for a couple of days. But that was before he had spoken with Ann Hartway. Now, rather than being comfortably settled around the house, his unrest had become increasingly more obvious.

"What are you thinking about? It's not Ann Hartway?"

Phil looked over at Maralyn, knowing there was little else he could tell her of their conversation and the suspicions he had after reading Frank Spalding's hospital chart.

"Is it that obvious? I guess that's partially it. It's hard to explain." He reached for a magazine nearby.

"You should look at yourself. I haven't seen you like this in ages, Phil. Are we going to play twenty questions? Don't you think you'll feel better if you talk about it?"

Phil pushed the magazine away.

"Honey, it's just that there's been a couple of deaths that I'm not sure should have happened. It has nothing to do with me or any of my patients. I just don't know if these cases should have been done and even worse, why they were done. I really don't know what else to say. I'm sorry."

"Is that really so unusual? Haven't you told me about that sort of thing before? It certainly has to be something more than that to make you this upset."

"These patients died."

"Well, that does make it more understandable. Was Jack Hartway one of them?"

"Is that your way of trying to find out who the surgeon is? You know I can't answer that."

"I'm just trying to get you to talk about it. Usually, when two people care about each other, that sort of thing helps, or so I'm told."

It was a very considerate, lighthearted reproach.

"You're right, but I really don't know what else to tell you. I'm sorry I'm letting it bother me this much, but I just don't know what to think, and unfortunately, it's not something that can be discussed right now. I just hope you can understand."

"Of course. I'd rather not see you this way, that's all." She walked over to him. "Tell you what. Do you think we might still be able to have a reasonably pleasant weekend together? The girls stayed home, and they've been looking forward all week to doing something with you. I wouldn't mind spending some time with you either."

Phil smiled and Maralyn helped him up. He gently embraced her.

"I apologize again. Get the girls and tell them we'll go out for lunch and then see what else we can do. I really shouldn't let this thing get to me this way, especially if it turns out that I'm wrong."

Maralyn gave him a quick kiss. Then she left to tell the girls they would all be going out for the day.

Everything went along pleasantly enough even though it was obvious at times that he was still preoccupied. Phil was less talkative than usual, and his daughters even remarked how he wasn't as much fun as he normally was in these situations. Nevertheless, everyone felt it was time well spent. It had helped to have spoken with Maralyn so that she had at least some insight into what was troubling him. Phil's biggest concern, however, was how to proceed further with Ann Hartway. He knew nothing more could be settled until he spoke with her again. He couldn't imagine, though, that anything would be said that would make him feel better.

He had planned to call her early that next week but on the following day he received a call from his answering service. The operator was very apologetic. She had told the caller that Dr. Berger was not available this weekend, but the woman insisted that she page him and say that Mrs. Hartway would like to speak with him and would he please call her. Phil waited until Maralyn left the house on a brief errand and then made the call. The conversation was kept short since Ann made it clear she would say very little over the phone. She had been wondering if Phil had been able to look into Frank Spalding's hospitalization and she also had some additional information she thought might interest him. She was going to be home the rest of the day and wondered if he might stop over. And, yes, she was feeling much better.

Phil had one consultation that he planned to do at the hospital a little later. The patient's physician had called him directly at home that morning and since it was a patient he had operated on before, he felt it should not be left to someone else. He could be at Ann's house between five thirty and six p.m. after having made his stop at the hospital. That would be fine, and he needn't rush. She would be home all evening even if he were late.

Phil arrived at the house a little after six and pulled into the driveway. He had been to her home on several occasions in the past for social functions and it was one that he liked very much. Jack Hartway had done very well in the family business of manufacturing steel gates for storefronts and the long brick and stone ranch reflected his success. With the burgeoning crime rate, he had branched out into security systems and alarms and had become even more successful.

Phil rang the doorbell and identified himself on the intercom. The door was opened by Ann Hartway. She was wearing jeans and a sweatshirt, which, for the moment, surprised him.

"I forgot you've probably never seen me like this. Well, if you can't be comfortable in your own home, where can you?"

She laughed and led him inside. She looked at him over her shoulder. "You make me wonder what kind of a reaction I would have gotten if I'd come to the door in a negligee."

Tactfully, she did not watch his expression and matter-of-factly took his coat and motioned for him to sit on the sofa She sat down herself rather heavily a comfortable distance away and folded one leg beneath her. Phil tried not to notice the bouncing of her breasts with all this movement, but he did anyway. He was afraid she saw this and was sorry now he hadn't been more discreet. Whether intentional or not, Ann was certainly being seductive, and Phil was not sure what was going to happen next. It was odd behavior, considering their recent conversations.

"You seem to be doing a lot better."

"I'm glad to see you. That helps. And the other day was really one of my worst. I do have to apologize. I felt very badly afterwards, having bothered you like that."

"You shouldn't. This has obviously been very upsetting for you."

Ann smiled faintly and then started to get up. "Can I get you something to ink? I haven't had company in so long I have to keep reminding myself of all the amenities."

"No, thanks. Maralyn's expecting me home for dinner after this."

"Does she know you're here?"

"Good God, no! She knows I talked to you recently and it was about Jack's death, but I didn't go into any detail. She's seen me upset before because of things that have happened in the hospital, so this is nothing new. She knows that's part of my nature, but she can also tell that it's worse this time. I'm sure she'd like to know more but she won't ask."

"Sounds like a very understanding wife. I'm not surprised. I always liked Maralyn. I always thought she was one of the nicest in that group. We haven't spoken to each other very much lately, but I guess that's to be expected in a situation like this."

"I'm not sure I know what you mean?"

"It's like being the odd man out. No one wants an unattached female hanging around, so you're never included in anything. I don't have much hope in a new relationship either. At my age anyone worthwhile has already been taken and anyone still out there can't be worth the trouble. I guess one of these days I'll have no choice and I will have to go after someone who's already married." She grinned coquettishly. "You can relax. I'm not ready yet and when I finally do have that in mind, I won't be foolish enough to give this much warning."

This kind of conversation made Phil uncomfortable. He understood the need for small talk, and laughed politely, but wished Ann would get to the real issue.

"You wanted to know if I had found anything out at the hospital and you also said you had some information for me."

Ann's mood immediately shifted. "Yes. I'm sorry we got a little sidetracked. I shouldn't be talking about my other problems. Did you find out anything about Sally's father?"

"I did. I found out he was like a lot of older patients who have medical problems and have surgery and later die of complications related to those medical problems. It's an old story and not necessarily one that suggests poor medical care, except that I'm not entirely sure he needed that procedure. I reviewed his record and again, it's whatever you want to make of it. I will say, however, that I didn't find anything that says it couldn't have happened as you suggest."

"Then you believe me?"

"No. I really can't go that far, but I am trying to keep an open mind. You have to understand how I have to look at this whole thing. I've gone over it time and time again. The surgeon certainly could have done a much better job building a case for his treatment, but I don't know if he didn't do that because he was sloppy or was in just too much of a hurry to get the operation done. It could also be the information just wasn't put into the chart."

"There's no question the patient had a hiatus hernia and was having symptoms. The GI series did show reflux. That goes along with the burning pain he was having since the acid contents in the stomach run up into the esophagus and cause that kind of pain. However, there are very effective medications today for dealing with this and surgery currently is very rarely performed for this condition. If a surgeon is planning to operate for this problem, then he really has to have the strongest possible evidence to support this approach. That just isn't there. There are no biopsies showing how bad the inflammation was. The x-rays do not show any severe changes. There isn't even a note from a gastroenterologist agreeing with the treatment even though he was supposed to have been seeing one. That should be very important in a case like this, and I'm surprised now that there hadn't been a lot more criticism at our conference. This case should have gotten a lot more attention. There's nothing else to say. Unfortunately, there's no way to know what was in Dr. Stallings' mind."

Ann was listening very carefully.

"I still think I have a pretty good idea."

"I'm sure you do, and no one can say you're wrong. I think there was every good reason why this outcome could have been expected. That's a very strong admission on my part but it doesn't mean this is what I think Dr. Stallings intended. A lot of surgeons can be criticized for their management of certain problems and the outcome can sometimes be just as bad, but I can't imagine anyone ever thinks of it as premeditated murder."

"Then can I tell you something else that I just recalled?"

Phil quickly shook his head and would not let her continue. "Before you do that, there's something I have to ask you."

"What?"

"You have to tell me why you're taking Mellaril."

Ann looked annoyed.

"I already did. I told you about the trouble I was having with Jack. Someone prescribed it for me.

"That's not enough. I don't want you to take this the wrong way, but you have to tell me more."

"Why? What more do you have to know?"

"Well, it's given most often for serious mental conditions. You may not be aware of that."

"Look, Phil, I took a lot of different things, Valium, Prozac, all the antidepressants. None of them worked. The psychiatrist didn't want to try Mellaril at first, but later gave me a very low dose, 25 milligrams three times a day. So far, it's the only one that worked, and he let me stay on it. Remember, I stopped it myself for quite a while after Jack died. You want to tell me what you're thinking?"

"The point I'm getting at is that it's often used for psychoses, when people have lost contact with reality."

Ann winced. "Is that what you think of me now?"

"No but think what you're asking me to do. You want me to believe this story which is incredible, and that's putting it as mildly as I can. Then you tell me you're on this medication that is used for some very serious disorders."

"You can say it. Very serious mental disorders."

Phil took a deep breath. "Ann, we have to be able to speak openly to each other about this. We can't let it turn into a fencing match. You have to know what my concerns are."

Ann looked away for a moment.

"Yes, Phil. I know I have to expect something like this. It just doesn't make it any easier for me."

"I'm not making a judgment, Ann. I just have to consider every possible explanation, especially when you tell me that's what you're taking. I assume this was a psychiatrist. What did he say was the problem?"

"What problem? The problem I was having, or do you mean the problem with me?"

Phil rubbed his eyes. "What did he think, Ann? You must have talked quite a bit. What did he say?"

"He said just what I've told you. I haven't tried to hide anything from you. I had a very lousy marriage. And there was plenty before that, that wasn't so good, either. Is that something you have to know?"

"I suppose not."

"You said something before about counselling if you don't feel this could've happened. Do you know how much counselling I've had already? I'm the one who tried to deal with this. No one made me go. I know I'm not perfect, but it was because of Jack. The psychiatrist never said he thought it was something else. I'm not crazy."

"I know that. No one ever said you were. These are just questions that have to be asked."

Ann got up from the sofa. "I'm going to have a glass of water. You're sure you don't want something?"

"No, thanks."

She called out from the kitchen, "Maybe what I really want you to tell me is that none of this could've really happened. Maybe I do want you to say it has to have been my imagination, it's totally impossible otherwise."

She came back into the living room and sat down on the sofa again.

"That would make it very simple. Unfortunately, I know better, and I'm still convinced it was just as I told you."

"I didn't say it was impossible, Ann. Hard to believe, but probably not impossible.

Now, what else did you want to tell me?"

Ann frowned. "Oh, I don't think I can tell you now, not after all this."

"Why? I'm here. I've already told you what I found with Frank Spalding's chart. If you think there's something else I should know, I'm telling you I want to hear it."

"You're going to think I'm concocting all this."

"Why don't you let me be the judge?"

"OK, but you have to understand. This man has me terrified. I can't stop thinking about this. Do you remember Marty Strumpf?"

"No."

"You're sure? I would think you'd have to. He was the one who weighed 400 pounds, at least. You must have seen him."

"Now I remember. Wait a second. Isn't he the one that had an intestinal bypass by Dr. Stallings? That was quite a while back."

Ann nodded her head.

"Sure, I recall that case. That was the first and last bypass for obesity done at Middle Valley. That had to have been at least five years ago and really caused a great deal of controversy at the time. Stanley bypassed a little too much intestine and the patient was having diarrhea twenty to twenty-five times a day. There were quite a few accusations with that case. Somebody said the patient was told that was normal and Stanley, I think, said he understood it was only six or seven times a day. The medical attending was really furious. I was in the emergency room when they brought the patient in. He had lost fifty pounds in about three weeks and his wife thought that was just great. Unfortunately, it was all water and he died of electrolyte imbalance and malignant hyperthermia about twelve hours later. They had to put two operating tables together to do the original surgery, which isn't done very much any more. There are newer procedures for this problem."

Phil looked at Ann. "You think this is another one?"

This time, he got up from the sofa and slowly began to walk back and forth.

"Pretty soon, Ann, you may have a case made for each and every one of his deaths."

"You asked me to tell you."

"Yes, but what do you expect me to say about this? This case was at least five years ago, and I can't tell you how much attention it got."

"You apparently know an awful lot about Marty's case, but if you'll listen to me for a moment, I'll tell you some things you don't know. I knew Marty Strumpf very well. I felt very sorry for him, and he knew it, so I guess he liked to confide in me a lot. He tried everything to lose weight, but nothing ever worked. He was the nicest guy and there wasn't anything he wouldn't do for Gladys and his kids. She insisted he have the surgery. She threatened she would leave him if he didn't lose the weight. He was terrified of surgery. The week before he was scheduled to go into the hospital. he was at my house every day actually crying and telling me how frightened he was but that he had no choice."

"The only thing you have to know is that less than a year after Marty's death she married Walt Pemberton, someone she had only known for several months even though they both lived in the same town for ten years. They met quite by accident for the first time in some resort down south where she had gone to recover from Marty's death. Walt was there because he was getting a divorce from his wife. Everybody thought it was just the most remarkable coincidence. So did I, I guess, until just now. Well, what do you think?"

"The same as anyone else would in a situation like this, a coincidence. But then again, I can't read as much into this as you can. I do know this procedure has been abandoned pretty much because of exactly the same complications your friend had, and quite a number of other surgeons had exactly the same problems with their patients."

"I think it would be unfair to say this situation was unique to Dr. Stallings. No one faulted him for doing the procedure or even the way in which it was done. Selecting the amount of bowel to bypass is critical but can never be done with exact precision and if too little intestine is left for absorption, severe diarrhea can result. I hate to sound like I'm giving you a medical lecture, but you have to understand why I can't be very suspicious of this whole thing. Furthermore, that was a long time ago. How can anyone believe that what you're suggesting could have gone on all these years? I think you have to be more objective, Ann."

"You're forgetting what happened with me," Ann said. "I have every reason to think this way. You've just told me he could easily have performed Marty's operation in a way that could cause some very bad complications, and no one would blame him. Don't you see why I'm so concerned? Don't you realize it's not any different from what he did to Jack? Why can't you accept that?" She bent forward and put her face in her hands. Then she looked up. "I'll bet I know why. It's not just that medication I'm taking. You think everyone in your profession is just like you, don't you?"

At first, Phil did not answer. There were too many thoughts going through his mind to allow any single response. He did hear himself say that wasn't it but remained too distracted to be sure what question he had just answered. They both sensed nothing further could be gained by continuing this. Ann wouldn't admit her assertions strained all reasonable sense of logic and credibility. Phil was conciliatory but not about to think otherwise. It was an impasse, at least for now.

Phil looked at his watch. "I'd better get going. You've given me a lot to think about."

Ann rose from the sofa. "I'm sorry for this, Phil. I know it's causing you a lot of aggravation. Believe me, if I thought there was anything else I could do, I wouldn't involve you. I know it's hard for you to think anything like this could really happen."

They stood for a moment, looking at each other.

"You're right, and another part of the problem is that I may not want to admit anything like this could happen. I realize that. All I can do is think about it. I can't promise you anything else."

He started to get his coat, but Ann suddenly reached for his arm and stopped him.

"Phil. If it'll make it any easier for you, you have my permission to speak with the psychiatrist. Naturally, I'd like to think you don't feel that's an issue, but I understand. I want to be fair."

"That's not necessary. I think you've explained it."

Ann smiled. "Anyway, it's Richard Terry. Do you know him?"

"Sure. I see him once in a while. He's got a good reputation. Maybe I'll have to see him myself, before all this gets resolved."

They both laughed.

"Actually, that's made me think. Before that happens, it might be a good idea to get away for a little while. One of the fellows at the hospital has been after me to go with him to a course. I think it's next week or the one after. I wasn't going to go, but now it might not be such a bad idea. He's not going to believe I changed my mind, but right now I think I might be better off if I just got away from all this for a while."

"I know I'll feel better if you're here," Ann said, "but I won't disagree. This is the first time you've laughed or smiled since you've been here."

"I was that bad?"

"You're basically a very serious person."

"This may be a very serious matter."

"I know."

They stood at the door. Nothing further was said just then. Somehow their meeting had come full circle and some understanding had been reached, albeit one that was still unclear.

"I'll call you in a few days."

Ann smiled graciously and helped him with his coat.

"I'll let you know what I'm going to do. If I do go away, it will only be for three or four days."

"You know I'll be anxious to hear from you. Please don't forget." She squeezed his arm as she opened the door. Phil managed a weak grin but said nothing else.

As he walked to his car a multitude of thoughts raced through his mind making it impossible to focus on any particular one. Perhaps taking a few days off was a good idea. He was surprised the thought had come to mind when it did. It was as if some inner mechanism had just found a way to protect him from all this duress. It was just as well. He had little idea what he should do next and without any sort of plan, he had no choice but to see what the next few days would bring. He arrived home a little late as usual, but his mood fortunately had improved, and no one was given reason to think something troubling had occurred. The remainder of the evening was uneventful.

Phil had only one operation scheduled for Monday. Before this, he had not bothered to check the rest of the procedures listed for that day. Now he looked for the cases Dr. Stallings had scheduled. In the past he often found it very disturbing that this surgeon seemed so quick to operate when he himself would always try to be absolutely certain his patients could not be managed some other way. At times he thought Stanley Stallings had clearly gone too far and had performed completely unwarranted procedures. There never seemed to be anything that anyone could do about it, though. That changed for a while after Jack Hartway's case. All that discussion had made Phil think that perhaps he had been too critical. He largely ignored Dr. Stallings' recent cases but now realized he would have to pay attention to them once again.

He found that Dr. Stallings had three operations scheduled for that day. One was a gallbladder and common duct exploration, which should have been straightforward with clear indications for the surgery. He was not so certain with the other two, a second-look exploration in a patient who had obviously had a previous resection of a malignant tumor and another exploration for a retroperitoneal tumor. Both procedures were sufficiently uncommon at Middle Valley Hospital to make Phil very curious. There was some rather specific information he would have liked to have had about both patients and he wondered if this was what he would have to do with each of Dr. Stallings' patients if this matter was ever to be resolved. The prospect of reviewing all his admissions in the short time between arrival in the hospital and surgery was disturbing and seemed unworkable. Unfortunately, he didn't have a better idea. As an afterthought, he also wanted to talk with Gary Barlow about the course that he was now planning to attend.

He found Gary later in the morning and told him he was thinking seriously of attending the colonoscopy workshop. Gary was both surprised and very pleased and provided him with all the necessary information including a phone number to call since it was getting rather late. The course was scheduled for the following week. Phil called and was told there were places still available and that he could probably register the first day of the course but that it would be better if he got his money in earlier. He promised to do so before the end of the week and requested the same hotel accommodations that Gary Barlow had.

That evening he told his wife that he probably would be taking a course the following week and would be gone Wednesday through Sunday. At first, she wasn't sure if he was indicating that he'd like her to make some last-minute arrangements so that she could accompany him. Phil, on the other hand, wasn't quite able to suggest that it might be best if he went alone because he'd probably be poor company. In the end Maralyn seemed to sense the situation and decided it would be too late to settle the girls somewhere. Las Vegas wasn't one of her favorite places.

The next two days did nothing to change Phil's decision. He had some small cases to do and found it difficult to keep his mind on his work while at the same time trying to keep track of Stanley Stallings' activities.

This, of course, was a very uncomfortable situation and made his decision to take time off even more appropriate. He rearranged his schedule for the following week and on Thursday phoned Ann Hartway to tell her when he'd be away. Her tone was initially quite perfunctory, but warmed quickly, and after a short while she began to express her concern for him. Had he been able to accomplish anything in the hospital? The answer was no. Did he have any new ideas since they last spoke? Again, the answer was no. Was his wife going to accompany him on the trip? No, he was going with another doctor. That last answer seemed to please her, and she made certain he promised he'd call as soon as he returned.

Nothing of real significance occurred over the ensuing few days before his departure except for another decision that Phil made. Since this was possibly not just a hospital matter, he would get legal advice when he got back. Mel Silverstone was a close friend and very knowledgeable attorney and would be a very good person with whom the entire matter could be discussed. Besides, he was also a distant relative through marriage. Phil made a note on his calendar to call him the following week. Three days later he and Gary were safely settled in adjoining seats on a flight heading for Las Vegas.

V

"Can you believe this course?" Gary said. He and Phil were relaxing comfortably at poolside. "I'll bet you were wondering how I found this no-brainer. This is old stuff and no one's giving courses on this junk anymore but this manufacturer has a new line of instruments and is footing most of the cost, so why not increase our repertoire. Anyway, another advanced laparoscopy course was more than I wanted to handle right now. Glad you agreed although you did surprise me."

Phil did not answer, preferring not to nurture another monologue. He kept his eyes closed to the sun. Nevertheless, he knew there would be the inevitable stream of consciousness and was resigned to letting it take its course. If he had to, he would leave, using the excuse that he wanted to avoid sunburn.

"Have you ever noticed how these medical conferences are always in places like Las Vegas, Hawaii, Cancun, St. Thomas? I wonder why that is?" Gary paused and seemed to be reflecting. "I guess it must be the same travel agent each time. I remember there was a conference I once wanted to attend. It was pretty important. It was on something like GI tumors or breast, something pretty useful, but it was in Omaha, Nebraska. So, I went to a conference on office management techniques instead, in Puerta Vallarta." He paused again, but getting no response, went on. "I don't know if I handle the GI tract or breast any better, but I know my billing's improved."

Phil managed a weak smile. He caught some of Gary's banter but was more interested in resting quietly and feeling the warmth of the Las Vegas sun. His mind was not completely relaxed but he felt better being here. It was a well-timed change, and the surroundings were perfect. Still, he could not totally ignore Gary.

"Why don't you try to get some time in front of the microphone at the nightclub tonight, Gary? Using your material on me is a waste. With this sun, I'm not paying attention to anything else."

"All right, but you've got to pay attention to this. Look what just walked over. Is that all one person?"

Phil removed the sun protectors from his eyes and after several seconds for his eyes to adjust, looked around. Just off to the left he saw the object of Gary's concern, a blonde, very spectacularly constructed young woman.

"Quick, what do you think?" Gary asked. "Whose work is that or do you think it just might be all real? Look for scars. Where are they making them these days, still infra-mammary or do they have a new place? I think they have a new place. The anterior axillary line. Look at the anterior axillary line."

He couldn't stop.

"We're too far away. Can you see better? You didn't bring binoculars, did you?"

"No, and I don't have a microscope either. Gary, can't we just accept things as they are, and enjoy them, and relax at the same time?"

"No, I'm sorry, Phil. We're doctors, surgeons, and we owe it to our colleagues back home. We have to be able to tell them what we saw out here, not only at the course, but everywhere, even at poolside. If it were reversed, we'd want them to do it for us. We need a camera. Where's your camera?"

"You need Valium. You don't need a camera."

"I can't do this by myself and you're obviously not going to help. I'll bet she had circumareolar incisions. You're a big disappointment, Phil. You're not good in the clutch. I'm going to get Blind Bob."

"Who?"

"Watch her carefully but don't make it obvious. I'll be right back. She's got to be going into that locker room over there at some point. See if you can at least do this. And don't worry about Blind Bob. I'll tell you all about him when the time comes."

Gary quickly got up from his lounge chair and headed towards the hotel entrance. Along the way he gave a thumbs-up sign. Phil braced himself. He had no idea what to expect. That he and the young lady were about to be surprised was a very fair and reasonable assumption.

Gary came back within ten minutes carrying a medium-sized bag. "We're all set," he said. "Nothing to do now but wait."

The next twenty minutes were uneventful. The woman swam a few lazy laps and then stretched out on a lounge at one end of the pool. Phil had almost forgotten that Gary still had something further in mind. He seemed relaxed but his frequent glances at the woman betrayed a sense of readiness, an impending denouement.

Gary suddenly tensed. "This is it. She's going for the locker room. I knew it. Now it's time for Blind Bob to take over."

Phil looked up. The young lady was indeed walking towards the ladies' locker room. At the same time Gary and bag were heading in the opposite direction. Phil watched him disappear around the building. When he didn't return for several minutes, Phil began to lose interest and went back to putting on his eye protectors and enjoying the sun. Suddenly he heard a tapping sound which seemed to be coming closer. Phil looked up and saw Gary wearing sunglasses and a Hawaiian-styled short-sleeved shirt heading straight for the ladies' locker room, a long, thin, red, white, and blue cane held in his right hand rhythmically tapping along the pavement. Phil could only imagine what was about to happen. Something told him this might be a good time to leave the pool area. He quickly picked up his few belongings and walked briskly towards the hotel. Something also told him this might be a good time to change hotels.

Gary, for his part, could not have felt more at home. Confident that he was carrying the standard for all the great figures of medicine both past and present, he made his way slowly and resolutely into that one place where no man is likely to have gone before. He braced himself for what he knew would be the first unsettling outburst of recognition. Although he wore sunglasses, he knew to keep his eyes closed at first because no matter how well-disciplined, no matter how well-prepared, the initial vision would be staggering, and he knew he could not avoid at least some reaction that would give him away.

"It's a man!"

Amidst all the screeching and screaming, he could at least make that out, which is what he expected to hear. He held his ground, not retreating, waiting for the next key words, which were not long in coming. "Wait, I think he's blind." He could then smile to himself, and he knew that he was home. Behind the sunglasses, he opened his eyes.

He had tried to prepare himself for this scene. The magnitude of this moment was not lost on him. Few men, if any, had ever attained this, the acceptance of his male presence in a ladies' locker room. He knew what he had to do now as he tried to find the girl from the pool. He had to convey the growing realization that he had made a dreadful mistake, that in his world of total darkness he had somehow mistaken the ladies' locker room for the mens', and so his first words naturally were, "Where am I?"

The commotion was settling down, as he expected. Women were no longer grabbing for towels to preserve their modesty, and most were now disregarding any need to keep covered, completely or otherwise. This too, he expected. He waited for the first indications that his plight was recognized and the sympathetic offerings that would be forthcoming, but since no one stepped forward he knew he had to over- come this inertia.

"Is this the wrong locker room?" he asked, and then haltingly, "This isn't the women's, is it?" Following quickly on that, reacting as though he sensed the correct answer before any reply could be made, he began to waver and said, "I think I'm going to faint."

Gary was immediately surrounded by eager helping hands and bodies. He allowed himself to be led to a nearby bench partly leaning his weight on two soft, semi-clad ladies on each side. He sat down slowly.

"See if he wants something to drink… If he's feeling faint now, imagine if he had his sight… He's cute… Somebody put some clothes on so they can help him out."

The voices came from all directions. He waited for the one inevitable outcry that would enable him to crown his performance with the final brilliant masterstroke that would once and for all silence even the staunchest skeptic. The voice came quickly.

"Wait a minute. I'm not so sure he's blind."

With that, Gary slowly removed his glasses, brought his other hand across his face and as his eyes gradually emerged, stared sightlessly straight ahead. It was an ability he perfected long ago used mostly to entertain and amuse. He liked to think it was probably similar to the technique used by the guards at Buckingham Palace who never seemed to flinch regardless of the distraction. The empty gaze continued, awaiting the appearance of the one among them who was the least convinced, and very quickly, she soon appeared. A very statuesque, well-proportioned red-headed woman made her way to those in front of Gary and then gradually moved between them until she was the closest to him. It was nose-to-navel and then as she slowly bent over, it became nose-to-nipple, and yet, through all this, his eyes never moved, his expression never changed. Afterwards, he would be able to recount every identifiable characteristic of her anterior anatomy, but she would never know it.

The redhead held her position, gently swaying to each side, her breasts gliding past Gary's eyes, and then suddenly she straightened, turned, and walked away.

"He's blind all right," she said. The others echoed her remark.

"He really is blind... The poor man ... How awful."

To Gary these words were the equivalent of a standing ovation, but he couldn't take satisfaction in his performance yet. He still had to find the blonde.

"Could I have some water, please?" He held out his hand waiting for a cup of water to appear, and when it did, he made certain his hand remained at least six inches from the cup. Someone took his outstretched hand and the cup and brought them together. He drank very slowly, being sure that a certain amount of trembling would be noticed. This wouldn't do in the operating room, but here it was very effective.

"If someone could help me, I'll leave now. I'm very sorry. Someone directed me in here when I asked for a men's room." Some women gasped when he said this but there was also some snickering and comments he couldn't quite hear. Gary began to stand, trying to see the blonde, making sure his head and eyes moved as one. "Can someone find my cane?" A hand took the cup from him and replaced it with his cane. A bench was in full view just in front of him. He put his sunglasses on, took two steps and purposely stumbled over the bench.

"Oh, you poor thing," someone said as he felt himself being helped to his feet by softer, yet sturdy bodies on either side. He slowly shuffled forward, guided by the women supporting him. Whenever he faltered, his equilibrium was quickly restored by gentle, firm pressure from either a hip or breast on the appropriate side. He couldn't help but think how his apparent misfortune had brought out the best in these gloriously virtuous women. Certainly, they would all be the better for this, but before he could reflect further, he saw the blonde. She stood just to his right, holding a towel in one hand, but loosely at the side of her body. A brief pause, a slight feint to the right as he pretended to go limp once more and as his sagging body was again bolstered by those on either side, he quickly surveyed the blonde. Not a scar was to be seen. He quickly realized he had just become witness to one of nature's finest achievements. Any urge to express how elated he felt was quickly suppressed as he was gently guided closer to the door. "The doorway is just ahead of you," he was told. "Will you be all right?"

"Yes, thank you very much," he answered. "I'm so sorry I've caused so much trouble."

"Please don't think that," someone said. "It wasn't your fault."

Gary was now at the doorway. Ten or twelve tap-taps with his cane would very convincingly get him to the corner of the building where a quick ninety-degree turn would miraculously restore his sight. He glanced over at the pool area where he had left Phil. He was still there, transfixed to a spot closer to the building, staring back at Gary, following his every step with complete disbelief. Turning the corner, Gary tap-tapped one or two more times, then collapsed his cane and walked briskly towards the hotel entrance.

Gary lay sprawled on his bed for about fifteen minutes before Phil got back to the room. He anticipated his reaction.

"Before you say anything Phil, I want you to be one of the first to know that blonde is absolutely a hundred percent for real. Now I know you just can't wait to start thanking me for that bit of information, but it won't be necessary. I didn't just do that because I had to. I wanted to. Or maybe it's the other way around. Anyway, your thanks isn't really necessary, and besides, I embarrass easily."

Phil could barely speak. "Did you do what I think you did?"

"You bet, old buddy. I really wish you could have been with me, but two blind guys might have been a little too much to pull off. Besides, there's a few little tricks you have to know, and they take a little practice. The most important thing is to keep your eyes looking straight ahead all the time. You can't move them no matter what the distractions are, and boy, were there distractions in that room! There was this one redhead. She had two distractions that almost made me forget about the blonde."

The words came slowly. "They really thought you were blind?"

"Phil, I had them in the palm of my hand, figuratively speaking, of course. That was one of my finest performances. I'll bet there wasn't a y eye in that locker room after I left. You have to understand, Phil, that I used to do this sort of thing all the time. There's really no better way to pick up girls.

"When I was in medical school, if I got horny, I used to take my sunglasses and cane down to a bus stop and wait for some decent looking chick to come along. I'd pretend I heard her footsteps and stop her for directions. I'd make it sound like I thought I was on the east side when I was on the west side or downtown when it was uptown and then I'd ask how to get to some godawful place. It worked best when the weather was lousy. I never struck out when it was raining. The girl always took me to her place. What the hell, you can't leave a blind guy stranded at the mercy of the elements, especially when there's no way he can get where he wants to go by himself. Care to guess how often I got laid doing that sort of thing? You know, there's got to be some special satisfaction girls get from screwing a blind guy. I guess it's like giving to the church, or maybe they feel he never gets it, so they're doing him a big favor. Anyway, it works."

Gary paused, waiting for some sort of accolade. He was disappointed. Phil said nothing. Certainly, by now, his performance in the locker room and his description of his technique should have convinced Phil that he deserved some amount of praise. Regardless, Gary's recollections made him become more expansive and graphic.

"You know, it's funny how girls will act when they're alone with someone who's blind. Some act as though they think you can still see and go into another room to change. Others do all sorts of things right in front of you. I had more girls strip all the way down right in the same room with me while I just sat there waiting for the coffee to perk. Everyone feels they have to make you coffee. Some of them even put diaphragms in while I just sat there holding on to my cane. Of course, that was before AIDS. Then, of course, there was also the perfume all over the body. Flavored douches came along a little later."

"I really had only one bad experience. I let this really good-looking girl take me back to her place once and while I'm sitting on the couch waiting for the coffee, she starts to undress. She goes into her bedroom but when she comes out, she still has her bra on, but she also has the biggest cock and set of balls I've ever seen on a woman. She's a goddamn transvestite, or rather he is, and that was the only time I ever let on that I could see. I was jumping up and down swinging my cane and cursing that son of a bitch. He couldn't figure it out at first. Then he realized I wasn't really blind, and he started screaming at me calling me every name under the sun for pretending that I was. I'm screaming back at him for pretending to be a girl. We had one hell of a screaming match. It's a wonder the neighbors didn't call the cops. I guess that sort of thing must have happened pretty often up there. We never did settle it though, which one of us was worse, I mean. It took me a good couple of months before I tried that sort of thing again."

Phil was not amused. "If I'm supposed to believe all this, and I'm beginning to think there's very good reason I should, this is one of the most stupid and dangerous things I've ever heard. Do you realize what kind of trouble you could have caused yourself? What if someone in the hotel had recognized you? You could have been arrested?"

"What's your problem?" Gary responded. "I'm a doctor. I'm allowed to look at naked women." He wanted Phil's mood to lighten. "C'mon Phil, no harm ever really came of any of this. Just think of me as a student of human nature. Forget about it. Let's go to dinner. I promise I'll behave. Temporary blindness always had a very stimulating effect on my appetite."

"It's still not right," Phil insisted. "Nobody goes around behaving like this. You're taking too much of a chance."

"OK, Phil, I promise I'll be good from now on. You'll be proud of me."

Phil started toward the bathroom. "I'll shower first." The look of disgust on his face quickly faded. He looked back at Gary. "It must have been pretty funny."

"I just wish you could have been there, Phil. You'd have been hysterical." They both laughed.

Later, after they had dressed and were about to leave their room, Gary had to add. "Just think, Phil, if somebody does recognize me, could you imagine the reaction? It would almost be worth it."

"In that case," Phil suggested, "maybe we shouldn't eat in the hotel."

Gary quickly settled the question. "Can't do that. It's included with the room." He grinned and they both walked to the elevator, Gary in front, at Phil's insistence.

They arrived in the restaurant well before the larger crush that would be expected later in the evening and were shown to their table. It was in a good position although Phil would have preferred one that was less conspicuous. They placed their orders with the cocktail waitress and were given menus, which they perused at length. They were still totally engrossed in making their selections when the waitress returned, not with the drinks they had ordered but with a fairly expensive bottle of wine instead, and a note from two women at a table some distance away. The note was handed to Gary and after he read it, he gave it to Phil. It read, "Congratulations on your total recovery. If you would care to join us, we would love to help you celebrate."

Phil looked up, only to see that Gary had already spotted the sender, a very attractive dark-haired girl and her dinner companion seated six or seven tables from theirs.

"I've got to find out what this is all about," he said. "I'll be right back." Before Phil could say anything, he got up and walked over to their table. From the very outset their conversation seemed to go quite well. There was quite a bit of laughter and frequently either Gary or the women would look over at Phil and smile. After about five minutes Gary came back to Phil's table.

"Grab the bottle, Phil baby. We have company for dinner."

"Do you mind telling me what's going on, Gary?"

"Well, it's very simple, Phil. The worst of your fears has been realized. I've been found out. That dark-haired girl was in the locker room this afternoon and she recognized me. I'm embarrassed to admit I didn't recognize her but, as she herself puts it, she wasn't exactly dressed the same way then. Anyway, she thinks that was just about the craziest thing she's ever seen anyone do and she and her friend would like us to join them for dinner. We pretty much have to now, Phil. If we didn't, it would be very rude and ungentlemanly, and that would not be like you at all. So let's go, old buddy." He handed Phil the bottle of wine. "The girls are waiting."

Phil got up slowly. He managed a smile knowing the women were watching, but he wasn't happy. "I'm coming over, Gary, but something tells me I'm going to regret this. First, the swimming pool, now the dining room. Pretty soon there won't be any place that's going to be safe with you."

The introductions were made quickly, and Gary and Phil sat down at the table. The two women had been at the bar when they saw them walk in and Ronnie, the dark-haired girl, recognized Gary almost immediately. After what he did today, she knew she had to meet him, so it was her quick thinking that was responsible for this. Everyone at the table then agreed they were indebted to her, everyone, that is, except Phil. Ronnie then repeated for Phil's benefit how she thought Gary's antics in the locker room were the funniest thing she had ever seen although everybody had felt so sorry for him at the time. As she went on, even Phil had to admit that it did seem to have that quality. After that topic had been pretty much exhausted and everyone agreed that the wine had been an excellent choice, the rather expected questions were asked about occupations and what each was doing in Las Vegas. The girls, it turned out, lived, and worked in Las Vegas, Ronnie as a receptionist and Jan, her friend, as a beautician. They also admitted to occasionally working here in this very same hotel as well as some others. In fact, even now they weren't sure if this evening was going to be all business or pleasure.

Phil didn't appear to catch on, but Gary certainly did and his look of elation was all the girls had to see. When asked what they did, Phil said they were surgeons here to take a medical course. Gary had to be more explicit.

"We're taking a colonoscopy course," he said. "We are going to be experts in the use of the colonoscope."

"What's a colonoscope?" Jan asked, her pronunciation surprisingly correct.

"Well, it's a long black thin thing with white stripes on it every few inches and a light on its end."

"Gee, I know some guys with long black things, but they don't have any lights on the end," Ronnie said thoughtfully.

"Or stripes," Jan added.

"What do you use it for?" Ronnie asked.

"Well, to be honest," Gary said, "you use it to look up someone's backside."

"Gee," Ronnie said, "that's sort of the same way they use theirs, too."

Gary couldn't stop grinning, but Phil was not amused and was noticeably uncomfortable. The women had been in this situation before.

"Fellas, I'd like to make a suggestion," Ronnie said. "I see no reason why we can't be completely honest. You seem very nice, and we think you're both very cute and Gary's very funny. If you'd like to buy us dinner and a show or some drinks afterwards, we'll spend the night with you, and it won't cost you anything else." She looked at Phil. "If you have some trouble deciding, Jan and I will step over to the ladies' room for a bit and let the two of you talk it over." They both smiled and then got up leaving Gary and Phil at the table.

"Phil, did you hear that? I knew it! This is it, Phil. We've got it made!"

"Now just a second, Gary," Phil said. "You may think you have it made but there's no way I'm going to get involved with these women."

"Phil, please, this is no time for you to start trying to be funny."

"I'm not joking, Gary. I'm not interested in that sort of thing right now and even if I was, the last thing I'd need is to bring something home to Maralyn. You might want to think about that yourself."

"Hey, if that's what you're worried about, forget it. We're doctors. They have to expect us to practice safe sex. If not, we can tell 'em it's in our oath. I'm not going to get carried away and do something stupid. I've got half-dozen condoms in my jacket pocket, four for me and two for you. I'm upset that you might think I wasn't prepared for this."

"You're really serious about this."

"Damn right! Did you really think I wanted to come out here just to learn how to do colonoscopy? I couldn't care less about colonoscopy. I have never been able to understand what attraction anyone could ever have for the insides of somebody else' intestines. Phil, this, *this*, is what I'm here for. I've never admitted this to anyone else. Not even my travel agent knows. And you're going to stand in my way and keep this from happening. I don't understand you."

Phil said nothing and Gary continued to eye him warily. He tried another approach.

"Phil, look at it this way. We have a once-in-a-lifetime opportunity to get laid in ways we've probably never dreamed of or thought possible, and we're also going to get 24 Category I CME credits at the same time. How can either of us pass this up?"

Phil still would not answer but shook his head negatively.

Gary threw himself back in his chair with disgust. "I can't believe you. You're really going to screw this whole thing up. They're going to be back here any minute. Do you know what you're really doing? Really? Let me tell you something. You go to nursing homes, don't you? You ever notice the old guys they have out there? Ever notice the expressions on their faces? Notice how almost all of them are sad, with pathetic, miserable, unhappy faces, but every so often you see one who always seems to be smiling. Know why that guy is smiling, Phil? He's smiling because he's thinking way back to experiences he had, just like the one we can have later on tonight if you don't fuck it up. I don't want to be like those other guys, Phil. When I'm senile and can't remember the last time I had a bowel movement, but can remember what I did forty years before, I want to remember the time you and I got laid by two broads in Las Vegas."

Gary paused and waited until Phil looked up. He was very serious now and would not continue until they were looking squarely at each other.

"Phil, I've got to make you realize just how important this is. You were never in combat, were you, Phil? Well, you know I was in Vietnam and this is like combat. Make no mistake about it. You never leave your wounded at the mercy of the enemy without leaving him something to fight back with or to put himself out of his misery. You're doing the same thing right now. If you mess this thing up, you are going to have to come back and find me in whatever nursing home I'm in and if I'm not smiling, you know what you're going to have to do. Now that seems like an awful lot more bother, but if you want that responsibility, you've got it. I rest my case."

Gary pushed further back in his chair and stared at Phil. Then he noticed the two women who were now making their way back towards their table and he leaned forward. "You know what your problem really is? You can't stand health. All you can relate to is sick and that over there is health, real honest to goodness motherfucking health." He motioned towards the women. "Man, is that ever health! All these years of taking care of sick people has really perverted you. No question about it. I really feel you're totally incapable of any type of interpersonal relationship unless that person is covered with lumps or is draining pus or whatever other ungodly thing turns you on. It's a real tragedy but regardless, with or without you, tonight I am going to get me one hell of a lot of health."

"That's a good idea, Gary. You take them both. That way you'll be happy, and I'll be happy. I might even pick up the check for dinner."

"I'm way ahead of you. That was going to be my next step even before you mentioned it. Just do me one favor and let me handle it." He rose from his chair to assist the ladies in his most gentlemanly manner.

"Did we take too long?" Jan asked. "Did you miss us?"

"Every second," Gary answered and grinned in his best, most engaging manner. "Did you decide what you'd like to do for the rest of the evening?"

"Ladies, I certainly know what I'd like to do for the rest of the evening, but Phil has reminded me that he will have to be leaving shortly so unless either of you have an objection, I would like to suggest that after dinner the three of us just sort of wander off into the night and kinda just take things as they come."

The women looked skeptically at each other. "That wasn't exactly what we had in mind," Jan replied. "Is there something wrong, Phil?"

Phil could only look up without answering.

Gary quickly interjected. "I had almost forgotten. Phil's been so good about this trip and everything we've wanted to do while we're here, but he had a bypass just a few days before we came out here and the one thing his doctor said he absolutely had to do was get at least twelve hours of uninterrupted sleep at night." He looked at his watch. "It's getting pretty close Phil, if you want to make tomorrow morning's session on time."

The women looked at each other and smiled. It seemed that Gary was progressing very nicely in the right direction.

"Does it still hurt very much?" Jan asked in a half-serious tone.

Phil thought he had a good answer and started to reply but Gary cut him off. "He's on a lot of pain medication."

"My goodness, Phil, don't you ever answer for yourself?"

"He doesn't like to talk about it. It's been a very big blow to him having this happen at such a relatively young age and only two years after the transplant."

Even Phil's eyebrows arched with this revelation as Gary went on, the women sitting there were probably confused but certainly amused.

"It's a wonder he's still here and yet through all this, his only goal is to improve his skills so that he can better tend the sick. That's why he's in Las Vegas. This man has never once thought of himself or the terrible illnesses he has been forced to suffer, so it is we who must be constantly on the lookout for his well-being. I think, Phil, as soon as you finish your main course, you should quickly order dessert and then hurry up to your room so Ronnie, Jan and I can get on with some very serious discussion."

"Hold on. You're being very nasty to Phil," Ronnie said. "Phil, I take it you really don't want to go with us?"

"I'm sorry but I really don't."

"That's OK We understand. We've been through this before and it wouldn't be the first time that we both went home with one man. But how do we know, Gary, that you're the right man? We're two pretty healthy women ourselves. You say Phil has the bad heart, but we wouldn't want to see yours give out or anything else, for that matter, that might be important."

Gary thought about their concern and then quickly answered. "I can appreciate that. You probably have the image of physicians being relatively delicate intellectual types who have little going for them when it comes to really physical things. Well, I jog five to six miles three times a week and lift weights the rest of the time. I can operate all day and night and never break a sweat. If I have to have a delicate touch or resort to brute force, I can do that too. Ladies, I can really go!" He waited for their reaction.

"Is that really the truth, Phil?" Jan asked.

"The brute force thing is. I've operated with him enough times to agree with that."

"See. I'm leveling with you. I guarantee you won't be disappointed. Look, I've been in mass casualty situations where I had to take care of fifty or even a hundred badly injured people. Can't you just imagine what I can do with just two women who are healthy and all in one piece? We could make medical history."

Gary sat back. Timing was very important and now he remained silent awaiting their response. Still smiling, Jan spoke first.

"That's a pretty effective line you have there, Doc. I'm game."

"Me, too," Ronnie added. "I have no idea what kind of time we're going to have but I do know I'll never forgive myself if I miss it. At least we'll have some good laughs."

Gary nodded at the two women, a very satisfied smile on his face. He purposely avoided looking at Phil.

The remainder of dinner was very pleasant. The women were actually very charming, and there were times when Phil thought perhaps he should have considered staying in their company. However, nothing further was mentioned suggesting he would be welcomed if he were to change his mind. Dinner ended with a round of liqueurs after which Gary and the two women left, presumably to catch a show at another hotel. Phil was left with the check.

After having walked about the hotel arcade for about thirty minutes and having been approached four times during that period, he went up to his room and straight to bed.

Phil awakened in the morning to find that Gary's bed had not been disturbed. He was not too surprised and expected that he would see him at the morning session. He wondered what kind of shape he would be in. As a more remote possibility he also wondered if he should turn on the news to see if any madcap adventures by a visiting tourist were being reported. However, Gary was already waiting for him when he arrived at the room where the course was being held. He looked surprisingly refreshed.

"*Buenos dias, compadre.* I beat ya but I can't really stay. I just came in to sign the register and show you I made it through. I gotta get back to the room and get some sleep. I know you're just dying for the details, but it would take too long. I also owe you an apology and have to ask a favor. The apology is for being pissed off at you because I thought you were going to fuck up the evening. Actually, you guaranteed the biggest perpetual shit-eating grin that's ever going to be seen in a nursing home some thirty or forty years from now. The favor is for you to help me take a colonoscope out of here after this afternoon's session. As much as the girls really enjoyed the activities, there's a matter of economics here and I pretty much had to guarantee that I'd bring a colonoscope if we were going to see each other again tonight. They're actually pretty smart and after I filled them in, on the colonoscope, that is, they really wanted to see one. They also have some great ideas how we can broaden its use. I really need to get my hands on one and I need some help, like from some real good, reliable, old buddy. What do you think? You may speak."

"Good morning, Gary."

"Good morning, Phil. Does that mean you'll help?"

"Did you have an enjoyable evening, Gary?"

"Yes, I did, and thank you for asking, Phil. Thank you also for being so nice to me now. Can I tell you how I think we can do this?"

"I'm very sorry you won't be able to stay this morning, Gary."

"Aw, Phil, will you quit breaking 'em. I promise I'll be good after this. I just need your help this one time."

"Gary, I'm trying to keep from really getting angry. Last night you pressured me about those girls. This morning you're pressuring me about some damn colonoscope. Last night it was consorting with admitted prostitutes, today it's theft. What are you anticipating for us tomorrow, mass murder?"

"Gee, you changed your mind already. I guess that's a negatory. For a while there, I thought you were going to help."

"No, Gary, I was never going to help. You were only hoping I would help. What I think I will do, however, if this keeps up, is have my room changed, probably to another hotel, maybe even another state."

"Oops, I don't want that. I really need your maturity and wisdom as a stabilizing force. I'm actually a very weak person and I certainly wouldn't want to go to jail where I could be brutally ravished and dehumanized. God, what you just saved me from. From this moment on I am forever in your debt. If it's OK with you though, I'm still going to go back to the room to get some shut-eye now. I'll be back this afternoon.

In the meantime, you can give the mannequin a big kiss for me, your choice whichever end you prefer."

Gary left and Phil worked pretty much by himself the rest of the morning and then into the afternoon after the lunch break. Gary did not get back until the afternoon session was almost over and even then, he wasn't too interested in operating the instrument. He became more concerned though when it was time to put away the colonoscope and teaching model. They returned to their hotel room a short time later and were just about to get in some pool time before dinner when Gary remembered something he had to do and excused himself. He would definitely be back for dinner but one hour later Phil heard himself being paged at poolside. It was Gary on the phone explaining that something even bigger than last night was about to happen and that his future as a nursing-home patient was about to be secured for all time. He probably wouldn't see Phil at all tonight, but he'd be at tomorrow's session on time. In the event, however, that he might be a little late and Phil should have some trouble finding the colonoscope and its light source, he shouldn't let on. All would be put in order forthwith. Phil hung up.

True to his word, Gary was already at their table the following morning when Phil arrived. He patted the colonoscope that lay on the table. "It's still warm," he said with a smile. "You can do all the work this morning. I got all my practice last night. Want to know how I got the stuff out of here?" He pointed to a large plastic bag. "I told security our mannequin died, and I was turning him in for another one. Honest."

Phil looked at him. "Do you think you're finished now?"

"Oh, absolutely. The girls can't possibly see me tonight. This is their last chance to make some money before they go back to work on Monday. It looks like I'm going to be all yours."

"I'm thrilled."

"I know you don't want to hear any of the details but I gotta say I made a mistake when I didn't bring along the polaroid attachment. The girls were awfully disappointed when I told them they could have had polaroids of their internal parts. Would have been a nice memento for me too."

"I don't doubt it. That would also have been perfect for their business cards."

Gary laughed. "Hey, that was really funny. One day left to go and you're just now starting to get with it. Maybe there's hope." He paused and looked at Phil. "You have to admit it hasn't been all that bad. Look at what we've learned. First of all, besides its obvious uses, a colonoscope can be the best ice-breaker for a party that you'll ever find. I don't care how boring a party might be, just trot out a colonoscope and guaranteed within minutes you'll have the social event of the year. And you know what else I learned. It really doesn't hurt that much."

"You mean you actually let them put that thing in you?"

"Only up to the second mark."

"Jesus, are you crazy? You could have been perforated."

"Hey, relax. I was only kidding, but I must admit they did try. Gosh, I really am going to miss them. Not too many girls like to have fun like that anymore. You know, if I could gross another fifty or sixty thousand a year I'd take 'em both back with me to work in the office. Ronnie does do office work and Jan could probably just lick the stamps and the envelopes. She'd really be terrific at that."

"OK Gary, I see you're really going to be heartbroken without your friends, so I'll be a real good guy and go easy and not tell you what I really think of all this."

"Gee, thank you, Phil. I'm not really sure I deserve all this but anyway, you don't have to go too easy. They're going to drive us to the airport tomorrow. Should I ask them to come to our room a little early?"

This time Phil just walked away. "I'll get the mannequin and set up myself," he muttered.

VI

Gary and Phil arrived home late Sunday evening. Their departure from Las Vegas earlier had not been without some anxious moments. The girls never did arrive to take them to the airport and Gary refused to leave until the very last moment insisting all along that they would eventually appear. He was convinced their relationship had taken on too great a meaning to have it all end this way. Only when it appeared certain they would miss their flight did Gary allow Phil to call a taxi. Naturally he was deeply hurt by this. It had been a very painful lesson. For much of the flight he went on about relationships, trust, educating the public and the sharing of knowledge, particularly current technology. He vowed never again to be so careless with his feelings. Phil tried to offer solace. He suggested that Gary invite both women to his home for a weekend. Certainly, his wife would understand. It was the only time during the entire trip that Phil was able to retaliate, and he made the most of it. By the time the plane had begun its final approach, Gary had already begged for mercy several times. It had been a very effective distraction, but now, as the plane was about to land, all that was expected to change.

They took a cab from the airport, and since there was little traffic at this hour arrived home in very good time. Gary lived the closer of the two and was dropped off first. Phil was to take care of the fare and Gary would pay his half in the morning. It was another ten minutes to Phil's home and Maralyn came to the door when she heard the cab on the gravel driveway. She was very happy to have him home and greeted him with a warm hug and kiss. She expected him to be tired from the flight and asked only a few questions about the trip before she suggested that he take a warm shower while she made a light snack. Tomorrow being a school day, the girls were already asleep, and he would see them in the morning. She did have to ask if he was glad he had made the trip, and Phil said that it had been worthwhile. Later, after having gone to bed, Maralyn carefully made it obvious that she wanted to have sex. Having been apart for three days, she did not feel it was a sign of a healthy marriage for the two of them to just fall asleep. Phil had some difficulty at first, which was quickly attributed to fatigue, but eventually they were both satisfied. Maralyn was asleep in a very short time, but Phil stayed awake longer. His sluggish response could well have been due to the long flight but at one point he had found himself thinking of the two Las Vegas women. That hadn't helped and he was at a loss for an explanation. Then he had begun thinking of Ann Hartway and that troubled him even more. It took much longer before he finally drifted off.

He began the next day very early, going first to the operating room to check the times scheduled for his cases that week. As he passed the lounge, he heard repeated laughter and when one nurse walked by and said she had heard all about his trip, he knew where he would find Gary. When another nurse poked her head out of the room and said, "It's him," it was only seconds before Gary bounded out from the lounge, coffee in one hand, toast in the other and a very broad, mischievous grin on his face.

Phil took him aside. "You haven't been telling them about the trip, have you?"

"Sure I have. You know what it's like. They live for these vicarious thrills. I've gotta go back in. I'm not finished."

"You can't be telling them everything?"

"Of course not. How could I? It's just like I just told them. Don't you remember? I was in bed every night by nine. You were the one who kept going off by yourself. How do I know what you were doing? Sometimes I didn't see you until the next morning."

Phil could only shake his head. He wondered if there'd ever be a time when Gary didn't have an answer.

"I'm just doing a lymph node biopsy under local anesthesia now, but I may need your help tomorrow. I just got a positive report back on a breast biopsy and the patient is trying to make up her mind. Can you help if I have to do a modified?"

"Sure. What time?"

"I'm holding a ten o'clock time. Oh, and I almost forgot the biggest news. I scheduled my first colonoscopy for Friday."

"What? You were hardly there for the course."

"Hey, fella, you seem to forget. Remember what you were working on in that lab? Well, keep in mind, I'm already up to humans."

Phil grimaced and muttered good luck. He was just about to ask Gary for the money he owed him when his beeper began signaling. Gary took it as his cue to go back into the lounge and Phil called the operator. The emergency room wanted him and while calling that extension, he checked the OR book. He had only a few small cases scheduled later that week and he made a mental note of the times. He then got through to the emergency room and was informed that a rather serious hand injury had just arrived, and his services were required. He was one of the few general surgeons on staff who had had additional training in hand surgery and was permitted to treat such injuries.

Moments later, he was in the emergency room attempting to stop some rather brisk arterial bleeding in the mangled hand of a young man who had been attempting to repair a snow blower. Unfortunately, at some point the machine had been accidentally turned on. The bleeding was considerable, and it was difficult to achieve adequate local anesthesia. The pain remained intense, and Phil's initial efforts were ineffective and he finally had to resort to a tourniquet. There wasn't much he could do under these conditions. He was finally able to control the bleeding with well-placed suture ligatures after the patient had gotten substantial temporary relief with intravenous Demerol. Everything else would have to be deferred until he could take the patient to the operating room later that day. He had eaten breakfast and the surgery could not be done any earlier. Phil ordered antibiotics and dressed the hand. He knew he had many hours of meticulous surgery ahead of him and began to rearrange his schedule for the day.

What should have been a very slow morning that would allow him to catch up with the work from last week was now anything but that. He canceled his office hours, briefly discussed the case with the resident who would be admitting the patient and then spoke at length with the patient and later, with his parents. He outlined the procedures that would have to be done and made it clear that although he had not been able to thoroughly examine the hand, he was certain there would be considerable loss of function and they would have to be prepared for this. Although he never liked to paint a bleak picture for any patient, the current liability climate left him no choice. He assured them he would do everything possible to preserve the maximum amount of use. The patient accepted his recommendation and signed the operative permit with his good hand. Phil promised he'd be checking on him again in a very short while and left to begin his much-delayed rounds.

The patient was brought to the operating room at one p.m. but with all the preparation, the surgery didn't start until quarter to two. It was over a little after six p.m. Phil was satisfied that he had done the best possible repair of the injuries and the OR staff was very complimentary, but the accident had been very destructive, and he felt badly about the eventual result. The patient did not have any insurance, was only nineteen years old and would now be significantly handicapped. He explained this to the family and emphasized the importance of future physical and occupational therapy. He also explained there might be further benefit from additional surgery later on but that could not be determined now. The family thanked him, and Phil left to change into his street clothes. It was already early evening and thus far he had had to cancel office hours, had not completed his rounds, and had spent five depressing hours attempting to salvage an irretrievably damaged hand. In his first day back, he was already as harried as he had been before he left, and he hadn't even begun thinking about Stanley Stallings. He still hadn't called Ann Hartway or Mel Silverstone. He hadn't let his wife know he'd be late for dinner. He did call his office, but his secretary had left much earlier. Answering service took the call and gave Phil what seemed to be the more important messages. He jotted them down but then thought they could wait until the following day and uncharacteristically stuffed the paper in his pocket and went home.

He did not make his calls until the next afternoon. He would have liked to have spoken with Ann Hartway earlier but was afraid to call from home. He couldn't be sure how their conversation might transpire and if Maralyn were to overhear anything peculiar, he'd find it very hard to explain. After he had spoken with the half-dozen or so patients who had called, he made an appointment with Mel Silverstone's secretary to see him the following afternoon at three p.m. Then he called Ann. He wanted to keep the conversation very brief.

"Hello, Ann. It's Phil."

"Hi, Phil. How was the trip?"

"It had its moments, but I don't think we should go into that now. I can tell you more about it when I see you."

"Are you more rested?"

"I think so but yesterday was very hectic. I had a pretty nasty emergency that took up the whole day and I'm already way behind schedule."

"Is that why you didn't call yesterday?"

"As a matter of fact, yes. Look, I just want to tell you, I'm going to speak to someone tomorrow, just to get some advice." He did not mention that it was an attorney.

"Is that what you feel you have to do?"

"Yes. I have to do something."

"How much are you going to tell him?"

"As much as I think I have to, but I won't mention any names. I don't think we should discuss this anymore right now."

"You will be careful? This is the sort of thing that makes me very nervous."

"Of course. I'll try to stop by to see you sometime afterwards. You haven't had any more problems, have you?"

"No. Do you know what time? I'll be sure to be home then."

He thought of his schedule.

"Figure about four thirty."

"Good. I'll be home. Bye."

Phil hung up. He was pleased that was done but now had to think about his meeting with Mel Silverstone. Much would depend on just how he would be able to present these allegations. He had no way of knowing what his reaction might be. He was well aware of the one possibility that Mel might just think he had lost all sense of reason. Of course, there were already times when he thought that himself.

Mel Silverstone was waiting for him when Phil arrived at his office the next day at three p.m. Somewhere in his mid-fifties, more than ten years older than Phil, he nevertheless always kept himself very fit, well-groomed, and well-dressed, the complete personification of a successful attorney. He rose from behind his desk to greet him.

"Phil! You're looking great," he said as they shook hands. "You must've just been away. You have a tan. Very nice. This is quite a switch. Whenever we've seen each other professionally before, it's always been because I've needed your services. Thank God the boys haven't been putting any more holes in their heads lately. Sit over here." He pointed to a small conference table in an adjoining room. "This is more private."

Phil still hadn't said a word since entering the office.

"This must be a pretty serious matter, Phil? It usually is when the party is very quiet, and you haven't said a word yet. Of course, I've also been known to talk so much at times no one can get a word in edgewise."

"It may be, Mel. I'm not sure. This may be hard to follow, and I know it's going to sound absolutely crazy, but I have to explain it to someone who can give me some advice. I don't want you to think I've lost my mind but there's a possibility that one of the surgeons at the hospital is in some way purposely causing the deaths of some of his patients. That's just about the best way that I can possibly put it."

He watched as Mel's eyebrows arched and his eyes widened. He gestured at Mel's facial expression.

"That's why I was so quiet. I know it's going to be very hard explaining this."

Mel regained whatever composure he had lost. "I'm listening."

"Well, it all started when a patient of mine had surgery by someone else on our staff. I didn't think the surgery had to be done and the patient died. That was about five or six months ago. About three weeks ago, I saw the patient's wife and heard a story that I couldn't believe then and can't really now, either. Maybe you can. I don't know. Anyway, she told me that the surgeon had offered to make sure her husband did not survive the surgery, for a considerable fee. They were having very serious marital problems, so she accepted, and he died. She also told me about two of her friends who had family members who were operated on by this same surgeon and both these patients died. In both these instances you could make the case that he caused these deaths on purpose. Now, another thing has me bothered. I have time and again been very critical of this surgeon. I've often felt that he is too quick to operate, that his decisions are very frequently based on other considerations and not the welfare of his patients.

"You mean, financial?"

"I would think so. What other reason would there be?" Phil paused, but Mel said nothing more, so he continued. "I honestly have to say, if there's anyone on our staff who could believe this, or anything else derogatory about this person, that would have to be me. Other surgeons know about him, but they just laugh it off. It's uncanny. It's as if this woman knew just who the one person on staff would be who would take this seriously. That's been on my mind a lot. There's probably no one else who would have paid any attention to her."

"That's interesting. Do you know her well?"

"I guess fairly well. You know, socially, that sort of thing."

"Did you ever talk with her about this surgeon?"

"No."

"Never? You're sure. You've never told anyone how you feel about this surgeon?"

"Maralyn knows. It's pretty hard to keep your feelings to yourself all the time. She knows how I feel about some of the people at the hospital."

"Of course. I take it she's friendly with this woman, too."

"Yes, but she'd never discuss anything I say about the hospital or the staff."

"Well, you never know."

"I think I know what you're getting at, Mel, and that's not it. I think there are some other very good reasons why she confided in me and not someone else. I did operate on her daughter. She trusts me. I don't think she had any idea I really didn't like this surgeon."

Mel listened carefully. "It's something we may have to think about. There's got to be a very strong reason why this woman would admit to you that she's an accomplice. I take it, this is what you're telling me?"

"Yes."

"Then why did she tell you?"

"I know why she did. She's afraid he's going to keep doing this and will eventually be found out. When that happens, she's afraid her name is going to come up. She wants him stopped, for her good and for the good of the profession. She thinks I can do that. Now, can you believe this?"

"You're the surgeon. If you tell me he could do what she claims, then of course, I can believe it. I don't believe there's any criminal act that hasn't been committed already. All you have to do is look in the law books. In other words, if somebody can dream it up, I think it's probably already been done."

"Then you say this isn't too farfetched?"

"I still don't know what 'this' is. I need more details. Before we go any further, though, I will tell you I'm already having a problem."

"What's that?"

"I can understand the woman's concern, but I find it hard to believe she'd tell anyone, at least, for that reason alone. I think there has to be more to it, don't you?"

Phil nodded. "That's exactly what I said. I told her I thought she was feeling guilt over her husband's death. I thought it was pretty obvious. I could never get her to agree."

"What did she say?"

"She admits something's bothering her now, but she won't say it's guilt. She says she was fine for a while but now she has to take sleeping pills. She's also on Mellaril and that could be for depression or agitation. She has seen a psychiatrist."

Mel looked up. "Now you're getting into something else. This is another question I had. Is it possible she's unstable? You know, that would change this considerably."

"I really don't think so, Mel. The feeling I got from talking to her was that her marriage was very stressful. I think she needed help to cope with a very unpleasant situation and saw the psychiatrist for that. I think the medication is what finally worked for her. I could be wrong, but she doesn't impress me as someone who's disturbed in that sense."

"It's still not clear, but we can come back to that." Phil shrugged.

"OK, do you want to try to fill me in further, or do you want me to ask some more questions?"

"Maybe it would be best if you just asked, and I'll add anything else I think is important."

"Fine. Do you mind if I take notes? And I take it you don't want to name names. Keep in mind anything you say is kept in the strictest confidence."

"I don't want to mention any names right now, if that's OK?"

"Sure. Then I guess what we want to do now is look at this thing more closely and make sure we don't come up with any missing pieces. Let's start with the motives. You say there were three separate incidents. Tell me about the first one."

"That was the man who had been my patient. I told you about that one. His wife was very unhappy. She was extremely depressed, not suicidal, though. She didn't think she could handle a divorce and she wanted to be rid of him."

"She told you all this?"

"Yes."

"OK, we'll get back to that." He continued writing. "Now, what about the next one?"

"That was an elderly man who was in poor health. His daughter and son-in-law had serious financial difficulties and the father had quite a bit of money. I don't think they were able to wait until he parted with it naturally."

"Good. Now the third."

Phil was now getting into the flow of Mel's line of questioning.

"That was another man. The patient was an extremely obese individual and his wife preferred another man. They were married a little while after he died."

"You've got one more."

Phil looked puzzled. "No, those were the three."

"You forgot the doctor. He has to have a motive, too. If you or someone else is alleging that he's done something pretty gruesome, he really should have a very good reason for that. You'll agree with me that whatever his actions are, they would be abhorrent to any other physician. So, what is his reason? We've already suggested it might be financial. It might be a good idea to find out if he's having some money problems, if he's had investment losses. Is he divorced and paying large support payments?"

"He is divorced. Other than that, I don't know anything about his financial situation. You have to realize that for years I've watched him do cases that I don't think should have been done. I've never been able to think of another reason for this other than just to collect the fees. I think you should also be aware that most of us are finding it a lot tougher these days to make ends meet. Reimbursements have been going down and many insurance plans now have very low fixed payment schedules. What with the economy being the way it is and expenses still being very high, a lot of doctors have very serious financial problems. Maybe he's one of them."

"Well, maybe that's just it then. Anyway, it's something for you to look into. He could have a very expensive girlfriend. Just another thought."

Mel jotted some additional notes and then went on.

"Now, it looks like we may have motives for the doctor and the others who want these people dead. Remember, this is all very sketchy but let's say we're this far. Essentially, these are contract killings. The next big question is how these arrangements were reached. I don't imagine he had this on his business cards or advertised it in physician's directories."

Phil was disturbed by the remark. "You're not being sarcastic, are you?"

"No, not at all. I apologize if it sounded that way, but you understand what I'm getting at. This is what I may have the most difficulty with. Convince me that the parties could reach an understanding in some plausible way and if the rest fits, I'd say you may very well have something very serious to worry about. Now, you tell me."

It was a valid question that Phil had asked himself many times.

"This woman was very open about her unhappiness in her marriage. She made no effort to conceal it from the surgeon. She feels he picked up on it and realized that she was vulnerable. Apparently, he's pretty shrewd at this and gradually he got her to accept the idea that he could eliminate her husband, and no one would be the wiser and she'd be a hell of a lot better off. Remember, she didn't feel she had any other option. I think he was probably able to do the same thing with the others. They all had reasons why they'd consider this, and I think he may just be the one person who's despicable enough to do this sort of thing and get them to go along."

"Mmm. I'm impressed." Mel beamed his approval. "I thought you'd have trouble with that, and we'd be going around for a while trying to come up with an answer, but you've gotten the point across. It's a reach but I can buy it. Morality is almost a forgotten word today. You're getting me into this now and I can't stop thinking what kind of a pitch this guy must have made. It must've been a beauty. This may have taken preying on one's vulnerability to its highest art form. Very good."

He underlined what he had just written.

"Now, what about the method? In other words, how were these acts committed? Here I want to warn you that I'll be out to impress you. Assisted suicides, lethal injections and turning off life support systems are very hot topics in legal circles these days and I've done my reading."

"It wasn't that way, Mel. He did it by operating on these people."

"You mean I can't tell you what I learned about potassium chloride and curare and succinylcholine? You're going to have to start at the beginning then."

"Mel, I think what he's done is either operate on people who were such poor risks that there was a good chance they wouldn't survive the surgery or during the operation he somehow created problems that, again, would not allow their survival. Believe me, I never would have imagined anything like this before. Now, I just dread the thought that all this has really happened."

"I guess you just answered my next question. You really feel this is a credible method for killing someone?"

"I wouldn't have until now, but yes, you're damned right. I just don't want to believe any surgeon would do this. It's not like holding a gun up to someone's head and pulling the trigger, but if you have a reasonably high-risk surgical patient and you subject him to a major operative procedure that's going to compromise some marginal organs, you damn well can expect you may wind up with a dead patient. The big trick is getting your colleagues to agree that the surgery is necessary." Phil was getting angry. "I can tell you our friend is a master at this."

"I guess he'd have to be. Each of these patients was a bad risk?"

"No, with two patients I think he did the operations improperly so there would be complications afterward. You're not a surgeon so I have to make you understand something now. When you're operating, you do so with a great deal of intensity. You do that so everything is as near to perfection as the conditions and human capability will allow. You do this so the chance for complications will be reduced to the smallest possible degree. You want your patient's recovery to be a smooth uninterrupted progression. Now, it stands to reason, if the intensity of that effort is ever lessened, then the chances for complications must increase. And if a surgeon ever purposely performed a procedure carelessly or indifferently, you could almost be assured there would be problems. And then let me tell you, sometimes those are problems that you just can't correct. Just imagine now, what someone could do in that very same situation, if he didn't want to see the patient survive."

Mel sat transfixed. "Christ, Phil, you should have been a lawyer. You mean he purposely botched the operations?"

"If we can ever be sure he purposely caused the deaths of these patients, yes, that's what I would say. I'm not quite sure how he did it in one case, but in the other he made a segment of intestine too short. I know that for a fact because it was discussed in conference, and he admitted it."

Mel was even more surprised. "You mean he admitted doing the operation incorrectly?"

Phil raised his hand. "Don't get excited. That's not unusual in medicine. It's not an exact science. Most often it's considered a noble gesture, not an admission of guilt. It's usually taken to mean the person making that admission is forthright and honest and above reproach. Obviously, it's not an infallible generalization."

"Is there any disciplinary action?"

"No. That doesn't warrant that sort of thing. You have to understand that he was doing an operation on a very obese person to get that person to lose weight. He had to bypass most of the small intestine so that most of what the patient ate would not be absorbed and he would lose weight. Now if he doesn't bypass enough small intestine, too much is absorbed, and the operation doesn't work. If he bypasses too much and leaves the segment for absorption too short, as in this case, the patient can develop all sorts of serious problems and many of these patients have been known to die of their complications. Determining the precise length of the segment is not an exact measurement and you're never sure the right length has been chosen until after the operation. I think he purposely bypassed too much intestine knowing he could never be strongly criticized for it since so many other surgeons have done the very same thing, with the best of intentions." He watched Mel for his reaction, and then continued. "You see, that's what makes this whole thing so difficult. With any of the things I could claim he's done; the same things could have happened purely unintentionally. How do I know what the truth is?"

"Well then, tell me. Do you buy this or don't you?"

"I just don't know. I guess that's why I'm telling you."

"OK, you're right." Mel put down his pen and rubbed his hands. "That is the question, and that's why we have juries. We don't have to prove the case right now; we just have to see if we have a case. Anyway, I'd like to leave that be for the moment. Tell me a little more about that intestine case, the obese fellow. I'm curious and in a moment, I'll tell you why. How far back was this operation done?"

"About five or six years ago."

"And this person was extremely heavy?"

"Extremely."

"You're talking about Gladys Pemberton's husband, aren't you, when she was Gladys Strumpf?"

That completely surprised Phil. Reluctantly, he confirmed Mel's suspicion. "Yes. I should have realized you'd be able to figure that one out. There haven't been too many people around here that size."

"Who died about five years ago, I might add. But I had one other advantage you're not aware of. I'm the one Walt Pemberton came to for his divorce."

"Really?"

"Yes. Don't forget this is not a very big community. And I remember he was in quite a hurry. I had just stopped doing matrimonial work, so I sent him to a friend of mine who was able to work out an agreement in very short order. Apparently, his wife did not object and must have gotten a rather good settlement. Anyway, the divorce came through very quickly and I recall he married Gladys Strumpf just a short time after that. I must admit, since Walt had come to me first for the divorce, I was very curious about the whole thing. I had heard they never knew each other before her husband's death but I can't say I ever believed that." Mel paused for a moment. "You know what we should do? Let's see when I saw him in the office, and when you're back at the hospital you can find out exactly when her husband died. It would be interesting to see what the dates were."

"I can do that right now," Phil said. "Can I use your phone?"

"Go right ahead. And while you're doing that, I'll get my secretary to check my records."

Phil called the medical records department at the hospital and requested the date Marty Strumpf died. He was put on hold and while waiting for the information, Mel went out to speak with his secretary. A short time later the record room clerk returned to the phone with the information.

"Martin Strumpf expired on September 16, 1987."

"He died September 16, 1987," Phil said when Mel returned. "When did you see him?"

"September 17."

Phil got up from his chair and began pacing the room. He kept looking at the carpet and didn't say anything.

Mel scribbled hurriedly and flipped the page on his pad.

"Just a moment while I get this down. I must admit this is a pretty impressive piece of information. I'm sure you're thinking the same thing I am, that this is quite a coincidence for two people who didn't know each other." He shook his head. Phil looked at him and still didn't reply.

Mel continued looking at his notes for a moment. "OK, I think we have enough information for now. I don't think it's going to do any good to rehash this any further. If we have any holes, and I'm sure I'll be able to think of some, we can deal with them later. Right now, we have motives, we have this woman who's implicated herself and the reason why and why she has involved you in this. We also appear to have a method albeit one that really stretches our sense of belief. Here I have to defer to you. You're the expert. If you say it can be done this way, then I have to take your word. Knowing how you feel about this individual, this other doctor, I also have to assume you feel he's quite capable of doing this sort of thing." He looked at Phil closely this time, waiting for his response.

There wasn't any answer at first.

"Yes. I honestly have to say, if anyone is, it would have to be him. But it can't be left at that. I have to know the truth. I can't go on thinking that he may be killing his patients and not do anything about it." He looked down.

"I understand," Mel said.

"No!" Phil's head shot up; his face flushed. He was on the edge of his chair. "You can't understand. You're not a doctor. You haven't lived with the responsibility that we have. You don't know the feeling I have for my profession and that's in spite of all the goddamned aggravation we have today. I should tell you what I have to put up with, the endless crap. That's really what it is. You want to hear about it? I can tell you about the enormous amount of paperwork, the duplications because insurance companies have this wonderful tendency to 'lose' forms, low reimbursement rates. They don't even begin to compensate you for your time, much less your effort." He made a point of looking directly at Mel. "Have to include malpractice."

"In the past, when I felt a patient needed surgery, I simply scheduled it. Today, I have to get pre-certification for many of my patients. I have to convince their insurance company I'm doing the right thing. Forget the fact I've just done this with the patient, his family, his friends, and the hospital. Patients come to the office today with almost an adversarial attitude. Your profession has had a lot to do with that, and you know exactly what I mean. You feel challenged and very often unappreciated. Many of my colleagues have become very cynical and resentful. Yet I still feel this is a privilege we've been given. Granted it's a privilege we've trained for, just like someone who trains to fix cars or broken pipes. But with us, it's the human body and now we have a trust and forgive me if I sound carried away with self-importance, but I consider this a sacred trust, to do all we can for the well-being of our patients. It's not something that can ever be taken lightly.

"We are the only ones who have this privilege to enter the human body and restore it to health. This is an enormous power. You can't possibly have any idea how much thought and consideration goes into every decision I have to make. I don't operate unless I'm absolutely certain in my own mind there is no other way to deal with a patient's problem. I would never want to think that I might have harmed someone because of an improper decision that I made, and yet, here we may have someone with the same responsibility and trust, completely disregarding this and then purposely causing injury to his patients." His tone softened but he remained adamant. "This simply cannot be allowed."

Mel was solemn, obviously very moved, but still with his objective in mind.

"Knowing you, Phil, I wouldn't have expected anything else in a situation like this. However, we still have to have some idea how we're going to deal with this. Emotions have to be set aside and we have to look at this thing logically. It's clear that you feel these events could have happened and after all that's been said, I have no reason not to agree with you. Do I think all this did happen? That's not as important as you might think although the stronger our personal convictions are, obviously the better it is for our case. Nevertheless, that would ultimately be for a jury to decide, and I must tell you, right now you would not get this before a jury. I'm not saying this to discourage you. We just have to be realistic. In order to go before a jury in a criminal matter, and this is a criminal matter, you have to have an indictment, and in order to have an indictment you have to have evidence, and you simply do not have any evidence. What you have is hearsay, coincidence, and innuendo and that will not get you into court. What will get you into court would be your lady friend coming forward and agreeing to give testimony against the surgeon. Of course, that means she'll be incriminating herself and in spite of laws safeguarding against that and any possible deals that could be worked out, if she didn't have to serve at least some time in jail, at the minimum, her reputation would be very badly damaged. I can't imagine anyone giving up their security for that, and apparently that's her biggest fear."

He lifted up his notepad and gestured with it.

"You know, I still have a problem with that. If that is her concern, why draw attention to something no one would ever suspect and from what you say, would be even harder to prove? That still bothers me."

"I told you what she said. She obviously doesn't see it that way."
"You buy that? You don't think there has to be something else?"

"I've told her a lot of this could be guilt and paranoia, but she says no. She's hinted at some other things, but she won't talk about them. I don't know. How can you ever know what goes on in someone else's mind?"

"You have to admit that has to bother you. There's another thought I just had." He raised his brow as he said this. "Was something going on between them? Is she trying to get back at him now?"

"I never thought of that. I can't answer you. They're two completely different people. I'd have to say no."

"It could explain a lot of this."

"Yes, but I also have to admit this is a pretty incredible story that she's telling us. How could someone like her come up with something like this if it didn't really happen?"

"Good point. But I was going to say, he could've confided in her, if they were having a relationship. That would really give you something to go on. Either way, we're telling each other there's probably something here."

"So now you want me to try to find that out, if they were having a relationship? That should be a pretty neat trick."

"I'm trying to get some logic into all this, Phil. Remember she didn't tell you exactly how it happened. That was left to you, right? You're the one who figured all the rest out."

"So, it's the two of us?" Phil had to smile. "That sounds just great."

"You wouldn't be here now if that wasn't the case. But just keep that in mind. There's a lot more you have to think about, and not just that. No matter what happens with her, going to trial is no guarantee that justice will be served. It would be her word against his and I'll tell you right now credibility would be on his side. Why, just the fact that the hospital has never taken action against him would give his lawyer all he needs to work with. I have to say, Phil, if you want to put this fellow out of action, your best bet lies within the hospital. If he's causing patients' deaths with surgery, I can't believe that he's not in violation of enough hospital regulations to cause suspension."

"That's just it. He probably isn't. On the surface there probably isn't anything he could be accused of except poor judgment and there's the feeling everyone is entitled to that from time to time."

Mel was very skeptical. "You mean you'd stand a better chance of convicting someone of murder than you would disciplining him for operating improperly?"

"I don't know if I would necessarily agree with that," Phil answered, "but in this instance, I'm afraid that would probably be correct. You have to know the system. First of all, it's assumed everyone is acting out of the most ethical considerations. In other words, whatever the physician does is what he feels is best for his patient. Basically, every other activity in the hospital is monitored. We have committees for everything that goes on. We have a committee or service that decides if a patient's admission to the hospital is appropriate, if the length of stay hasn't been too long or too short, if the care rendered has been satisfactory. The dietary service will even determine if the number of calories is adequate. For the most part, patients are probably eating better than I am. Indirectly, this is a yardstick for measuring the quality of care a physician is rendering, but we don't have anything that evaluates the individual practitioner's motivation and intent, and we probably never will. How do we know the test that's been ordered or the treatment that's been recommended is the best possible choice for that patient? How do we know the physician isn't really just adding to his financial return? There are arguments to be made on both sides, so then, how could anyone have suspected what this particular surgeon had in mind, when he operated on these people?"

Phil expected a reply, but Mel remained silent and contemplative, so he continued.

"There was a time when I thought the best way to control questionable practices was with the chief of service. It probably still is, but unfortunately, in many institutions it's very difficult for that individual to be effective. We don't have any full-time chiefs in our hospital. All our department heads are in private practice, and they don't want to antagonize too many people. They depend on referrals just like the rest of us. Even the old-time, crusty department chief who was a full-time, salaried hospital employee who didn't care who he pissed off as long as he was right would have problems today. Nobody wants a chief who's too heavy-handed and is likely to cause a major controversy, especially with the legal recourse everyone has today. That kind of person wouldn't last too long. The board of directors would see to that. Everyone today has to be a mediator who has to find the answer that sends everybody home happy. There is nothing more devastating for a physician than to have his privileges suspended. Everyone wants to avoid that, and no physician ever accepts that without one hell of a legal fight. It's really a very difficult situation."

He stood quietly, thinking. "I suppose it has gotten better. I remember when patients were being brought to the operating room who didn't have more than a few days or weeks to live whether they had surgery or not, just so some goddamn surgeon could get his fee before it was too late. You would think when someone's time has come and there's really nothing else that can be done for them, you'd want to keep them comfortable and just let them go. Fortunately, there are quality assurance committees today and that sort of thing doesn't go on as much. You'd be amazed, though, at the garbage we still have to listen to when somebody tries to justify going in on patients like that. I guess someone might think that's their version of euthanasia just like this guy seems to have his." He threw his arms up and abruptly sat down again. "Aw, what the hell."

Mel looked over at him. "The thought crossed my mind, but it's not quite the standard definition of euthanasia, is it? Frustrating, huh?"

"Yeah."

"Well, I can appreciate that. We have more than a few similar problems with my profession."

Phil laughed when he heard that.

"Wait a minute, Mel. I didn't ask for any comparisons with your profession. Don't put us in the same category. I'm not implying this applies to most doctors. Most doctors are very ethical. It's not like your profession. It's really just a very small number that bends the rules and abuses the system." There was a smirk on his face.

"OK, now it starts getting ugly. I was wondering when the name-calling would begin. Do you think our kind will ever be able to live in peace?"

"Not until you get your hands out of our pockets."

Mel looked at the smug expression on Phil's face. "Surprised yourself with that one, didn't you?"

"Yeah, that was a good one."

"I'll concede that, and I'll even acknowledge that you had the advantage, on one condition."

"What's that?"

"That when you leave here you promise never to tell anyone this was a freebie. I'd never be able to live it down if it got out that an M.D. was in my office and didn't get soaked real good."

Phil laughed as he stood up. "Agreed."

"One last thing. I can appreciate the problem you think you'll have at the hospital. I still think that's your best bet. I don't think you stand a chance with a criminal action, but we could get another opinion. I do know someone in the district attorney's office, and I could give him a call and see what he has to say. I wouldn't want to do that now, but it's a thought. What you can do is find out a few more things about the surgeon. Try to find out about his financial condition and look into those operations that he's done. See what you can find out about his technique in those cases. That's going to be very important." He gave his notes one last look. "I suppose we could also try a long shot and ask this woman if she'd be willing to make a statement." He was not very convincing when he said that. "I guess that's about it." He stood up. "Call me over the weekend and we'll compare notes."

The two men walked to the outer door of the office and shook hands. "I wish there had been some way you could have prepared me for this, Phil, but I guess there really wasn't. I'm a bit relieved, though. I had no idea what this was going to be when you first called and then when you came in here and I saw your expression, I really thought you were going to tell me something had happened between you and Maralyn. I'm glad it wasn't that, although this is bad enough. You give her my love." He squeezed Phil's hand tightly. "I want you to know I will help in every way that I possibly can."

"Thank you, Mel. I appreciate that."

Phil started to leave but Mel stopped him one last time. "I don't want you to worry about this later. Since I know who one of the patients was, it won't take much effort to find out who the surgeon is, but I will keep that to myself."

"Damn! I forgot about that." He grimaced. "Thanks for telling me."

Phil left, grateful for Mel's candor and advice. He knew he had done the right thing in speaking to him. Although Mel had not been overly encouraging, he had somehow made Phil feel better. He looked at his watch. He still had ample time before Ann Hartway expected him and he debated going back to his office to check his messages. Instead, he decided to drive directly to her house. He intended to be straightforward about his discussion with Mel Silverstone. It was her reaction that concerned him now.

Phil pulled into the driveway just as Ann Hartway's car rolled to a stop in front of the garage.

"You're early," she called to him as she waited so that they could walk to the front entrance together. She was dressed in a gray business suit and Phil wondered where she had been to warrant that type of attire. With an almost clairvoyant sense she explained that she had been going to the factory almost every day to learn its operation and had been dressing as befits its top executive. Did he approve of her new image? Of course. Did she also know that the boss left work early today so that he wouldn't be kept waiting? No, but he did appreciate it.

Phil waited in the living room while Ann took a few minutes to freshen up and then they both went into the den where Ann made a vodka Collins for herself, and Phil agreed to the same.

She had removed her jacket earlier and now she kicked off her shoes and sat on the couch, one leg bent beneath her. Phil remembered she had sat that very same way the last time they talked. She appeared very much at ease and smiled at him.

"Which do you want to tell me about first, your trip or the meeting? I can already tell you had good weather. I'm very jealous of your tan."

"It was a nice change, but I think you'd really prefer to hear about the meeting, wouldn't you? The trip was strictly medicine, not very interesting." He knew he could have been more truthful, as some of Gary's antics flashed through his mind, but they would have been hard to describe, and he wasn't in the mood.

"Of course," Ann said.

"First of all, I just wanted to see how all this would sound to someone else. You know it's been very difficult for me to believe this could happen. I discussed it at length with this person and we went over a lot of the details. Of course, I didn't mention any names. I must admit I was very concerned before I went in to speak with him thinking he might just laugh at the whole thing and then I don't know where that would have left us. Anyway, you'll be glad to know he seemed to accept everything I told him. The big difficulty will be what to do next. He made some suggestions but I'm not sure if they'll do any good. I'll just try to do what I can."

Ann had been listening very attentively. "I really would like to know what you told him. Having someone else know about this makes me very nervous. I really wanted to tell you not to speak with anyone after you called me, but I know you're only doing what you think is right and I trust you."

"I really didn't say that much. He needed to know enough details to see if it made sense, and I didn't tell him anything more than that. He doesn't know who's involved and doesn't really want to know, so there's no reason for you to worry. We just went over what happened, how we think it happened and what we should try to do about it now. A lot of this had to do with the legal aspects since these probably are crimes that have been committed."

Ann looked puzzled and concerned. "Did you really think you had to talk about that? You know I'm frightened to death of this thing ever being found out. I just want you to keep him from doing this again. I don't want you thinking of doing something else."

"Nothing else is being done, Ann. I assure you. That's just one of the things we thought should be considered, regardless of what we decide to do. This person's a lawyer so you have to expect that's going to be a concern."

Ann suddenly sat forward. "A lawyer! Why did you have to see a lawyer? I thought you would have spoken to another doctor."

Phil was caught unawares. "It's all right! He's not going to do anything. He didn't think we had any kind of legal case. He agreed whatever we do will have to be done through the hospital. You don't have to be so worried."

Ann was standing now, and Phil started to go to her but her expression made him stop. Her eyes never left his and she looked angry and distraught.

"I just don't know why you had to see a lawyer. I thought for certain you were going to talk to another physician. I never expected this."

She sat down, but quickly got up again. She reached for her drink but then decided against that, too.

Phil watched her. "Ann, there really isn't any problem. I just thought I should have some idea what the legal responsibility is in a situation like this. I wasn't trying to make it more difficult. The attorney was a good choice. I thought he was the best one to help me with the questions I had. I still do. He told me what my options are, I'm sorry, what our options are, and he agrees with you. Whatever is done should be done through the hospital. This shouldn't upset you. It should make you feel better. What's more, I found out something from him that I think is very important and I wouldn't have if I hadn't spoken with him. This was pure luck, but it just shows how we're going to have to get the information we need. I'm sure you'll find this very interesting. Did you know that Walt Pemberton inquired about a divorce from his wife on the very next day after Marty Strumpf died? You know what that suggests, don't you?"

Ann's face suddenly became very pale. "How did Walt Pemberton's and Marty's names come up? I thought you said you hadn't told the lawyer any of the names."

Phil sat very quietly. He realized his mistake and now he struggled for an explanation.

"The lawyer was able to figure out who one of the patients is." His tone was apologetic. "I had to give some description of these cases so he could have a full understanding and when it came to Marty Strumpf, he realized who I was talking about. As he pointed out, there haven't been too many guys that size around here who died after surgery. I guess I should have been aware that could happen, but I don't know how it could have been avoided. I'm sorry. He also had on record a visit to his office by Walt Pemberton the day after Marty Strumpf died. He was there to discuss a divorce."

Ann remained standing, watching Phil closely. "This is not very good, Phil. If he knows any patient's name, then he's certainly going to know the name of the surgeon. That's going to lend suspicion to any of his patients who died. Do you know where that is going to leave me? This is exactly what I was trying to avoid."

Ann closed her eyes and shook her head. "Who is this attorney?"

"Mel Silverstone."

"Oh my God! He just finished settling Jack's estate." She buried her face in her hands and fell back on the sofa.

For a short time, she sat there shaking and Phil could not tell if she was crying.

Then she was very still. "Are you all right, Ann?"

She did not answer at first. After a while, she raised her head. Her eyes were red and moist, but there were no tears.

"No, I'm not all right, Phil. I honestly couldn't feel any worse right now. Mel Silverstone knows a lot about Jack's death. His will be the first one he thinks about as soon as he realizes Stanley Stallings is the surgeon. This is exactly what I've been afraid of. To answer your question again, no, I'm not all right. I really hope you understand what this is doing to me."

She got up again and paced back and forth briefly.

"I'm terribly sorry, Ann. I just didn't think of all this before. I understand your concern, but I don't think it's something you have to worry about." Phil was also on his feet now. "Mel Silverstone is not going to think that every one of the deaths in Stanley Stallings' practice over the past five or ten years was planned, and Jack's is one of the hardest to explain in that way. He died because he wouldn't agree to an amputation. No one could have foreseen that. Maybe there was something else Stanley Stallings had in mind once things started going bad, but we'll never know that. Of all these cases, I would say yours is the least likely to arouse any suspicion. Mel Silverstone is not a fool. He's far from being convinced."

"You're beginning to sound like you're not very convinced, either."

"I need to constantly reassure myself. I admit that. That's why I have to talk to other people. And I try to be very careful when I do speak to them."

"You didn't describe Jack's surgery?"

"As I remember, not at all. He could have been any one of the patients who died, and I'm being completely truthful. The only one we discussed in any detail was Marty Strumpf. It wasn't necessary with the others, and we really didn't have the time."

Ann took a deep breath. "I certainly hope that's true. Maybe I overreacted but all this frightens me terribly. I know you mean well but sometimes I think we may not have the same thing in mind. I just want him to stop doing these things, so he doesn't get caught. Sometimes you sound as though you want to build a case against him so that he can be punished. That's something I could never want."

"You don't want to see him really hurt by this?"

"No, I've told you that before."

"Well, I can't deny I wouldn't like to see something like that. If there is any truth to all this, then it would only be right that he's punished, but there's very little chance that'll happen. I think it's pretty obvious that will be impossible to prove, so I'll settle for just what you want. But don't misinterpret the way I go about this. If I'm to continue to feel I'm doing the right thing, I have to keep convincing myself he's really done what you say, so in that way, I am continuing to build a case against him. That's something you have to understand right now so we don't have this happening again. And I don't want to see you hurt by any of this."

"You really mean that?"

"Yes, of course I do. You know that."

Ann came towards him.

"Oh God, Phil, this is making me feel so awful. I always feel so alone." She was standing very close. Phil had never seen her look so forlorn. "Please hold me."

She reached out her arms to him and he gently drew her close to hold and comfort her. They stayed that way, holding each other, Ann's face against his shoulder. He waited for her to draw away but instead she clutched him more tightly, pressing her body into his. She lifted her head, and he felt her cheek against his face. Her skin was smooth and warm and her fragrance, heady and enticing. At first, Phil was surprised by Ann's unmistakable ardor, and not unpleasantly so, but this quickly turned to confusion and then concern that something eventually quite regrettable might happen. He slowly lowered his arms and tried to step back. Ann finally relented and turned away. Neither looked directly at the other.

"I'm afraid I have to go," Phil said softly. "It's getting late."

"Yes, I know. I kept you longer than I should have. I'm sorry."

"No, Ann. Please. You don't have to say that. A lot of things have happened. We just have to do the best we can to deal with them."

Their eyes met once again.

"What will you do now?" she asked.

"The only thing I can do. I'll talk to whomever I can and find out whatever I can and watch him very carefully. What else can I do at this point? And I promise to be very careful. I'll try not to make any more mistakes."

That brought a very faint smile.

"I still have all my faith in you. My entire future is really in your hands."

"I don't think it's like that at all, Ann, but I'll do whatever I can."

Nothing further was said and Phil left. His arrival home was not viewed as anything unusual, nor was his mood the rest of the evening. He may have been a little quieter than usual but that was always understood and accepted. Maralyn had her own obligations for that evening and had to leave shortly after dinner so very little time was spent with each other. Phil did have some trouble falling asleep that night but otherwise, the day's events did not seem as troubling as might have been expected. He had already decided on his next course of action, and for the time this put to rest any other thoughts he might have had.

VII

Phil was scheduled for the operating room at nine the next morning, but his mind was much more on getting to the record room and learning who the assistant was for Jack Hartway's bypass. He began rounds before eight and as soon as the record room was open, he hurried over. The sooner he knew who that was, he knew he'd likely see that person during the course of the day and tactfully try to get the information he needed.

The clerk brought the chart and on both operative procedures Dr. Stallings was assisted by Dr. Thaddeus Pindyck. This was not unexpected. The two often worked together on vascular cases. Ted Pindyck was the third generation of his family to practice surgery at Middle Valley, his grandfather, also Thaddeus, having been one of the founders of the hospital. This role had been clearly bestowed upon him from his earliest days and had never been questioned or challenged. Phil was of quite the opposite lineage; no other physicians ever having been produced in his family for as long as anyone could remember. This had the advantage of making him the most admired among his family members but at the same time very much aware of the other's more noble family tradition. Phil's future had never been in doubt by virtue of his talent and hard effort. Some distinctions, however, would always remain. Ted Pindyck never set foot in the hospital before ten a.m. so Phil knew it would be pointless to look for him now. Resigned to this, he continued rounds finishing with his last patient just before being called to the operating room. He had to close a colostomy for a seventy-six-year-old woman who had previously perforated herself while self-administering an enema. That was one month ago, and she had tolerated the emergency procedure very well. He was quite certain he would not have to resect the colostomy, and so had requested one of the family practice residents to assist him.

The surgery went smoothly with the colostomy over-sewn and then placed back within the peritoneal cavity and the abdominal wall defect securely closed with a drain. The entire procedure took forty-five minutes and after talking with the patient's family and writing the post-op orders, Phil changed into his street clothes and waited for Ted Pindyck. He had devised an approach he hoped would not allow any suspicion of his real intent and true to habit, at just a few minutes after ten, he watched him come in through the doctors' entrance. He timed his own arrival at the coatroom door to coincide with that of his more privileged colleague. Ted Pindyck spoke first.

"Hi ya, Phil. Looks like I'm coming in and you're going out."

"No such luck, Ted. I've just got to get a form I left in my coat pocket. I'll still be here for a while."

"Too bad. It's a beautiful day out there. A little nippy, though."

"Try the coffee on One West. You'll forget it's winter outside, guaranteed. If you're heading that way, I'll walk with you." With that, both surgeons headed down the corridor toward the nursing units.

Phil waited for just a short while and then spoke again.

"By the way, Ted, I've been meaning to talk to you. I've been thinking of reviewing our vascular complications and I was told you assisted Stanley on that case he reported six months ago. I don't know if you remember. It was Jack Hartway."

"Oh yes, I remember."

"I was thinking of asking you because I'm not sure I'll get a straight answer from Stanley. What really went wrong with that case? I saw the angios and I would have sworn he'd get a good result."

"I thought so, too. You know, you're the first person to ask me about that case. I obviously couldn't say much at the conference but if you really want my opinion, I'd say he just did a terrible job. I've helped him with a fair number of those cases before and he's always done a very competent job but this time it was like someone else was operating."

"It was that bad?"

"It had to be for me to remember it so well. First of all, the vein was very narrow, almost hypoplastic. Then at some of the areas where he had to ligate its branches, he narrowed it even further. I never thought it would stay open, but he kept saying it would dilate and I think he must have really believed that. I know I would have taken it down and put in a prosthesis. I kept telling him that, but he kept saying you get better results with the vein. It's true, except not with that one. There was a pulse when he finished but one area was so narrowed, you could feel a thrill just beyond it."

"You think that's where it occluded?"

"It must have. I helped him when he went back in and he couldn't even get a Fogarty catheter down from above. We took the vein out and put in a Gore-Tex graft, but the leg was very bad by then. That surprised me too, because the patient didn't have that bad a problem to start with and I thought if that graft occluded, he wouldn't be any worse off than he was before the operation. It just goes to show you that you never can be sure about these things. I guess that clot just propagated all the way down his leg. The arteriogram we got after that second procedure didn't show much at all going into the lower leg. It was really too bad."

"You feel it was all technical, then? No chance that heparin or anything else could have helped?"

"No way. It was just a technically poor operation. Actually, very poor. And I'd never seen him operate like that before or since. So, what do you say? Nothing. You figure he just had an off day, and you leave it at that."

Phil seemed to be very understanding.

"Well, Ted, I appreciate that information. I want to be accurate with the reasons for the failure and I knew you'd give me an honest opinion. I don't know if I'll have enough material for a paper but so far it looks promising. There're a few other cases I'm particularly interested in, but you're not involved. Maybe I'll come up with something worthwhile. Who knows? Anyway, it's time to see some patients. I'll probably catch you later. Thanks again."

"Anytime."

Phil spent some time at the nurses' station and when Ted Pindyck was no longer in view, headed back toward the coatroom. He wasn't sure what he should be feeling now but the implications were obvious. A sense of anticipation was slowly building. If Stanley Stallings had truly intended to harm Jack Hartway, this was precisely how Phil theorized it might be done. Clearly, these complications could escalate to bring about the desired result. If it appeared these would not be enough, Phil had every confidence some aspect of the patient's further management could be manipulated to achieve that outcome. It could have been high-dose antibiotics needed to fight a critical infection that could lead to an overwhelming superinfection. These same agents could cause liver or kidney failure. There were many such options.

This was very disturbing, but also very crucial. It seemed to bring much-needed credibility to Ann Hartway's allegations. His first reaction was to call her but then he reminded himself she had maintained this all along. He decided, instead, to wait for the weekend and contact Mel Silverstone for his reaction. There was other information he had been asked to get, in particular, information about Dr. Stallings' financial status. He hadn't but that didn't seem as important right now. A very strong link had just been forged and with it came a feeling of great satisfaction and others as well, of anxiety and foreboding.

Phil called Mel Silverstone at his home on Saturday morning. Mel was very impressed with Phil's description of Jack Hartway's operation and also considered it very crucial. He again emphasized that knowledge of Stanley Stallings' financial situation would be very pertinent and somehow should be obtained. He had also taken the liberty to speak with an assistant district attorney. He admitted this was probably premature, but perhaps not that premature, after having heard the description of Jack Hartway's operation. In any case, as skeptical as that person was, he did say that he would like to meet directly with Phil. His name was Gordon Mulcahey and he was very highly regarded. A meeting could be held in Mel's office this Monday or Tuesday afternoon if Phil could be available. Phil said he would be there, and they decided on Tuesday at three p.m.

The rest of the weekend was busy. Phil was on call and there was a fairly steady stream of lacerations and assorted minor trauma that required his services in the emergency room. He also had one person with an incarcerated inguinal hernia that received prompt surgical correction and an automobile accident in which two of the four people involved were admitted for further observation and treatment. On Monday morning, he did a colon resection and a breast biopsy and, in the afternoon, saw twenty-three people during office hours. It was a very grueling three days and yet little of it seemed to have impacted him. Unbeknown to any others, his thoughts were elsewhere and seemed to make him oblivious to the stresses of those three days. On Tuesday afternoon at precisely three p.m., he walked briskly into Mel Silverstone's office.

Mel was seated at his desk. Sitting across from him in one of the large brown office chairs was a pleasant looking, rather husky professional type complete with three-piece suit and full mustache. Phil guessed his age to be about forty-five and assumed this must be Gordon Mulcahey.

Mel got up from his chair and extended his hand.

"Phil, you made it. Good. This is Gordon Mulcahey." The two men shook hands and Mel shut both doors to his office.

"I'm very glad to meet you, Doctor. Mel has been telling me quite a story about these allegations at the hospital. I think I should be very candid with you. The very least I can say is that it stretches the imagination a bit."

Mel stepped between the two men and led Phil to a chair. "Gordon and I were talking for a while before you got here, Phil, and I did my best to give him an unbiased picture of what you say happened, but I don't think he's ready to buy it. Is that a fair statement, Gordon?"

"I'd say so."

"You'll also find him to be very blunt."

Phil sat there without saying anything.

"Doctor, when Mel first called me and described these so-called events to me, I thought he was putting me on. However, I know Mel doesn't joke like that and then I realized he was serious. I still wouldn't be here if I didn't respect him as an attorney. Another reason, frankly, is that I'm curious. It's very hard for me to believe what you say happened, but you're welcome to try to convince me. I'm here to listen."

"What can't you believe?" Phil asked.

Gordon Mulcahey leaned back and laughed. "We'll be here all day, Doctor." He laughed again but then sat forward in his chair and his expression immediately changed. "OK I'll tell you right at the outset. The woman who told you all this, she's seeing a psychiatrist, right? You feel she's someone who can be believed?"

"Yes."

Gordon looked at Mel and then turned back to Phil. "She's also on this medication, Mellaril. I've dealt with people who have been on it. That's usually given to the ones that are very disturbed, isn't it?"

"Usually, I suppose, but not always. In her case, it's what seemed to work best. She had a very troubled marriage and other medications were tried first. There are a lot of people like that. I don't think they're disturbed in the sense you're suggesting."

"She told you this?"

"Yes."

"You know the name of the psychiatrist?"

"Yes. She's been very open about all this. She hasn't tried to hide anything."

"You haven't tried to speak with this psychiatrist?"

Mel was trying to get Gordon's attention at this point. Finally, he looked over.

"Yes, I know, Mel. You don't think I should be this hard on the good doctor." He turned back to Phil.

"Don't pay any attention to the way this may sound. These are questions that will have to be cleared up. Don't forget what you're asking us to believe. Now, you didn't speak with this psychiatrist?"

"No. I'm satisfied with her explanation."

Gordon pursed his lips and sat staring for a moment. "Mel also tells me you don't particularly care for this other surgeon. You have a very poor regard for him."

"Yes, and that's why I'm trying to be so careful."

Gordon put a hand to his face and then quickly glanced at Phil. "Excuse me, Doctor! I think if you really meant that, you would speak with the psychiatrist and find out precisely this woman's emotional state. Not doing so, it seems to me you may be more anxious to involve this surgeon than you're willing to admit. What if the psychiatrist tells you she's really off the wall?"

"I don't think so. She's never given me that impression."

Gordon scowled. "Come on, Doctor. Even Mel and I know better than that. You're not an expert. Maybe psychiatrists really aren't either, but aren't they the ones to decide this? You're a good surgeon. Mel told me. Isn't this what you'd normally do?"

"Yes."

"Well, then, why don't you call this psychiatrist and find out how reliable this woman really is? Let him convince us. I don't think I'm being unreasonable."

"That's fair," Phil said.

"OK Now let's talk a little more about the case that seems to have started all this. How did this woman and the surgeon arrive at the decision to kill her husband? Did she come right out and ask him or was it the other way around? I'm kidding, of course. Mel says that was very vague."

Phil answered slowly and deliberately. "I'll tell you the same thing I told Mel and that was what the woman told me. It was vague and it was mostly implied. I'm not going to tell you it was more explicit, if she tells me it wasn't. When the surgeon told her of the risk of the surgery her husband would require, she passed a remark that she didn't really care what happened to her husband. Now, that remark could have been passed absentmindedly and without thinking. She was probably just ventilating about her unhappy marriage, and I think any surgeon would have passed it off as just that.

"But this particular surgeon doesn't do that. Before this he wasn't particularly in favor of surgery. Now he's willing to operate on the patient even though he may be open to criticism for doing a procedure that may not really be required. And, of course, the fee has to be very substantial, thirty thousand dollars, in this particular case."

"He never does actually say that he is going to kill the patient?"

"No, he doesn't."

"And she never asks him directly if that is what he is going to do?"

"No. According to her, it was all very subtle, but she claims it was clearly understood her husband would not survive the surgery. She even told him at one point that paying the thirty thousand dollars would not be a problem if it came out of her husband's life insurance money."

"What did the surgeon say to that?"

"She didn't say he said anything. There was another time, though, when he asked her if they still had an agreement."

Phil waited for a reaction.

"That's it?" Gordon looked at Mel and then Phil. "Doctor, even if this patient's wife took the stand, what you've told me wouldn't even get us in the courthouse door. I suppose she paid cash?"

Phil nodded affirmatively.

"Of course," Gordon said.

Mel interrupted. "I told you what this was going to be, Gordon. I think we have to be fair about this. Phil is in a very difficult position."

Gordon Mulcahey frowned and took a deep breath. "Don't take my reactions as anything personal, Doctor. This is a very troubling situation, for every conceivable reason. Let me ask you something. Do you think this surgeon has been knocking off his patients?"

"I'm not sure," Phil said. "That's the one question I keep trying to answer every single day."

"OK Then let me ask you this. Do you think he could have killed these patients?"

"Yes."

"OK then, tell me this. You claim he is doing this with the surgery he performs, again, if this is indeed what is happening. Mel tried to explain this to me and although I know something about lethal injections and turning off life support systems, and now these assisted suicides, your theory is entirely new to me. I can certainly understand operating on someone who is a bad risk and having that patient die of complications. I just went through that with my wife's grandfather who had to have surgery for his gallbladder and then died of pneumonia. But what about someone who is younger and basically much healthier? How do you get them to die without being obvious about it? I must admit, this is what I'm most curious about.

"Convince me that this is possible and maybe together we can work out something on this."

"All right. I've already discussed this with Mel to some degree, but I think I can be more specific now. Just this past week I was able to speak with the surgeon who assisted on the bypass procedure. I wanted to know what he thought of the operation since any one of us, I think, would have expected it to be a success. He told me it was one of the worst procedures he'd ever seen. He described one after another instance of poor judgment, poor technique, just plain lousy surgery. Now this surgeon is technically very competent. I'll even admit that. His assistant said he's never seen him operate as badly either before or after that case. Now why should this rather technically sound surgeon do such a poor job? And why do I say that kind of surgery could be used rather reliably to bring about a patient's death? Because just as the surgeon knows how to avoid complications, he can also cause them if that's what he wants and if those complications will not lead to the patient's death, of and by themselves, then he can help that along in the guise of treating those complications. For example, this patient's leg became gangrenous. When that occurs, the patient needs intensive antibiotic treatment either to prevent infection or treat it. Antibiotics have side effects. Some will injure the kidneys if administered in very high doses. Others may destroy the bone marrow. They can even cause a different infection, one that's worse than the original one.

"The surgeon orders high doses because he's dealing with a serious condition. Pretty soon he has other problems. That makes the infection even more difficult to treat or there may be other totally different complications that require other drugs, all with their own particular side effects. He can keep ordering one thing after another until he gets just the result he wants, and everyone is thinking he's pulling out all the stops to save the patient."

"Nice," Gordon Mulcahey said. "That's what you think he did?"

"Not entirely. It looks to me that he acted like this only to a point. Then something else happened and I'm not sure the surgeon expected it. The patient refused treatment that would have saved his life. If this is what he intended, it certainly made the surgeon's job a lot easier although I'm sure he would have found another way."

"You sound very positive about this person now. A little while ago you didn't sound as certain. Anything change all of a sudden?"

The tone was derisive causing Mel to glance disapprovingly in Gordon's direction.

Phil shook his head. "No, not really. It's just the way my thinking goes from one minute to the next. I'm totally frustrated, that's all."

"Well, this thing is not going to do that to me," Gordon said and laughed. Then, more serious again, he looked at Mel and then at Phil. "You have no idea how you're going to prove this, do you?"

"No."

"And you think he may have acted in this very same way with these other cases?"

"Yes."

"Judging from what I've heard so far, I don't think we have to go into those details right now. I think we'll be left with the same level of suspicion and nothing really concrete. Even with what this woman has told you, all this is still just supposition? Correct?"

"Yes."

"Then I have one suggestion that I feel is really worthwhile. Let's forget the woman for the moment. Her testimony eventually will be needed even though any decent attorney will be able to make mincemeat out of it. It will have its purpose. Right now, however, you need something to tell you that you're going in the right direction. My thought is that you try to tape him in a conversation with another patient. Now this is strictly off the record, but you could consider sending someone to this surgeon's office wearing a wire and pretending that they wanted someone knocked off with an operation. You'd have to be pretty slick about the whole thing, but you might just get him to say something on tape that could be incriminating."

Phil looked at Mel.

"What Gordon is saying, Phil, is that you plant a small microphone on someone and send that person to the surgeon's office with some sort of story about needing surgery that he will believe. Then you try to set up the same type of situation you had with the woman and her husband, only this time, you try not to make it so subtle. This idea has some merit and in your particular situation, this is probably the only option you have."

"Look," Gordon said, "you get everything down on tape. I don't know just what you'd get or even if you'd be able to use it in court, but it might be something that could help your case. I could give you the name of someone very good who we've occasionally used. The expense, of course, would have to come out of your pocket."

Phil mulled it over for a moment.

"You really think that's something that should be done?"

"You really haven't got anything else," Gordon said. "My first reaction would have been to advise you to try to do something about this guy through the hospital, but Mel has told me you don't feel that would work. I'm not sure I really understand that. One would think he had to break some of the rules of good medicine before he had actually broken our criminal laws. If any of these allegations are true, I'm sure there must be ample grounds to report him to some committee. I still don't see how you could do any worse if you reported him to someone."

Phil shook his head. "No, I'm afraid you're wrong. This person is very shrewd, and you just have to listen to him talk. He can be very convincing. It would all be explained to everyone's satisfaction as just being poor judgment. Everyone is allowed that every so often, as long as it doesn't become a frequent thing."

"With all due respect, Doctor Berger, that sounds like the old saw, whenever the chips are down, you guys will always cover for one another."

Mel raised his hand trying to get Gordon's attention and at the same time mollify the tone of his comment, but Phil was already on his feet.

"Damn it! Don't you realize what's going on here? Some bastard is going around killing his patients while the rest of us spend twenty-four hours a day, seven days a week ripping our guts out trying everything and anything to keep our patients alive. This isn't just some deviation from the so-called standard of care. This is a goddamned abomination! To me, this is blasphemy. If this is what is happening, it must be stopped!"

Suddenly his voice trailed off as he became aware of the intensity of his emotions.

The two lawyers watched him closely. Phil regained his composure.

"I've told you whatever I can right now. I realize it may not be very much but it's enough to cause me enormous concern. I know I can't do anything about it within my profession and you've told me I can't within the legal system, either. That leaves me with very little recourse and that is very upsetting. Bad as it is, you have to make it worse with a totally uncalled-for remark about doctors covering up for one another. What that tells me is that I still haven't gotten the point across to you and you don't really understand what I've been saying."

Mel started to answer but Gordon stopped him.

"Wait a second, Mel. That was meant for me. That remark may have been out of line so I will apologize, but you better understand what you have here. This is just a lot of unfounded suspicions and the allegations of one woman, which even you admit are so vague as to be questionable. This doesn't mean that I think you should give up or that I won't try to help you. I'm going to give you my card. It has a direct number to my office. Anytime you feel you have something worthwhile; I want you to call me. We'll go over it and see what it sounds like. I'll tell you right now. If this guy is that bad, he's not going to stop and one of these days he'll make a mistake. If you watch him, you just may catch him."

"That's going to be hard," Phil said. "Surgical patients usually aren't in the hospital very long before they're operated on. That doesn't give me much time to check on his patients."

"You'll have to do the best you can." Gordon stood up and handed Phil his card and reached for his coat. He suddenly turned and faced Phil again.

"Christ, do you know how many people we know who have committed crimes, without there being any doubt whatsoever, and we can't prosecute them because we don't have a case, crimes as bad as this one, if not worse? You have just one. I hate to tell you how many we have." He headed for the door but then stopped. "Now I sound like I already have this guy convicted." He laughed, but that quickly changed.

"You know what I think? I don't think it's guilt and fear that made her come to you. I've got a much different feeling about this whole thing. I'll bet there was something going on between the two of them, the wife and the surgeon. Nothing else makes as much sense. Maybe it happened the way you say, but I don't think so. Let's face it. Regardless of what she says, she wants to get back at him. Don't be surprised if they had something going at one time and maybe he called it quits. How often have we seen that, Mel?" He glanced over at him and then at Phil. "It also wouldn't surprise me one bit if it turns out she was one of his patients."

He opened the door. "Mel, I'll talk to you. And Phil, I expect you to call."

Mel gestured to Phil to sit down after Gordon left.

"He's a good man. He'll try to help."

"Do you think he believed anything I said?"

"You heard what he just said. He's trying to. You just have to remember he's a district attorney. Unlike the rest of us who can try to bluff our way from time to time, his cases have to be very solid. With us, if they ever made a rule that a lawyer had to believe his client before he could take the case, we'd all be out of work. He has serious doubts. We all do. What's important, though, is that he recognizes there might be a problem, and he's willing to try to help you resolve that. He's already given you one good piece of advice, the wireless microphone. You really ought to think about that."

Phil remained silent. He sat forward, looking at the floor.

"There's something else you should think about. I mentioned it the first time we spoke, and Gordon also brought it up. It's just conjecture, mind you, but try to follow this. There is a conspiracy to kill this one patient, but it's not subtle or vague. It's a very clever scheme devised by the surgeon who's involved with the patient's wife. It's a mutual decision. Both are completely willing participants, and the plan is successful. After a while, he loses interest in her and wants out. She doesn't want that and now she wants to get back at him. In their more intimate moments, he may have told her how he gets along with some of his colleagues. She goes to one who she knows does not care for this surgeon. She wants to convince him that what he's done to her husband, a truly criminal act, he's done to some of his other patients. That may or may not be true. She will not allow herself to be implicated, but she can be reasonably certain this surgeon will make trouble for her ex-paramour. Serious trouble. Sound familiar?"

"Yes, Mel. You make your point, but that's not the way I see it. Unfortunately, you don't know this person the way I do—not the wife, the surgeon. I don't know if he's done the things she's said, but I do feel he's capable of it. And I think I know why she came to me, and it's not for the reason you think. There's probably a lot of different ways you can explain this, but there's only one real answer. That's the one I must have."

He slowly got to his feet.

"That's OK That's why you have to keep working on this and we have to help. It's going to take time. We know that."

Mel was standing now, ready to accompany Phil to the door. "Let's see what we can do. Don't forget the wire."

"Thanks, Mel. I don't know what I'm going to do, but I'll keep you posted." With that, he took his coat and left.

He went straight to his office and called Ann Hartway. There was no answer and he assumed she must be at work. He wanted to tell her he had met again with Mel Silverstone and there had been further discussion but without mention of any names. He thought she would find this reassuring. Nothing would be said about anyone else's presence. He decided he'd call her later, after his rounds. Then he placed the call to Richard Terry. No one was in the office, and he left a message on the answering machine. A little while later, he was back in the hospital.

He was still seeing patients when he heard his name on the overhead page. Phil excused himself and went to the nearest phone. It was an outside call.

"Hello?"

"Hello, Phil. It's Dick Terry. Your office told me where I'd find you. You surgeons never leave the hospital, do you?"

"It seems that way, sometimes. Thanks for calling back."

"No problem. How can I help you?"

"I have a question about one of your patients, Ann Hartway?"

"Funny you should mention her. I hadn't seen her for months and then she called me. Wanted to have some medication renewed."

"Yes, I know. Mellaril, 25 milligrams T.I.D."

"She told you?"

"Yes. You saw her while she was having a lot of marital difficulty. I know you tried other medications before the Mellaril. She said I could speak to you."

"Hmm. Sounds like she did. Is she having a surgical problem now?"

"Yes. That's precisely what she's having. I couldn't have put it any better myself."

"Is that your way of saying you're having trouble with the diagnosis? I think I detect a little humor."

"Right again. I am having a lot of trouble. All of a sudden, I find out she's been on Mellaril and now I'm not so sure she's giving me a clear picture of her problem."

"Phil, I'm usually not at liberty to discuss this type of information without the patient's consent, even with another physician. She does seem to have confided in you. Well, with what you've told me and what you're asking, I don't think this would be a breach. As I recall, she's quite stable. I wish I had my notes with me. It's not a matter of misleading you. There may be some other pertinent information I can share with you. Will you be in tomorrow afternoon? I can call you."

"Sure. Thanks a lot, Dick."

Phil did not feel this was necessary but agreed. He went back to his patient, Ann's stability no longer an issue.

He arrived at the hospital later than usual the following morning. The hospital was again having problems with its discharges and a number of the day's admissions had to be cancelled because of lack of beds. This included the varicose vein stripping Phil had scheduled for that day. He decided he'd have an easy, relaxed morning. He had spoken with Ann Hartway around five yesterday afternoon and described his conversation with Ted Pindyck. She wasn't at all surprised and hoped he'd be encouraged by this. She was less pleased when told there had been a second meeting with Mel Silverstone even though no additional names had been mentioned. She was still apprehensive, but hopeful that all would work out for the best. Nothing else was mentioned and Phil promised to call again or stop by in a few days.

His first stop this morning was the surgical unit on the second floor of the Humboldt Pavilion. As he began to turn the corner into the main corridor, he heard Gary Barlow's familiar voice.

"I don't care if it is only ten dollars. That's not the point. I can name a dozen nurses in this hospital who'll go a lot further for a heck of a lot less."

Phil didn't know if he should continue in the same direction or quickly turn around, lest he be drawn into another embarrassing situation. Before he could decide, Gary saw him.

"Hi, Phil. Be right with you." Then he turned back to the pretty young nurse he was berating.

"OK, I'll pay your ten dollars, but this is the last time. Here! Imagine, taking money for that."

And with that, Gary turned to join Phil. People who had passed by either heard the conversation and left with their mouths gaping or pretended not to hear and double-timed past with their heads buried in their chests. The poor nurse, of course, was every shade of crimson and absolutely speechless.

"My God, Gary, how could you embarrass that poor girl in front of everyone like that? How is she going to face those people after this?"

Gary looked puzzled. "What are you talking about, Phil?"

"What am I talking about? I'm talking about whatever it is that's going on between you two. You just broadcasted it throughout this entire hospital."

"I'm sorry, but I don't follow you, Phil. I just sponsored that nurse in one of those March of Dimes walkathons. I gave her a dollar a mile and she walked ten miles, but now I find out most of the other guys were giving 25 and 50 cents a mile and their entries walked a lot more. It cost them a lot less and I feel like I've been had. Now, what did you think I meant?" Gary waited but Phil remained silent. Finally, he began to smile and pointed a finger at Phil. "Don't tell me you were thinking there was something going on between me and that nurse. Shame on you, Phil. You actually had your mind in the gutter. Does that mean there's a new you that we're finally seeing?"

Phil would not answer. He knew his only recourse now would be his continued silence. Still, Gary would not be deterred.

"Hey, you wanna see a really great case? I mean it. You've never seen anything like this before. Come with me."

Reluctantly, Phil followed. This could be another prank but then again, no one ever knew when Gary was serious. They came to a semi-private room. A very attractive brunette occupied the bed next to the window. Gary was smiling.

"Say, Rosalind, did you see it this morning? It was there when I pulled in and it should still be there now."

"You mean it? Darn, I didn't." The brunette rushed from her bed to the window. She was wearing a thin, sheer yellow nightgown, which was now silhouetted against the window and with the bright sunlight shining through was rendered completely transparent. The two surgeons were treated to this scene of a very well-built, essentially nude young woman straining at the window to see something that apparently was not yet in view.

"I don't see it, Dr. Barlow. Are you sure it was there?"

"It certainly was when I came in." Gary winked at Phil. "Keep looking. It was in the far row."

"The far row. Oh, I don't see it. I must have missed it again." The brunette turned to face the two men and paused momentarily in front of the window. It was actually difficult to find fault with Gary at that precise moment. The scene was almost reverential. She walked slowly back to her bed. Every movement was carefully observed.

She sat on her bed and pouted.

"Dr. Barlow, sometimes I think you're teasing me."

"Don't be silly. It's been there. I'll come back later, and we'll look again, together."

Gary's smile was rapturous and widened even more. With that, he turned to leave the room, Phil close behind. Both men glanced at the woman in the other bed. Her look was clearly disapproving as she mouthed the words, "You're terrible."

"Uh-oh," Gary said, nodding towards the roommate. "She wasn't here before. There was some old gork in that bed who was totally out of it. I'll bet this one is going to shoot her mouth off. Now I guess I'll just have to discharge her. I really should, I suppose. I took her appendix out about a week and a half back and she's been ready to go home for the past four or five days. I just can't bear to see her go. She's some sort of sports car freak and I keep telling her someone has a Lamborghini that he brings to the hospital once in a while. She's never seen one and I just love to watch her look for it, especially when it's really sunny. I guess now I'll have to send her home. It's just as well. The utilization committee was getting after me, anyway."

"Boy, you never stop, do you? I just wish they'd get after some of the others. There are no empty beds again and most of the elective surgical admissions were cancelled."

"You don't have to tell me. I had two people cancelled yesterday and only one is getting in today and I practically had to beg the admitting office for that one. Hey, if it isn't this kind of aggravation, then it's something else. Last week I found out a patient I operated on two months ago forgot to pre-certify his admission, and now the insurance company won't pay. He won't either. He says my office should have done it for him. Doesn't even return our calls now. You know, you really can't afford to overlook anything these days. I have a case being reviewed by our esteemed peer review committee right now because I didn't change an antibiotic after the sensitivities showed the organism to be resistant. It didn't make any difference that the patient did fine."

"None of that is going to get any better," Phil said. "I have my secretaries check everything on the patients' insurance and I document everything in their charts. You don't have a choice if you want to stay in practice."

"You think it should be this way?"

"No. I think sometimes it does make for better patient care but most of the time it's just too much unnecessary extra work. I'm not happy with the way things are but there's obviously a lot of people who don't think we can be trusted. I'm not sure they aren't occasionally right."

Gary nudged Phil. "Whose side are you on right now? I can't tell."

"Don't worry. I'm on the right side, our side. It's just that I feel we're responsible for some of our problems and I won't deceive myself by always blaming someone else. Look at the way some people practice in this institution. Do you mean to tell me every patient that comes into this hospital receives good, sound advice and treatment? You know that's not true."

"Who are you talking about?"

"Who do you think?"

"I don't think that's fair," Gary said. "He's a very unusual individual. I don't think there're very many like him around."

"We're talking about the same person?"

"I'm sure. Stanley. Right?"

"Yes."

"Everyone knows. I just got off the tissue committee. Half of the cases that came up were his. Most of the gastroscopies and colonoscopies that he does are questionable. He has more normal appendectomies than any other surgeon on staff. It's the same thing with his breast biopsies.

Almost everything is fibrocystic disease. What can you do about it? He always has some sort of answer."

"Who's doing the surgical mortalities now?"

"You putting me on? C'mon now. You mean you really don't know?" Phil shrugged.

"It's me. I'm the man. Mal Mueller gave it to me right after I got off the tissue committee, in more ways than one. I hate that damn job."

"I really didn't know," Phil said. "While we're on the subject, have any more of his cases come up for mortality review?"

"Not since I've been doing 'em, but that's only been since the first of the month. I guess the last one was that vascular case you knew about. Speaking of that, I have one upstairs right now that's almost like that one. It's a seventy-eight--year-old man with ischemic changes in his foot with an occluded aorta and iliac arteries. I'd like to do an aortofemoral bypass, but he's had some EKG changes. Anesthesia won't put him to sleep unless a cardiologist puts a note in the chart that he absolutely hasn't had an MI. He feels fine, never had any chest pain and his enzymes are all normal. If they won't clear him for general anesthesia, I can swing a graft from his axilla to both femoral arteries under local anesthesia, but his daughter can't make up her mind. She runs the show, and she wants me to guarantee that there won't be any risk. She can't decide if he should have a bypass and run whatever the risk is of an MI or wait for gangrene to develop and then have an amputation. In the meantime, I'm stuck in the middle. Isn't that something like Stanley's case? Wasn't the patient trying to tell him what to do?"

"I think his was a lot different."

"Well, maybe, but you can see it's getting a lot harder to treat this type of patient with all the input you have to get. I'm not so sure I'd be that hard on Stanley, at least in this case."

"That's your opinion. I'll tell you what. You let me know the next time Stanley's name comes up in mortality review and let's talk about that case. Then let's see what we both think. Maybe we'll find that we're perhaps a little too understanding when it comes to some of his cases."

Gary winced. "Man, you really do have it in for that guy. Don't you think that should be someone else's job? Isn't there some guy named

Malcolm Mueller who's supposed to be the chief of surgery? Isn't that what he's supposed to do?"

"I think you just said it when you said 'supposed'. Can you ever remember him doing anything when it came to a quality issue?"

"I've seen him try," Gary said. "I think it's just his personality. I don't think he likes to deal with problems. That still doesn't mean someone else should try to do his job for him."

"Meaning?"

"You know damn well what I mean, Phil. Look. I'll let you know when he has another death if you don't hear about it first. I'd just be very careful what you make of it. Stanley's been around here a very long time and nobody else has tried to make trouble for him. That should tell you something."

"I'm not trying to make trouble, Gary. I just have trouble understanding some of the things he does." He rubbed his face and eyes. "I don't want to keep talking about this, so let's just drop it. What are you going to do with the man with the bad foot?"

"I don't know. Wait for the daughter to make up her mind, I guess. Everything's documented in the chart."

"The patient can't sign?"

"I think he understands but no one wants to do anything without her consent. She can be an awful lot of trouble. She's either in the nursing office or administration every single day bitching about one thing or another."

"You smell a lawsuit?"

"Very possible. I wouldn't put it past her. Look, if you get a phone call from me at three in the morning within the next few days, you'll know she's decided and we're going to be doing something. That way you'll have your name on the chart, and when they sue, you'll know the same time I do. How's that?"

"I guess I couldn't ask for anything more from a real friend. Thank you, Gary."

"Don't mention it. By the way, want to hear my idea for improving the tight bed situation?" Gary did not wait for an answer. "Improve the hydraulics on the beds. Make 'em into a sort of catapult. Face 'em towards the windows. I got the idea watching the news the other night.

They showed a nursing home fire, and they were tossing the patients out the windows. Seemed to work pretty well."

"Same old Gary," Phil commented. "For a while there, you seemed serious. I was getting worried."

"Anybody can have a lapse now and then," Gary said, then winked and walked away. Phil continued on his rounds.

He saw the patients at a very leisurely pace, and after that was finished, he dictated a number of charts and then attended a noontime pathology conference where sandwiches were served. Gary was there but left promptly after all the food was eaten. Phil stayed to the end and then it was time for office hours. There weren't any last-minute additions so even that wasn't rushed. He wondered if Dick Terry would remember to call. He was pretty sure he would, so wasn't surprised when the secretary called over the intercom at quarter to four that Dr. Terry was on the phone. He asked the patient to get dressed while he went next door to take the call in private.

"Hello, Dick. I'm glad you remembered to call."

"I said I would. I have my notes in front of me now. I didn't even bother to call Mr. Hartway. With what you've told me, I'm sure this is all right."

"I appreciate that."

"My pleasure. Now, just what was it you asked? Why she's taking the Mellaril, right?"

"That was it."

"Well, according to this, we tried Valium, Xanax, Ativan, Elavil, Prozac. Mellaril was suggested only because we had no success with the others. She said it helped."

"It was only because of her marital difficulty."

"As far as I can tell, yes. Let me just look here. Oh, yes. This was a terrible marriage. Here's what I was looking for. I really felt her husband needed counselling. I suggested to her that he come in, either with her, or alone. The next week she had a large bruise on her cheek. I have it here in my notes. She said her husband didn't wish to see me."

"You think she was a battered wife?"

"She said he didn't do it. In my notes I have down that someone else might have done it. Don't ask me why. That must've been the impression

I got then. She was insistent it was an accident. That's underlined. I never saw any bruises again. I watched for them because that marriage wasn't going well at all. To answer your question, she didn't feel she had to see me after her husband died, so it would seem he was the source of her problems. Don't ask me why she needs Mellaril now. I offered to see her again."

"What did she say?"

"She'd try to work it out herself, first. If you're seeing her now, maybe it's organic. Maybe you have the answer."

"Not yet."

"Well, let's see what else I can tell you without overstepping my bounds. You're really hung up on that Mellaril, aren't you? Well, she's not delusional. I have here, strong-willed, manipulative, flirtatious. That reminds me. She is an incredibly beautiful woman. Why her husband didn't appreciate her is beyond me. I'm not saying she ever came on to me. I guess 'outgoing at times' would have been more appropriate."

There was a lull.

"Let's see. You're not interested in this. I shouldn't tell you that. Oh, yes. Frequently indulges in fantasies. I thought I recalled that. That's the sort of thing that should interest you, Phil."

"Why?"

"Well, because of the distinction you have to make. As long as you know it's a fantasy, you're OK. If you think they're real, then you have a problem. Ann knew what her fantasies were. Obviously, they helped her cope with this very difficult marriage. They were a means of escape. I'd say any symptoms she has now are real, and not imagined. Gee, look at this. Infatuation, question mark, physician. I forgot about this. And now I'm sorry I read it out loud. These are the things we shouldn't be discussing. I apologize."

"That's OK It wouldn't mean anything to me anyway."

"Well, I still shouldn't mention anything like that. In all fairness to her, there was never anything about an affair and this infatuation thing, possibly with a physician, a supposition, something she may have said and the way I took it. I think we covered it, Phil. She's with it. She's OK."

"Thanks very much, Dick. I appreciate it."

"My pleasure."

Phil put down the phone. Sometime in the next few days he would tell Gordon exactly the same thing. Ann was quite rational and very much in touch with reality. No one else had to know the rest. That he would leave to mull over himself. He went back to his patient.

There wasn't much else Phil could do over the ensuing weeks but go about his usual activities and watch and wait for anything else that might happen. Initially, he called Ann Hartway frequently to maintain their contact but as little of consequence occurred, the intervals between the calls became longer. She seemed to understand and as each exchange became more like the previous ones, she had less and less to say. It was frustrating but Phil was reconciled to this.

One morning he was scheduled to help Gary with a low anterior resection of the colon, which was expected to be unusually difficult. On the way to the operating room, he noticed an extremely decrepit, elderly patient lying on a stretcher apparently waiting to go into another operating room. His curiosity aroused, he was told this was Dr. Stallings' patient who was to undergo revision of a malfunctioning gastro-jejunostomy, hence the advanced state of debility. Phil looked back at him once more. He thought it was a minor miracle the patient had survived the elevator ride to the OR suite.

There would be a brief delay so after changing into his scrub suit he decided to wait in the lounge. Gary was already there leafing through a magazine and seemed oblivious to all else. The others, doctors and nurses, were passing the time in their usual fashion, their conversations animated and at times boisterous. Val Rogoff was among them and seeing Phil, smiled and waved. It was a very typical scene as the day's schedule progressed. Suddenly, Gary grimaced, and his head recoiled.

"Jeez, look at this!" He waved the magazine overhead. It was opened to a full-page picture of baby harp seals being bludgeoned, their blood in stark contrast to the whiteness of their fur and the snow-covered ice floes.

"Everyone's seen that," someone said. "They do that every year to keep down the size of the herds, or they were doing it until some environmental group got after them."

"That's called 'culling the herd,'" someone else said. "All that blood shouldn't bother you, Gary. We've all seen you operate."

Gary acknowledged the laughter with a wry smile.

Val Rogoff raised his voice over the others. "That's real not culling," he said. "Culling is when you kill off the sicklier animals to ensure that the healthiest ones have the best chance to survive. I hate to sound pedantic, but I just wanted to set the record straight." He looked smug.

There were some catcalls, but Gary quickly caught the group's attention again.

"Hey, I think I see something here. How about culling the population? I betcha it could be a specialty, but I don't know whether it would be medical or surgical. What do you think of that?"

"Gary, you're an imp and only an imp could think of something like that."

"That's probably true," one of the other surgeons, Paul Markham, said. "But even if he is an imp, I'm not so sure he's so terribly wrong." He grinned in Gary's direction. "We may just find ourselves having to do this in another few years. There's no way we're going to be able to afford the very best medical care for everyone. We may very well be called on to make choices."

"Understood, but if that's going to be the case, we're going to have to be a little more sophisticated. They were using baseball bats in that picture." Rogie still had his smug look.

Gary nodded his head vigorously in agreement. "That's why it would have to be a separate specialty. You would need a residency to get the right training."

"You're a sick group," one of the nurses said. She got up to leave the room but was smiling.

"Hey, if there's a buck in it, I'm sure we could get the administration interested. We could be the first hospital to offer culling."

Just then, Stanley Stallings, in scrubs, appeared in the doorway.

"Wait! Here's our average man in the street," Gary called out. "Let's get his opinion. Excuse me, sir, but could you tell me exactly what you think of population culling?"

"Culling what?" Dr. Stallings asked, with a good-natured smile. Phil looked at Gary and then Stallings.

"Culling the population. I just came across a picture of hunters killing baby seals because there's too many of 'em and we got on the subject of culling, which means—"

"I know what it means," Dr. Stallings said. "I guess this is another one of your jokes, Gary, but I'll play along. Who says we need that?"

"Paul says we may not be able to provide medical care to everyone who needs it. We're looking at ways to solve the problem."

Stallings thought for a moment. "I suppose that's one solution. Maybe it'll come to that. I don't know what you've all been saying, but maybe in time we'll come to think it's not such a bad idea."

"Uh-oh, that doesn't sound like you, Stan," Gary said as some of the others were shaking their heads. "Does this mean you have a dark side? What would your patients think?"

"You asked me, and I gave you my answer. Don't think that's not already an issue. We just don't want to deal with it. Is this a serious discussion or are you just joking around?"

Rogie grimaced. "Looks like you finally did it, Gary. You may have actually gotten us on to a serious issue. What are you going to do now?"

"Help me, someone." Gary made a half-hearted effort to get up from his seat. "Maybe they're ready for my case."

There was scattered laughter, then relative quiet. No one seemed interested in carrying the matter any further.

"I'd like to hear more about this," Phil said finally. "I'd be very interested in hearing what you have to say, Stan. Why don't you finish what you were saying?"

Stallings hesitated only for a moment.

"I'm flattered, Phil. I didn't know you held my opinions in such esteem." He turned to the others, leaving Phil to wonder if he was the only one to sense his sarcasm. "I don't think this should surprise anyone. How much longer do you think we can go on pouring all our resources into patients who have little chance of pulling through, or if they do are only going to be back with us again and again with the same problems? Half the money we spend on medical care is for people in the last six months of their lives. Doesn't that tell us something?"

"We know that" one of the others said, "but what are we supposed to do about it? God forbid one of us ever takes less than the very best care of a patient. Peer review will be on us in nothing flat and they understand just one thing: standard of care. You don't want to give them any reason to come after you."

Phil moved so they could clearly see each other.

"Let's say we all agreed on the problem, although I'm not sure that would be entirely true. What would you suggest, some sort of rationing, maybe in the form of something like culling?"

"I get the feeling you're trying to put me on the spot, Phil, but I'm not afraid to say it," Dr. Stallings said. "It may well be that we won't have any other choice."

"Do you think our society would accept this?" a nurse asked. "Don't you think they'd feel someone would have to be really twisted to think that way?"

"I don't think so," Stallings said, "not if the reasons are rational and valid."

"I'd like to remind you someone has already tried something similar," Paul Markham said, "and our legal system hasn't taken too kindly to his reasoning."

"You're talking about assisted suicides. That person obviously wants the publicity and is just flaunting this in front of the public and the media." Dr. Stallings paused and seemed to be reflecting. "I think someone can accomplish exactly the same thing without anyone else realizing it. He would just have to be smarter than anyone else." His voice was much lower now and it was much more difficult to hear him.

"What the hell are you saying, Stan?" George Bigelow asked. "Did you hit your head on the way into the hospital today?"

"I'm just saying if someone wanted to do this sort of thing, until it was legalized, there could be another way. I think it's reasonable to assume that someone really smart could figure it out. If it makes you feel any better, think of whatever I said as being strictly hypothetical."

"Then I have another question for you, Stan, strictly hypothetical, of course." Phil looked straight at him and spoke very deliberately. "Do you think this idea, culling or whatever you want to call it, should also apply to people no one else seems to want, aged parents, unwanted spouses?"

Stanley Stallings met his gaze and remained silent.

"This is getting out of hand," he finally said. "I thought you were having a sensible discussion. My error. I think I'll see if they're ready for my case."

He smiled and moved from the doorway.

Gary looked surprised at the sudden departure but then, in one motion, shook his head and started to get up.

"I guess that means the interview is over." He sighed in his best theatrical manner. "In that case, I think I'll check on how they're doing in my room, too. See you in a little bit, huh, Phil?" he said as he left.

Val Rogoff motioned to Phil to sit next to him. "That was very strange, coming from Stanley. That didn't sound like him at all."

"Maybe that *is* Stanley," Phil said. "Maybe we just saw the real Stanley for the first time."

"Aw, c'mon." We've all seen the way he fusses over his patients, especially the old ones. They love him. He's the last person I'd ever expect to talk like that."

Phil looked at his colleague for a moment. "Then maybe we don't know him as well as we think." He sat quietly a little while longer and then patted Rogie's knee. "I think I'll see if Gary's ready for me now." He left Rogie sitting there, looking rather bewildered.

Gary was already prepping the patient when Phil finished scrubbing and entered the room. He was in the midst of reciting the litany of the patient's previous surgical encounters to anyone who might be listening. There had been an appendectomy for perforated appendicitis as a teenaged girl, a cholecystectomy as a young woman, a uterine suspension when somewhat older, various procedures for a noninvasive carcinoma of the cervix followed later by a total hysterectomy with removal of both tubes and ovaries, a bladder suspension and then most recently, lysis of adhesions for an intestinal obstruction. They would now have to make their way through the residua to remove a malignant tumor quite low in the rectum. Adding to all this was Gary's insistence that he would make every effort to avoid a colostomy. As long as it was technically possible, this patient was going to be hooked up below and would continue to have bowel movements just as before.

As expected, the case was very difficult and proceeded very slowly. All the organs had to be carefully separated as dense adhesions had formed everywhere. Both surgeons were very quiet, concentrating intently to avoid injury to the intervening structures. After they had been working for well over an hour, there was suddenly a great deal of commotion in the hall outside their room.

"What's all that racket?" Phil asked.

The circulating nurse peeked into the hall. "I think one of the patients had an arrest." "I'll bet I know who that was."

"You better keep quiet," Gary said.

"Looks like he's got himself another scalp."

"I really think you should keep quiet."

Phil leaned further over the operating table.

"Do you want to bet that I'm right?" He looked over his shoulder. "Marlene, why don't you go out and see whose patient that was?"

"Marlene, don't you go anyplace! I want you to stay right here." Gary looked up for an instant.

"I've got my hands full here, Phil, and I don't need an assistant who's more concerned about what's going on in someone else' room. Now I know what you're thinking but save it until after this case."

Phil retracted more of the small bowel. "OK Gary. I'm sorry."

There were no further distractions during the remainder of the case. Phil gave Gary his undivided attention and after the tumor had been mobilized and resected, Gary was able to bring the two ends of the bowel together with the EEA stapling device. Just prior to the closure the circulating nurse leaned over towards Phil and told him that it had been Dr. Mueller's patient who had had the arrest but seemed to be all right now. Gary quickly glanced up at Phil, but Phil pretended not to notice, and Gary went right back to his work without making a comment. Phil left the operating room just as soon as he was no longer needed with most of the wound closure still not completed.

Phil was not happy with his conduct in the operating room. He was glad Gary had not made more of an issue of it. It made him more careful and much more sensitive to any future ill-advised remarks. It also made him study his options more closely and he went over these in his mind innumerable times.

There were a number of agencies and organizations concerned with the conduct of physicians and standards of care. These ranged from committees within the local medical society to regulatory bodies of the state and federal governments each with designees having local jurisdiction. Phil had even served on two committees for the local Professional Review Organization. Originally established to monitor hospital and physician practices for the purpose of improving efficiency and reducing soaring medical costs, it was now very heavily involved in the investigation of physicians thought to be responsible for substandard care. Its current mandate made it seem like an appropriate agency to hear the allegations, at least initially.

However, there was the matter of the clearly obvious criminal nature of these acts. In addition, objective evidence would have to be submitted and Phil simply did not have that.

He was learning to be patient.

VIII

Phil was totally immersed in the care of his patients over the ensuing weeks. Some of the problems were quite complicated and there were stretches when it seemed that he never left the hospital. This kept him in a much better position to hear of any further incidents, but it also made for additional strain at home, in spite of his family's understanding and acceptance. Thus far, nothing of note had occurred. Then one morning Phil was sitting at one of the nursing stations writing progress notes.

He was distracted by two people who seemed to have been waiting at the desk for an unduly long period of time. Finally, the young man approached one of the nurses.

"Excuse me, but could you tell me if Dr. Stallings will be here soon? He told my mother and I that he would meet us here at eleven a.m. to speak to us about my father, Mr. Olekewicz. We've been waiting for over twenty minutes."

"I haven't seen him, but I could page him for you," the nurse said. She went to the phone and a short time later a tall, lanky figure could be seen briskly striding down the hall.

Mrs., Tommy. I'm so sorry I kept you waiting," Dr. Stallings was smiling. He apparently did not see that Phil was seated close by. "We can talk right here."

His expression became more somber.

"I'm not happy with the way things are going with Henry right now."

"We aren't either, Doctor," Tommy said.

"He doesn't seem to want to eat," Mrs. Olekewicz said.

"I know, and I think it's his gallbladder that's giving him this trouble. You remember after I did his surgery, I told you that in addition to the tumor, he also had gallstones. I think that's the problem now."

Tommy looked first at his mother and then, Dr. Stallings.

"But you said you would never take out his gallstones. You told us there was too much tumor."

"Yes, I know, but conditions change. I didn't think he'd ever get to the point where he would have this much trouble."

"Then you're talking about another operation," Mrs. Olekewicz said. "Oh, I don't want to see him go through that again. He's suffered enough." She began to cry.

"He's suffering right now, Mrs. Olekewicz."

The young man put his arm around his mother to comfort her.

"How can you be sure it isn't the tumor causing all this? he asked.

"I'm not absolutely sure, but if it is the gallbladder, I'd hate to think we missed a chance to give him some relief."

"He's my father and I don't want to see him suffer either, but when we asked you after the last operation what we should expect, you told us he would lose his appetite and begin having pain, and if he began to turn yellow, it wouldn't go on for more than another few weeks. He's been yellow for two weeks now."

"I know, but gallstones can also cause that."

Tommy couldn't stop biting his lip. "Doctor, you keep telling us you want to take out my father's gallbladder but what if you get in there and find it's the tumor that's causing all this? What have you done for him then?"

"I can't guarantee what I'll find, but if you'd rather I just keep him comfortable, I'll do that. I'll give him enough pain medication if that's your wish." He looked at the wife and son, who clearly could not make that decision. "Maybe it would be easier if we asked Henry what he wants."

"My father will do anything you tell him to do, Dr. Stallings. He would never question anything you say."

"I'm not going to tell him what to do, Tommy. I'm just going to tell him what choices he has at this point. The three of you can then make the decision. I think that would be the best way and probably the easiest on you and your mom."

Tommy looked at his mother, but she was unable to respond. She stood mute and stared straight ahead.

"OK but be careful what you tell him. He knows it's bad. Don't make it any worse than you have to but be honest with him."

"I always am," Dr. Stallings replied, and all three started down the hall towards the patient's room.

Phil was very disturbed by what he had just heard. If the patient did have very extensive tumor involvement within the abdomen, then there could not be any justification for even thinking of removing the gallbladder. Indeed, another operation at this time in just such a patient might cost him whatever time he did have left. They returned after just a few minutes.

"Nurse, may I have an operative permit?" Dr. Stallings asked when he reached the desk. The wife and son stood behind him as he filled out the form. Tommy Olekewicz had his arm around his mother the entire time.

"There's nothing else to do, Mama. Papa doesn't want to leave us yet."

His voice broke and he hid his face on his mother's shoulder. Both were crying. Dr. Stallings watched the two for just a moment and then motioned to the nurse to follow him to Mr. Olekewicz' room to have the operative permit signed and witnessed. Phil used that opportunity to slip away before Dr. Stallings returned. Mr. Olekewicz' surgery had now become his highest priority and he would not let it go unheeded. He would find out what was done and how the patient fared. There could well be additional material for the next surgical conference.

Phil had a very short case scheduled for the next morning and was finished by nine thirty. He kept his scrub suit on so that he could move back and forth freely between the floors and the OR suite. Henry Olekewicz' surgery had been booked as an added case, which placed it at the end of the day's schedule. It was listed as a laparotomy with a cholecystectomy and possible common bile duct exploration.

Because of cancellations and an unexpected break in the schedule, he was brought to the operating room at ten thirty. Phil made certain he'd be close by at the end of the procedure. At 12.10, Mr. Olekewicz was wheeled into the corridor and then to the recovery room. Phil waited until he saw the scrub nurse emerge from the operating room.

"How's it going, Betty?" he asked casually. "I haven't had you on any of my cases for a while. Whose case were you doing just now?"

The scrub nurse looked over.

"Oh hi, Dr. Berger. Dr. Stallings' added case." She managed an uneasy smile. "I'll tell you how it's going just as soon as someone tells me why we just operated on that poor man." She leaned much closer so that she could lower her voice. "In my seventeen years in this operating room, this has to be the worst. I would just like someone to tell me what we were supposed to be doing for that man."

"What was the problem? I saw today's schedule. He was just taking out the man's gallbladder and possibly exploring the duct."

"What gallbladder? Everything was replaced by tumor. Oh, he managed to take something out all right, and I even saw a big stone, but don't ask me where it came from. I think he just chopped something out where he thought the gallbladder might be. And it must have been a good guess because he did find a stone. But no way are you going to convince me that did any good. There was just so much tumor and he never did stop all the bleeding when he closed."

"Who helped him?"

"Dr. Linfield."

"Did he say anything?"

"Nothing. He never does. You know how he is. The only way we know he's really there is that his glasses fog up every once in a while."

"You don't think that patient's going to make it, do you, Betty?"

"No way. I figure two or three days, that's all. It's a shame too, because he didn't have very long, and he didn't need another operation just for the hell of it. Sorry, but I've been around too long to think anything different."

"That's too bad. I still wouldn't go around telling anyone else about this, Betty."

"Don't worry, Dr. Berger. I never do, and neither does anyone else. Maybe that's the problem around here."

"Well, maybe something will be done about it this time, Betty. We'll have to see. Thank you."

Phil went into the locker room and changed into his street clothes. It might have been more prudent to have obtained this information from someone other than a nurse, but Phil trusted Betty Strong's judgment and considered her the most reliable source in the room. He was also certain a very objective evaluation would be carried out by Gary Barlow who would review the case as a surgical mortality. He just had to be certain the case would be presented at the next mortality conference. As he left the hospital, he wondered what Stanley Stallings had told the family after the surgery.

Phil learned of Henry Olekewicz' death two days later while making his morning rounds. The patient had expired late the previous evening never having regained consciousness after his surgery. He had continued to bleed both from his wound and the drain site and failed to produce any urine after the first hour in the recovery room. Phil was told the family took it very hard. There would not be another mortality and morbidity conference for almost three weeks. Phil knew he would just have to bide his time. He did call Ann Hartway to tell her he planned to pressure Stanley Stallings at the conference in several weeks' time. She seemed to be only moderately interested and Phil attributed this to the recent businesslike tone of their conversations and possibly some mood fluctuations, which he could understand. She did ask that he call her afterwards to let her know what happened.

Leaving nothing to chance, Phil made sure Gary reviewed Henry Olekewicz' case in time for the conference. Although it was expected that each surgeon would volunteer the deaths on his or her service that month, occasionally one would fail to do so. Gary had the prerogative to advise Malcolm Mueller beforehand about which cases should be discussed. After considerable baiting and teasing, Gary assured him the case would be presented. In fact, he was quite upset, himself, with Dr. Stallings' decision to perform surgery on this patient. There would not be any argument this time. By chance, almost the entire surgical staff was present for the next M & M conference. Occasionally, the participation would be very poor, and Malcolm Mueller would vow some punitive action that would never take place. Today, however, the attendance was almost 100%. After the usual brief introductory remarks, the surgeons were polled and any who had deaths or complications to report gave appropriate, concise accountings. For the most part these meetings had come to have the atmosphere of a play rehearsal. Rarely was there any real controversy. Only when it came to Stanley Stallings did this seem to change.

"Do you have any cases?" he was asked as a formality. Referring further to his notes, Malcolm Mueller added, "I'd like you to present, Henry, how do you pronounce this, OLE K E W I C Z?"

"Olekewicz," Dr. Stallings replied. Having been told beforehand the case would be discussed, he immediately began his presentation.

"This was a sixty-four-year-old retired factory worker who was operated on for carcinoma of the pancreas six months ago. At that time, I found positive lymph nodes, liver metastases and some local extension.

"He had gallstones. He wasn't a candidate for a resection and there wasn't any obstruction so I just biopsied one of the nodes and didn't do anything else. He came back about three weeks ago with decreased appetite, weight loss and jaundice. He had also been on chemotherapy but that had been stopped. I didn't think he looked that bad considering all his problems and I didn't think I'd do anything more than put him on IVs and analgesics and get him into a Hospice program somewhere. After being in the hospital for approximately one week he suddenly developed severe right upper quadrant pain. I was pretty sure that was caused by the tumor, but I did mention the gallstones to the family as a very remote possibility. I felt they should be aware of his entire condition. I'm afraid they just didn't want to give up hope and were very insistent I do everything that might improve his condition. I was concerned he might have an obstructed gallbladder, but I did not realize how far the tumor had spread. I suggested getting a contrast study through a catheter in one of the bile ducts to get more information, but his family didn't want to put him through that. I suppose I should have been more insistent, but I thought at the very least, if I operated, I could do a bypass to the gallbladder. I did remove the stones but there was too much tumor to do anything else. I must admit now, it was not the right decision. He deteriorated very rapidly after the surgery and died, I think, about two days later. Fortunately, I did make it clear to the family just what could happen, and they did accept the outcome pretty well. I must tell you I was very concerned how they would react if I missed an obstructed gallbladder. I think that is real grounds for a malpractice suit. By the way, they wouldn't permit an autopsy." At this point he paused and waited for any comments.

Phil sat looking downward, listening to every word. This was absolute nonsense but as usual sounded as though it had some merit. He waited for any remarks the others might have but there was only continued silence, even after Malcolm Mueller had made a plea for comments, any comments. Phil finally spoke.

"I would like to know how this patient could be operated on when he was considered inoperable six months ago and had a disease that statistically, if it hadn't killed him by now, would certainly do so in a matter of weeks, at most?"

Dr. Stallings hesitated briefly and then answered. "I can accept that, but I don't think that is necessarily correct in this case. There's no absolute certainty this patient would have been dead in several weeks and he had developed what I thought was a new problem. This was a significant setback for him, and I thought it could possibly be relieved with surgery. I think this was reasonably sound judgment."

"But when you operated, you found tumor had replaced all the major structures outside the liver. Isn't that correct?"

"Yes."

"Then I have to say that I don't think there was anything else that you could have expected to find at surgery. We've all had enough experience with this disease to know it has one of the worst prognoses and that was very clear six months ago. If this man wasn't dead by now, he would be in a very short time regardless of what you did, and I don't think this kind of patient warrants surgery." Phil looked around the room. "If anyone here disagrees with this, I certainly think this is the time to speak up."

Everyone remained silent until Paul Markham raised his hand. "Well, I can't argue with wanting to do something about an obstructed common bile duct, if you can. Obviously, it's tumor and not stones that are a factor here. Now I know a CT scan or one of those dye studies of the ducts you do through a needle in the liver doesn't always show you what you find at surgery, but they are reasonably accurate. I sure as hell wouldn't operate unless I did one of those first, and I wouldn't care what the family said. Let 'em get someone else if that's how they feel. I have to agree with Phil. I don't think you should have expected to be able to do anything for this patient and if you had gotten one of these studies, I'm sure you would have seen this and you would not have operated."

Dr. Stallings thought for a moment. "That may be true, but you must remember I was under very great pressure from the family to do something. I tried to be very cautious, but they were very unrealistic in their expectations and I don't know how anything other than surgery could have satisfied them."

Phil could not listen to this any longer. His hand shot up so abruptly it almost lifted him from his seat. It startled those sitting around him and easily caught Malcolm Mueller's attention.

"You have something else to say, Phil?"

He wanted to blurt out everything he knew but immediately realized he had to be careful. Straining to choose just the right words, he quickly regained his composure.

"We all know what it's like to deal with patients' families. The more grief we get from the lawyers and the media, the more difficult it becomes. There's more distrust and almost everyone today has just enough knowledge about medicine to have an opinion about any one of our cases. Stanley mentioned pressure from the family a couple of times. I know that's a valid consideration, but I don't think that should be a valid factor in determining how we manage our patients. I think it's very dangerous to let that influence our judgment. They are not our consultants. They are not that knowledgeable. I think there's a difference between listening to their requests and listening to their opinions. Neither should alter our objectivity although a sensible request could temper our actions. I don't want to get too philosophical about this, but it just makes me too uneasy to think our decisions could be influenced this way. Furthermore, it's not something that can be quantified."

"What do you mean?" someone asked.

"I mean it's not something you can look at and measure, or interpret, like a lab value or an x-ray. Even with an x-ray, there can be differences of opinion. With the other, it's too subjective. It's hearsay. Its accuracy could always be questioned."

This was getting into an uncomfortable area and brought a look of reproach from several surgeons.

Dr. Mueller interrupted. "I think we're getting away from our objective here. I think this has been a worthwhile discussion and the appropriate clinical issues have been addressed." He was very abrupt. "Let's move on to another case."

Phil heard him call another surgeon's name, but he did not pay attention to anything else that was said. He was aware that Stanley Stallings had been watching him very carefully throughout. Otherwise, he remained very detached during the rest of the conference and left at its conclusion without speaking with anyone. This continued until Malcolm Mueller caught up with him in the corridor.

"Got a minute, Phil? Is there something going on between you and Stanley? That was a rather unusual display. Is there something I should know?"

Phil kept his pace. "No, I don't think so."

"You started to make a pretty strong statement in there. I think you owe me an explanation."

Phil stopped and faced Dr. Mueller squarely.

"You really want an explanation. You have some place where we can talk? I'll be happy to give you an explanation."

"My office."

"Fine."

Dr. Mueller's office was on the same floor and only a short distance away. It was just a small room and was a courtesy extended to him as chief of the department. It was used only for hospital business and his patients were seen at his much larger private office outside the hospital. He unlocked the door and went to his desk. Phil took the only other chair in the room.

"Now, what was that all about?"

"It was just the way Stanley presented his case. First of all, everyone knows that patient should never have been done. He was inoperable and no amount of rhetoric can change that. What is really tragic is that the family didn't want the surgery. I heard what Stanley said to them. He talked them into it."

"You heard what he said?"

"Yes. I happened to be sitting at the nurses' station when he met with the family. He obviously didn't see me. I actually heard him tell them it might be the patient's gallstones that were causing his problems. That's how he got them to go along with the surgery. They really didn't want it. They knew how bad he was. You should have heard how he answered their questions. It was disgusting."

Malcolm Mueller looked exasperated. "I wish I had known this."

"What difference would it have made? Stanley always finds a way to do whatever he wants. You've heard some of his other presentations in conference. Frankly, I think it's become a joke."

"Now, just you stop right there! This is beginning to sound like a criticism directed at me."

Phil was unfazed.

"A lot of us know there are cases presented at conference that are not entirely accurate in the way they're described. I think you're too busy with your own practice to pay much attention to what the other surgeons are doing. I think if you did, there'd be a lot less questionable surgery being done here."

"So, you think we have that big a problem here and I'm part of the problem, too?"

"I don't think it should be ignored, Mal. I'm not trying to upset you and I'm not accusing you. I just think it's a problem and we should be dealing with it."

"You can't expect me to be looking over everyone's shoulder all the time."

"No, only the ones you know who need that kind of attention."

Malcolm Mueller leaned back and looked at the ceiling.

"You know, Phil. Ever since I've known you, you've always had this self-righteous thing about you. I don't know what to say about it. You're an excellent surgeon. There shouldn't be anything wrong with that, but somehow you make it a little hard to take."

He was quiet for a moment and then sat forward.

"I'll tell you what. I'll try to reach some sort of understanding with you. If you become aware of anything else where you feel something improper has been done, I would ask that you come to me first and I promise to look into the matter promptly. I will handle it. You try to help me with my job and maybe I can make you a little happier."

"Fair enough," Phil said. "Just one other question. What are you going to tell Stanley?"

"I'm going to tell him that I'm disappointed with the judgment he used and that he should not have operated on that patient. I'm going to tell him that I expect him to be much more careful in the future. Is that satisfactory?"

"Yes, it is. For now."

Phil waited for his reaction.

"You don't ever give up, do you?" Mal said.

"I have my reasons."

"And I take it you've told me all of them?"

"For now."

Phil excused himself, and left Mal sitting at his desk.

He did not remain in the hospital very long after that. He saw two other surgeons and neither seemed inclined to discuss the conference. Had he seen Gary Barlow, he was certain a lot more would have been said. He wanted to call Ann Hartway but thought she would be at work. For the first time in a long while he had what he thought was something very worthwhile to tell her. He went to his office and decided he would try her home just on the chance she might have left work early. To his surprise she answered.

"I made sure he'd have to present that case at our conference today. Naturally he didn't describe things exactly as they happened, and I was able to get the chief of surgery to agree with me that the surgery shouldn't have been done and that he used bad judgment. Now if I see something else that I don't like, our chief wants me to tell him about it and he'll take appropriate action. Maybe that doesn't sound like very much, but at least it's a step in the right direction and it's the best we've been able to do so far."

"It almost sounds like kids in school," Ann said, "but yes, I think that does sound very good. Maybe that will make him more careful and take fewer chances."

"We'll just have to wait and see."

"I'm curious about the patient, Phil. What was wrong with him?"

"He had advanced cancer. There was nothing that could be done."

"Oh. I guess he must have waited too long before seeing a doctor."

"Maybe, but some conditions are very difficult to catch while they're early."

"I see." Ann paused for a moment. "By the way Phil, I was going to let you know I've made plans to go away for a while. Actually, you saved me a call. I was pretty sure you'd say the way I'm feeling is because of some sort of a downer so what could be better treatment than a complete change of scenery in a nice warm climate. You agree?"

"Sounds good to me. How long will you be gone?"

"I'm planning about three or four weeks if I like it."

"That long?"

"I think I need it. I would write to you but I think you might have some trouble explaining the letters. Everything OK with you and Maralyn?"

"Oh yes, just fine. I think you'd probably be right about the letters, though. Anyway, you be sure to have a good time. When are you leaving?"

"Next week. Wednesday or Thursday. I'm going to spend the end of the week with the girls at their school."

"Sounds very nice. Just be sure you let me know when you get back."

"I will, Phil, and good luck with what you're doing at the hospital. I know it's hard and I appreciate everything you're trying to do. Bye now, Phil."

Phil put down the phone but didn't get up from his desk just yet. Their conversation had been very pleasant. Perhaps this whole matter would resolve itself without further misfortune for anyone. Of course, one could never be certain about Stanley Stallings, but some measures were now being taken, and justifiably so. Whether he harbored a much greater guilt might never really be known. That would never stop running through Phil's mind, but all in all this had to be one of his better days.

He still thought he might hear some comments the following week regarding the conference but his colleagues apparently either chose to ignore the matter or decided it wasn't worth further discussion. Even Stanley Stallings remained cordial the few times they encountered each other either on the floors or in the OR. Gary Barlow, of course, would be the exception. Phil had approached him early in the week for help with a case.

"You had a good shot at Stanley's jugular at the meeting. How come you let him off? I really thought you were going to do a number on him. What's next? You gonna duel him with proctoscopes?"

"Yeah, right, Gary. As if I'm the only one in the department who's supposed to speak up. Look, do you want to help me with a case today?"

"Sure. What have you got?"

"It's an eighty-year-old lady who's obstructed. Her colon is really distended, and I can feel a mass on rectal exam. I'm just going to do a colostomy as soon as the OR can give me time. They said it should be between eleven and twelve."

"Great. Another poor unfortunate who can't even do something as simple as have a decent bowel movement. I just love those cases. I don't care how often someone tries to tell me heart disease is our number-one health problem. From where I stand, it's constipation. If you need someone to help wage war on this scourge, you can count on me, Phil. I'll be there."

"Thanks. I'll see you upstairs, then."

"You bet. In the meantime, I gotta find some food. I can't remember the last time I ate."

"Yeah, sure. There're bagels in the OR."

"I'm on my way."

They met in the OR locker room two hours later and changed for the case. Gary playfully harassed the nurses while Phil checked the patient in the OR and spoke briefly with the anesthesiologist. A resident had been assigned to the case and was already gowned and gloved and waiting. Gary was almost euphoric when he recognized Greg Falcone.

"Look at this, Phil. They've given us the eminent Dr. Godfrey Falcone to show us the way. We're in luck."

Gregory Falcone was no stranger to Gary's usual demeanor, particularly in the operating room, and often played the role of the reluctant participant.

"It's Gregory, Dr. Barlow. My first name is Gregory. My parents don't like it when I tell them someone keeps calling me Godfrey. They're simple hard-working people from the old country who only wanted to give their son a name they could be proud of. They know there was a Pope Gregory. There never was a Pope Godfrey."

"You're arguing with me again, Falcone. Didn't the last time we scrubbed together teach you anything?"

"Yes sir, it did, and the director of our program let me go on a three-day retreat immediately afterwards, so I feel much better now."

Gary looked at Phil.

"This is gonna be great, Phil. There isn't a better straight man in any residency in all of medicine. You two have met before, haven't you? After he finishes here, Dr. Falcone wants to do a couple of years of family practice in a deprived area and then become pope."

Phil pretended not to hear and after he scrubbed and was gowned and gloved, moved to the right side of the operating table. Gregory Falcone positioned himself on Phil's left and Gary and the scrub nurse stood on the opposite side. Phil noticed an unusually wide gap between Gary and the nurse. Undoubtedly, she had scrubbed with Gary in the past and was trying to protect herself. Phil wondered how successful Gary would be in narrowing the space as the case moved along. He was handed the betadine solution and a prep stick and began to paint the abdomen. Even with the relaxation provided by the general anesthesia, the abdomen remained enormously distended, of which Gary duly took note.

"Dr. Falcone, as I look at that which is before us, do you know what I find myself irresistibly compelled to do?"

"Mess with the nurse, like you tried to do the last time we scrubbed together?"

"No, you errant, misguided neophyte! I am going to teach. In the great tradition of Hippocrates, Galen and Halsted, I am going to pay homage to their noble memory, and you will be the ultimate benefactor. I am going to ask you just one question. Get it right and the duck will pay you fifty dollars. Now, what is the number-one health problem in our country today?"

"You are, sir."

The laughter that followed was so uncontrolled that Phil had to wait until everyone had settled down. Most were in tears. Gary was unperturbed.

"Wrong. You are dead wrong, fella. It's constipation. It's something our government just won't admit. That's why you keep hearing about heart disease. You think all these other countries are going to trust our technology and buy our products if they know our workers can't even go to the bathroom regularly. Use your head. Maybe they should teach it in school. I've been thinking about this. They could call it lavatory science."

At this time Phil was carefully gaining entry into the patient's abdomen. He had made a small transverse right upper quadrant incision and Gary, in spite of his constant chatter, kept pace clamping and tying bleeders and directing Dr. Falcone's efforts at retracting and providing exposure. Phil incised the fascia overlying the rectus muscle and before he could do anything further, Gary's hands darted into the wound and with his index and middle fingers he split the muscle fibers and brusquely pulled them apart, exposing the deeper fascia. The resident groaned.

"What are you, some sort of wimp? This is a man's work. Grab that retractor and give us some help while we try to get inside without getting the bowel."

Dr. Falcone reached for the Richardson retractor that lay on the field, but it slipped from his grasp and slid off the drape onto the floor.

"Goddamn paper drapes!" Gary said. "Everything slips off these things. Anything to save money. I hope you're taking all this in, Godfrey. Later on, when you're pope, maybe you'll get our cloth drapes back, and gowns, too. I hate these paper things."

"It'll be my first edict."

"Good. Anyway, I didn't mean to get off the subject. This patient is a perfect example. She wouldn't be here now if she'd been regular."

"The patient's obstructed, Gary," Phil said. "She's got a tumor in her rectum."

"A weak excuse. You wait until I finish my definitive work on constipation and the universe. You'll see how all this ties together. I go into constipation and politics, constipation and the economy, constipation and the arts. This has never been done before. My big thing now is constipation and crime. You'll be amazed at the connection."

While Gary rambled on, Phil was having difficulty maneuvering a segment of transverse colon into the wound for construction of the colostomy. The bowel was filled with liquid stool and stretched paper-thin. Disruption of the bowel and leakage of its contents into the abdominal cavity had to be avoided. The consequences to the patient could be disastrous.

"Gary, I know you're giving me great assistance, but you are distracting me. I wish you would just hold off until we get the bowel out of the abdomen."

Gary remained quiet but as soon as the loop of intestine was elevated above the skin, he started again.

"You have to listen to this. Crime is our number-one problem today, right? What is the most blissful thing you can think of? Remember, the key word here is bliss."

"Do we really have to discuss this now?" the scrub nurse asked.

"Hey, c'mon," Gary said, "this is the nineties. Everything is out in the open now. Let's not take a step backwards. Now, do you think anyone could be capable of doing something bad after he's had a good, erm... I'm trying to be delicate. Anyway, you have the idea. That was my plan for ending the Vietnam War. You know how rice binds. I thought we should manufacture Metamucil in the form of little rice kernels and drop fifty-pound bags all over the place. No way they would have fought the way they did. I mean it. You start asking the people in our prisons. See how many have suffered this agony. Of course, lawyers could start using this as a basis for their defense. Mmm... Maybe I have to give this a little more thought."

Phil had begun to complete the case, much to everyone's satisfaction, and Gary had apparently concluded his, as well. He closed the layers of the abdominal wall securely around the colostomy and then the skin, both to seal the wound and support the colostomy.

"Do you want to open it now?" Gary asked.

"I think we'd better, don't you? I think the bowel's too distended to wait."

"OK, but we better have plenty of lap pads and you better make sure the suction's working."

"It's working," the circulating nurse said.

"OK, I'm going to open it then. Two Babcocks please."

Phil applied the Babcock clamps to the colon and with Gary providing traction, made a small incision in the wall of the bowel with the cautery. Gary quickly inserted the suction cannula into the bowel.

"Drink, Igor, drink!" Gary exhorted the suction, and liquid, yellow-brown stool immediately began to speed through the clear plastic tubing towards the suction bottle nearby. But then just as suddenly, the flow began to falter and then stop. As it did so, the contents of the bowel began to well up around the suction tip and spill onto the drape.

"Goddamn suction!" Gary cursed. "Will somebody get this damn thing unplugged!" He handed the clogged and bespattered tip to the scrub nurse.

Phil had placed a stack of lap pads on the right side of the patient abruptly reversing the course of the liquid stool which now flowed to Gary's side and onto the floor. "Goddamn paper drapes! Everything runs right off them." Gary moved back several steps.

"Where are you going?" Phil said. "I need you up here to help me with this."

"It was starting to go into my shoes. Anyway, you're taller than I am and I don't want to be the first to go. You can't swim in this stuff, you know."

They stared at the continued flow. The odor was nauseating. There was nothing they could do until another suction was ready. It seemed to both that it should have started to slow down by now, and yet, if anything, it seemed to increase.

"Jesus Christ, look at everything that's come out so far," Gary said, "and her belly hasn't even begun to go down yet. I think she's making the stuff just as fast as she's putting it out."

"Faster," Greg Falcone said.

Gary and Phil were too busy trying to dam the flow to respond.

Greg Falcone's voice droned, "Maybe she's not of this earth."

"Goddamn it, Falcone, is that all the help you're going to be? The least you could do is help us bail." Gary then turned to Phil. "Shall I ask damage control for a report, sir, and should we have them begin the bilge pumps now? It does seem to be getting worse." Gary motioned to the circulating nurse who was busily trying to get a fresh suction operating. "Have all the bulkhead doors tightly sealed. It's our only chance to save her." After a short pause he declared, "It's rising too fast. Have the crew prepare the lifeboats." Turning again to Phil, he said, "I take it you'll be staying with your patient, and you will be going down with her, Captain? It's traditional, you know. If I may suggest, sir, at the very end when the muck begins to swirl around your neck, don't try to fight it. I know it sounds unpleasant, but it will go much better for you if you just duck under and take rapid, big, deep gulps and get it over quickly. God bless you sir, and it was a privilege and an honor to serve with you."

Phil nudged Greg Falcone. "I guess we've seen everything now. Stool does turn him on."

A new suction was working now and even though it clogged occasionally, most of the drainage went into the suction bottle. It gave them an opportunity to clean the operative field somewhat.

"I think we're OK now," Phil said. "Her abdomen's a lot flatter." He removed the remaining saturated lap pads and let them fall to the floor.

"OK, notify the bridge and cancel the mayday," Gary said.

"Enough already, Gary," Phil said. "Just look at this mess." Towels and bed sheets had been piled around the operating table to prevent anyone from slipping on the wet floor. Large yellow-brown stains were everywhere, and the odor lingered in spite of two cans of air freshener.

Greg Falcone stared at the patient.

"I still think it's possible that she's not human. Maybe if we work her up further, we'll find she's missing some of the basics, like chromosomes. They had this movie on TV the other night, *The Green Slime*. That stuff came from outer space."

Gary nodded approvingly as he pondered that thought.

"Maybe our man Godfrey has something here, Phil. Maybe it's something you should consider. Where was this patient before she came to the hospital?"

"She was in a nursing home," Phil said.

"That would certainly fit. What better place is there to hide an alien without raising suspicion? Ever see some of the people they have in those places. You know what this probably means, though?"

"No, what?" Greg Falcone said.

"It probably means that constipation is also a serious problem in other parts of the universe."

"Damn! I'll bet that's why all those rockets we shoot into space are shaped like giant suppositories." A revelation had come to Greg Falcone. "Simply amazing," he said.

Phil had enough. He quietly asked the circulator to apply the colostomy bag, thanked the anesthesiologist and after removing his contaminated shoe covers, left the operating room. Gary could go on indefinitely and he left his two assistants still trying to out-humor each other. The last words he thought he heard were something to the effect that the movie *The Green Slime* might have actually been produced by the Defense Department. He couldn't quite hear Gary's reasons for thinking this. He wondered how much longer they would keep at it. As he got out of earshot, even this thought quickly passed.

IX

With Ann Hartway leaving for vacation and Stanley Stallings presumably chastened by the surgical hierarchy, Phil expected it to remain quiet and uneventful. Malcolm Mueller had met with Dr. Stallings and expressed his displeasure with the manner in which he had handled Henry Olekewicz' case. He made certain that Phil was aware of their conversation. Dr. Stallings had, of course, reiterated the pressure he alleged to have felt from the family and his honest belief that the patient could benefit from the surgery. Malcolm Mueller felt he had made it clear he did not feel this was sound judgment and that he did not expect any future repetitions. He thought Phil would be pleased with this and was certain in his own mind that this incident would not be repeated. Phil had to think he was probably right.

Several days earlier, Phil had repaired an incisional hernia on one Bonislaw Wladiscewski, a gardener who had emigrated from Poland and now worked on one of the nearby estates. The patient was very proud of the rapid progress he had made postoperatively and on Thursday, his third day post-op, went to considerable lengths during rounds to impress Phil with just how active he had become. Phil did not appreciate the significance of this until he was introduced to his patient's new roommate. It was a gentleman who was to undergo surgery the following morning for the same condition.

"Dr. Berger, I want you to meet my new friend, Nunzio Battaglia. He's havin' the same surgery tomorrow and I been showin' him there's nuthin' to it. You gotta see the size of his, though. I ain't seen nuthin' like it. It's twice the size mine was."

"Yeah, Doc. Take a look at this."

Mr. Battaglia slowly got up from his bed and turned sideways lifting his pajama top. Although thin almost to the point of being emaciated, Mr. Battaglia's abdomen protruded outward as an enormously bloated, incongruous extension of his torso. On closer inspection a long scar could be seen from just below his breastbone to his pubis and it was obvious his entire abdominal wall had given way allowing his unsupported organs to spread out in a huge paunch.

"Ain't that somethin'," the gardener said.

"That's quite impressive," Phil replied. "How did you get that, Mr. Battaglia?"

"I got it after they took my stomach out. I had bleeding ulcers and the operation got infected. I had this thing for a while, but the doctor says I should get it fixed now. It's a pain in the ass anyway. Whenever I stand up it looks like I'm gonna have a kid." As the patient spoke, Phil could not help but notice that he paused after every few words, inhaling deeply, as if to catch his breath. Each time he exhaled he pursed his lips. Patients with emphysema frequently did this.

"Are you a little short of breath?" Phil asked.

"Yeah, a little, but what do you expect? Look at this gut I been carryin' around. Dr. Stallings says I should feel twenty years younger after he gets me fixed up. I might even try to find me some young girl, if this operation gets everything else to work better. What do you think, Doc?"

Mr. Battaglia grinned and his roommate began to laugh, sharing his rather obvious joke. Phil, however, was not paying attention. He vaguely heard his own patient remark that Mr. Battaglia should have had Phil for his surgeon, that there was no one better. But Phil now had a much greater concern.

"Are you a very heavy smoker?" he asked.

"Not anymore," Mr. Battaglia said. "I used to smoke three or four packs a day, but I stopped when I decided to have the operation. I was starting to cut down even before that and then I found out you can't smoke in the hospital anyway."

Phil glanced at a pack of cigarettes lying nearby. Mr. Battaglia saw it too.

"Those are from my visitors," he said, and put the cigarettes aside.

"Sure," Phil said. "Did any other doctors check you out before you came into the hospital?"

"Yeah. I had to see another doctor and he said all my tests came out OK and I could have the surgery if that's what I wanted. So here I am.

Well, what do you think, Doc? This operation gonna make me a new man?"

"Well, I don't know about that, but it should get your hernia fixed. Good luck tomorrow."

He spoke for a short while with Mr. Wladiscewski and told him he thought he could go home the following day. He then left the room and went straight to the nurses' station. He found the little he knew about Mr. Battaglia very troubling. If he did have significant respiratory insufficiency because of emphysema, the hernia repair would force his organs back into his abdominal cavity and increase the pressure against his diaphragm. Its already limited movement would be restricted even further, and his respirations made worse. The outcome could be fatal. It was hard to believe that Dr. Stallings could have overlooked this. In view of all that had recently happened, it was even more inconceivable that he would have ignored it. There had to be an explanation.

Phil found his chart and quickly leafed through it. Surprisingly, the arterial blood gases were within the normal range. The medical consultant's note also mentioned this but since these results were normal, he saw no reason why the surgery should not be done. Pulmonary function studies would have been useful but were not ordered. The chest x-ray was read as showing advanced emphysematous changes. Phil was certain there had to be an error in one of the reports. Mr. Battaglia's physical appearance alone had convinced him that he couldn't possibly have normal blood gases. Something was wrong, and at the very least, it should be discussed with Malcolm Mueller.

Phil checked with the page operator and found that Dr. Mueller was no longer in the hospital. He called his office number and left a message that Dr. Mueller should page him at the hospital as soon as possible. The call was returned some twenty minutes later, and Phil took it in the laboratory area where he had been reviewing pathology reports.

"Hello, Mal. Thanks for calling back."

"That's OK Phil. "What can I do for you?"

"It's one of Stanley's patients. I'm sure you remember you asked me to call you first if I thought there was a problem. Well, I don't know if I'm crazy, or he's crazy, but I think someone else should take a look at this."

"What's the problem?"

"He has a patient in the hospital now with a very large incisional hernia. He's on the schedule for tomorrow and he has very bad emphysema. I'm afraid if Stanley repairs the hernia it's going to cause too much pressure on his diaphragm, and he won't tolerate it. The problem is that he has normal blood gases, and I can't believe that."

Malcolm Mueller did not reply at first.

"I don't think I follow you," he finally said. "you say the patient has an incisional hernia and emphysema and normal blood gases. I don't understand your concern."

"I don't believe the blood gases, Mal. This patient is in a room with one of my patients. That's how I got to know him. He can't even hold a conversation without huffing and puffing. This incisional hernia is enormous, and he's had it for years. If Stanley tries to stuff all his guts back into that abdomen, he'll never be able to move his diaphragm. I don't even think you'll keep him alive on a respirator."

"Isn't there a medical consult?"

"Yes, and he's surprised the gases are normal, but as long as they are, he says Stanley can go ahead with the surgery."

"You really don't think the case should be done?"

"I'm certain it shouldn't, Mal. I wouldn't have known anything about this person if my patient hadn't introduced me to him and gotten him to discuss his case with me. I can't see how he could possibly make it post-op."

"Well, I guess I'm going to have to take a look at this fellow. I hope you realize you're putting me in a bit of a spot. You say the blood gases were normal. I don't suppose there were any pulmonary function studies, were there?"

"No."

"I wouldn't have thought so. With normal gases no one would figure the other is indicated, so that's no help. Well, I'll tell you what. I really don't want to come back to the hospital tonight if I can avoid it. What time is the patient being done tomorrow? If it's not a first case, I'll be in before he goes to the OR and if things don't look right, I'll tell Stanley he'd better hold off. Do you know the schedule?"

"Hold on," Phil said. "There should be one close by."

He put down the receiver and walked to the blood bank. The surgery schedule for the following day was there as expected, and Nunzio Battaglia was listed as the second case in room 3, the first being a thoracotomy and lobectomy. He returned to the phone.

"The case should be around ten, Mal. There's a lobectomy scheduled first and he's to follow."

"OK That's perfect. I don't have anything tomorrow, so I'll be there about eight thirty. Don't worry, Phil. If I have any reason to feel as you do, I'll cancel the case. I made a commitment to you before and I intend to stand by it. I'm sure there's some sort of explanation. I can't believe Stanley would get careless after the talk we just had. Is that satisfactory?"

"I guess so, Mal. I think I'd feel better if we had this thing settled tonight, but tomorrow morning should be OK I appreciate it. Thanks."

"I'll talk to you in the morning, Phil. So long."

Phil was uneasy with this decision but was resigned to it. He thought it would be more considerate for both the patient and the staff if the case was cancelled now rather than at the last moment, but it was not his choice. He might have some trouble falling asleep later that night, but he did have the assurance the case would be reviewed before any harm could be done. There was really nothing more he could do.

He intended to be at the hospital before eight the next morning to make sure all went as planned. At 7.20, however, he received a call that one of his patients had been in a minor automobile accident on the way to work and was in the emergency room with a small laceration of the nose. By the time Phil arrived at the emergency room, reviewed the x-rays, and completed the repair and the paperwork, it was eight fifteen. He went straight to Nunzio Battaglia's room, reaching there just before twenty past eight. Bonislaw Wladiscewski was sitting at his bedside, eating breakfast. Nunzio Battaglia's bed was empty.

"Where's your roommate?" Phil asked.

"They took him upstairs. He's having his surgery now."

"Are you sure? He wasn't scheduled until ten o'clock."

"Yeah, I know, but they came for him early. They said there was a cancellation, so he didn't have to wait. He was glad because he didn't want to have to watch me eat breakfast."

He laughed but Phil was no longer there to share his joke. He was already racing down the corridor.

He ignored the elevators and sprinted up three flights of stairs reaching the OR short-winded and perspiring. The supervisor was busy on the telephone, so he approached two nurses standing nearby. His voice was choked.

"Do either of you know how far along Dr. Stallings is?" The two nurses appeared puzzled and looked at each other. "The word must be spreading awfully fast today," one of them said. "They're still waiting for the results of the blood gases. No decision has been made yet."

Phil did not understand. He was still feeling the effects of his sudden exertion and his anxiety when he first entered Mr. Battaglia's room. "What happened? Is the patient in trouble?"

"Not yet," the same nurse replied, "although Dr. Bigelow thinks he will be if Dr. Stallings goes ahead with the surgery.

"I don't understand," Phil said. "Isn't the patient being operated on now?"

"No, Dr. Berger, he isn't," the other nurse answered. "Dr. Bigelow isn't happy with the way the patient looks and wants the blood gases repeated. That's what they're waiting for now."

Phil leaned back against the wall and took a deep breath.

"Are you OK?" one nurse asked.

"Oh yes, I'm fine," he said. He was considerably relieved but only for the moment. He was grateful to the anesthesiologist, George Bigelow, but this had been too close. Just then the door to the Operating Room Suite opened and this time it was Malcolm Mueller who rushed in. He headed straight for the supervisor's desk but then on seeing Phil, quickly walked over to him. He looked equally disturbed.

"I'm sorry, Phil. I really am. I didn't think the case might be moved up. Any idea how much he's done so far?"

"We got lucky, Mal. He hasn't done anything yet. George Bigelow is giving anesthesia and must feel the same way I do. He's having the blood gases repeated before he goes ahead with the anesthesia. I don't think the results are back yet."

"Really? He hasn't been put to sleep yet? That's a relief." He turned to one of the nurses who was nearest to him. "Would you do me a favor, please, and walk down to Dr. Bigelow's room and ask him to come out and speak with me?" The nurse nodded and promptly complied. She returned a moment later with Dr. Bigelow.

"Good morning, George. What kind of problem do we seem to be having this morning?"

The anesthesiologist shrugged and was expressionless in his reply. "I'm not having any problem, Mal. It's you surgeons who seem to be having the problem. I'm just trying to prevent one."

That annoyed Dr. Mueller. "Please, George, I'm going to have enough aggravation with this without your help. Can't you just tell me what you think is wrong?"

"Of course. This guy's got lousy lungs and I can't believe those blood gas results are correct. He gets short of breath just trying to tell you his name. Anyone should know fixing this hernia is going to put tremendous pressure on his diaphragm.

"I'm surprised no one in my department picked this up in pre-surgical testing. I hate to think we still have people who don't know how to evaluate a patient before surgery. This guy's a walking time bomb. I suppose we could call downstairs for the results now. It should be enough time."

Dr. Bigelow picked up a phone and was waiting to get through to the lab when Reggie Green, one of the inhalation therapy technicians, entered and started towards the supervisor's desk. Phil surmised that he had the new results and motioned to Malcolm Mueller.

"Do you have something for us, Reggie?" Dr. Mueller called to him. "Some lab results?"

"Yes, I do, Dr. Mueller. I have the gases on Mr. Battaglia."

"Would you give them to Dr. Bigelow, please?"

George Bigelow looked them over quickly and then handed the slip to Malcolm Mueller. He looked at Phil. "The pO2 is 51," he said. "What was the first result, 91?"

Dr. Mueller shook his head.

"We ought to get Warren Duncan up here. It's his lab. Maybe he can explain this. In the meantime, somebody better tell Stanley his patient's pO2 is 51 and we don't think he should do his case."

"Perhaps we ought to move away from here and find a quieter place to discuss this." Phil said. "You know how excitable Warren can become if you tell him you think there's been a lab error."

"Good thought," Dr. Mueller said.

A call was put out to Dr. Duncan and the group moved to one of the unoccupied side rooms. Reggie Green asked if he could be excused and was allowed to leave. The group was soon joined by Dr. Stallings who was still wearing his OR gown. Phil tried to casually separate himself from the other physicians.

"Well now, it seems you can't even trust the lab. I really must say I didn't expect this," Dr. Stallings said. His usually cheerful manner was only slightly daunted. "Of course, I've cancelled the case and we'll get the patient completely worked up. I can't understand how the two results can be off by so much. At this point we really don't know which is correct." His demeanor remained buoyant, inappropriately so, and the other physicians were perplexed. George Bigelow shook his head.

"You shouldn't be surprised, Stanley. Anyone should have been able to recognize severe lung disease in this patient. I'm appalled you apparently didn't and even now think the original blood gases might be the more accurate ones. This man's a respiratory cripple. He should never have been considered for surgery."

"The medical consultant cleared him," Dr. Stallings insisted.

Dr. Mueller stepped between the two. "I haven't seen the patient so I can't comment but you should get pulmonary function studies. If they are consistent with the low pO2 I think you had better review this case at length with your consultant."

Dr. Stallings looked over at Phil.

"How did you get involved in this, Phil?"

"Phil is not involved in this, Stan," Malcolm Mueller quickly said. "He and I were discussing another matter when this came up and he's here completely by accident.

"As a matter of fact, Phil, there's no point in keeping you any longer right now. Why don't I call you later today?"

Phil was just about to agree and leave the room when he heard the voice of Warren Duncan. Seconds later, the pathologist entered the room and closed the door behind him.

"OK gentlemen, who's badmouthing my laboratory again? I already know what's going on here this morning and I don't have any answer for you right now but be careful before you start placing the blame."

"Well, how else could this have happened?" Dr. Mueller asked. "You know we have two very different results on this one patient."

"I don't know. They're obviously both arterial specimens and even if there was an error in calibration, the results wouldn't be this far apart. I really don't know at this point. I certainly would like to talk to the technician who drew the blood the first time. It shouldn't happen but maybe there was a mix-up."

"Can you find out who that was?" he was asked.

"I should. It has to be one of the inhalation therapy techs. The regular lab techs don't do arterial punctures. I just have to find out where the specimen was drawn and who was working in that area on that particular day. If you like, I can call right now."

"If you would, please," Dr. Mueller said. Dr. Duncan left the room to make his call and Phil took his cue to leave at the same time. He didn't want to go too far so he decided to wait in the main corridor outside the OR suite. Like the others, he was at a loss to explain the wide disparity in the lab results. The more he thought about it, the more intrigued he became with the irony of all this. Laboratory errors were uncommon but apparently one had occurred. This one had to happen to a patient whose surgeon was the most likely to use it to his own advantage. At the same time, chance would have it that this patient was placed in a room with one of Phil's patients, thus permitting suspicion to be aroused in the one person capable of that. If there was a grand design to all this, some higher power was probably having a very good time with it.

These ruminations were suddenly interrupted when Phil saw the tall figure of Reggie Green step from the elevator at the end of the corridor. The technician hesitated momentarily as he passed the waiting area and then quickly approached Dr. Berger.

"What's goin' on, Dr. Berger? I hope they're not going to ask me to stick that poor man again. I'm gonna have to go back downstairs and get my stuff if they do."

"No, Reggie. If they called you, it's just to see if you can help them figure out why there's such a big difference in the blood gases."

"I don't know, Dr. Berger. I been thinking about it, and I know they're ticked off because something got screwed up, but I honestly don't know how it could have happened. I know I must have drawn that blood because I been doin' most of the outpatients lately. I even think I remember the guy's name, but y'know what?" He shook his head emphasizing his uncertainty. "Even though I know he's gonna look different in a hospital gown under all those lights, I don't think I've ever seen him before. He ain't the guy I remember. I don't know what it is, but somethin' ain't right about that guy." He frowned.

Phil was confused. "What are you trying to say, Reggie?"

The technician shrugged. "Maybe I really don't know what I'm trying to say, Dr. Berger. Maybe the guy's really OK and maybe I'm the one who's really got a problem. You wanna hear something else that's crazy? Twice now I've gone past the waiting room and twice I seen someone inside that I know I seen before, but I just can't remember where. It's like the guy I should recognize, I don't, and someone I shouldn't, I do. Something is really wrong, and I don't know if it's with them or if it's with me."

"I don't know either, Reggie. Maybe you should just go inside and do the best you can. Just try not to make it too confusing. I'm going to wait out here. After you're finished, I'd appreciate it if you let me know how everything seemed to go."

"Sure," Reggie said, "if they don't try to get me all mixed up. I'll do my best." With that, he disappeared into the OR suite.

Phil did not have much time to think about what Reggie had said. He was surprised when Reggie reappeared only a few moments later.

"Well, what happened?" he asked.

"Nothin'," Reggie said. "I told them I was the one who drew the blood in the lab because I had that rotation and I thought I remembered the patient. I told them I couldn't see any way that I could've mixed up the specimen. That was it. What else could I really say?"

Phil shook his head. "But you really don't think it's the same patient, do you, Reggie?"

The technician winced. "Here we go again. Look, Dr. Berger, I don't know how I can explain this to you. Sometimes I may spend some extra time with a patient. We may get to shootin' the shit about somethin', usually somethin' about sports. That's one of the things I like about this job. This guy came in the day after that double-overtime game last week and I noticed he had a newspaper and was readin' the sports pages, so we started talkin' about the game. He's a real big basketball fan and I still play a lot. We talked for a pretty long time and I gotta say that's not the guy in the operating room right now. This guy was a lot younger lookin' and didn't look sick. I even wondered why someone ordered gases on him. The guy in the operating room is sick and he looks it. I'll tell you somethin' else. I didn't have any trouble with that guy gettin' blood from the radial artery. This guy today was impossible. I finally had to use his brachial artery. The guy was so easy the first time, I never should have had any trouble today. Maybe there was a mix-up, but it was the right name. Why he ain't the same guy, I don't know. Somebody else is goin' to have to figure that one out. I only know what I seen an' I ain't gonna make myself look crazy to any of those doctors."

Phil had been listening carefully and knew that he didn't have any explanation either. As Reggie finished speaking, Phil became aware that they were being approached by a young man who had previously been standing in the doorway of the waiting area. The man came directly up to Phil.

"Excuse me, sir, but perhaps you could give me some information? I saw you come out of the operating room a little while ago and my uncle is having surgery in there right now. Perhaps you could tell me how he's doing? His name is Nunzio Battaglia." Phil quickly glanced at Reggie Green. His own reaction notwithstanding, the technician stood transfixed, mouth agape, staring wide-eyed at the young man. For his part, Phil also studied the young man who was almost a mirror image of Nunzio Battalia, but younger and considerably heavier. He also seemed rather nervous. Phil did not know how to answer him at first and the man repeated his request.

"If you know any way I can get some information about my uncle, Mr. Battaglia, I'd really appreciate it?"

"I'm not at liberty to give out information on other doctors' patients," Phil said finally, "but I do know Mr. Battaglia. He's in the same room with one of my patients. I'm Dr. Berger. I believe your uncle's operation was cancelled this morning, but you should wait to speak with his surgeon. He can give you all the proper information."

"Are you sure? He really didn't have the operation? You're sure we're talking about the same patient, Nunzio Battaglia?"

"Yes. He's Dr. Stallings' patient and he's the one who was cancelled. I'm sure if you wait right here Dr. Stallings will be out to explain what happened."

The young man slapped his thigh with the newspaper he was holding and scowled.

"Naw, I'll talk to him later." He turned and began to walk away. He muttered something further to himself and Phil thought he overheard him say he was afraid something like this would happen. Phil called after him.

"If the case was cancelled, it was only because it was best for your uncle."

The young man did not answer and quickly passed from sight when he found the nearest stairwell. Phil suddenly remembered the expression on Reggie Green's face and turned to the technician. He was still motionless, his mouth only slightly less agape.

"What's the problem, Reggie?"

"That's him. That's the guy I drew the blood from. I knew I seen him someplace before and now I'm sure of it. As soon as he said Mr. Battaglia was his uncle, I remembered.

"I kept looking at him in the waiting room, but I just couldn't place him. He's the one. I'm positive. But why would he tell me he was the patient?"

Phil couldn't be sure, but he was beginning to have suspicions. "You seem pretty certain, Reggie, but you could be wrong, couldn't you?"

"Hell, no! Didn't you see that newspaper he was carrying? I saw it. Same damn paper, same damn sports pages. I tell you, he's the one. I really should tell those doctors I know what happened now."

Phil reached for his arm.

"I'm not so sure that's a good idea right now, Reggie. That fellow could just deny it and then it would be your word against his and I don't think anything would be accomplished. I'd like to ask you to do me a favor and just not say anything to anyone about this right now. Let's see what I can find out. I think that would be a lot better."

"Gee, I don't know, Dr. Berger. I don't want anyone to think I screwed up and that's probably what they're all thinkin' right now."

"No, I don't think so, Reggie, but I do know they'll be wondering about you if you tell them something as far-fetched as this. How would you prove it?"

The technician thought for a moment and then agreed. As they parted, he had one last question.

"You believe me, don't you, Dr. Berger?"

"Yes, Reggie. I do."

Phil wasn't able to do anything more until early that afternoon. Nunzio Battaglia had been kept in the recovery room for a while as a precautionary measure and then was sent back to his room. If Reggie Green had any doubts about Phil's sincerity, he had only to know what was going on in his mind at this time. Phil was very anxious to speak with Nunzio Battaglia, but he did not want his interest to be too obvious. He still had to discharge Mr. Wladiscewski and chose the time right after lunch for what would appear to be early afternoon rounds. As he strolled into the patient's room, he was immediately set upon by Mr. Wladiscewski who first told him the surgery had been cancelled and then gave forth a multitude of theories as to why this happened. His main thrust was that Mr. Battaglia had not used the same good judgment as he had in selecting Phil as his surgeon. With considerable time and patience, Phil was finally able to calm his patient and approach Mr. Battaglia.

"I'm sorry your operation was cancelled, Mr. Battaglia. Any idea what happened?"

"Yeah, my doctor says one of my blood tests got worse since I been in the hospital, and they got to check that out first. It should only take a few days."

"That's too bad, but it happens. You had some other tests before this, didn't you?"

"Yeah. About a week ago."

"I'll bet you had a lot of tests, too. I hope they won't have to repeat all of them. How many times did you have to be stuck when they drew the blood for all those tests?"

"Just once. They filled up a whole bunch of tubes from this one big vein here." He pointed to the crook of his left arm. Being so thin and with emphysema, his veins stood out as enormous cords.

"Did they try to get blood from anyplace else, from your wrist, for example?"

"You mean like they did today. Hell, no! That hurt like a bitch! Then that didn't work and they had to do it in my arm. The other day they did it once and that was it."

"Well, I hope you won't have that problem again. I think as long as you're going to have to spend some time here, you might as well try to enjoy yourself. If you're a basketball fan, there should be some pretty good games on TV."

"Who, me, a basketball fan? Hell, no, I can't stand the game. My nephew, Nick, he can watch basketball all day and night. He bets on the damn games too, and that's something I don't like. He's a good worker and the only real blood I got left but forget it when there's a game on. I got three pizzerias that probably make more money than ten of you doctors and I promised him they'd all be his, but only if he gives up that goddamned gambling. Except for that, he's a terrific kid and he worries about me all the time. His name really is the same as mine, Nunzio, but he likes to be called Nick. I just wish he'd stop with all this basketball crap, but then it's baseball, or it's football. See why I ain't no fan."

"My mistake," Phil said. "I didn't mean to offend. I think I did meet your nephew this morning outside the operating room and you're right, he does seem very concerned about you. Looks a lot like you, too. Was he with you when you had your blood tests the first time?"

"Yeah. He wanted to come. I told him he didn't have to, but he didn't want me to come alone."

"Sounds like you have a really wonderful nephew, Mr. Battaglia." Phil smiled and Nunzio Battaglia looked pleased. Bonislaw Wladiscewski seemed to be enjoying all this too, but now it was time for him to be discharged and Phil gave him his instructions and an appointment to his office the following week. A few more pleasantries were exchanged and then Phil excused himself. Once outside the room, he stopped momentarily. Even though everything had been said so quickly, Reggie Green, the nephew, Mr. Battaglia, he knew what each and every word meant. This had been altogether unexpected and yet his presence of mind finally seemed to have provided him with what had always eluded him before, actual corroboration of Stanley Stallings' activities. He had to speak with either Mel Silverstone or Gordon Mulcahey.

He made his way directly to the pay phones in the hospital's lobby and decided to try Gordon Mulcahey first. Someone in his office said he was still in court and would probably not be back in his office before four p.m. Phil said he would call back. He next tried Mel Silverstone, but his secretary said he was gone for the day. She offered to try to reach him, but Phil said it wasn't necessary. He continued on his rounds trying hard not to be distracted. He thought how Ann Hartway would react to all this. It was just as well she couldn't know. It certainly wouldn't have added to her vacation.

He finished rounds and went to his office. There were a few messages that required his attention and then he placed his second call to Gordon Mulcahey a little before four thirty. This time he was in.

"Hiya, Doc. I was wondering when I'd hear from you again. What can I do for you?"

"How are you, Gordon? Are you busy right now? Do you have time to talk?"

"Sure. Has your friend been up to something?"

"That's why I called. We had another incident at the hospital today. He was going to operate on someone who shouldn't have had the surgery. He was a terrible risk, and the operation would easily have killed him. He did something else, though, which I never would have imagined anyone doing. He had someone else take a blood test for this patient. The test would have shown how bad the patient's lungs are and no one would have permitted the surgery. I have the technician who drew the blood, and he identified the patient's nephew as the person who took the blood test for him. I know I'm going very fast, and I hope you can follow this. The man's nephew has a gambling problem and is in line to get his businesses, which are very profitable."

"You got all this today?" Gordon said. It was uncertain if his response was one of great admiration or profound disbelief. "Let me see if I understand this. There's this patient who's a very high risk and shouldn't be having surgery. Your guy tries to operate on him today, right? A blood test would have shown he was too sick for the surgery, so your surgeon has someone else take the blood test for him. That person is the man's nephew, and he has a gambling problem and gets his business if anything happens to him. Does that sound about right?"

"Yes."

"Damn. I followed all that. I must be good."

"You do understand what I'm saying?"

"Yeah. Don't forget you primed me before and although you don't know it, I have been giving this a lot of thought. Mel and I have spoken about this several times. There're more than enough nuts out there to make anything possible."

"That's another thing, Gordon. This is the last thing I would have expected now. He just had a case that was very strongly criticized for the way he handled it. I would have thought he'd be very careful now. He knows he can't afford something like that again. I really don't understand it."

"But now you think he really did kill those other patients?"

"Yes. Right now, I really think he did."

"Well, I guess we can forget my theory. Maybe he's sick?"

"Maybe. I just don't know."

"How's the patient doing?"

"He's OK We managed to prevent the surgery."

"Yeah. How'd you do that?"

"I guess it was luck. The patient was put in a room with one of my patients. I could see he would've had a very big problem if he had the surgery that was planned. I spoke to the chief of surgery. We now have an understanding about this particular surgeon. I'm supposed to let him know if I see anything I don't like about any of his cases. One thing led to another, and the case was cancelled. We repeated the blood test, this time with the patient's blood. The results were very poor. The operation would have killed him. He'll never have the surgery now."

"This surgeon knows how involved you are in all this?"

"I think he suspects but I don't think he knows anything more than that."

"You may want to start thinking about being more careful. You don't know what else this man's capable of doing."

"You think something like that is possible?"

"Anything is possible. You told me yourself you didn't expect him to do anything like this now. If all this is true, I think you have a real problem on your hands." Gordon did not wait for Phil's response. "I'm sure this isn't all there is to this. I'm sure you have a lot more you can tell me. We're going to have to get together and talk further about this. There was one thing you told me that was very important. What was that? Oh, yes. The technician that drew the blood. You didn't let on what you suspected?"

"No."

"He's very important. Don't lose him. Do you know if the nephew actually identified himself as being the patient?"

"I assume so. That's what the technician thought."

"I think you may have something now. I think if you could also get that patient's wife to testify, we'd really have something to work with. Have you spoken with her recently?"

"She's away on vacation right now. She really doesn't want any part of this. She wants him to stop what he's doing, and she just wants to be kept out of anything that happens. That's the reason she came to me in the first place."

"How do you feel about that? You keep going with this thing and she's involved, no two ways about it."

Phil did not have to give that any thought. "He has to be stopped. I'll deal with the rest when the time comes." It was the only decision his conscience would allow.

"Well, keep working on her. People change. Situations change. We can work with her. This may also be the time to start thinking about sending someone to this doctor's office with a wire and see what we can get. It might be something incriminating. Let's think about getting together. It would have to be late in the afternoon. Is that OK?"

"Sure. Any day would be fine as long as it's late afternoon."

"Good. I'll try to line up Mel's office and I'll get back to you. That's as good a place as any and I'd like to have Mel there, too. I don't know if you're aware he used to be in our office before he went into private practice. He was very good."

"I've heard that," Phil said. "I guess I'll just wait then until I hear from you."

"I'll call you. You don't expect this guy to do anything in the meantime, do you? Then again, you never can know with this guy, can you?"

"No, you really can't," Phil said. "So long, Gordon." He put down the phone and sat there for a long time. Many thoughts came to his mind, not the least of which was Ann Hartway and what this would mean to her. It was very disturbing.

With Bonislaw Wladiscewski discharged, Phil no longer had an excuse to visit with Nunzio Battaglia. He was still able to follow his course, however. Pulmonary function studies were performed and showed very marked deficiencies in all parameters. A subsequent consultation with a pulmonary specialist resulted in the recommendation that the patient immediately stop smoking and that he should be discharged from the hospital with no thought ever to be given to repairing the incisional hernia.

It was suggested, but not urged, that an abdominal support might be tried but if it hampered his breathing it should be discarded.

Phil wasn't entirely pleased with this outcome. He hadn't expected the matter of the widely disparate blood gas values to be resolved, but he also didn't expect it to virtually eliminate the criticism of Dr. Stallings, which should have been forthcoming. He found this very disturbing. He was even more disturbed by the man's unrelenting persistence. It was inconceivable to him that Stallings would attempt something like this now, much less any other time. These feelings lingered through the week and when the meeting with Gordon Mulcahey took place that Friday, they were obviously still troubling him. Mel Silverstone had made his office available and agreed to be present. They were both there to greet him when Phil arrived shortly before five p.m.

"Gordon took the liberty of filling me in as best he could, Phil. Aren't people beginning to ask questions about this guy at the hospital? What do you think is really going on with him?"

"You're right. There is some concern now and he has to know it, but it doesn't seem to make any impression on him. I really believe he had someone impersonate a patient while blood tests were being done so none of the results would prevent him from doing the surgery. He has to be crazy."

"Maybe he is," Gordon Mulcahey said.

"What exactly happened this time?" Mel asked.

Phil described the circumstances of the past month in very careful detail. He began with Henry Olekewicz' case and subsequently his reaction and that of the others at the surgical conference. Nunzio Battaglia's case was recounted even more thoroughly. Both attorneys were very attentive with Gordon taking notes quite frequently. It took Phil almost twenty minutes to cover all the essential information. He looked squarely at both men when he finished.

Mel was the first to speak. "What do you think, Gordon? Can we do something now?"

Gordon hurriedly finished jotting his notes, put down his pad and looked up.

"Let me tell you how I see this thing. I'm sure we're all thinking right now we could bring this technician in, get a statement from him and take things from there. This is probably the first solid thing we've had to work with, and Phil has made it very clear how the nephew was able to have his own blood substituted for the patient's. It sounds like it would be a good start but unfortunately, I think it would fall apart. The nephew is not going to incriminate himself and it would be the technician's word against his. It wouldn't get us anywhere and it would tip our hand. You agree, Mel?"

"I agree. I think at the right time, with enough other information, this can be very crucial. I see the problems with it now, especially if the nephew has a decent lawyer."

"This leads us to a point I will get to in a moment," Gordon said. "First, I want to clear up some other concerns. Number one, this is no longer a matter that should be handled at the hospital level. We talked about this before but if all this is as you say, this clearly belongs in my office. I'd rather you kept things quiet, so the hospital doesn't jeopardize any case we're trying to build. That means you have to keep that technician from saying anything to anyone else until we take his statement. Can you do that?"

"I think so," Phil said. "I talk to him almost every day."

"He's not getting a little antsy? I mean, he doesn't feel everyone thinks he screwed up and he's got to absolve himself?"

"No, he's still confused as to what he should do, but he's willing to listen to me and wait. I've known him for a pretty long time, and we've always had a good relationship. How long would it be before you would want to talk with him?"

"I don't know," Gordon replied. "It would depend on what other progress we make. Certainly, if we could get some knowledgeable party to make an accusation, we'd be ready right then and there. The only person that fits that description right now is that patient's wife. I'm glad that medication thing is cleared up, but I don't imagine she's changed her mind."

"No, she hasn't," Phil said. "And she's still on vacation. I'm not sure when she's getting back."

Gordon scowled, but then thought the better of it. "I guess there's nothing we can do about that. At some point we're going to have to at least try to get her to come around. I know you're trying to protect her, Phil, but pretty soon we're going to have to get some names. This is becoming much more serious, and we can't have any delusions about medical confidentiality or any other misguided notions about protecting anyone who's involved. We have to start making some progress."

Phil remained contemplative but Gordon didn't wait for an answer.

"Mel and I have talked several times and we had a chance to discuss this before you got here. We both think this would be a good time to try to get something on tape that might incriminate this guy. He seems to be on a roll, and he doesn't seem willing to back off. We think if you create a situation similar to the ones you've been telling us about and have someone wear a wire who's involved in the discussions with the doctor, we might just get him to commit himself. We really think it's worth a try and this is a good time to do it. If he's become cautious you will not have lost anything, except we'll probably be a bit less convinced. But if he really opens up, this can be a big help. How do you feel about that, Mel?"

"I've already said I think that should be the next step. I think it's important that we have the opportunity to see for ourselves what this person is all about. This should give us that chance."

Gordon nodded in agreement. "You're going to have to work this out, Phil. You're going to have to find a patient and concoct the right kind of story that will be convincing to this surgeon. By this time, you should know what we'd like to have. We'd like him to go as far out on a limb as we can. It's got to be a patient that definitely should not have surgery but someone else has to push for it and the surgeon has to go along. They'll have to play word games, but it has to come across as clear as you can make it that this guy intends to do in this patient. I can supply a couple of investigators from my office to impersonate relatives or whomever and they would know what to do. Everything else would be up to you. At this point I could not use any other resources of my office so you would have to acquire the services of someone to provide the eavesdropping equipment and bear that expense personally. I can recommend someone to you who is very competent and would be very reasonable. It would probably run around five hundred dollars for what we need. You have to realize until we have enough to begin a formal investigation, this is how we have to operate. Can you handle this?"

"I think so," Phil said. "The expense is no problem, but I will have to find a patient. That may not be so easy. I'd like to find someone who's not from this area."

"Sorry, but I can't help you there," Gordon said.

"I was thinking, Mel. I usually see your Aunt Edith each year when she comes up to visit. I know it's not until the weather gets warmer, but do you think you could get her to come up sooner? She'd be ideal and anyone local would present a lot of problems."

"I could try," Mel said. "You'd be afraid the word might get out if you used a patient from around here?"

"Sure. I have to find someone with an obvious surgical problem and whatever explanation I have to give could reach the wrong people. Aunt Edith would be perfect. Her doctors are in Florida; she's got a very obvious rectal prolapse that I would never repair, and she's got serious medical problems. It would be a lot easier for me with someone like her."

"It's OK with me," Mel said. "I'll speak with her. I'm sure I can come up with some reason to get her up here now. I'll call her this evening and let you know."

"I hope you can work it out. She's always had at least some rectum prolapsed whenever I've seen her, so that will be very convincing. I don't think we could find anyone better."

"I hope it works out too," Gordon said. "I'm no trained expert but Aunt Edith sounds like a good one to me, too."

He sat back in his chair.

"I'm very impressed how this whole thing has managed to play itself out. I have to tell you, Phil, and I've said this to Mel. You always manage to be in the right place at the right time. At first, I found this very hard to believe. This woman confides in no one else but you. You're in just the right spot to overhear the conversation about that cancer patient, Mr. Olekewicz. The hernia patient, Mr. Battaglia, gets admitted to a room with one of your patients. Clearly an awful lot of coincidences, and I would have meant that sarcastically, but Mel reminded me that perhaps this is all we know about. Perhaps there's more and this is just the tip of the old proverbial iceberg. Maybe you weren't really so lucky, after all."

"It's a small hospital," Phil said.

"That's OK. I want to move on this thing now. I don't know what we're sitting on. I don't care how serendipitous all this sounds, and Aunt Edith may be just another example. Let's get her up here soon if she's going to be the one. Now I think it's time we knew who this surgeon is. We will be making an office visit very soon."

"Stanley Stallings." Phil answered without hesitation.

"I don't know him," Gordon said.

"You knew who it was, didn't you, Mel?"

"Yes, but I wasn't going to say anything until you did. I knew it after we talked about that one particular surgery he did. He's got a decent reputation, but I have heard people say he's pretty quick to operate whenever he can."

"OK guys, I don't want to interrupt, but we've got to keep going," Gordon said. "As soon as you know who it's going to be, Aunt Edith or whomever, I'll arrange a meeting with a couple of my staff members, and you can put together your scenario. You can be thinking about it in the meantime. I wouldn't set anything else up, like the wiring, until that's been done. Now you two have to get it arranged with Aunt Edith just as soon as you can. I'd like to be in that doctor's office in two weeks, three, tops. If she won't work out, you have to have someone else ASAP. We can't fool around."

He was much more serious now.

"Depending on the way this thing turns out, I could be in for a lot of criticism later on if I mishandle it now. I'm trying very hard to avoid that." Then looking at Mel, he said, "How about it, counselor, is that the way you would have done it back in the old days?"

"Absolutely," Mel said, with a very big grin.

"Then we're all set," Gordon said as he rose from his chair. "I'll leave you two guys to work out some of the details and I'm sure we'll be talking again soon." They shook hands and Gordon excused himself. Phil left no more than a few minutes later.

There was little for Phil to do over the weekend, and he spent most of the time with his family. The recent events had energized him so he filled the time with a variety of activities. Everyone enjoyed themselves and afterwards, he wanted very much to be alone with his wife. It was a long time since he had felt any real desire and it left them both very loving and gratified. They slept well.

Monday morning was a return to the matters at hand. There were rounds, two minor surgical procedures and a number of phone messages at the office. There had been a terse call from Mel Silverstone that all was being arranged and that he would speak with Phil later. Phil decided he'd try Ann Hartway's home again. He thought she might have returned from her vacation by now and had been calling from time to time, never getting an answer. At some point he expected someone to pick up the phone but no longer anticipated when this would happen. He usually let it ring for a while but this time the receiver was lifted after the second ring.

"Hello. Ann?"

"Hello."

He recognized the voice and it startled him. He had no longer been thinking what he was going to say to her and now was at a momentary loss for words.

"Ann, it's Phil. I've been calling you almost every day. I was beginning to think you weren't coming back."

"I don't think you were expecting me now, either. I think I surprised you. That's very flattering, Phil. You sound as though you really missed me."

Phil was slow to answer and intuitively, Ann quickly said, "Tell you what, Phil. I'll settle for just having you tell me you're glad I'm back."

"Of course. How long have you been home?"

"I got back yesterday. I'm still settling in. I was getting ready to call you and would have if you hadn't called just now."

"Well, I'm glad I finally got you. We have a lot to talk about. You'll be very surprised at some of the things that have happened."

He knew he could only be partially truthful and would need time to decide what Ann could know and what she couldn't. Fortunately, for the moment, she made it very easy for him.

"I'd like to hear about everything, Phil, but not just now. You're welcome to come over any time you can. I don't plan to return to work for at least another week. Actually, I don't really feel up to it now. This wasn't as much a vacation as I would have liked. I was pretty sick for a while."

Phil was immediately concerned. "What happened?"

"I guess they finally wound up blaming it on a parasite but for a while they thought I might have colitis. I was in a hospital for ten days. Most of that time I couldn't have anything but IVs. I lost fifteen pounds and I've only now started to put it back so I'm warning you. I look pretty bad."

"I could never believe that," Phil said.

"You'll see. I spent the last two weeks in Puerto Rico. Once I got out of the hospital, I wasn't going to take any chances on that Mexican water again. And I wasn't coming back home in the kind of shape I was in. So, I checked out of my hotel and flew to San Juan. That helped and I do feel much better, but you'll see that I'm still not back to normal. When would you like to come over and survey the disaster scene?"

"It can't be that bad."

"I'll let you be the judge. Just don't say I didn't warn you. When can I expect you?"

"I'll call first." Phil said. "Either tomorrow or the following day."

"Good. That gives me at least another twenty-four hours to fatten up. I'm looking forward to seeing you, Phil. Bye."

"Bye, Ann," he said and hung up. He was glad she was back and was anxious to see her. Certainly, this was as it should be and Phil shouldn't have given it further thought, but his feelings were not that easy to dispel. They were a concern and very difficult to gauge. Just speaking with her gave him warm satisfaction and intensified the deepening attachment he felt for her. He was confused by this, particularly after last night with Maralyn. Perhaps his feelings were more than he was willing to admit. Could they reach a point where he would no longer be able to control them? This was a question that he might soon have to ask himself. Then there was the deception that he would have to carry on before he could deal with her truthfully and tell her of everything that was being planned. He found this very disturbing and knew these were conflicts that somehow, he would eventually have to resolve.

His thoughts were interrupted by Mel Silverstone's return phone call. Aunt Edith was thrilled by his invitation and couldn't wait to leave. This was a lot earlier in the year than she was accustomed, and Mel was afraid the cold weather might deter her. Actually, she was excited at the prospect of seeing the snow at this time in preference to the spring when there was usually a lot of rain. Mel called her other relatives in the area to let them know she'd be staying with him. He told them it would be his turn this year and this was a convenient time for him and his family. Regardless of what other reasons he gave, the two of them agreed this was probably the best way to have everything go smoothly for the visit to Stanley Stallings' office. Aunt Edith would be accessible at all times and could be coached as much as needed. It wouldn't be as easy with Ann Hartway.

Ann came to the door wearing a loose-fitting warm-up suit. Her face was deeply tanned and her eyes gleamed as she smiled at Phil and beckoned him to enter. He hesitated momentarily. She had lost considerable weight and although forewarned, her appearance startled him. Her face was no longer full, and her skin was now taut with her features much sharper and more pronounced. It was hard to believe a recent bout of dysentery could bring about such a drastic change.

"Do doctors always try to cheer up patients by staring at them so hard?" Ann's chiding was good-natured. "You really ought to see the expression on your face, Phil."

"I'm sorry, Ann. You did tell me, but I guess I was still a little surprised. I was sure you were exaggerating."

"Change your mind?" She gently guided him into the living room.

"A little, but it's not as bad as you made it sound."

"Sure," Ann said. "I watched your face. I know how I look. I told you I was very sick but I'm getting back to myself now. I figure another two weeks in this outfit, and I'll be ready to join the human race. These sweats hide an awful lot, but all the important things are still there, I assure you."

Phil quickly tried to allay his embarrassment.

"You're not having any more trouble now, are you? Did they ever tell you exactly what you had?"

"Some bug. I can't remember the name. It doesn't make any difference. I'm over it now and I'll never go back there again, but that's not important. Tell me what's been going on back here. You said you had a lot to tell me. By the way, can I get you something?"

"No, thanks."

He looked at her again and sat down. Leaning forward, he moved to the edge of his seat.

"Well, our doctor surprised us and tried to do it again."

Ann quickly realized what he was saying and became visibly upset. She remained quiet however and paid rapt attention as Phil continued and went into many of the details much as he had with Mel Silverstone and Gordon Mulcahey. She showed particular dismay when told of the abrupt change in the scheduled time for Nunzio Battaglia's surgery and gasped audibly when Phil described how the patient had been taken to surgery before being seen by Dr. Mueller. When he finished with all this, she breathed a long sigh of relief, but this was not because she was any less concerned.

"He's really not stopping, is he?"

"It doesn't seem so, and I really don't understand it. He knows there's been considerable criticism and he must be concerned that his cases are being monitored."

"That frightens me. Now someone else, that technician, knows what he's been doing."

"Not exactly. He really doesn't know what else has been going on and he isn't going to say anything to anyone. He knows it's possible no one will believe him, and then what's he done? I can't say we shouldn't be worried, but not about that."

"And what about the lawyer, Mel Silverstone? He knows something."

Phil had to be careful. "He doesn't know very much and whatever he does know, he's told me is hearsay. He doesn't put much stock in it. I haven't spoken to him recently."

He had responded deliberately, and this was a good, if less than honest, reply. He knew what he was saying would trouble him later, but he didn't feel he had a choice. He didn't want to say anything else if it was going to further upset her.

"This is going to end badly," Ann said. "I should have known it. These things always do. It was fine for the first few months after Jack's death but that couldn't last. I just know it's going to get worse."

"I think you're wrong, Ann. I can tell you that it's going to be very difficult to show any wrongdoing on his part. Believe me when I tell you this. He could go on for a very long time like this. I hate to think that may be true, but I've looked at every possible way to deal with him and I don't know what else can be done. No one is going to suspect what we know about him. If you hadn't spoken with me, I certainly wouldn't. You're worried about being implicated and…" His voice trailed off.

Ann looked up expectantly. "And?"

"I don't see how that could happen. It still isn't something anyone else is going to believe."

"Maybe you're right," Ann said. "I hope so. I still don't feel so well and sometimes I can't think straight. Maybe it won't seem as bad once I'm back to normal." She managed a faint smile, and it was time to discuss other things. "What's been happening with you? Anything?"

"Not really. Work, family, this thing."

"How are they, your family?"

"Everyone's fine. They're even starting to think about the summer. I don't know what Maralyn is planning to do with the girls, but I'm sure she has something in mind. I'm usually the last to know, anyway. Have you thought what you're going to be doing with your daughters?"

"They'll be home for a couple of weeks and then they'll spend most of the summer with Jack's parents."

"Are they looking forward to that?"

"Probably not, but they realize it's something they should do."

Phil stood up. It seemed the appropriate time. "I should be going now, Ann. Please don't get up. I'll let myself out." He took his coat and started towards the door. "You take good care of yourself, Ann. I don't want you worrying. If you have any more problems, I want you to call me."

"You mean with my stomach?"

"Yes, of course. That, and anything else." Ann's gaze followed him to the door.

"Thank you, Phil. If I'm having any more problems, I will call you."

X

Phil began to prepare for Edith Skolnick's arrival. He reviewed her office record at great length. At one point he realized he had not taken the precaution of having another patient in mind if a problem developed with Aunt Edith. His immediate reaction was that of mild panic. In the end she arrived on schedule and his fears were allayed. Mel brought her to the office for her evaluation. As in the past, she brought with her copies of treatment she had received during the year and Phil added these to his records. This time he suggested that she have a second opinion with another surgeon who had devised a new low-risk operative procedure for her condition. He would schedule the appointment himself and if Mel was unavailable that day, he would have someone else take her. This was in keeping with the plan he had devised and now he was able to call Gordon Mulcahey and schedule their next meeting. This was hurriedly arranged in spite of heavy work schedules and the greater number of people involved. It would be held in two days at eight p.m. in Mel Silverstone's office.

Although Phil arrived early, he had only a few moments to chat with Mel before Gordon arrived with his associates. They were introduced to Donna Moreland and Kevin Schneider and then Mel ushered everyone into the adjoining room where they all took seats around a large conference table.

Gordon placed a yellow notepad and pencil on the table before him. "I'm glad we were all able to make it this evening. I thought we might have a problem with the hours Donna and Kevin have been putting in, but they made it. I really appreciate it, you two." He turned to Phil. "I've filled them in as much as I can, and they want to help. I think it's fair to say they have some skepticism, which all of us have had initially, but now we agree it's time to find out what's going on. I told them they can ask any questions they wish."

Phil nodded at the pair, but they chose to remain silent for the moment. Gordon continued.

"Donna and Kevin know they will accompany the patient to the surgeon's office. One or both will try to get the surgeon to make as many incriminating statements as they can. These will be recorded. How successful they will be will depend on just how well they understand the medical aspects of this case and how far they can push the doctor without having him become suspicious of our real purpose. We really need you to guide us at this point."

Phil sat forward in his seat and leaned over the table. "I think we have the perfect case to get our surgeon to commit himself," he said. "This particular patient has what we call a rectal prolapse. This is a condition where several inches or more of the rectum hangs out of the anus causing any one of a number of symptoms. There can be pain, bleeding, inability to control the stool or there may not be any symptoms at all. Our patient really has not been bothered by her condition, but our surgeon is not going to know that. Instead, he is going to be told the patient is incontinent of her stool and has been bleeding and this is causing all kinds of problems at home such as soilage and so forth. One of the impressions that you'll give is that you're fed up of taking care of her and all her mess and that she refuses to go to a nursing home. You'll also imply that she's getting more senile although this particular patient is anything but that.

"Now we come to the most important part of the scenario. So far, we've described a bona fide surgical condition, which, by the way, the surgeon will clearly see for himself when he examines the patient. This woman's rectum is always prolapsed when she's up walking around so he will be convinced there definitely is a problem. What makes it perfect for our purpose is her medical history. I have a report from her internist in Florida dated last year, which fortunately is addressed to whom it may concern, and cites all her medical problems. On paper she is a very poor surgical risk and I'm certain no reputable surgeon would operate on this patient with her medical history. You will, of course, have that report with you when you see the surgeon and you'll be certain he reads it. After that, there's only one other thing I want you to do, and that is also very important. You must tell him that although you don't have this other report with you, you do know that the patient had another heart attack in Florida four months ago and was hospitalized. I don't want any decisions reached in this case to be a so-called matter of judgment. I want it to be absolutely clear to everyone that this patient is not a candidate for surgery. There is a general rule that you don't do elective surgery within six months of a documented myocardial infarction because studies have shown there's a very high incidence of additional infarcts after surgery within that time period. If our surgeon agrees to operate knowing she's had a recent infarct, then I think we will have gotten pretty much what we want from all this."

At this point Phil interrupted his discussion to allow the others to ask questions but no one seemed inclined. He looked over at Gordon, but he only smiled, so Phil continued.

"I know this is rather sketchy and we have a lot of details to work out, but I wanted you to get a general idea of the plan as I see it. The next area I think we should get into and one where I'm not sure how much help I can be is the matter of getting a positive response from the surgeon. In some way you have to make it clear to him you'd rather not see the patient survive the surgery. You're going to be completely on your own with this one and I don't know how he's going to react and reply. I can only tell you what impressions I have from talking with one patient's wife who had just such a conversation with this doctor."

Donna Moreland raised her hand. "I think Gordon has briefed us very well before this meeting, Doctor, and I believe Kevin and I have a good idea of what we're supposed to do, but I have some questions. You may be about to cover this, but it would help me understand this a little better if I can clarify a few things."

"Certainly."

"The purpose of all this is to get this doctor to make certain statements that will make him liable for prosecution. Isn't it more likely he might do this if he were talking to just one person rather than both Kevin and I?"

"Yes, I would think so," Phil said.

"Then don't you think we ought to decide now who that should be? I know it would help me get a better idea of what I think I should know as we go along."

"I agree. I do think this person would be more cautious with two people than he would be with one. I was going to give you my thoughts on this a little later, but we might just as well get into it now. I have a feeling, Donna, since you brought this up, you and I may be thinking alike. You're probably the one who should do the talking and I'll tell you why.

"Our patient doesn't know anything about all this. All I've told her to say is that her backside hurts. God forbid she should mention my name. That's why I'd like you in the examining room with her and obviously that leaves Kevin out. I've asked her not to say that she's seen me. I've told her I want a completely impartial recommendation and that I would speak with the doctor later. But I don't want her to tell him that and you could quiet her if she starts to say something. She's intelligent and I have to keep her in the dark. Fortunately, she's very trusting. I can't be sure what he's going to ask or what she's liable to say, so someone has to be in the examining room so the two of them are not alone together. That way you can deal with any question or answer that is liable to get us into trouble. If you get into any real bind with something she says, you can always use her alleged senility to bail us out. I also think a female might be more sensitive to the problems Edith's condition can cause so that's another reason I think Donna should wear the microphone and go one on one with our surgeon. Do you agree with that, Kevin?"

Kevin Schneider shrugged good-naturedly and smiled.

"I think those two may already be one step ahead of you, Phil," Gordon said. "I think they already decided that when we sat down and talked earlier, unless you were going to have an objection."

Donna's face reddened and she seemed a little embarrassed by the remark. "You shouldn't make it sound that way, Gordon." You know these things seem to work better if it's a female dealing with a male."

Gordon nodded but otherwise remained expressionless. "I just thought Dr. Berger would find this consensus reassuring," he said.

Turning to Phil, Donna's look of displeasure quickly faded.

"When Gordon outlined this situation to us, both Kevin and I thought it sounded as though it would be better if it was just me who spoke with the doctor. I've given it considerable thought and have some ideas, but there's a lot of information I need, and I'd like to know what you think would be the best way to approach this?"

"I do have my own ideas," Phil said. "You realize I did speak numerous times about this with one person who had just such a conversation with this surgeon, and I feel I do know what type of person he is. I'm quite certain if you give even the vaguest hint that you don't care about the risk of surgery, and that the patient's death is a chance, you'd be willing to take, our surgeon will pick up on this and you'll be able to take it further. That's how this whole thing developed with this other patient I've alluded to. I will admit though, that he's very clever and is very careful with what he says. A lot will be suggested, and I think any actual intent will be implied rather than clearly stated. That means you'll have to be equally clever to get him to say something incriminating for the tape without arousing his suspicion. One thing you should expect if he goes for it will be his request for a very high fee, probably thirty thousand dollars. That's for risking his reputation if anything should go wrong operating on this type of patient. That, of course, is just a pretext. Is this helping you, Donna?"

"Yes, but why do I want the patient dead? Am I going to get some of her money? I think I need some good answers here, either to get the conversation going or make it more convincing."

"Absolutely," Phil said, "and for that reason you'll have to clearly establish several things. Number one, you're going to have to make it perfectly clear you find the patient's condition intolerable. You can liken this to an infant who isn't toilet-trained and keeps soiling itself."

"But the patient lives in Florida and we're up here. How does that follow?"

"That concerned me too, at first, but all you have to say is the relatives in Florida couldn't look after her anymore and you offered to help. Now you're finding it more than you can handle, too. Even though our patient doesn't have the problem, many patients with her condition cannot control their stool and you're going to make it sound awful. You're going to complain of having to do loads of laundry because her clothes and bedding are always being soiled. You can say she won't wear diapers and your furniture is even being ruined. Complain about odor and whatever else you can think of that I haven't. Number two, you're going to picture her as being senile and you'll make an issue of the so-called quality of her life. That's a favorite of a lot of people these days.

Grandma has some medical problems and isn't always with it so what's the point in keeping her around. Third, you'll imply that Aunt Edith has a lot of money that no one is really enjoying while she's alive. If he ever mentions a large fee, make it clear there won't be any problem seeing that it's paid. You might even try getting his response to a veiled reference that you'll find it easier to pay the fee if the patient doesn't survive. I'll let you use your own judgment. That was said to him once before, but I don't think it would make him suspicious and we might get something worthwhile on tape. Basically, those would be the areas I think you would want to cover, if you're going to convince him you really don't want the patient around any more. I'm willing to elaborate further if you wish."

Both Kevin and Donna took notes as Phil spoke but even as she continued to write, Donna indicated she had another question.

"How explicit do you think I can be in trying to get our surgeon to commit himself? I know I can't come right out and ask him to kill the patient but how close do you think I can come?"

"I really don't know the answer to that. You'll have to go along with him very cautiously trying to get as much from him as possible without making him suspicious or scaring him off. I know this is very vague, but I don't know how else I can help you. You're going to be completely on your own. I will say, however, that he could make it much easier for you than we're anticipating. If I tell you that just recently, he went as far as to have a relative of a patient impersonate that patient so that a blood test would not prevent the patient from being operated on, then I think you can appreciate the type of person we're dealing with. He hasn't been scared off and he's still pursuing these high-risk patients and he's going to some very extreme lengths to ensure that he gets to operate on them. He may just take your cue and say quite a bit with very little prodding. I just don't know, and I think you'd better be prepared for any possibility."

Donna had another question. "How about a little clowning around? Do you think that might help keep him off balance? I was just thinking that all this about soiling clothes and furniture and odor could be made to sound pretty funny depending on how it was presented. That might make it less likely that he would get suspicious." Donna looked at the others at the table, but no one seemed to react to her suggestion.

Phil hesitated as well and then replied. "Again, I'll just have to say I don't know what's going to work and what won't. You're going to be completely on your own and you're going to have to decide everything for yourself. Maybe a little humor would work to our advantage. This is a surgeon who likes to laugh a lot, sometimes at the damnedest times, but I just don't know. Anyway, let me ask you a question. After all this, do you think you can do it?"

Donna eased herself back into her chair. She spoke very deliberately. "When we first sat down, Gordon mentioned there was skepticism. Speaking for myself and I don't know how Kevin still feels, I think it's fair to say I'm still skeptical. That's not a problem, though. On this job you learn everything is possible and you don't pre-judge. I don't have to think about guilt or innocence to do my job although it usually helps.

"What does bother me is credibility and here I have to rely on your expertise. This is where I could have a problem, but you've made me very curious, so much so that I feel I have to do this. With enough of an understanding, I think I can do it very well."

Kevin Schneider smiled. "I wasn't sure if Donna would give me an opportunity to say anything." There was polite laughter and he glanced quickly in her direction. "If Gordon had told you what we said the first time he spoke to us, you'd wonder how we could possibly be here now. I honestly thought he was just putting us on. But I think Donna will agree, the more we listened, the more we both wondered if this could really happen. I know I'd sure as hell like to find that out, if we can."

Phil nodded his thanks. "I appreciate your candor," he said, "and your help. Now that we've resolved this much, I'd like to move on to some other areas. The patient's name, in case I haven't mentioned it already, is Edith Skolnick, and the relatives with whom she usually stays when she's up here are Sylvia and Stanley Wasserstrom. That's who you will be. This time she's staying with Mel for obvious reasons, but they know she's here. I'll give you their address, phone number and so forth. They're Jewish."

"I've been Jewish before," Donna said.

Phil smiled. "Sylvia is a housewife and Stanley is a jeweler and operates his own jewelry store. They have two grown children. That's right, isn't it, Mel?"

"Yes."

"They're Mel's relatives and we don't want them involved in this at all. When we make the appointment, we'll use Mel's home phone number for any calls in case the doctor's office wants to confirm or change the time. If any questions are asked, we'll explain that Edith will be visiting several relatives while she's here and this is the best number to use. I've tried to think of everything but if something has slipped past us, you'll have to do some quick thinking. The one thing that scares me is Edith and what she might say. She knows nothing about this and thinks she's just having a second opinion. We've agreed it's best to keep her in the dark. I don't want her left alone with the doctor and if she starts to say something wrong, interrupt. I've asked her not to mention my name and if you think she's going to, for God's sake, don't let her. Get her out of the office as quickly as you can. She doesn't have to wait around while Donna speaks with the surgeon, and she certainly can't be in the same room with the two of them. Kevin can take her out using any excuse you want. If she hears the name Wasserstrom have some story ready for her. Mel will tell her you're friends who are helping out because there won't be anyone at home to take her. You're Stan and Sis. You won't give her any last name. I know there are things I've left out but I can't think of anything else right now. I just hope it works."

They waited for Gordon to comment. He looked at Mel. "Think it'll work?"

"I think it should." Mel said. "The story is good. I'll try to prompt Edith a bit. That's the only possible screw-up but we can't let her in on this. I'll explain we just want to get her in and out and she probably won't even speak with the doctor afterwards. We'll say we're giving him time to prepare his report. She may feel like she's been steamrollered, but it has to be. There's too much at stake here. Donna can say some things to her afterwards."

"OK guys, that much is done," Gordon said. "Now we just have to schedule the appointment and set up the monitoring. Donna and Kevin, let Phil know what your schedule is. I've already spoken with our old friend, Barney Lemlich, and I've told him to expect a call from Phil. You'll have to show him the office, Phil. If you've ever been in it before, you can describe it to him. It'll help him know where to park his equipment to get the best possible signal. When all this has been done, we'll just need Donna to make the appointment and get everything coordinated one last time for the big day." He hesitated for a moment as he looked at each one. "I guess there's only one other thing to say. Mazel Tov."

"Where'd you learn that?" Phil said. It was a welcome opportunity to tease someone.

"Aw, c'mon Phil. Give me some credit. You know how they say there's a little Irish in everyone. Well, I think it works both ways."

"Very good, Gordon," Phil said.

"OK" Gordon said as he stood up. "This has gone very well. I'd like to see Donna and Kevin tomorrow just to talk this over a little more. Here's Barney Lemlich's card, Phil. Call him as soon as you can."

They shook hands all around and the three left. Phil stayed behind for a short while with Mel.

"Well, what about it, Mel? You really think it's going to work?"

"It should. The only question is that you don't know what you'll be able to get this person to say. That's what you really want to know and you just can't worry about that now. You just have to keep working on it."

Phil agreed. They talked a while longer, particularly about Aunt Edith and then he left. He felt some trepidation, but he also felt very optimistic.

Donna made the appointment shortly after Phil met with Barney Lemlich. He was shown the office building and Phil pointed out the exact location of Stanley Stallings' suite and described the interior layout. He had been an occasional visitor when they were both first starting out and were on more friendly terms. Barney didn't foresee any problems. He had learned his craft working first for a radio station and then for the telephone company. His work now was mostly for private investigators and occasionally for law enforcement agencies. Phil could see how he could be very effective. He was probably the most nondescript individual he had ever met and he thought if he saw him again the next day, he probably wouldn't recognize him.

The office visit was scheduled for the following Tuesday afternoon, and this coordinated well with everyone but Gordon. It was almost certain he would be in court that entire day. As the time grew near, Phil became increasingly apprehensive. His wife and daughters noticed a change but Phil said that was because he had some very sick patients in the hospital. He spoke with Ann Hartway several times but only to inquire how she was feeling. He kept any other conversation very brief and even she asked if he was all right. Fortunately, he could sleepwalk through most of the things he had to do and even though the concentration wasn't there, his patients did well. He was relieved when Tuesday finally came and everyone met in Mel Silverstone's office.

"Hi, Dr. Berger," Donna called out to him. She was talking to Barney Lemlich who came over to shake hands. Kevin Schneider smiled and waved. They each appeared so calm and relaxed that Phil actually felt annoyed.

Mel came out of his private office. He did not see Phil at first. "Donna, do you want to use this to put on your gear?" He motioned towards the doorway behind him and then saw Phil. "Hi, Phil. I guess it's game time. How are you doing?"

"I'm nervous, Mel."

"So is everyone else. They just won't admit it. It's that professional thing. Ordinary folks like us would call it pride."

That brought some laughs and catcalls and made Phil a little more comfortable.

"Why don't you get yourself hooked up, Donna," Mel said, "so Phil can see how this stuff works. It has to be tested anyway."

Donna smiled in reply and began walking towards the vacant room motioning to Barney to follow. They went into the room, Barney carrying a small bag, and partially closed the door. They came out about five minutes later.

"We're ready to test," Barney said. "Want to see how it works, Dr. Berger?"

"I certainly would," Phil replied.

"OK then, just follow me."

They left the office together with Barney carrying on most of the conversation.

"That's a great bunch you're working with, Doc. That Donna is something else. I don't know what kind of material you're looking for, but if she can't get it, no one can."

"You've worked with them before?"

"Yeah, this has got to be the third or fourth time."

"They all seem so unconcerned."

"That's their business, Doc. That's what they do."

They had walked only a short distance when Barney stopped at a very inconspicuous green van. He unlocked the passenger side door and climbed inside. He moved to the rear motioning Phil to follow. One side of the van was lined with electronic equipment. Barney unfolded two small chairs so they could be seated and handed Phil a set of headphones. He began flicking switches and adjusting controls.

"It should be coming in loud and clear in a second," Barney said.

Phil suddenly heard Kevin and Donna speaking as though they were just outside the van. The clarity was very impressive.

"You won't find better equipment anyplace else. That's why the law uses me every once in a while. They don't have the money in their budget to get the kind of stuff I have and sometimes what they've got breaks down, and I've got to fix it for them." He motioned to his equipment. "I'll let them go on for a little longer and then I'll play back what we've got. No matter how good the signal, it won't do you a bit of good if it doesn't record."

A moment later he pushed the stop button and then the rewind and two cassettes sped in reverse.

"I always have a back-up machine going just in case there's a problem with the first machine I don't know about. I consider it disaster insurance."

The replay was perfect and Barney removed his headset. "I guess we're all set." He shut off the equipment and folded his chair and moved towards the passenger door. When he was sure Phil was ready, he opened the door and both men stepped out.

"We'll try to get as close as this when we get where we're going. The closer I am, the better the tape quality." As they walked back to Mel's office, he had another thought. "You know, you mentioned before how loose Kevin and Donna are but I noticed there wasn't any clowning around when they knew I was listening. Usually, they'll tease or crack jokes but there wasn't any of that. They didn't say much at all. I'll just bet they're a lot more concerned than they've let you think."

"I hope so," Phil said. "I know I am."

They were greeted by expectant looks when they returned to the office.

"Everything is working fine, boys and girls," Barney called out. He added to Phil, "Kevin's never forgotten the time they were using their own equipment and it broke down. They got zilch. Ribbed 'em a little for that one and they're still trying to get even."

"Did he show you his collection of dirty pictures?" Donna said. "That's his real forte, you know."

Barney groaned. "See what I mean?"

At that point Mel came out of his office. "How did it go?"

"Very well," Barney said. "Clear as a bell."

"In that case, we should be ready to leave. How much time do we have?" Phil had been glancing at his watch repeatedly. "A little less than an hour."

"Let's not cut it close," Mel said. "We have to get to the professional building on Bradford Boulevard and that can take fifteen minutes or so. Donna and Kevin have to pick up Edith and Barney will want time to set up. I think we should leave now."

Everyone reached for their coats and Mel left instructions with his secretary while he would be out of the office. They went out to the parking lot in the rear of the building where Donna and Kevin had left their car.

Phil handed Kevin a slip of paper. "You know how to get where you're going, but just in case, I've written directions to Mel's house and the office on Bradford Boulevard. Dr. Stallings is in suite 207. Just be careful of any conversations you have with Edith while you're there. It's a small waiting room."

Phil was trembling but it was also very cold, so the others probably didn't notice. Donna and Kevin drove away, and the rest walked back through the building to the front where Barney had parked the van. Mel had decided earlier to go along and all three got in. It was a short ride to the office but then they had to wait until a parking space became available close to the building. They almost lost the space when another driver tried to pull in, but Barney would not be deterred. He turned off the engine and waited for Donna and Kevin. When they finally arrived, he moved to the back and switched on a small electric heater that ran off a battery. He began putting the equipment in operation and when he felt all was in order, he handed headphones to the others.

At first there were just some occasional remarks by Donna or Kevin and muffled conversations from elsewhere in the room. The receptionist could be heard giving instructions for completion of a questionnaire and a Medicare form. Donna took charge and virtually dictated verbatim the information Edith put down. Edith herself said very little, and Phil was beginning to worry that she might be taking her instructions too literally. This went on until Dr. Stallings' nurse was heard introducing herself.

"Dr. Stallings will be ready to see Mrs. Skolnick in just a few moments. I'd like you to come with me now, Mrs. Skolnick. The doctor will want you in a gown for the examination."

"This is it," Phil said. All three listened intently to catch every word.

"Can I go with her?" Donna was heard to ask. "I think she'll be more comfortable if I'm in the room with her," and in a lower tone, "I also brought some fresh clothing, just in case."

"Good move," Phil said, breaking into a broad smile.

"Of course," the nurse answered. "I'm sure the doctor won't mind. Just follow me." There was a short period of silence and then the nurse could be heard giving instructions to Donna and Aunt Edith after which she excused herself. The transmission remained very clear. Donna kept making cheerful remarks that probably were keeping Aunt Edith at ease. It didn't help the tension in the van, however. It almost reached a bursting point a few moments later when the nurse announced her return with Dr. Stallings.

"This is Mrs. Skolnick and her niece, Dr. Stallings."

Phil held his breath. The nurse introduced Donna as Edith's niece. He braced himself for Edith's response.

"Hello. I know those paper gowns are clumsy, but could you just walk over to that table? Help her, Ruth."

"Is that your man?" Mel asked.

"Yes," Phil said. There was still no response from Edith and Phil's expression remained puzzled as he looked at Mel.

"How long have you had this prolapse?" Dr. Stallings asked.

"A long time, Doctor," Edith said.

"Has it been getting worse?"

"I don't think so, Doctor. Maybe it has, but I haven't really noticed."

"Do you have any pain?"

"No, Doctor."

"I'd like you to turn on your left side, if you would, please, Mrs. Skolnick." The rustling of paper could be heard. "Well, you certainly do have a prolapse. This may be a little uncomfortable, Mrs. Skolnick. I'm going to try to put it back in. Please stay as you are. All right, that wasn't too difficult. Sphincter tone isn't that bad, either. Cough, please. It seems to be staying in although I'm sure it will be back out again soon. Do you have any trouble moving your bowels, Mrs. Skolnick?"

"No, I don't, but sometimes it comes out when it's not supposed to."

"I understand." There was a pause. "Well, we can talk about this now but I prefer that we go into my office. I understand you brought some records, which should be on my desk. I'd like to look at those."

"I'd also like to speak with you privately," Donna said. Phil did not know if Edith could overhear. "I think it would be easier if just you and I talked. I can explain everything to Edith later. If you'll give me a few minutes to get her dressed, I'll take her out to my husband, and they can wait someplace else. That'll be a lot easier, believe me."

"If that's what you prefer, that's fine. It will give me some time to look over those reports."

They heard a door close. Donna had all sorts of encouraging words for Edith as she apparently helped her dress. She was going to take Edith to Kevin, and they would wait while she spoke to the doctor. Edith said nothing and a little while later they heard Donna's brief conversation with Kevin. There was further quiet and then Donna asked for Dr. Stallings. Another voice directed her and after a brief pause, she spoke again.

"I didn't want to say anything in front of her, Doctor. She gets very annoyed with me and says I'm only trying to embarrass her, but the situation has really become intolerable. She doesn't realize she's soiling herself continuously and she often has an odor. She's probably gotten so used to it that she doesn't notice it herself. We can't take her anyplace with us and she can't be left home alone, so she's made us virtual prisoners. I'm sorry I sound this way, but I just can't deal with it anymore. There must be something that can be done?"

Mel nodded his approval to Phil.

"I wouldn't think it would be that bad," Dr. Stallings said.

"Then you should spend some time at my house. She refuses to wear any sort of pad or diaper. I had plastic slipcovers on my furniture when my children were small. I took them off when they got bigger. By the time I realized I had to put them back on, she had practically ruined all my furniture. You have no idea how she is destroying my life, not to mention the amount of laundry I have to do each day."

"Why don't you consider a nursing home if she's such a problem?"

"She won't hear of it. She has all the money in the world and in the beginning, all her relatives wanted to take care of her. Most of them are in Florida and she likes it better there anyway. I guess they thought they could get more from her that way. They used to compete with each other, but not anymore. They probably don't feel it's worth it now. We thought we'd give it a try, but it's become impossible. We want to believe there's still some sort of solution."

"You're making it sound as though surgery is your only option."

"That's why we brought her to you. Someone suggested we look into this."

"There's a problem if that's the route we're going to take. I looked through these reports from Florida. Your aunt has pretty severe coronary artery disease. She's had a previous heart attack and her medical doctor considered her a very poor surgical risk and that was last year. That's going to make it hard to justify surgery on her. I notice she's on digoxin. She doesn't take a diuretic, does she?"

"Is that what Lasix is?"

"Yes."

"She's been taking that too, since she got out of the hospital in Florida four months ago. They thought she had another heart attack, but it must have been a mild one. I'm sorry I don't have that report. She came up to stay with me right after that. The others were afraid to take care of her down there."

"This is really going to limit anything I can do."

"Why, Doctor?"

"Because there's too much of a risk of another heart attack if this patient has surgery now. That's been well established for many years. I'd be taking an enormous responsibility."

"Something has to be done, Doctor."

There was a pause. Mel and Phil looked at each other. The discussion had reached a very critical point, and this was reflected in their faces.

"On the other hand, I never like to take away all hope from a patient or the patient's family," Dr. Stallings was finally heard saying. "This is a dilemma but there may be a way I can deal with this surgically. There would have to be an understanding."

There was another pause.

"You realize the surgery could be successful, but the patient might not survive, don't you? That has to be a very real concern here. Would anyone have difficulty understanding or accepting that?"

"If you mean, would I?" Donna said. "The answer is no. I know that, at her age, anything is a risk. She's had a long life and I don't think she's enjoying it very much anymore. I know I'm not. How much longer does she have anyway? It might hurt your ego, Dr. Stallings, but there are far worse things than a sick old woman dying from surgery. I don't know if I'm as heartless as I am practical. I also know I can't take having her around the way she is, and I often think, if it's not this now then it's going to be something else later. I can't keep going through this."

"I think I understand what you're saying. I also want you to know that basically I'm probably quite a bit more aggressive towards certain types of surgical problems than my colleagues are."

"Then you will operate?"

"I would give it very serious consideration. I'll have to find a way to get her cleared medically but I should be able to do that. She looks pretty good on the surface. I will certainly give it a lot of thought, but I want you to hear my conditions. I will be putting myself at risk to take a case like this, so for it to be worthwhile my fee will have to be considerable, and it will have to be cash and paid in advance."

"How much?"

"Before we get to that, let me ask you a question and we'll consider it off the record. Remember, this is not a small problem that you have, and the risk isn't to you. It's to me. I seem to be getting a sense from you that you have a very particular preference for the outcome, and I want to be sure I understand that."

"What do you mean?"

"Well, it would seem the surgery on your aunt is going to have a positive benefit for you no matter what, but just how much I think will depend on how well she does. This sounds like one of those situations where you'll do even better if she doesn't. Am I correct? Is that the impression I should be getting?"

Donna answered promptly.

"Yes, and I don't think there's anything wrong in that. I didn't give her this condition. I just want to get my life back and if I can make it a lot better at the same time, then I think that's just fine."

"So, you wouldn't be terribly upset if the surgery turned out to be too much for her, if she had another heart attack or something like that? You could accept that?"

"If that's the risk we have to take, yes, very easily. I think I've already made that quite clear."

"Yes, I think you have. I just wanted to be sure of that. Then there's really not much more we have to discuss right now. If I can work all this out, can you get your aunt to agree to the surgery?"

"I'm sure I can. I'm certainly going to try, and I think I can get her to go along with it."

"Then I think it's time we discussed the fee. It's thirty thousand dollars. Can you handle that?"

"It's a lot!"

Another pause followed.

"Do you know anything about me?"

"A little. You were recommended to us by some friends. You don't know them. Several of their friends spoke very highly of you."

"There's a reason some people bring patients to me. I take cases other surgeons won't. And I don't think any of them have been unhappy with my results. I just try to be sure everyone who comes here, like yourself, has reasonable expectations. I don't feel my fee is excessive. I believe it's entirely appropriate for the service I provide."

"I wasn't disagreeing with you," Donna said. "It's just that it's a lot, but I know you're doing something for me no other surgeon would. I appreciate that. I'm sure I can do whatever's necessary. Depending on the way things turn out, it may become very easy to take care of that and a lot of other things as well. She's changed her will since she's been up here, and I've been told we're mentioned rather prominently now. Again, there was silence and Phil began to feel a little uneasy. Then he heard Dr. Stallings.

"In that case, you should be enjoying your good fortune very soon. I'll keep these records with me. You don't have any others, do you?"

"No."

"Good. From the looks of things, I don't think that last coronary did any damage. I'll even bet there's a strong possibility her doctors weren't sure she really did have a coronary. In cases like that a lot of the time they only think there's been a heart attack. I'm not even sure there's any point in bringing that up. I could go on, but I think you're beginning to see how the situation can be improved."

"Dr. Stallings, I can't tell you how much better you've made me feel."

"I'm glad to hear you say that. You were right. It was best just the two of us talked. This is a complicated matter, and I don't think it could have been handled any better. I'll keep in touch with you regarding the arrangements. You can be reached easily?"

"Yes."

All this time Phil sat transfixed, his fists clenched, straining to hear every word. He marveled at the way Donna had been able to manipulate the conversation and there were times he wanted to cheer but didn't want to miss anything that was being said. He felt she had gotten what they needed. There was a danger in being too obvious. He heard chairs moving.

"You look as though you still have questions," Dr. Stallings was again heard to say.

"I know it's foolish, but I keep wanting to ask what Edith's chances will be. I guess I'm just looking for a guarantee before I leave here that I won't have to deal with any of this anymore. And I think I'd like to say, I'm not talking just about the prolapse."

"People in my profession don't give guarantees, so you must realize I can't say any

thing more. I can assure you though, her problem… *your* problem, one way or another will be eliminated. You will not have to deal with it any further. I think I'm being pretty explicit. If that's not good enough, then perhaps we should both reconsider."

"No, Doctor, I'm satisfied. I'm sure we understand each other."

"Very well, then. I think it's time now for you to collect Aunt Edith. Start getting her used to the idea of surgery. I'll want to see the two of you again in about one week and then I would like you to have at least a partial payment."

"I will, Doctor, and thank you."

There were several minutes of relative silence interrupted only by the receptionist making the next appointment and then Donna was heard speaking with Kevin.

"I think that was it," Mel said. "I don't think there's going to be any more."

"Can I wrap it up?" Barney asked.

Phil listened a while longer and only when he was certain they had left the office would he allow Barney to stop recording. Barney quickly rewound his equipment and listened briefly to one of the tapes. He rewound that one again and handed the two cassettes to Phil.

"Here you are, Doc, working perfectly. You can keep the back-up for a spare and now you're in business."

"Thank you, Barney. I can settle with you now, if you like? I brought a check with me."

"Great, Doc. I can see by your expression you're happy with what you got. I'm glad. Why don't you make it out for $400, if that seems OK, and make it out to cash."

"That's fine," Phil said. "I wasn't planning to use this as a deduction anyway."

They all laughed, and spirits remained high as Barney moved behind the wheel and began the trip back to Mel's office. Phil could not stop talking about their apparent success and Mel agreed what they heard seemed to confirm all that Phil had been telling them. His demeanor, however, was much more reserved. They arrived well before Donna and Kevin who had to take Edith home first and waited in Mel's office. Phil was even more exultant when those two finally walked through the door.

"Donna, you were terrific!" He embraced her with a big hug.

"Thanks. It did go well, didn't it? I gave him every opportunity I could, and I think he's made a believer of me. You heard what he said. He's some piece of work."

"You did a beautiful job, and thank you for all your help too, Kevin."

"You're welcome, and we shouldn't forget Aunt Edith did very well too."

"God, I almost forgot!" Phil said. "You got her home alright? This didn't bother her too much?"

"Well, I think you're going to have to sit down and talk to her," Donna said. "She's really such a sweet thing and we did make her awfully confused. She handled it well, though."

"I'll say she did," Phil said. "How did you manage when the nurse introduced you as her niece? I thought for sure Edith would say the wrong thing and that would be it. I kept waiting for her to say something."

"That wasn't a problem. I just told her they might not let anyone stay with her in the examining room unless it was a relative, so we agreed I could tell them I was her niece."

"Fantastic. And then at the end you tried to get him to say just a little bit more. I was afraid he might feel he was being pushed a little too much and get suspicious and back down. It worked out OK, though."

"You're right. He didn't like that, but I thought it was worth a try. Hey! We wanted to get everything we could, right?"

Mel was motioning to them. "Hey, you two! I hate to break up this love affair but Barney wants to get his stuff so he can get out of here. You're holding him up."

Donna handed Barney the microphone with some bits of wire and tape. "Here y'go, Barney. I took it off in the car."

"Kevin kept his eyes on the road the whole time?" Barney said. "God bless you, Kevin. I don't think I could have done that." He stuffed the material into his bag. "It's been a pleasure, everyone." He shook hands all around and left.

"We really should be going, too," Donna said. "Gordon should be back at the office by four and he asked if you could meet him there, Dr. Berger. I can take one of the tapes back with me and he can listen to it before you get there. He wants to go over it with you today."

Phil hesitated in handing over either of the tapes and Donna quickly recognized his reluctance.

"On the other hand, it might be just as well if you hold onto both. I know they're important to you and this way you'll know exactly where they are. If you like, we can give you directions to the office."

"I can tell him," Mel said.

"Great. In that case, we'll see you there at four."

Phil sat down after the other two had left. He and Mel looked at each other.

"So, what do you think Gordon's going to say?" Phil asked.

"Oh, I don't want to second-guess. You certainly made believers of a lot of people today but let him tell you. Just don't be disappointed if he says you still have a long way to go. If you can, try to think like a lawyer."

"You don't think we did that well today?"

"You did very well. You just didn't wrap up your case all in one afternoon. My opinion isn't that important. Hear what he has to say first."

Phil remained silent as he gave that some thought.

"Are you going straight to his office?" Mel asked. "You still have a lot of time."

"No, I think I'll stop at my office first. I'm sure there'll be messages."

"Don't they beep you?"

"Only for emergencies when my secretaries are in. It's a different story when answering service takes over. Then I get called for everything."

"I only asked because I never hear your beeper go off."

"I've got them trained."

"OK You know the County Court Building on Harwood Drive? It's in that group of buildings two blocks before you get on the interstate. He's in the Major Crimes Unit, second floor. Very easy to find."

"I know where that is." Phil got up from his chair, but he wasn't quite ready to leave yet. "I guess I did let myself get a little carried away." A tight grin formed. "I still think we got some awfully good stuff."

"You're doing a very good job," Mel said. "Stay after this guy. Someone has to find a way to close the book on him, and you'll be the one."

He walked Phil to the door. "Call me after you speak with Gordon."

Phil had just enough time to make a stop at his office, attend very quickly to several semi-urgent matters and then drive to Gordon Mulcahey's office. Gordon had already been there long enough to have been thoroughly briefed by Donna and Kevin. He took one of the cassettes from Phil and placed it in a small recorder he had on his desk.

"Donna says you have some real good stuff here. I'd like to listen to it first and then we can talk about it. You're going to have to tell me, from a medical standpoint, just exactly what you think we have."

He switched on the playback and turned down the volume so that only the two could hear. He listened very carefully. When he was finished, he rewound the cassette and looked at Phil. "That's not the typical conversation a doctor has with a patient or the patient's family, is it?" He didn't wait for an answer. "Frankly, I'm very surprised. He says a lot more than I would have expected and he really gets right into it, doesn't he? Forget what he said for the moment. What possesses him to assume this is what this family member really wants? If I recall correctly, this is very similar to the conversation you say he had with that patient's wife. It's as if he's aware of something the rest of us are not, some type of basic human aberration. Apparently, it's a lot more widespread than any of us would think and he's developed his own sales pitch to take advantage of this. He's made this into a regular cottage industry." For a moment Gordon had a faraway look. "I must be losing it because I generally never have this reaction." His fingers drummed forcefully on the table. "I apologize. We're getting ahead of ourselves. Let's backtrack.

We really should start with the significant medical improprieties here. Why don't you tell me what they are?"

Phil had to quickly gather his thoughts. Gordon's reaction had momentarily confused him.

"The whole tone of this thing," he said. "Stallings clearly shouldn't be operating on this patient. The worst thing he's doing from a medical standpoint is to conceal the recent heart attack Edith is supposed to have had. That puts her at a greatly increased risk. I think it's obvious why he's doing that. The other improprieties? Probably the fee. Thirty thousand dollars is certainly not what would be charged for a routine surgical procedure. And then there's the question he asked about preferences. Since when is someone asked about their preference for the outcome of a surgical procedure? And how about his answer to Donna when she asked about a guarantee? If you ask me, I think the whole thing was an impropriety."

Gordon shook his head. "You have to be more objective. You have to distinguish between an actual breach of acceptable medical practice and the *appearance* of such a breach. Here, I'm the one telling you about medical practice and you're the doctor. That's a switch. But I don't think you really understand this. Withholding information concerning the heart attack is obviously an impropriety but I don't think you can be as certain about the rest. That may well be the impression a lot of people would have but no lawyer would let that stand in court. You can be sure he'd give a much less sinister meaning and be very convincing, at that. I would have to listen to the tape quite a few more times before I can say what I really think it does for us. As an initial impression I would have to say it certainly justified your efforts. It's given you credibility where everything up to this point was based only on your say-so. This was our first chance to put our skepticism to the test. Remember, we're lay people and even though we find Stallings' conduct incomprehensible, he's still a doctor. We needed convincing and you and he did a very effective job of that today. We're just a long way from going before a grand jury."

Phil looked disheartened.

"I thought he had said just about everything we wanted him to say. Donna even agreed. I thought things went perfectly for us."

"Short of him coming right out and saying that he was going to commit murder, I would have to agree. But we're still missing the main ingredient. Everything we have is for the most part circumstantial. We need someone to pull the trigger. What are we to say when we're asked how all this came about? A little birdie told us? We figured it out for ourselves? The fact is, someone came forward but now won't testify. You see where that leaves us?"

"Do you think it would be worthwhile to go back again, to see if we could get something more a second time?"

"To his office? I doubt it. From what I just heard, he's too smart, too cautious. He could just decide to bail out completely, and then how would you use that tape?"

Phil thought for a moment. "Well then, what if we actually let Aunt Edith go into the hospital for the surgery. We could allow everything to continue right up until the time she is to be anesthetized. Then the procedure would be stopped, and he could be confronted with the tape. I was wondering just what that would accomplish?"

"You would know better than I. You're the one who knows how your disciplinary system works. The impression you've given me is that it's not too reliable and then you have to deal with your colleagues knowing that you set him up. You'll probably put yourself in a very difficult and unpleasant position and you'll lose whatever advantage we have at the moment. Right now your Dr. Stallings doesn't know we're on to him and that's our biggest plus. I wouldn't want to give that up because we still want to make this a criminal case and get the evidence that will bring an indictment against him."

Phil sank back in his chair. "I thought today was going to do that. Now I'm not sure there's anything that can be done."

"There is one thing," Gordon said. "I brought it up just a little while ago. I don't think you want to talk about it, but I think you have to keep it in mind. You could keep trying to get that woman to testify. That's really what we need. Then the rest of it, including today, would fall in place."

Phil halfheartedly raised his arms. "She would never do that. I could never do that. That was her whole point in all this, to get him to stop so that he would never be found out and she would never be found out.

That's all she worries about. She trusts me to see that never happens to her. How could I possibly ask her that?"

"I don't know. Maybe you have to decide what's more important to you. Then again, if you're so sure she won't testify, maybe it's just as well you don't antagonize her. I can't tell you I have the answer."

"Neither do I, Gordon. I just wish you knew how much this is eating me up inside. I see this person every day and I don't know how to react towards him. I try to be civil but then I feel I'm betraying my responsibility. There's so much to be considered here. It bothers me no end that there are so many committees in the hospital that are monitoring the most picayune details and here's a surgeon who's actually killing his patients and no one knows it. I don't know how much longer I can keep this up."

"You'd better take it easy," Gordon said. "This is a very unusual situation. It may even be the so-called perfect crime, so far. It's going to take some unusual maneuvering on our part to get this guy and that's going to take time, lots of time, plain and simple. I have a pretty good intuition about these things. One of these days the whole thing will break in our favor. Mark my words. We just have to be patient."

"I hope you're right," Phil said. "I just hope you're right."

Gordon tilted back in his chair. "Let's relax a little and get away from this aspect of it for a minute and let's talk about reasons. Why do you think he's doing all this? It can't be just for the money. He'd be throwing away too much if he got caught. Do you think it's an ego thing, that he's found a way to beat the system and he just keeps thumbing his nose at it? You never found out about his finances, did you?"

"Not yet."

"This is what I find most intriguing. I wonder if he thinks this is a way to show his superiority, that he can take the unthinkable and carry it out time and time again with no one ever the wiser. Maybe it is just a head game with him. Sometimes, when you can get into the head of a person like that, it's the first step in putting him away."

Phil had a wistful look. "I don't know what to tell you, Gordon. I wish I knew." Neither man spoke for a while and then suddenly, Phil broke the silence.

"There was something he said a while ago and I've never brought it up. I wasn't sure what he really meant or how you might have taken it, but I think I should mention it now. A number of us were waiting for our cases to start in the OR and someone brought up the subject of culling. Somehow that got shifted over to the general population."

"You mean us?"

"Yes, a sort of euthanasia. Some of the people there agreed something like this might become necessary. It's the argument that medical costs are so high not everyone will be able to get the best care and some sort of selection will be needed. Stallings agreed with this."

"I follow you, but so what?"

"He also said someone could do that and not be found out. He would just have to be that much smarter than everyone else, he said."

"A physician?"

"I think he probably meant a surgeon."

"You didn't want to tell me about this before?"

"I wasn't always thinking about it and to be honest, I didn't know how you'd react."

"God, if that's it, this guy's a real sicko." Gordon waved the cassette in his hand. "Let me keep this so I can listen to it again. You keep the other one in a safe place. I'll certainly keep in mind what you just said." He slowly rose from his chair. "I'm sorry I disappointed you but let's keep on top of everything. My feeling is this man is not going to stop and now that we're on to him, it's only a matter of time before we'll get him."

Phil had nothing else to say. Gordon gave him a reassuring pat on the back when they shook hands. Neither mentioned another time to meet. Phil went back to his office, but it was after five and everyone had left. He knew he had to call Ann Hartway. He just needed time to decide what he would say to her.

There was no answer at Ann's home the first two times he called. She finally answered when he tried again later that evening from the hospital. She was feeling better and had gone back to work. Not everything was back to normal, however. She still tired easily, and her waist size surprisingly was larger than it had been. A program of fewer rich desserts and more exercise was being considered. She reminded Phil that it had been a while since his last visit. He told her that was the purpose of his call, and a date was tentatively set for that Thursday evening. Once again, he was at an impasse and although the thought disturbed him immensely, asking Ann to testify had clearly become his only hope.

XI

A strategy of sorts had been formulated before the visit to Ann Hartway. Phil was going to tell her that Dr. Stallings apparently had no intention of discontinuing his activities and he was rapidly running out of ideas how to deal with this. He was also going to tell her about Aunt Edith's visit but would not mention that Gordon Mulcahey's office was involved. Depending on how Ann reacted, he might also mention that it could become necessary for someone to come forward if Dr. Stallings was ever going to get what he deserved. He was anxious to get her reaction. Waiting had become the most nerve-racking experience he had ever had, and he just wanted it to be over.

He arrived at Ann's home at six thirty. She met him at the door with a big smile, obviously very glad to see him. She gave him a light kiss on the cheek and took his coat. It was also obvious that she was feeling better. Her face was fuller, and her color improved but still not what it had been. She was aware that Phil was watching her closely. They went into the living room.

"I know, Phil," she said, "it's still not the old 'me'. Give me a chance. It's getting better, though, isn't it?"

Phil laughed. "I'm sorry. You're right. You do look much better. It's just that I've been so puzzled by this recent trouble you had. It certainly seems to have taken its toll on you. I don't think I would have expected that."

Ann shrugged. "I don't know either, but I do feel a lot better. You may have to get used to some of this, though. I don't think I'm going to put all the weight back on. I think I may have been a little too heavy before. My color should get better. It's still a little pasty but that should get back to normal when the weather improves. My complexion is naturally very dark, and I can't wait for the sun. You look well."

"I'm OK You realize we still have a few months before the warm weather."

"I know. I'm just trying to be very positive."

Phil smiled. He wasn't quite ready to get into the real matter at hand. "How long have you been back at work?"

"A few days. It feels pretty good. Jack always had a very good staff, so I can honestly say I wasn't really missed. I guess that's both good and bad. How about yourself? How's your practice?"

"A little slow right now. It runs in spurts. Even our friend hasn't been very busy, but that doesn't mean he hasn't been trying."

"I was going to ask you. Could I make you something first? I think I'm going to have something."

"Anything cold would be fine. A soda would be perfect."

Ann disappeared into the kitchen and then brought out a small tray with glasses, a bucket of ice and an assortment of mixers. Phil poured a Coke for himself while Ann mixed a scotch and soda. She sat down a short distance away.

"This is still a big problem, Ann, and I really don't know what to do. He doesn't show any signs of backing down. I told you about that latest incident at the hospital when he had a nephew impersonate the patient so he wouldn't have a problem with the blood test results. Well, I went one step further. I sent a patient up to his office with a problem but also with a very bad cardiac history. I wanted to see what he would do. It was the same thing. I have it on tape."

Ann didn't seem to know what to say. She sat staring at Phil, her mouth open with a pained look on her face. He thought she looked a little pale. He wasn't about to say anything else until she did.

Ann took a deep breath. "I guess it really was time for us to have another talk." She hesitated again and this time looked at him searchingly. "Why did you do this? Don't you believe me?"

"Of course. I just had to have something more. I had to hear it for myself."

"You weren't convinced?"

"I was convinced but let's just say I wanted to be more convinced. Please, Ann. I don't think that should be so hard to understand."

Ann was obviously thinking very carefully. "Explain to me just what you did."

"I'll try to make it as clear as I can. I have a patient who lives in Florida and visits me every year. She has a rectal condition that I've been watching. She's had it for years. It doesn't really require surgery and she does have a very bad cardiac history. No reputable surgeon would ever operate on her. It occurred to me this was just the kind of patient he would operate on if—"

"If what I was saying was the truth."

Phil sighed. "No, Ann. If it was suggested to him the family didn't want her around. That's what I wanted to make him believe. It wasn't a matter of what I believed. I wanted to see if he would still try the same thing again even after everything else that's happened, and he did. That's why I'm still so concerned."

"I'm sorry," Ann said. "You had me frightened. Didn't you think you were taking a big chance? What did you do to keep him from connecting you with this?"

"I was never mentioned."

"If I think I'm really beginning to understand all this, who went with the patient?"

"I had a young couple pretend they were her relatives. The woman did all the talking with Dr. Stallings. She had the recording device."

"Then they know what's happened?"

"Not really. It was all arranged through Mel Silverstone's office. You know I've spoken with him before about all this. The patient is actually a relative and she's staying with him right now. The other two people do this sort of thing for a living. They didn't have to be told very much."

Ann shook her head. "I think I understand what you're doing but I'm not sure I agree with it. You're still keeping me out of all this, aren't you?"

"Yes, of course. No one knows anything about you, who you are. Nothing."

"I still wish you hadn't done this. Somehow it makes me very nervous. It's as if you're trying to trap him, and if you do, everything will come out. Do you understand now why this upsets me?"

"Yes, but I don't think anything like that will happen. I'm even beginning to believe he can go on like this forever and no one will ever be able to do much about it."

"Do you really mean that?"

"Yes. They may slap him on the wrist at the hospital a few times, but they'll never believe the magnitude of the things he's done. Besides, it's gone beyond that. This is no longer a question of improper or substandard medical care. These are criminal matters, and the hospital is not the forum for this. This belongs in the criminal court system. If anything is ever going to happen to Dr. Stallings, I think someone is going to have to step forward and point an accusing finger at him and then the legal system can take over. Since there's very little likelihood of that, I don't think anything is going to happen to anybody for a very long time."

"Listening to you, Phil, I can't help thinking that may be what you want me to do. Is it?"

"I never said that."

"Obviously, you must be thinking about it. There really isn't anyone else. Answer me. Is that what you really want? Do you want me to be his accuser?"

Phil tried to choose his words carefully.

"I don't want you to be hurt. Yes, I have thought about it. I'm always thinking about it. What he is doing is abominable. If there is a way to have you expose him without being hurt, yes, I would hope you'd come forward. There just doesn't seem to be a way to do that and protect you at the same time. I wish there was. Right now, you're a very important concern."

"But that could change." She raised her hand, admonishing Phil not to reply. "I understand. You don't have to say anything. Better yet, there are some things I should tell you and this is a good time. I want you to listen to me, please." She stared into her drink and swirled it several times.

"I was all right for a while after Jack died. Back then I didn't really think I had anything to do with his death. Patients had complications and sometimes they died because of them. I guess that's what I wanted to think had happened, whether I had those conversations with Dr. Stallings or not. It wasn't until I learned of the others

that I understood what I had done. That's when I first spoke to you. I really was terrified someone would find out what he was doing, and they would eventually know about me. I couldn't handle this alone, and you were the only person I could think of who could possibly help."

She sipped several times from her drink finally finishing it, and then shifted her position.

"There was another reason that you should know. It doesn't embarrass me to say this. I was becoming very lonely. I wanted another relationship, but I was very unsure of myself. I realized what I had done. I didn't know if this would ever allow me to have any kind of meaningful relationship with another man. I thought if you accepted me, knowing all that you did, then it meant I wasn't that terrible person who should never be with anyone else. I hoped we'd become close. I know in a way we have, but I mean as close as two people can be. I know you have something very good with Maralyn and I didn't mean to come between that. I only knew if someone as good as you could accept me completely as a woman, I'd have a chance someday with someone else. If only men understood us better. If Jack did, then I know none of this would ever have happened."

She had glanced only occasionally at Phil while she spoke, but now she watched him very carefully. He in turn, completely surprised by all this, could only listen, incapable of any response.

"I had hoped we could have a physical relationship. That would have been very important to me, but I realized you didn't want that. I'm not saying that to be bitter. That's just you and I probably respect you even more for it. Most men, I think, would have been only too happy to accommodate 'the grieving widow'. To me, that would have meant your total acceptance of me as a woman and regardless of the past. That was very important to me then, but it isn't any longer and now I wouldn't want it. There's a good reason for that and someday you may know what it is. I can't tell you now, but it has nothing to do with my regard for you. That's never changed.

"I know what you would like me to do. It's hard for you because you still want to protect me. I may have to make that decision someday, but I can't right now. I know what kind of a person he is and that he has to be stopped. I may even know that better than you. Many things have changed for me and there may be a lot more later on. I have an awful lot to think over. I know this sounds very mysterious but just try to be patient with me. This is a very difficult time."

Phil had not been prepared for this and he could not fully understand all that Ann was saying. Many thoughts went through his mind at once. When she spoke of her feelings and desire for him, he immediately thought of his own but could not admit this. It took a little while before he could respond.

"I want to help you, Ann, but I'm not sure I know how. There's a lot you said, but there's probably more. I think I know why you were upset before, but this is different. I don't want to pry. I'm not comfortable with that. You have to tell me if there's something else. If not, would you consider going back to the person you were seeing before?"

"You know I can't do that now. Anyway, if I ever do need someone else, it's not going to be that kind of doctor."

"What do you mean?"

"It doesn't mean anything, Phil. I meant it as a joke, a very poor one, I'm afraid." She got up and walked back and forth a few times and then sat next to him.

"Look, Phil. I don't think there's any point in continuing this right now. We said a lot to each other and I'm very glad we did. I feel very close to you and I'm very grateful for that. I couldn't get through this without you. You may think I'm exaggerating but believe me, I'm not. Let's just see how things develop. Keep doing whatever you have to do. I just can't push things along any faster right now. I want to keep seeing you. You're my one bridge to whatever's good in my life right now."

"But I don't like it when I see you like this, Ann."

"I'm really all right. I just get a little melancholy sometimes. I'm a woman, right? Well, don't forget it. I may just want to appeal to that part of our relationship again sometime." She stood up and took his hand. "C'mon, Doc. It's time to go home."

There was nothing else Phil could say. He got up and walked quietly to the door. Ann tried to help him with his coat, but he took it from her and put it over his arm. She put her hand on his cheek and smiling at him, held it there. He put his hand over hers and with his eyes closed, moved it to his lips. Pleasant warmth surged over him and then slowly ebbed away. When he looked at her again, she was still smiling, and her eyes were moist. She said thank you very softly and opened the door for him. The bracing cold air jolted him and by the time he reached his car, much of his composure had returned.

The drive home was nonetheless unsettling. He could not quell the turmoil in his mind. Ann had spoken of thoughts and feelings he had never fully realized. Nor did she react as he expected when he spoke about confronting Dr. Stallings. He thought she would be infuriated. Instead, she talked of this as a possibility at some later time. Phil was very surprised. He had not expected to hear this. Although he found this encouraging, he also felt very uneasy. He was bewildered by many of the things she said. He would not have characterized her as disconsolate or despondent but there was an unmistakable sense of resignation. It disturbed him very deeply that he didn't know the precise reason for this.

When he reached home, he tried to put all this out of his mind. Maralyn thought they could have a quick snack and try to take in a movie if there was still time. She did not want to stay home, and the girls could look after themselves. Phil decided she couldn't have made a more perfect suggestion. He certainly wasn't going to be a pleasure to have at home. He didn't even ask what movie they would see.

On the way to the theater Maralyn mentioned she had tried to reach him earlier to see if they could make plans for the evening. Phil said he must have been in the hospital. Maralyn said she paged him there. Phil said he was probably in the medical library at the time and that was one area where the page system frequently didn't work. Maralyn said he should have let the page operator know where he would be if he knew that was a problem. Phil agreed and the conversation ended. Afterwards, Maralyn said very little about the movie, which was just as well because Phil could not remember very much about it. It was no different later even after they went to bed. Phil's only consolation was that it would have been much worse if they had stayed at home.

In the morning he was awake and dressed well before the others. He had been restless through most of the night and hadn't slept well. Maralyn offered to fix breakfast for him, but he said he'd get something at the hospital. She asked if he was all right. Phil said there were problems with some of his patients and it was just the usual distraction. He apologized for his mood and Maralyn gave him an understanding hug and kiss. Phil left, feeling grateful that he hadn't caused a major upset at home.

The day went quickly enough and when Phil thought he might be able to reach Gordon Mulcahey, he put a call into his office. He was now very familiar with his schedule and after a very short wait, Gordon was on the phone. He lost no time in detailing the conversation with Ann Hartway but was unable to explain the cryptic references she made. He did say several times that Ann had not totally rejected the possibility of testifying against Dr. Stallings. In fact, he said it was something she admitted she eventually might have to consider. Gordon confessed he didn't know what kind of spin to put on this but felt it represented movement in the right direction. He urged Phil to keep working on all avenues that could help the case. He was sorry there wasn't anything he could do at this point but would always be available if there was something Phil wanted to discuss. He wished him luck and emphasized that he wasn't losing interest in the matter. He expected Phil to keep him well-informed of any and all developments. Then he asked how Phil was going to handle the matter of Aunt Edith's surgery with Dr. Stallings' office. Didn't he recall correctly that another visit had been scheduled? Phil's intention was to have Donna call the office and cancel the appointment presumably because she couldn't convince Edith to have the surgery. Gordon thought that was a good idea and said he would relay the message. That basically concluded the conversation, and it wasn't long after he hung up that Phil realized once again all his efforts would have to be totally reassessed.

The only course of action left to him now was a more careful monitoring of Stanley Stallings' case material. There didn't seem to be an alternative. He didn't feel he could just stand by waiting idly for some chance occurrence that might or might not come to his attention. This meant a considerable amount of additional work that would have to be performed in a rather clandestine manner. Phil was very familiar with chart review. He had done this for many years for different hospital committees and certain outside organizations and had become very adept at determining deficiencies and improprieties. More would be needed if he was to maintain the momentum that seemed to have peaked with the visit to Dr. Stallings' office. Each patient's hospital record would have to be examined, particularly the treatment rendered and its results. Recognizing that there could be inaccuracies at times for whatever reason, input from the floor staff and OR personnel would also be obtained whenever possible. All this would have to be done without raising suspicion and would be very time-consuming because of the large census Dr. Stallings usually had in the hospital at any given time. It was not a task he welcomed but rather one he felt was absolutely necessary.

During the course of the next several weeks he managed to look over a considerable number of cases. There were two deaths on Dr. Stallings' service in that period and none seemed suspicious. One had been the result of massive injuries sustained in an automobile accident and that patient died in the emergency room. The other was an elderly patient with terminal carcinomatosis who had lived long beyond reasonable expectation. The rest of the cases were routine although there were some that deserved further scrutiny and possibly some corrective action. One patient had the removal of a lipoma, a benign fatty tumor, but Dr. Stallings reported this as an incarcerated hernia, which carries a much higher reimbursement. Another was admitted as an emergency with an incarcerated inguinal hernia resulting from a work injury. The hernia was apparently reduced manually in the emergency room and then repaired electively the following day. Those present in the operating room, however, saw no evidence of a hernia and were quite willing to speak about it. The compensation carrier could not be aware of this, and of course, would eventually pay the full charges. There were some others but none of those would be of any use to him. Still, he kept his vigilance.

He continued to see Ann on occasion during this period, but these visits seemed destined to be less frequent. Their recent conversations never had any real significance and in addition, she began having her daughters travel home to be with her on the weekends. She apparently wasn't ready to make any important decisions at this time and always managed to keep their discussions from moving in that direction. She looked reasonably well but Phil continued to feel she was having even more difficulty dealing with all this than she was willing to admit. She did make it clear, however, she would accept only so much help, and nothing more.

He was home one evening, around this same time, and he and Maralyn were having dinner. He had been late, and the girls had eaten earlier and were off somewhere doing their homework. Their conversation covered the usual topics and then took a most unexpected turn.

"Is everything all right with Ann Hartway?" Maralyn asked. She purposely avoided looking in his direction.

Phil was startled. "I'm not sure what you mean."

"I'm just asking if there's anything wrong with her. Someone has seen your car at her house a number of times and asked me the same thing. It was rather awkward. I didn't know what to answer."

The question wasn't any easier for Phil to answer and he hesitated.

"Is she having a problem?" She looked at him now, very earnestly.

"There is a problem. I can't tell you what it is, not right now. I'm trying to work it out. It has to do with Jack's surgery but that's all I can say. It's a very sensitive matter."

"It's not something between you and Ann?"

"No, and I think you know me better than to ask that."

Maralyn's eyes glistened but otherwise her expression remained unchanged.

"Yes, I do think better of you than that, but I also know anything is possible. She's very attractive and now she's a widow. Someone tells me they keep seeing your car at her house. I think how it's been with us lately when we're in bed. There's been a change and you can't tell me there hasn't. What would you expect me to think?"

"I'm sorry," Phil said. "I hoped this wouldn't come up. I knew it would be hard to explain."

Her anger exploded. "Explain what! You haven't explained anything!"

Phil was startled by her reaction but quickly responded. "I can't, Maralyn. It's a medical thing, that's all. I know it's not fair, but I can't tell you anything more about it right now. I've had to see her at her home a number of times but there's no relationship. I don't think I could have one even if I wanted it."

Maralyn had a puzzled expression. "I'm trying very hard to be understanding, Phil, but you're not making it any easier. What did you just mean?"

"I just don't think I could allow myself to get involved with someone else. I don't think there's anything worse that you can do to another person and I would never do that to you. I have too much respect for you and too great a sense of what's right and what's wrong. Besides, you mean too much to me. I don't think I would ever risk any of that."

"There really isn't anything between the two of you?"

"I've told you. No, there isn't. I feel very badly you have to think that. That's why I never said anything to you. I don't know how else to make you believe that."

"Do you still have to see her, for whatever you say the reason is? Do you still have to go there?" She abruptly drew back in her chair, her head tilted upwards. "God, I sound just like some schoolgirl!"

Phil reached for her and grasped her arm. "This is getting foolish, Maralyn. There is nothing going on between Ann Hartway and myself except some very serious questions about her husband's death and some other patients' as well. I didn't even want to tell you this much but you're my wife and I love you very much and I owe you at least this. I can see why you're upset but you have to put a stop to it. There's no reason for us to have this kind of aggravation right now."

Maralyn studied his every word and expression.

"You are telling the truth, aren't you?"

"Yes, and I want this to mean that you believe me."

Maralyn nodded. "I haven't handled this very well, have I?"

"It's my fault. I should have found some way to tell you. When did you first find out about this, anyway?"

"Today." She finally smiled. "Did you think I was going to let this go on for a while? I was getting to the bottom of this right away. I should tell you all the thoughts I had, the excuses I made for you. Everything went through my mind just so I wouldn't think the two of you were carrying on. I was sure she had this terrible illness, and you were treating her. I kept thinking there had to be some reasonable explanation and that had to be it. It just made me feel so awful when I thought it could be something else. I had to ask you tonight. I'm sorry. Deep down inside I always knew it couldn't be anything bad." An apologetic look crept across her face. "I knew I could trust you."

That brought a smile from Phil, a bit skeptical but playful. There was an unmistakable gleam in Maralyn's eyes. He watched her for a moment.

"What would you like to do now?" he asked.

"I think it might be nice if we went upstairs."

"The girls are still up."

"We could lock the bedroom door."

Phil pushed himself back from the table.

"I think that's an excellent idea." He and Maralyn left the dining room and climbed the stairs hand in hand.

Phil was much more relieved over the following days. Maralyn had actually been very reasonable although she probably didn't think so herself. Some of the things she said occasionally suggested some lingering personal embarrassment. She also made it clear she'd understand if he still had to see Ann at her home from time to time. Phil had already decided there would be much less chance of that. Ann was becoming increasingly more distant, and Phil did not want to pressure her. He would stay in touch, but she would have to indicate when she was ready to come forward. In the meantime, he would try to spend more time with Maralyn. He was grateful to her. There was no way of telling how great a breach this could have caused in their personal lives even though nothing improper had occurred. He accepted that he had feelings for Ann but also that these were out of sympathy and concern for her. It was his wife who he both loved and respected and he felt deeply indebted to her. At this moment, he considered himself very fortunate. It helped maintain his resolve.

XII

It wasn't as busy at the hospital as it had been. The volume of surgery always seemed to run in cycles for some unexplained reason, and right now the surgical caseload was low. Phil had begun to keep a record of the information and material he had been gathering and this was hidden away in a very secure place with the cassette tape. He had the time to do this now and took to the task with a great deal of enthusiasm and energy but usually at odd hours when he was less likely to be seen by others. As a result, he had much less contact with the staff, including Gary Barlow. This had at least one disadvantage since there was always the chance Gary had heard something Phil hadn't. That didn't mean, however, that they still weren't having their typical confrontations from time to time.

During rounds on one particular afternoon, he spotted an unopened tin of cookies that someone had left at one of the nurses' stations. Unexpectedly, he found himself thinking back to a recent wildlife program he had seen on television. It depicted the basic instincts that were common to all forms of animal life. That being the case, he could laughingly surmise at some point certain others might be attracted to this spot. He left for a short time and when he came back, he found Gary foraging through the cookie tin.

"I thought I might find you here."

"Oh, please, Dr. Berger, take him away before he eats all our cookies," one nurse pleaded.

"Damn! Imagine! In this entire hospital with all the patients we have, this is the extent of the appreciation we're shown for the care we're giving. One tin of cookies! That's it! I know. I've been to every floor. And they expect us to still be nice to everyone."

"Any chance I can talk to you now, Gary, or should I get a dart gun?"

"Oh, great. It gets slow around here, we stop working, the tension eases and you develop a sense of humor. I really need this now."

"I just thought I'd ask how it was going."

"Well, don't. It's been dead, or perhaps you have another source of income and hadn't really noticed. I've got one little thing to do later today, on one of the nurses. That's it. Even your buddy, Stanley, hasn't been doing anything."

"That's one of the things I wanted to ask you. You haven't come across anything or heard anything?"

"About him? Nope. No, everything has been very quiet. I've been spending most of my time trying to straighten out a bunch of bills in the office. Damn insurance companies keep losing the forms or change the codes and knock down the amounts. I take care of the patients, but they feel they can tell me what I did for them. If that's not bad enough, these HMOs are trying to get me to sign up and their fees are ridiculous. I'd be busting my ass for nothing. Patients aren't paying either. You having this problem?"

"Of course. I thought you were going to tell me something new."

Gary began to smile, and the smile became wider and wider. Since there wasn't any polite way that he could hastily make his exit, Phil knew he had to prepare himself. Another discourse was about to start.

"You really want to hear something new? Then listen to this. I've been thinking about this for a while. With all the changes going on, we have to come up with some new ideas or we're dead meat. A lot of this trouble is because of the economy, right? How about little surgi-centers that are run on the barter system? A lot of people have pretty lousy insurance, don't they? Why not make up the difference with stuff they own and don't use very much? People could bring in lawnmowers, furniture, old clothes. The stuff's gotta have some value. We'd put these surgi-centers next to small warehouses and every so often we dump the stuff. The bigger the procedure, the more stuff they have to bring in. I'd even like to see big signs outside like 'Surgery While You Wait'."

"That's a bit redundant, isn't it?" Phil said.

"So what? It emphasizes the whole thing. Hey, don't try to knock this idea. You know how we lose cases to the big centers in the city. This will give us a big advantage. Do you think some guy who needs his hernia fixed is going to drive all the way into the city with a lawnmower and an outdoor barbecue strapped to his car, find a place to park and then carry all that stuff into some fancy office to do a little bargaining? Never!

Not when it's just a short hop to one of our convenient redemption centers located throughout the suburbs where your negotiations are handled quickly, carefully, and courteously by our trained staff of experts. I don't think this can miss, but if you don't like it, I got another idea."

"How long will this one take, Gary?"

"Phil. I'm giving you an opportunity to be one of the founding partners in all this. I would think you'd at least want to listen. What do you think of bronzing patients' surgical specimens and selling them as mementos of their hospital stays? I had in mind either wall-mounted plaques or different walnut bases suitable for someone's desk or mantelpiece. You only need a little bit of tissue for a diagnosis and there's always plenty left over that never gets used and just gets thrown away. Now people could take 'em home and put 'em next to their first set of baby shoes. If you have had multiple operations, you could display all that stuff in one room specifically set aside for that purpose. As a matter of fact, with some surgeons I can think of, like your friend, there could be more of the patient hanging on the wall then there would be shuffling around the house. If someone came looking for you and you weren't home, they could still be told you're in the such-and-such room and they wouldn't really be wrong. I think that's a pretty good idea."

"Great, Gary." Phil started to draw away. "I'll really think about all this."

"Wait! I got one more."

Phil groaned and stopped abruptly.

"How about colonoscopy? How many have you been doing?'

"Not very many."

"Same here. Hardly made it worth taking the course, wouldn't you say? Then again, I do have memories that will last a lifetime." His expression could best be described as cherubic when he said this, but then became more serious. "Regardless, that's not what's important here. We gotta start using modern-day business practices. Right now, we're scoping only patients that really should have it done. I say we should loosen up a little. I'm reminded of a slogan Muhammad Ali made famous a number of years back. Why not a weekly 'scope-a-dope' campaign? Or we could start appealing to a whole different segment of society. We could lighten up on the sedation and hire girls in white latex uniforms with names like Monique von Pain to work in the endoscopy units. We'd still be taking care of sick people."

"Who's going to be taking care of you?" Phil asked and as he said this, a nurse passed them in the hall and she and Gary immediately burst out laughing. Phil was completely at a loss.

"Don't be flattered," Gary said. "I wasn't laughing at your little witticism. That's the nurse who has this little thing on her thigh that I have to take off later today." He pointed to his right upper thigh just below the groin. "She told me a little while ago she just got her period and she asked me if that was going to be a problem. I told her no, that I'd just work around it. That's all. Nothing improper. As a matter of fact, that's a big improvement over the way things were a few weeks ago. She wasn't even talking to me then. Remember the old lady you helped me with, the one with the small bowel infarction? Well, I happened to be on the floor when she expired, and they asked me to pronounce her. Carol came into the room while I was listening to her chest, and I suddenly got a brilliant idea. I asked her to get me another stethoscope because I thought the one that I was using was broken. I couldn't hear anything with it. She came back a few minutes later and was handing me another stethoscope when she figured out what I just pulled. She threw the thing down, stormed out of the room and didn't talk to me for days. I finally apologized and that's how I wound up taking this thing off her thigh. It's just a little nevus, kind of ugly, though. Certainly will make her thigh look better. One more endeavor to keep America beautiful."

"How do you manage to come up with all this stuff every time I see you, Gary? All I asked was how things were going and the next thing I get is a monolog. I think I get this from you every time I see you. Are you sure you're in the right profession?"

"A man's gotta do what a man's gotta do. In other words, Phil, it's just my way of coping with all this crap, and that's all I'm going to say." That was his reply and he said nothing more and simply walked away. Phil thought he was being pretty funny himself and this response surprised him, but he didn't feel it meant anything. A short time later he left, too.

There is a well-accepted idiom in medicine that the busy times come in spurts and just as it had been very quiet for nearly a month, there was now much greater activity throughout the entire hospital. Phil had begun seeing a substantial number of new surgical patients in his office and coupled with the usual emergencies, there had been a considerable increase in his workload and the hours spent in the hospital. This had the added benefit of keeping him busy and distracted but didn't allow him much time now to keep track of anyone else's activities Many of the other surgeons were just as busy and he saw them frequently in either the operating and recovery rooms or on the floors. Stanley Stallings was a constant fixture in all these places and it seemed that Phil was never able to avoid him. He was very uncomfortable in his presence but remained cordial, albeit reserved. Dr. Stallings, on the other hand, was always the opposite, smiling and outgoing even to the point of being effusive much of the time. Phil found it sickening but apparently Dr. Stallings' patients didn't and this, in Phil's opinion, probably accounted for most of the former's success. He went about everything much the same way as all the others, just more friendly and more considerate. Watching him only further antagonized Phil, but at least he knew what he was doing at that particular time. It was his one consolation.

It continued like that for weeks. Maralyn saw very little of him, but he made sure she knew it was the hospital that was taking so much of his time. He saw Ann again, but just once and only for a very brief visit. There were several phone calls after that, but Ann always ended their conversations very quickly. The constant demands of his schedule and Ann's reticence began to take its toll. Unable to adequately pursue the matter, Phil began to lose confidence it would ever be properly concluded. He confided this to both Mel Silverstone and Gordon Mulcahey but neither could offer any worthwhile advice. Both urged him not to get discouraged. Then he found himself unable to reach Ann Hartway at all. He made numerous calls to her home over a two-week period, but none were answered. This was even more distressing, and he wondered if she had gone away again without telling him. He couldn't afford any distractions at this time, however, and he continued to see patients at a very hectic pace.

He had just finished the last of three cases one morning when his office called to tell him Dr. Paul Metzger was looking for him and wanted Phil to call him at his office as soon as he could. Phil promptly placed the call.

"Hello, Phil. Thanks for calling back so soon. I know you just got out of the OR."

"It sounded urgent, Paul."

"I have a woman I'd like you to see. I had a call from Jeff Carlisle at University Hospital this morning. He had just seen this patient who he had operated on five or six months ago for an ovarian carcinoma. He thought he might have gotten it all, but he wasn't too optimistic. When he saw her today, she had obvious ascites and probable small bowel obstruction. She's from out here and didn't want to go back to University Hospital and since Jeff doesn't have privileges here, he asked if I'd admit her. He told her she'd probably need a general surgeon and she mentioned your name. She says she knows you."

"Oh, really. What's her name?"

"Ann Hartway."

There was a long silence.

"Are you still there, Phil?"

"Yes, Paul. I'm sorry, but that name threw me. There must be some mistake. The Ann Hartway I know couldn't have had any surgery. I've seen her pretty often this entire past year. The only time she was away, and that was about six months ago, was on a vacation to Mexico."

"Well, I don't know, Phil. That's what Jeff tells me. Maybe there're two Ann Hartways. Anyway, I haven't seen her. I sent her straight over to the emergency room to be admitted from there. I ordered x-rays and bloodwork and put in a consult for you. She's probably in her room by now."

Phil was puzzled but not concerned. This could not be the Ann Hartway he knew. It had to be someone with the same or similar name or some other sort of mix-up.

"I'll see her right away, Paul. Do you want me to get back to you?"

"No, I'll be over later, and I'll check your note. You order whatever you have to. I doubt if there's much I'll have to do and I'll probably transfer her over to your service. I'll just give Jeff Carlisle a call that you're going to evaluate her."

"I'll look at her films right now. I'll try to catch you later, Paul."

Phil went directly to the emergency room. The patient had already been taken to Room 242, but her x-rays were still there. He checked the name on the folder, and it was Ann Hartway but that didn't seem to bother him. He placed the films on the view box and immediately noted the generalized haziness throughout the abdomen, which had to be the result of ascitic fluid. Even though this obscured most of the detail, there was the unmistakable dilatation of much of the small intestine. These findings, occurring not long after surgery for an ovarian malignancy, had to mean recurrence of the patient's disease and a very dismal prognosis. Phil could be reasonably certain of this, even without seeing the patient, but it still didn't mean very much to him. He couldn't connect Ann Hartway to this and as he took the stairs to the second floor, there was no apprehension, no sense of foreboding.

He passed the nurses' station on the way to the room and hesitated, thinking that he should check the patient's chart first. Then he decided that it probably hadn't been put together yet and that he wouldn't be able to find the information he wanted. It was at this point that he began to feel uneasy. He started down the hall, but his pace slowed and became very deliberate. He suddenly felt very warm, and his heart began to beat rapidly and forcefully. He began to perspire, and his limbs became heavy and weak. A wave of nausea overcame him as he stood outside Room 242 and lingered before passing. Even before entering the room, he knew the deception had ended.

Ann did not hear Phil when he first came in and he watched her for a moment. The head of the bed was raised slightly, and she appeared to be resting quietly with her eyes closed. She looked waif-like except for the bedcovers that rose paradoxically over her abdomen. The IV had already been started and was dripping slowly. She turned her head, apparently sensing his presence, and opened her eyes.

"I thought it might be you, Phil."

Phil moved closer to the bed.

"I don't know what to say, Ann. I'm totally overwhelmed by this."

She held out her hand. "I'm sure you are, and I'm very sorry. I didn't want it to turn out this way but there wasn't anything I could do. Please come closer."

He stood at her bedside and took her hand.

"I really didn't think it could be you at first, Ann. It's still hard for me to believe this."

"I just didn't want anyone to know about the surgery, Phil. I didn't think anyone should be feeling sorry for me, not after everything that's happened."

"But you were always here. I know. I always called or stopped by. You were away only for that vacation." Then suddenly he understood.

"That's when I had the surgery, Phil."

"Yes, I just realized that. I guess I'm not as quick as I thought. I was just about to argue with you. I saw you when you got back. You were just getting over that intestinal thing, and you had a tan. I was going to point out you didn't get that in a hospital. That's not the way it happened though, is it?"

"No. I never had that intestinal problem. I made that up after the surgery, so I'd have an explanation for the way I looked. I was in the hospital for two weeks and then I left directly for Puerto Rico. I never did go to Mexico. I thought if I was going to convince all my friends that I had really been away, I'd better look the part. I even sent them cards. I thought about sending you one, but then I thought it might cause a problem. I guess I did a pretty good job of keeping everything a secret and nobody would have ever known if it hadn't been for this. Oh, Dr. Carlisle said there might still be problems, but I guess I didn't want to believe him."

She reached for a damp washcloth on her night table and licked her lips. "Hand me that, please, Phil. My mouth is so dry and they won't let me drink anything. They said I can suck on a damp cloth. Isn't that great?"

She took the washcloth from him and pressed it between her lips. It seemed to help and she was able to continue.

"I honestly thought the operation would take care of everything. He found a mass on a routine exam so we both thought he caught it early. When you think of it, though, this really shouldn't come as any surprise.

You get what you deserve. I can accept that but I dread being judged by others. No matter. I don't feel so bad physically. I started having cramps just the past few days and he explained that it's probably from the obstruction. I vomited last night and that's what made me see Dr. Carlisle today. I knew if I didn't do something, it would get worse. Actually, the thing that bothers me the most is my damned stomach. It's so bloated. Do you remember how I told you I must be eating too much and not exercising enough? It's really fluid, isn't it?"

"Yes, but some of it is the obstructed intestine."

"That's a bad sign, isn't it?"

"It's hard to tell. I really can't be sure at this point."

Ann managed a smile, but it was more of resignation than assurance. "You'll do whatever you have to, Phil. I'm not afraid of another operation. All I ask is that you tell me exactly what you find and what my chances are. There are some decisions that I'm sure I'll have to make."

Phil looked very somber. "This is going to be very difficult for me, Ann. I'm not sure I'm the one who should be taking care of you."

"Why?" Ann said. She tried to raise herself, but it was difficult. "I don't want anyone else. You're the reason I'm here and not at that other hospital. I won't have anyone else." She was on the verge of becoming distraught. "Why did you say that?"

Phil had to look away. "I'm too involved, Ann. This whole situation is so complicated, and I don't know what's going to happen and how I'm going to react. I don't think it's right for me to take on this responsibility."

"I don't care!" Ann said. Her face had a look of anguish. "You have to. Don't you remember how I was the past few months? When I had the other surgery, I didn't want anyone to know there was anything wrong with me, especially you. I couldn't say anything to you, but now it's different. I think I know how this is going to turn out and you have to help me get through it. You're the only one who can."

This left him with nothing else to consider. "I'll do everything I can," Phil said, the words spoken so softly he wasn't sure she heard them, but then she seemed to relax, and he knew she had. He released her hand

and started to leave when he suddenly turned back, leaned over and kissed her lightly on the cheek. Then he left the room.

He sat at the nurses' station with Ann's chart in front of him, to write his consultation note and orders, but it was several minutes before he was able to collect his thoughts. Obviously, he would need time to bring his emotions under control. Finally, he composed his note carefully and in considerable detail and then methodically listed his orders. He walked back to Ann's room and leaned in from the doorway.

"I've ordered some tests for the morning, Ann. I also changed Dr. Metzger's order for the tube he wanted placed in your stomach. Instead of the nasogastric tube, I've ordered a long intestinal tube, which I think will be more effective. It's very easy to pass and as soon as it comes up to the floor, I'll put it down myself. The nurses will advance it every four hours and we'll follow your progress with x-rays. Dr. Metzger should be here later this afternoon to check you over and I'll talk with him then or in the morning. I think I'll hold off examining you myself until the tube comes up. I think I've had all I can handle for the moment." He smiled and Ann smiled back.

Phil came back quite a bit later when he was sure the tube would already be on the floor. He had very little difficulty inserting it after he had carefully explained to Ann its function and how it is passed. Almost a liter of fluid drained promptly and Ann immediately said she felt better. He then proceeded to examine her. She had never been exposed to him before and he was anxious to do this quickly and discreetly, keeping her well-covered even while performing a rectal exam. Her abdomen was quite distended but relatively soft and non-tender. He took note of the lower abdominal incision from the previous surgery and was relieved that he could not feel any masses, particularly during the rectal exam. He finished very promptly and smiled.

"I really don't feel anything, Ann. I'll have to check you over again tomorrow but right now we just have to wait and see. Maybe we'll be lucky."

Ann looked up at him. "I hope so. Whatever it is, I know you'll take good care of me."

He patted her cheek and then his hand remained in a gentle caress. Their eyes met but nothing more was said, and Phil turned away and quickly left the room. He would have remained in the hospital a little while longer seeing patients but felt rather depressed and decided to leave for home early, stopping briefly at his office to check for messages and the mail.

His mood was not any better later and rather than risk upsetting Maralyn and the girls, he thought a place with more activity might be worth a try. He asked Maralyn if she would like to go out for dinner and when she jumped at the idea, chose one of their favorite places, a small Greek restaurant that was always busy and crowded. They were very friendly with the staff and there were the usual greetings and small talk as they were being seated and later while selecting from the menu. The distractions helped but Phil knew at some point he would have to talk about Ann Hartway.

"Another lousy day?" Maralyn asked. "Maybe we should have two bottles of Retsina instead of just one."

"It's really very obvious, isn't it?"

"I'd have to be deaf, dumb, and blind not to have noticed. Is that the kind of wife you want?"

"No." He reached for her hand. "I only want what I already have." He looked straight at her. "Are you ready for this? Do you remember when you said to me you thought I might be going to Ann Hartway's house because she was very sick? I saw her in the hospital today. She has ovarian cancer."

Maralyn gaped at him in disbelief. Her body lurched and for a second, he thought she might slip from her chair.

"You don't mean that. When did you find this out?"

"Today. I was asked to see her in consultation."

"You didn't know this before?"

"No. She did, but I didn't. She never let on."

"Is she very sick?"

"I think so. I'll know more in a few days. She's probably going to need surgery."

Maralyn had a pained expression as she leaned towards him.

"I feel so terrible, Phil. That poor woman. Those poor girls. First Jack, and now her. That's just awful. Do you think I should go up to see her?"

Phil hesitated. "I don't think so, Maralyn. She has an awful lot going on right now." He took a deep breath and shook his head. "Then again, maybe you should. I don't know."

"This has you upset, hasn't it?"

"Yes. She's confided quite a bit in me since Jack died. She's had a pretty difficult time. I feel very sorry for her."

"It's not fair," Maralyn said.

"She might not agree with that."

Maralyn looked unsure. "What do you mean?"

"It's very complicated and I probably shouldn't have said that, but I think she may be having some guilt. Like I've told you, it's been difficult for her."

"I can't believe this. I know you never expect something like this to happen and it still seems so unreal. I don't know what else to say. I don't think I'll be able to have dinner now. My appetite's gone."

"We have to have something. That's why I suggested this. I thought it would be better than telling you about this at home. I feel very badly, too, but I can't let it drag me down. You shouldn't let that happen either."

"But I just feel so sorry for her, and then there were those things I thought about her. Can you understand why I feel this way now?"

"Yes, and perhaps one of these days I'll be able to tell you what this was all about, but now I'm not so sure. You aren't the only one who was completely floored by this."

"You'll do everything you can for her, won't you? I know you'll have to see a lot of her now and I want you to know I won't mind. That probably sounds stupid, but I was pretty stupid before, so this probably isn't out of character. I just want you to understand me, Phil. I'm usually not jealous, but I can be. I think you saw that. I'm proud of what you do, and I don't want to hold you back. I'm making excuses for myself this time, but I shouldn't have to. I'm a woman and I'm your wife. You can't hold that against me."

Phil grinned sheepishly.

"No, I don't hold that against you. In fact, I happen to love you very much and part of it is probably a lot of the things you just said. I think I'm very lucky."

Maralyn smiled. "I think I'm very lucky, too. Do you know who isn't lucky?" She gestured towards the waiter who was standing nearby. "Teddy isn't lucky. He's been waiting all this time to take our order and I think my appetite is back. Can he, finally? For some reason, I'm hungry now."

Phil flashed a big smile and motioned the waiter over. The selections were made and one bottle of Retsina was gradually finished and a second started when the food arrived. The mood was much more relaxed during the remainder of dinner. Maralyn brought up Ann's name from time to time in their conversation to assure him that he could speak freely about her. This conciliatory effort probably was no longer necessary but reminded Phil just how much it was in Maralyn's nature to be understanding. It made him feel better but naturally could not relieve all his distress. Later, after they had returned home, Phil said he wouldn't be going to bed right away. He expected he'd have trouble falling asleep and would read for a while first. Maralyn said she was sorry to see him this way but understood and hoped he'd feel better and get some rest. She gave him a reassuring hug and kiss and went upstairs without him. Phil was awake much of the night.

The following morning, again, he left very early. He met Paul Metzger shortly after he reviewed Ann's latest x-rays. The intestinal tube had not advanced beyond the proximal small bowel and had begun to curl in the stomach as the nurses continued to advance it through the night.

"What are you going to do to our girl?" Dr. Metzger asked.

"I put a long tube in, but it doesn't seem to be moving beyond the proximal small intestine. I thought I'd have them take her down to x-ray and put in some contrast to see where she's obstructed."

"Don't you think you're going to have to explore her?"

"I would think so, but I'd like to give her a chance to open up on her own first. I guess it's possible this might be adhesions."

Dr. Metzger made no effort to hide his skepticism.

"Come on, Phil. After a carcinoma of the ovary? You know what this is. Besides, I felt something on the pelvic I did yesterday. I'll bet she's got a lot of disease in there."

"You're probably right," Phil said reluctantly.

"You know I am, and CAT scans and barium enemas and gastrografin studies aren't going to do you a bit of good. The sooner you make a tissue diagnosis and get this girl started on chemotherapy, the better off she'll be. I also think you'll want to take out her omentum to cut down on the ascites. Why don't you schedule her for tomorrow?"

Phil could not fault Paul Metzger's opinion. He needed prodding. "OK, I'll schedule her but I also want to give her the gastrografin."

"Hey, do whatever you want just as long as you put her on the schedule. I'll go up there right now and put a note on her chart saying I think she should be explored, and I'll tell her."

"Why don't you wait until I've seen her and had a chance to talk with her?" Phil said. "I haven't been up there, this morning and I really think it should come from me first."

"Fine. I'll stop back later, then."

"Thanks, Paul."

Phil climbed the stairs and stopped at the nurses' station to schedule the gastrografin small bowel study and then went to Ann's room. She had raised the head of the bed as high as it would go and was sitting upright. She looked much better and smiled eagerly as he entered the room.

"Good morning!"

"Good morning, Ann."

"I have to compliment you. That tube sounded horrible when you described it and I don't like the nurses pushing it up my nose every few hours or so, but I don't have the nausea and cramps anymore and I do feel quite a bit better. Don't I look better?"

"Yes, you do."

"I've been at the mirror for the past hour trying to do everything I possibly can. No one's ever come up with a way to disguise one of these tubes, have they?"

"Not that I know of."

"I didn't think so. I know I couldn't, and believe me, I tried. Did you see my x-rays?"

"Yes, I have. We've made some progress, but not as much as I'd like."

"So, what's next?"

"That's what I want to talk to you about. While we're doing that, I'd like to examine you again. I should have been more thorough yesterday, but I just wasn't up to it."

"I had you pretty upset, didn't I?"

"Yes, of course."

"I was afraid of that. You have no idea how much I worried about your reaction while I waited for you. I was afraid you'd walk in, take one look, turn around and I'd never see you again. You'd be surprised how much I worry about our relationship. Nothing has been more important to me for a long time. Obviously, it's even more so now."

Phil looked down. Even if he knew how to answer her, he thought it better not to. He patted her arm reassuringly and reached for the controls to lower the head of the bed and then partially closed the curtains. He helped her lie flat and Ann opened her robe and raised her hips to lift her nightgown. The blanket covered her to her thighs. Phil moved the nightgown higher to just below her breasts and palpated gently. He could not feel any masses. The scar from the previous surgery was partially hidden in the pubic hairline. Her abdomen was moderately distended but soft and Phil could not help but notice how remarkably smooth her skin was, and free of blemishes. It was still fairly dark, and Phil did not know if this was her natural color or if some vestiges of her tan could remain after so many months. His hand moved over her abdomen again and again, pressing a little deeper each time overcoming his fear and reluctance that he might find something. He asked several times if he was hurting her and she said no. When he thought he had been as thorough as he had to be, he stopped. He drew her nightgown down over her abdomen and closed her robe.

"I don't feel anything, Ann," he said as he stepped back. "That makes me feel better, but it doesn't solve our problem. Dr. Metzger told me what he found on his exam yesterday and I have to agree with him that you should be explored. This type of situation after the kind of surgery you had is very worrisome. We're always afraid of recurrences in situations like this. The only way we can be sure what the problem is and what we should do about it is to operate and see exactly what is going on. On top of that, you're obstructed, and I don't think that will get better unless it's relieved surgically. I've ordered a small bowel series for later today to see where the obstruction is and if it's complete. But regardless of what it shows, I still feel it's going to come down to surgery and I don't think we'll gain anything by putting it off. I'd like to schedule you for tomorrow."

Ann had watched him very carefully while he examined her and then while he was speaking.

"I'll do whatever you say, Phil. I knew all along this was pretty serious."

"It may just be adhesions, Ann, scar tissue that's built up since the last operation. That's still a possibility and if it is, we'll have plenty to celebrate." Phil managed a not-too-convincing smile.

"That's not the kind of luck I seem to have." She reached for the damp washcloth and dabbed her lips. "I know what you'll find. Tell me, though. Why do you want to do this small bowel thing if you know you're going to operate anyway?"

"I just want to satisfy myself that we don't have any choi whatsoever. If the contrast we put in through your tube doesn't go through, then we know the obstruction is complete and will stay that way. You can't be left like that, and surgery is the only treatment. No one will be able to argue with me for operating and I won't be able to argue with myself. I told you I would have trouble making decisions about you."

Ann closed her eyes but quickly opened them again.

"I'm sorry, Phil. I don't want this to be an ordeal for both of us. You don't have to worry about your decision. I know you've made the right one. I knew when I talked with Dr. Carlisle that I'd need another operation."

"Then I can schedule it for tomorrow?"

"Yes."

Ann grasped the electric control and raised the bed, so she was once again upright.

"I'd better take care of that now," Phil said. "Do you want to call any of your family and is there anyone I should call after the surgery?"

"No."

"Are you sure? That may not be such a good idea."

"There's no one, Phil. Any notifying can wait until after the surgery. I'll have a better idea what to say then, certainly much better than now."

Phil looked at her for a moment but there was no indication she was about to change her mind.

"I'll be back later, Ann. I'll let you know what everything looks like and what I may have to do tomorrow."

Ann nodded her approval and smiled as Phil left the room. He had to schedule the case and then find an assistant who might be available on such short notice. His first choice of course would be Gary Barlow and he thought of a few places where he might find him before he would have him paged. A few minutes later he ran into him just outside the OR suite.

"Wait a second, Gary. I've been looking for you. I need some help with a case tomorrow. Do you have anything scheduled?"

Gary stopped and turned when he heard Phil's voice. He saluted, sort of, with his right hand.

"That's just what I was going to check on," he said. "Elliott Larkin has a patient with abdominal pain that he's going to laparoscope tomorrow. He wants me to help in case it's an appendix. I was just going to check on the time. What kind of a case do you have?"

"It's a friend of mine who has ascites and small bowel obstruction six months after she had surgery for carcinoma of the ovary. I'm really going to need help."

"That doesn't sound too good. I'll tell you what. Let's see if we can get it to follow the laparoscopy. As a matter of fact, I really don't think it's appendicitis. Why don't you look in while he's doing the thing and if it's PID or endometriosis, we should be ready to do your case right away. That way we can save some time. I have office hours tomorrow afternoon."

Fortunately, the OR staff was able to switch several cases making that a satisfactory arrangement. Ann was scheduled for a laparotomy, possible bowel resection and possible colostomy to follow in either Dr. Larkin's room or the next one that was available. Phil left the hospital for a while to tend to some other matters and returned later to review the small bowel series and Ann's lab work and discuss the surgery with her. She seemed to understand everything quite clearly and fully accepted Phil's recommendations although she did express her displeasure and repugnance at the prospect of possibly requiring a colostomy. Phil explained that this was purely a precaution and extremely unlikely. He felt he was being truthful. Now, as before, he tried to be honest and objective resisting any temptation to give assurances he couldn't keep. Ann sensed this and never pressed Phil for anything more. She did not even ask about the gastrografin study, which Phil had reviewed and whose results seemed inconsequential now. He did mention that very little contrast got through and only after considerable delay. Surgery remained the only recourse and was scheduled for late the following morning. Phil ordered a sedative to help Ann sleep that night and anticipated having considerable difficulty himself.

He almost welcomed the call just after midnight notifying him of a patient in the emergency room who had been injured in an automobile accident and had multiple contusions and a scalp laceration. He hadn't been able to sleep, and this provided a worthwhile respite. The patient wasn't seriously injured but required Phil's concentration as he evaluated the man's complaints and repaired the wound. It took a little over an hour after which he discharged the patient, completed the paperwork and returned home. He was finally able to fall asleep a little while later.

Phil began rounds a little later than usual that morning. Maralyn was up and about but he left without mentioning anything about Ann's surgery. He would do that afterwards. He avoided Ann's room at first knowing he would see her later in the holding area before she went into the OR. Then he thought she was probably expecting him much sooner and he should really see her now. He finished writing a progress note on

another patient and went to her room. Ann seemed very calm even though she had not yet received the premedication the anesthesiologist had ordered for her. She also had obviously been concerned about her appearance and had taken the time to put on lipstick and some make-up. Under these circumstances she looked very well, perhaps even beautiful, Phil thought.

"I didn't know if I'd be seeing you before the surgery," Ann said.

"I just wanted to see how you were doing and make sure everything was all right.

How do you feel?"

"Very well. I'm not nervous at all. How do you feel?"

"Pretty good. I was in the emergency room for a little while last night, but I feel fine. It probably helped settle me down. I was able to sleep pretty well afterwards."

Ann looked at him with concern.

"Is this going to be very hard for you?"

Phil said nothing at first. He stared at Ann's form beneath the covers. "Yes," he finally answered. "It is going to be hard, but neither of us seems to have any choice at this point, do we? We're both going to do fine, though. That much I can assure you."

Ann reached for his hand and squeezed it gently. Then she leaned back. "I'll let you go now," she said.

As he left, she called out to him, "Thank you for everything, Phil. In case I don't have a chance to say it later, thanks for all the things you've said and everything you've done for me."

That made Phil stop, and he walked back to her. He was even more resolute now. "I'll see you in the operating room in a little while," he said firmly, "and after the surgery you'll see me again in the recovery room. We'll see each other plenty after that and you'll be able to tell me anything you want. We have a long way to go together. I want that understood now. OK? I'm not going to let anything happen to you."

Ann looked away, about to cry, and reached for a tissue. Phil held her hand until she regained her composure.

"I'm sorry, Phil. I'll be OK. I just got a little weepy. You go do what you have to. You don't have to stay." She let go of his hand and glanced up at him. "I'll be OK. Really. I guess that just needed to come out."

Phil remained at the bedside, uncertain if he should leave but Ann was insistent and continued to reassure him. When he saw her smile, he gently put his fist to her chin and only then, knowing she'd be all right, did he leave. Suddenly, he had a renewed confidence. This last display had somehow reawakened him to his responsibility. For a while now he had felt sorry for Ann and lately, for himself, too. He knew this could only be detrimental but had not been able to withstand the feeling.

Now, faced with Ann's surgery and her fear of the outcome, he realized what he had to do. His objectivity had to be restored and he had to take control. This had always sustained him in the past and now was needed even more. In a short while Ann's surgery would begin, and he would have to be more than equal to whatever he might find. Much to his satisfaction, he felt ready and went directly to the OR suite to change his clothes and find out how soon he'd be able to start.

He went to the room where Gary was working with Elliott Larkin to see how far along they were. He walked in just as the cannula for the laparoscope was being inserted into the patient's abdomen below the umbilicus. Dr. Larkin attached the plastic tubing that would deliver the carbon dioxide into the peritoneal cavity and ordered the insufflation to begin as he monitored the pressure gauge. Gary watched the abdomen distend, unaware that Phil was now in the room, and then leaned over the drapes and called to the anesthetized patient, "Regular or high test, Ma'am?"

There was some snickering. When the appropriate pressure had been reached, the carbon dioxide was turned off and Gary again turned to the patient.

"Will that be cash or charge?"

"We have a visitor in the room, Dr. Barlow," the scrub nurse politely informed him.

Gary looked over his shoulder. "Oh hi, Phil. We should have an answer any minute now."

He again leaned over the patient as Dr. Larkin placed the laparoscope within the cannula and manipulated it back and forth attempting to identify the pathology. Every so often he paused to confirm his findings with Gary but the diagnosis continued to elude them. Gary began to fidget and Phil knew he was becoming impatient. Finally, Gary turned to the scrub nurse.

"How'd you just do that?" he asked.

"Do what, Dr. Barlow?"

"You know. What you just did."

"I have no idea what you mean, Dr. Barlow. What is it you're talking about?"

"You really want me to say? As a gentleman, I'd much prefer to be more discreet but if you insist, OK All I want to know is how you're able to handle the instrument table and whatever you're doing with my nether regions at the same time?"

When he didn't get a reaction, he said, "Nether regions. You know, my private parts."

"What! I beg your pardon, Dr. Barlow, but I've done no such thing. That's disgusting!"

Elliott Larkin straightened up with a groan.

"Jesus, Gary, I'm having enough problems and now you have to start."

"I'm sorry but she's the only other person on my side of the table. Wait, see, there it goes again."

"Oh, for God's sake, Gary, you're just leaning against the blood pressure cuff," the anesthesiologist said.

Mary Chen shook her head. "I should have realized someone was doing that. All of a sudden, the pressures started going all over the place."

"Well, I'm sorry," Gary said, his tone suddenly very prissy. "How am I supposed to know a blood pressure cuff can do that? I wasn't brought up that way."

"It can't be helped," Dr. Chen explained almost apologetically. "It inflates automatically."

"That doesn't make any difference. It feels like a thousand magic little fingers wafting across my you-know-what. What was I supposed to think?"

"Why don't you just step back from the table so your you-know-what isn't pressing into the cuff and then you won't feel violated each time?" someone suggested.

"Because then I wouldn't be able to help my good buddy, Elliott," Gary answered promptly and firmly.

"Oh, for crying out loud, will someone just take the cuff off that arm and put it on my side so we can get him to quiet down! Phil's in here waiting to see when he can do his case and I just want to get finished and instead, there's a vaudeville show going on. Put the damn cuff over here."

"No, wait a minute, don't," Gary said. "Don't take it away from me. I promise I'll be good. Is that asking too much," he whimpered, "just a little affection from a blood pressure cuff?"

Except for Phil, everyone was laughing now.

"Unless..." Gary continued. "Unless... Ah, I'm beginning to understand. You want it on your side, don't you, Elliott? Don't you realize you're much taller? It won't be the same for you but OK, you can have it, but only for five minutes. Then you have to give it back. I could never have it on my conscience if your brain went soft. I can't take that responsibility, nor could I live with myself if we wound up with another idiot on the GYN staff."

This struck Gary as exceedingly funny and he had to step back from the operating table, unable to control his laughter. He did not see Phil leave the operating room. Mary Chen asked for quiet, admonishing everyone to remember the patient and the procedure eventually resumed.

Phil waited in the hall and approximately ten minutes later, Gary emerged.

"I knew it wasn't appendicitis," he said as he approached. "It looks like she ruptured a small cyst and Elliott thinks she has endometriosis, too. They're going to follow with your case in the same room. They should be ready very soon."

"Thanks. You seemed to be in exceptionally good form in there today. I don't know if that would really help with the next case."

"Don't worry," Gary said. "I know she's a friend of yours and it doesn't sound very good. I probably got it all out of my system anyway."

They had coffee while waiting for the room to turn over and then Phil left to see Ann in the holding area. She had been sedated but was still very bright and alert.

"You doing OK, Ann?"

"Yes. There's one thing I didn't mention to you. I left something for you in the top drawer of my night table in case there's a problem. I told the girls I wouldn't be able to speak with them for the rest of the week so they won't worry if they don't hear from me. If I'm OK after this, you won't have to bother with it. It's just in case."

"You still don't want me to call anyone?"

"Not if I'm able to do it in a few days."

"OK You're the boss."

He stood by her stretcher a little while longer until they were approached by the circulating nurse.

"Gonna take your patient in now, Dr. Berger," she said.

They looked at each other again, very quickly.

"You go ahead," Phil said. "I'll be right in."

He watched as Ann was wheeled from the room and then went quickly to the lounge to use the bathroom. He took another drink from the water fountain in the hall before tying his mask and went back to Ann's room. She was already on the operating table and being very cooperative as monitoring devices and the rest were being applied in a very businesslike fashion. The floor was still wet in spots where it had been mopped following the previous case. The scrub nurse and circulator had apparently completed the instrument count, and all seemed in order.

"Come say hello to your patient, Dr. Berger, so I can let her take her nap," Mary Chen said as she inserted the syringe containing the sodium pentothal into the IV tubing.

"All set, Ann?"

"Yes, Phil. How about you?"

"I'm fine. You'll be going to sleep now, and I'll see you later in the recovery room."

Mary Chen took that as her cue to begin injecting the sodium pentothal and a moment later Ann closed her eyes. Her breathing slowed and became more tranquil. She looked very serene. Phil watched her intently until the anesthesiologist's movements disrupted his gaze and then he turned quickly to scrub. As he left the room, he asked to have a Foley catheter inserted, and this was done promptly. When he returned, he was handed a sterile towel and dried himself before putting on his gown and gloves. He stood at the side of the operating table and waited as Ann's gown was removed and the blankets drawn apart exposing her from just above her breasts to her thighs well below her hips. The circulating nurse then rearranged the blankets more discreetly and Phil began prepping the entire area.

"She's only thirty-nine according to her chart. That's very young for ovarian cancer, isn't it, Dr. Berger?" one of the nurses asked.

"Yes," Phil answered, "it's usually seen in older patients."

"Is that what you think she has now?"

"I don't know. I hope not," Phil said.

"Someone said her husband died in this hospital last year after he had surgery. Is that true?"

"Yes, he developed a serious complication after a vascular procedure."

"Was he that much older?"

"No, he really wasn't."

"This must be terrible for her. She's a very attractive woman. She must have been very beautiful before all this."

Phil did not answer this time. Until then he had thought only of the procedure that would begin very shortly. He had asked to have the blanket moved above Ann's breasts in case he had to make a long midline incision and extended the prepped area to just above her nipples. In spite of the abdominal distention and her recent weight loss, there was much that was still quite pleasing. He quickly reached for the towels to place around the operative field and hastily completed draping the patient. He was told by one of the nurses that Dr. Barlow was scrubbing and would be in the room very shortly. Phil just stood at the table waiting patiently, his eyes fixed on Ann's abdomen.

"Do you want to start now, or do you want to wait for Dr. Barlow?" the scrub nurse asked.

"I'll wait."

Phil heard Gary come into the room and then the sounds of the scrub nurse helping him into his gown and gloves. Gary came around to the opposite side of the table.

"How y' doin', Phil? Did you feel her abdomen now that she's relaxed?"

"No."

"Mind if I do?"

"Go ahead."

Gary quickly palpated the entire area.

"I can't be sure," he said.

The scrub nurse handed Phil the scalpel and he hesitated momentarily.

"You goin' in the midline?" Gary asked.

"Yes, I think so."

"Well, whenever you're ready."

Phil slowly made a six-inch incision above, around and below Ann's navel. He incised the thick fibers of the linea alba exposing the peritoneum underneath.

Gary asked to have the suction ready. "This looks like a good place here," he said, motioning with the suction tip. "Why don't we make a small opening right here and maybe I can get most of the fluid before it runs all over the place?"

They each placed Kelly clamps on the peritoneum and Phil made a small incision. Clear amber fluid immediately spewed out, but Gary was able to get the suction tip into the wound and the rest flowed into a large collection bottle a short distance away. It was as if Ann's abdomen was slowly being deflated. The flow stopped when almost three liters had been reached.

Gary removed the suction and quickly placed his finger in the wound. He palpated the undersurface of the peritoneum.

"The bowel's free," he said.

Phil carefully incised the peritoneum in both directions, up and down. Gradually, he was able to identify the structures within. Suddenly, an overwhelming feeling of despair overcame him. Directly in view were small dense white nodules randomly scattered over the surface of the bowel. As he opened further, more were seen. These were unmistakably areas of spread from the original tumor and it was obviously very extensive.

"We'd better extend the incision," Gary said.

Phil remained silent and it took a little while longer for him to react. The incision soon extended from just below the breastbone to the pubis. A Balfour retractor was inserted and now the entire abdomen was open. Gary took the initiative.

"Mind if I take a quick feel?" he asked.

Phil had no objection and Gary quickly began to explore Ann's abdomen. This went on for a short while and Gary seemed to have encountered some sort of difficulty in one particular area. Perspiration began to show on his forehead and at times his features appeared contorted beneath his mask. A little later he straightened up and took his hand, now quite bloody, from the wound.

"It's not too good, Phil," he said, "but I think we can do something. This is gonna have to go." He pointed to the omentum, which had been almost completely replaced by tumor and was now a mass of hard, ugly, gray-white tissue. He reached in again and began maneuvering the loops of dilated intestine.

Then, very abruptly, he lifted a matted, hemorrhagic segment into view. "That's it. That's what was taking me so long before. That's where she was stuck. If we take this out, she'll still have plenty of intestine to get by. You see what's in there, but I don't think any of that is going to give her trouble right away. We'll look again more carefully but I think she should do OK for a while."

Phil took the mass in his hands. Ann would have a year to live at best, and probably less. He studied the bulky, puckered, constricting tumor. On one side, the dilated, obstructed proximal intestine entered and disappeared into its core. On the other, empty, collapsed normal intestine emerged. He would correct this now, but the same problem would recur in time in other areas. Ann's fate had been irrevocably decided.

Phil began the process of resecting this segment. His movements were very slow and mechanical but gradually the pace quickened. The bowel was transected and removed from the wound.

"Are you going to sew the anastomosis or do you want to use staples?" the scrub nurse asked.

"Let's use staples," Phil said.

A side-to-side anastomosis was completed and the defect in the mesentery closed. Phil promptly turned his attention to the omentum, which was dissected from the transverse colon and handed off. Hopefully this would reduce the amount of fluid that was likely to reform in the future. Following this, once again they very carefully reexamined the abdomen. There were numerous additional deposits of tumor tissue, but most were no larger than millet seeds and none seemed likely to cause complications in the near future.

"I don't think there's anything else we can do," Phil said.

"Did you feel in the pelvis?" Gary asked. "There's still a fair amount of tumor down there. If you feel she's eventually going to obstruct her sigmoid, you might want to do a colostomy or put the colon under the skin for an easy colostomy later on."

Phil had already decided. "No, I talked to her about that. We'll do it when she needs it. Let's close."

"Sure," Gary said. "Maybe she'll get a good response from chemotherapy and do OK."

That was all anyone could hope for and Phil began to close the wound. Gary left after the fascia had been approximated and Phil finished the rest with the help of the scrub nurse. The drapes were taken down and the dressing applied. Ann's abdomen was completely flat, and he knew that would please her. That would not be true for anything else he had to tell her. He watched as she was transferred onto a stretcher and wheeled from the operating room. He followed a short distance behind to the recovery room where he wrote the post-op orders and checked once again to be sure Ann was all right. Then he went to the dressing room and found Gary changed and just about to leave.

"Thank you very much, Gary. I appreciate everything you did for me in there. I was afraid I was really going to need you on this one and I guess I did."

"That's OK, Phil. I'm glad I was able to help. How many times has it been that you've bailed me out?"

Phil held out his hand. "I wish I could explain."

"You don't have to. Every once in a while, somebody gets a case like this, and it can be pretty tough. You said she's a friend of yours. I understand."

"Her husband died last year. He's the one that refused an amputation after Stanley did a bypass. We talked about it."

"Oh, yeah, I remember. Jesus, that's rough." He patted Phil's shoulder. "Hey, you did her some good today. Can't ask for anything more than that." He gave a reassuring nod and started to walk away. "Any time you need me, just let me know."

Phil dressed quietly and spent the rest of the afternoon in the hospital making rounds and looking in on Ann frequently. She had awakened from the anesthesia but was kept well-medicated and was barely able to acknowledge his presence. Any discussion would have to wait. When everything else was done, he decided against going back to the office, phoned his secretary for messages and left for home earlier than usual. No one else was there when he first arrived but a short time later, Maralyn and the girls walked in. She had picked them up from school and had gone grocery shopping. Phil waited until the packages had been put away and they were alone.

"I operated on Ann Hartway today."

Maralyn had started to prepare dinner but now she stopped and looked at Phil.

"It wasn't good, was it? I can tell from your expression."

"No, it wasn't. She has recurrent tumor, quite a lot of it."

"What does that mean? You don't expect her to pull through? I mean, she's not going to get any better."

"For now, yes, but it's not going to be long term."

Maralyn was upset. She sat down on one of the kitchen chairs.

"How long does she have?"

"Six months. Maybe a year."

"I still can't believe this. Do you remember when I said I thought you might have been going over there because she was sick? This couldn't be more ironic. I feel terrible for her. I know it's taking its toll on you, too."

"Yes. It makes it a lot harder when you know so much about a patient. She's had to deal with an awful lot since Jack died. You have to feel sorry for her. I haven't even told her yet."

"I'm sure you'll do everything you can for her. I'd like to see her, but I know it won't be for a while. Tell me when you think I can. It sounds like you both probably need some time."

Phil thought this was a very odd remark and asked Maralyn to explain.

"I don't know what I mean," she said.

She remained quiet, but only for a very brief moment.

"Well, it's just that you seem to take everything that happens to Ann awfully hard. I find it very confusing at times. That's all. I really don't want to talk about it. This isn't the time. What happens next with her?"

"Chemotherapy. Radiation is out. She's going to have it pretty rough."

Phil watched her, waiting for a response, but Maralyn remained silent.

"I thought we had all this settled. You know I have to take care of her now and the rest of it has nothing to do with us or with Ann and me. I just wish I could tell you how all this got started. Do I have to go into that again?"

"No," Maralyn said, but her tone wasn't very convincing.

"Sure. For God's sake, Maralyn, I told you before she's made me aware of something that was done and until it's resolved, I really can't say anything more about it. Frankly, now she thinks she's paying for it. It's a mess and I'm stuck in the middle. I may not have had a choice but there's absolutely no reason for you to be hurt by it. There's a very good explanation and again, I hope eventually to be able to tell you what that is. In the meantime, I apologize for not having been able to handle this differently. All I'm asking is for you to trust me."

Maralyn was still not satisfied. "I didn't mean to get started on this, but I wish you could listen to yourself. You seem to think you have to explain but then you don't. I really don't want to keep up this discussion, but what did you mean when you said you had no choice?"

"She told me certain things, medical things, that I just couldn't disregard. Maybe someone else would have, but I couldn't. It has nothing to do with the person who spoke to me. It's the person she named. It would have been the same thing no matter who told me, Ann or anyone else."

Maralyn's tone softened. "I suppose. I've heard you say that before. I'm sorry we got on this, but maybe it was for the best. I guess there'll always be a certain amount of suspicion and it's probably better to talk about it. It makes it harder for me now that Ann is having this trouble. I feel very badly talking about her this way."

Her eyes had wandered as she spoke, but now they were focused squarely on Phil.

"I only hope when you are able to explain, I don't find myself angry with you. You make me feel very badly sometimes. It's like you have your albatross and I have mine and I'll tell you something, it's a damned shame if neither of us deserves this."

Phil started towards her, but Maralyn motioned him back.

"Let me start dinner, Phil. Neither of us is in that good a mood now. Go read the newspaper or watch TV."

Phil walked away but she still had more to say.

"Deep down inside I know that whatever you're doing you feel is the right thing to do. What really pisses me off is that you'll still do that even though you know it's upsetting me. There are times when I just can't accept that. I don't like it when that happens. Think about it."

He did think about it, but it was one bad thought on top of many others that day. Maralyn's reaction had been totally unexpected. Later, were it not for his daughters' giddy chatter, dinner would have been eaten in complete silence. The mood improved somewhat towards the end of the evening but was still strained. Maralyn was talking to him again but not too often and at a distance. She did wish him goodnight before she went to bed but it was a long time before Phil joined her and that too was at a distance.

The next morning was another of those times when an early departure for the hospital seemed the smart thing to do. Phil had not slept well and was up much before the alarm. He was anxious to see how Ann was but knew it would be unwise not to let Maralyn know he was leaving. She had just awakened and was either still very sleepy or the overnight passage of time had softened her resentment. She pulled him down onto her and hugged him, telling him she loved him and would try to be more understanding. Phil was surprised and somewhat relieved.

When he arrived at the hospital, he went straight to Ann's room. She had just been medicated and was about to fall asleep again but tried to stay awake when she saw him. She could barely speak, and her eyes opened and closed several times as she tried to respond. Phil asked how she was feeling but it was useless. She drifted off and Phil checked her dressing and the drainage from the intestinal tube and bladder catheter. He was pleased with the numbers on her clipboard and went out to the nurses' station to look through the chart and enter his note. He was there no more than a few minutes when he felt a hand on his shoulder. He turned and found himself looking up at Stanley Stallings.

"I see you operated on Ann Hartway yesterday. I heard it wasn't so good. How is she doing?"

Phil was curt.

"Pretty well," he said.

"I was going to tell you I operated on her husband last year, but I just remembered, you knew that. We had that little difference of opinion at the conference. I talked to her a lot back then and I was just thinking I probably should say hello to her. Do you have any objection?"

"This probably isn't a good time. She was just medicated, and I was in there myself and couldn't really talk to her. I don't think she has any idea what anyone is saying to her."

"She's really out of it, huh, saying all kinds of funny things? You know how they get."

"She's not saying anything right now, Stan. She's asleep. If she asks for you, I'll tell you. How's that?"

Whether Dr. Stallings recognized the sarcasm or not, the ever-present grin remained.

"I just thought that might be a nice thing to do. I remember her as very pleasant, but you're right. There's no point in going in there if she isn't making any sense."

Phil was growing impatient.

"I don't know if that's what I really said, but you're close enough. This isn't a good time to visit."

"OK, I didn't mean to bug either of you. One last question. How do you think she's going to do? Do you think she's going to make it?"

Nothing Dr. Stallings said could have made Phil angrier, but he tried not to show it.

"She's going to do fine, Stan. We took care of the obstruction and to answer your question, I think she's going to do very well. I wouldn't be surprised if I'm able to discharge her in a week, maybe ten days, tops."

Dr. Stallings straightened up. Until then he had been leaning over Phil's shoulder and most of that time, trying to catch a glimpse of the note Phil was writing.

"Glad to hear it. I always thought she was a very nice woman, and she certainly has had her share of grief this year." The grin widened. "You did your usual good job, Phil. Say hello to her for me when you can." He patted Phil's shoulder again and walked away.

Phil tried to ignore the entire incident.

His office hadn't booked any surgery for that day, so he was able to spend the morning making rounds and looking in on Ann from time to time. He didn't want her sleeping that much so he left orders to get her into a chair. That would be the best time to speak with her, but the nurses were busy, and Ann remained in bed drifting in and out. Phil used the rest of the time to catch up on his chart dictations and then left for the office. A heavy afternoon had been scheduled including several excisions and he knew he wouldn't get back to the hospital until that evening. The first patient was scheduled for twelve thirty and they continued in a steady stream after that. He finished with the last patient at quarter to six and was fairly exhausted by then. Nevertheless, he was determined to see Ann one more time before the day was out and made the trip back to the hospital. His fatigue quickly disappeared as he entered her room and found her not only awake but sitting in a chair and smiling.

"Sleepyhead! You finally decided it was time to get up. Congratulations." Grinning, he pulled up a chair in front of her, sat down and patted her knee. "You look good, Ann. You're doing very well."

Ann never took her eyes off him. She kept smiling even though it was not without considerable effort. The tube in her nose made it very difficult to talk. Her voice was weak and hoarse.

"Thanks to you, Phil," she said. "If I'm still here, it's only because of you."

"Did you notice your abdomen? It's flat."

"You're wonderful," Ann said. "Yes, I did see that." Her face was filled with gratitude. "You did the surgery yesterday, right?"

"Correct."

She raised her hand and then her index finger. "Good. At least I got that right. I'm trying to stay away from those shots. They help the pain, but they make you awfully groggy. Tell me, did you try to speak with me before? I think I remember seeing you here."

"No, you were sleeping. You wouldn't have remembered anything I said."

"Are you going to tell me now what you found?"

"I can, if you like, or it can wait until later when you're feeling a little stronger. We don't have to talk about it now."

"No, I want to know. I don't expect it to be good news. Don't let that hold you back. I want you to be completely honest."

There was nothing else Phil could say.

"It can't be good news, Ann. The tumor has recurred and that's never good, but we were able to remove the obstruction and some other tissue. That will certainly be an improvement and you should be able to get rid of all these tubes in a few days and start eating. There's still tumor that couldn't be removed and that will cause problems in time, but when that will be, I don't know. I definitely feel you should have chemotherapy and if you have a good response, you may do well for a very long time."

Ann winced. "I hate the thought of that chemotherapy. They talked to me about it the last time. I don't know if I can handle losing my hair and all those other things. What if I don't want the chemotherapy or it doesn't work, how long do I have then?"

Phil looked away as he answered. "I can't be sure. Six months."

"There's no chance this could be a mistake? Could some report come back that says you're wrong?"

"No, Ann," Phil answered softly. "I wish there was that possibility but there's no mistake."

Ann let her head fall back. "I'll bet you're asked that all the time. I can't believe I did." She brought her head forward and stared straight ahead. "When you think about it, what else could I have expected? What else could be more perfect for me?"

She looked at Phil again.

"I'm tired now. You don't have to come back later but I do want to speak with you tomorrow. I have something very important to tell you, but I don't want to talk any more right now."

Some of this was very perplexing but more than that, Phil was disheartened.

"I never wanted to tell you this," he said. "This was very hard for me."

"I know. I could see it in your face."

Neither said anything more and Phil somewhat reluctantly got up from his chair and made his way from Ann's room directly to the doctors' parking lot. A light rain had begun to fall, and it suited his mood perfectly and he stood outside for a while. Then he got into his car and drove home. It was another evening when he felt he shouldn't simply sit at home so he suggested they all go out for dinner. Everyone quickly agreed and after choosing Chinese over Italian food, they left for the restaurant.

Dinner was enjoyable and a distraction and no mention was made of patients or the hospital. Afterwards, when they were home and Maralyn and Phil were alone, she did ask how Ann was doing. Phil said he wasn't sure. She seemed to be recovering nicely from the surgery, but he didn't know how well she was handling the rest. Maralyn left the conversation at that and when they went to bed later, both fell asleep rather quickly, or at least, that's the way it seemed.

Telephone calls at night were not anything unusual and when the phone rang at two thirty a.m., Phil did not have any particular anticipation when he picked up the receiver. It was the nurse on Ann Hartway's floor.

"Dr. Berger, we've had a bad problem with your patient, Mrs. Hartway. I think you'd better come right over."

Phil was jolted upright. "What's wrong?"

"She's lost a lot of blood."

"From where?"

"Her central line came apart. There's blood all over the floor."

"What!" Maralyn was fully awake now. "How is she?"

"I don't know. The residents are in with her now. She's lost a lot of blood."

"I want to know how she is!" Phil screamed into the phone.

"Please don't yell at me, Dr. Berger. I'm not in the room right now. I came out here to call you."

"Is she in shock?"

"Yes. I couldn't get a blood pressure before. I don't know how it is now."

"Are you getting blood?"

"Yes, it's been ordered."

"Is the IV working?"

"Yes. I reconnected it."

"Run it wide open. I'll be right there." He started to hang up the phone but stopped. "She hasn't arrested, has she?"

"No, Dr. Berger. There's a pulse."

"Oh, God," he said as he slammed down the phone.

"What's wrong?" Maralyn asked.

"I don't know," Phil said as he hurriedly threw on clothes he grabbed from his closet. "They said she's lost a lot of blood. Her IV came apart. I can't believe it."

"Ann?"

"Yes. I have to run. I don't know when I'll be back."

He bolted down the stairs and into the garage. The door opened automatically, and he quickly backed down the driveway onto the street. He drove furiously slowing only at intersections when the light was against him but then racing across if no one else was there. He left the car at the emergency room entrance to save time and raced through the corridors and up the stairs. He ignored the others on the floor and burst into Ann's room. His fears began to ease only when he saw she was moving, and her eyes were open.

"How is she?" he asked the resident nearest to him. He saw the unit of blood that was already being transfused.

"Better. Her pressure's coming back."

"Is that the first unit?"

"Yes."

"How many more are you giving her?"

"At least two more. Did you see that?" He pointed to a stack of blood-soaked towels near the wall. "They were on the floor right near the IV."

"All that blood?"

"All that blood and the towels. They were saturated. It's hard to tell, but it looks like most of her blood volume. I think she's going to need more than three units."

Phil let out a deep breath in exasperation. He leaned over the bed. "Ann, you're going to be OK. Don't be frightened." He couldn't tell if she heard him. If she was conscious, she was just barely. Her breathing was rapid and labored. Oxygen was being administered through a nasal cannula. Phil reached for her wrist and felt for her pulse there and in her neck. It was very fast but stronger than he expected.

"Get the next two units of blood up here now and run them in as fast as you can!"

"Yes, Dr. Berger," someone responded.

"Tell them to set up three more. We'll probably need those too."

"Yes, sir."

Phil stepped away from the bed. "How did this happen?" No one answered.

He walked into the hall and found the nurse who initially called him. "What happened?" he asked.

"I don't know, Dr. Berger. I walked past Mrs. Hartway's room and I only went in because all the lights were off. When I turned the light on, I saw all this blood. I don't know how the IV came apart. I put it back together and then I called a code, she looked so bad. I don't even know if she had a pulse then. The residents came right up and took over. This has never happened before. Do you think she's going to be all right?"

"I think so. Who saw her last?"

"I did," the nurse answered. "She's in my section."

"Everything was all right then?"

"Yes."

"How long ago was that?"

"Twenty minutes, maybe a half-hour before all this happened."

"Did you have to give her something through the IV?"

"No, Dr. Berger. The IV was fine. Even if I did, I wouldn't have taken the cap off the central line. We have that new system, and you just plug into the cap. The cap was off when I came in here and there were towels on the floor just where the blood was going. I never put them there."

"Those towels I just saw in her room weren't used to get the blood off the floor?"

"No, sir. They were already there when she was bleeding. There was also a plastic chux pad right under the central line so the blood just kept pouring right off onto the towels. None got on the bed."

"What are you saying?"

"I'm not saying anything, Dr. Berger. I'm just telling you what I found when I went into Mrs. Hartway's room. Ask the residents. They saw the same thing."

"Who was here?"

"Myself, and the other two night nurses, and our one aide. Dr. Stallings was here for a little while. He saw one of his patients, but he didn't stay long."

"Who did you say? Dr. Stallings? Here, at this hour?!" Phil couldn't believe this. "Why?"

"He said he had to see someone in the emergency room, but they hadn't shown up yet, so he came up here to see one of his patients. He was here for only a few minutes."

"And you're saying he wasn't here when Mrs. Hartway got into trouble."

"No, I wish he was. I don't think I would have panicked as much. I didn't see him leave but it couldn't have been more than five or ten minutes before everything else happened."

Phil stood quietly for a moment.

"I see. Well, thank you for telling me this and I thank you for going into Mrs. Hartway's room when you did. I think you saved her life.'

The nurse was near tears.

"Thank you, Dr. Berger. I know Mrs. Hartway is your patient and I'm glad you don't blame me. I know some people will. I don't know how that line came apart, but I know it was fine when I saw her and it's not my fault."

Phil patted her arm. "I know it's not." He walked back to Ann's room.

The residents were working diligently. "That's the second unit of blood, Dr. Berger, and we've got the third one ready to go. Her systolic pressure's 80. Looks like we're getting there."

"Very good. Is she alert?"

"Yes, she's been trying to talk."

Phil moved close to Ann's side. "You're doing fine, Ann. A little bit more and you'll be right back where you were. I'm sorry this happened but it's OK now."

Ann tried to speak. Her voice was barely audible. "What happened?" she asked.

"It was nothing with you. Your IV came apart and you lost some blood. I don't want you to talk now. Just rest. We can talk about it later."

Phil stepped away from the bed and motioned to one of the residents. "Get a blood count after this third unit and start a fourth and then I want you to follow the blood counts every four hours. Get a stat EKG and cardiac enzymes. I want to be sure she didn't have an MI while all this was going on. Then I want her in the ICU."

"No problem, Dr. Berger." The resident started to walk away and then came back.

"Just one question, Dr. Berger. Do you think we should be doing all this, what with her diagnosis, all that tumor, I mean?"

Phil glared at him. "I want her in the ICU. I also want that lab work done."

He didn't say anything else or even look at the resident again. He went back to the bedside.

"I have to leave for a few minutes, Ann, but I'll be back. We're going to put you in another room for a little while. You'll have some extra nurses. Then we'll get you back here."

Ann didn't answer but followed him with her eyes. As he turned away, the blue chux pad under the IV suddenly caught his attention. He lifted one corner.

"Has this been here the whole time?" he asked the nearest resident.

"It was here when we got here. I guess the nurse put it there when she fixed the line."

Phil lifted the pad higher. There wasn't any blood on the sheet underneath. He put it back down and left without saying a word. He stopped in the ICU to be sure a bed was available for Ann's transfer and then went down to the emergency room. The staff already knew what had happened.

"How's your patient doing, Dr. Berger?"

"Better, now. You heard about it?"

"They called a code and a couple of us went up but they didn't need us. It was just the IV coming apart, wasn't it?"

"It looks that way." "Geez, that's scary."

"You're right, especially now, when there aren't that many people around. We were very lucky tonight. The residents did a good job but it's always nice to have some attendings in the house, too."

"Dr. Stallings was here."

"Really? When was that?"

"Not that long ago. Some patient with abdominal pain called him and said they'd meet him in the emergency room. He waited for him for a while and then said he was going to see some patients. He said to page him when the patient arrived."

"Did the patient ever get here?"

"Nope. He never showed."

"Did Dr. Stallings ever come back to the ER?"

"No. He never heard from us, so I guess he just left, probably just before your patient got into trouble. If he was still here, I'm sure he would have been at the code. You know how he is."

There was some murmuring and muffled laughter from the others.

"Got the picture," Phil said. "Well, I was going to go home but maybe I'll go up and see the patient one more time."

He smiled at the group. "Thanks for the help with my patient."

"For you, anytime, Dr. Berger."

Those were nice words to hear.

He made his way upstairs to the ICU. Ann had just arrived, and the nurses were getting her settled in, reviewing the order and hooking up her lines to the various monitors. Phil immediately noticed her pulse rate now was 90, a marked improvement. He waited until there was a little less activity around the bedside.

"Doing very well, Ann. Looks like we'll both be able to get some rest soon." He leaned closer to her and put his hand to her cheek. She had been, and still was, so terribly vulnerable. "I'm not going to let anything happen to you. You can get some sleep now. These nurses will be with you, and I'll be back and forth. I have one case this morning, but I'll be free after that. See you a little later, OK?"

Ann smiled and closed her eyes. Phil looked at the nurses who, at that moment, stood watching. He nodded to them and they immediately resumed their respective duties. One patted him on his arm.

"We'll take good care of her, Dr. Berger."

It was clear to Phil what had happened, but it wasn't until the ride home that he began to think of its implications. He would never have thought anyone could be capable of something like this. He remembered the earlier conversation with Dr. Stallings. Somehow Ann's condition had threatened him and left to his own thinking, he had acted quickly to avoid possible detection. There could be no other explanation. A more terrifying thought was the realization there was nothing he wouldn't do now. Nothing was too heinous.

It was too late to go back to bed when he reached home. He tried to be very quiet when he looked into the bedroom but Maralyn hadn't been sleeping and she heard him.

"How is she?"

"Better," Phil said.

"What happened?"

"The IV came apart and it was attached to a central line. She lost a lot of blood."

Maralyn was sitting up now, the covers around her waist. Light was just beginning to come in through the bedroom windows. One strap of her nightgown fell from a shoulder, but she didn't bother to put it back. She looked tired.

"That shouldn't happen, right? How does something like that happen?"

"I guess that's something a lot of people will try to find out. You're right. That shouldn't happen."

"Is she going to be OK?"

"After getting four units of blood and probably more later on, yes, I'd say she's going to be OK I put her in the ICU. I think that'll be better for her, too."

"Is this the fault of the nurses taking care of her?"

"I'm sure that's what everyone will say but I don't think so. I'm not going to say what I think. Let's leave it as one of those things that every so often just happens and no one ever really knows why. That's the way medicine is, sometimes."

Ann looked up at him. She was trembling. "You must be very tired." She looked at the clock. "You've been gone over three hours. Come here."

Phil walked around to her side of the bed. She pulled him down and pressed him against her. He felt how soft and warm she was.

"I know how good you try to be to everyone else," she whispered. "I know I have to share you, but I really want you all to myself. I get jealous." She kissed his ear. "I don't suppose you want to come to bed for a little while now?"

They held each other but then Phil began to draw away. He kissed Maralyn's shoulder. "I can't, hon. I have a seven-thirty case, and I have to get back. I just want to get cleaned up and change my clothes. I wish I could." He sounded very convincing. "You feel awfully good," he said.

Maralyn fell back on her pillow and smiled. "We'll save it for later."

Phil continued to stare at her, as if reconsidering the offer, but then he suddenly bent forward, kissed her on the lips and turned to go into the bathroom. Maralyn fell asleep and later Phil changed his clothes and left without awakening her. He passed two very sleepy young girls in the hall, kissed them and reminded them not to miss the school bus. Then he was on his way back to the hospital.

He went to the ICU first before going to the OR. All the activity at this hour would make it difficult for anyone to sleep and Ann was wide awake. She smiled when she saw him. Phil picked up the clipboard at the foot of her bed, looked at it quickly and smiled himself.

"Looks good, Ann." Her systolic pressure was now 120 and there was only a slight elevation of her pulse. He walked around to her side. "You're doing very well. I hope you know that." He gave Ann time to answer but she didn't say anything, and her expression never changed. "Give me a minute," Phil said. "I want to talk with your nurse. I'll be right back."

Ann's nurse had seen him at the bedside and had begun to walk towards him. There were certain orders she wanted to discuss. They talked at length. Ann's hematocrit was now 28 and Phil did not feel she needed any more blood. Her urine output was improving, and the EKG had been done and hadn't shown any change. Regardless how much better she was, Phil wanted her to stay on complete bed rest at least for today. He went back to her bedside.

"We're just going to watch you here for a little while, Ann. I want you to stay in bed today. I want to see you a little stronger before we get you up again. That doesn't mean there's a problem now. You're actually doing exceptionally well, and I really mean that. Anything you want to say?"

Ann's voice was still very weak. "I can't think." Phil had to strain to hear. "You said something before, but I can't remember. Come back later. I want to know what happened. I want to talk with you." There was a long pause each time she spoke.

"I have to go to the operating room now," Phil said, "but it won't take long. I'll be back later."

The case was an inguinal hernia repair, and it took a little less than an hour. Gary Barlow was busy that morning at the County Hospital and Phil did the surgery without an assistant. Just before he finished, he was given a message that Dr. Mueller wanted to see him. The two met in the corridor just outside the operating rooms and found a place where they could speak in private.

"What happened to your patient last night, Phil? I heard an IV came apart and she lost a tremendous amount of blood. Someone said she almost died."

"That's pretty much what happened. She probably would have if the nurse hadn't spotted it and called a code."

"How the hell can that be? She had a central line, didn't she? Those things are all screw-on. Hell, those things are so tight I usually can't get 'em off even when I try. I guess they never had it on right to begin with."

Phil did not answer.

"How is she doing now?"

"Pretty well. Blood pressure is back to normal and she's in the ICU."

"You had to give her a lot of blood, didn't you?"

"Four units and her hematocrit is only 28 now."

"Jesus, she really bled. You know, you're lucky she didn't get an air embolus when her pressure went way down."

"I know that."

"Hmm, well, yes. I guess you do know that. Well, too bad. I'm sorry this happened, but I'm glad it wasn't any worse. I understand she has a lot of residual tumor."

"Yes, she has."

"Well, that doesn't make any difference. She's a young woman. Her husband died here a year ago, too, so I'm told. He's the one that had the bypasses that failed and wouldn't let Stanley take off his leg."

"You know the whole story."

"Are you kidding? That's all I've been hearing from the nursing office from the minute I walked in this morning. They're going crazy over this. I think they may want to take some action with her nurse. They say there's been some problems with her before."

"I hope not," Phil said. "I hope they'd listen to her first. I don't think it's her fault."

"What happened then?"

"I don't think anyone can say at this point. I talked to her. She says the IV was fine the last time she saw it. I can't call her a liar. I wasn't there."

"Yes, but Phil, come on. Who else was there?"

"I can't say who else was there. Why don't you find out?"

Dr. Mueller looked puzzled. "I don't know what you're saying, Phil. If that was my patient, I'm sure I'd be very upset with the nurses, but if you're not, then you have a much different attitude. I think you're being very generous."

"Oh, I'm upset all right, Mal. I just don't know with whom. I'd rather know more, if we can."

"What else are we going to find out? The line disconnected. It wasn't put together properly."

"I'm not going to argue with you, Mal. Let's hear what everyone has to say after it's all been reviewed."

Malcolm Mueller shrugged, nodded his head, and slowly began to walk off. Phil watched him for a little while and then went to the recovery room to write orders for his patient. He could have said more but decided that would be unwise. Instead, he was much more anxious to tell Gordon Mulcahey all that he knew and get his reaction. It was a call that he wanted to make as soon as possible.

Phil had planned to keep Ann in the ICU for the next few days or at least until the central line could be removed. He didn't want any more 'accidents'. Then he decided it would be better to preserve the site for a more permanent venous access that could be used for chemotherapy later. That, her very rapid improvement and her repeated wish to speak with him persuaded Phil to transfer her back to her room after just two days in the unit. By this time both the intestinal tube and Foley catheter had been removed and Ann had begun to take short walks and take in limited fluids. Phil also ordered private duty nurses at night. Curiously, he didn't see Dr. Stallings at all during those two days. Ann was already back in her room several hours when Phil was finally able to come by and spend some time with her. She was sitting in a chair and stretched out her arms when he walked in.

"It's so wonderful to be back home," she said, her gestures exaggerating the very limited confines of her room.

Phil surveyed the room. "It's a big improvement over the ICU, no question about it. Can't say much for your decorator, though." He put another chair close to Ann's and sat down. "You look great. How do you feel?"

"Still very weak. I'm trying to move around as much as I can, but I never thought it would be this hard. I'm exhausted all the time."

"I know," Phil said. "This problem you just had didn't help. Don't forget what you went through. This was a tremendous stress placed on you twice in two days."

"I can see that now. I guess I don't want to admit it." Her expression changed. "What really did happen, Phil? That's one of the things I wanted to ask you. I know something happened to my IV, but nobody's really explained it."

"Apparently your IV came apart. Since one end was still in your chest, actually in the largest vein in your chest, there was nothing to prevent the blood from just pouring out. You lost an awful lot and went into shock. Fortunately, the nurse saw this before it became even worse."

"I was in pretty bad shape. I know that. You're saying I could have died."

"I don't want you thinking about it, but I'm afraid so."

"That's very frightening. Why do they make those things so they can come apart so easily?"

"That's just it. They don't. They can be tightened so hard they're actually very difficult to separate. What's more, the cap never has to be removed from that line you have in your chest. It has a small rubber diaphragm. It's always sealed, and the nurse just has to plug into it. It's designed to be very safe for you and for her."

"So, what happened to me?"

Phil hesitated. "I guess I'm doing the right thing giving you all these details. Not only did the line come apart, but the cap came off too. That's clear, but how it happened or who's responsible no one really knows. Do you remember anything from that night?"

"My God, no, Phil. I was so out of it. I was getting those shots and they were putting me in another world. My mind's a blank except that I think I was still having the same bad dreams, my usual ones, even here. Shouldn't they stop, when you're that sick?"

"What do you mean?"

"I never told you. I have nightmares almost every night, sometimes two or three times, about Dr. Stallings. It's been going on for months. I thought I saw him again in the hospital."

"When?"

"I don't know. After the surgery. That night. I can't be sure. When I remembered, I thought it was another dream. It'll probably happen again tonight."

Now very concerned, Phil moved to the edge of his chair and leaned closer. "What can you remember? Can you be a little more certain when you think this happened?"

Ann tried to recall. "It must have been before I lost all that blood the other night. I certainly don't remember anything after that. I thought I saw him standing over me. That's about all. It wasn't like a lot of the other dreams I have. Those are real nightmares."

"You think it was that night and that's all you remember?"

"Yes. It was after the surgery, and it had to be before the other thing, and it was at night. I remember it was very dark, but so what? It was a dream. Why do you keep asking me about it?"

Phil's expression was somber. "Because there's something else about that night that I haven't told you. I don't want to give you anything more to worry about, but it's something you should know. Dr. Stallings was on your floor that night, just before you got into trouble."

Ann sat there staring at him. Either she hadn't heard clearly what he said, or she did not comprehend. He repeated himself. "Dr. Stallings was here that night. He said he was called to the emergency room and then he came up here to see a patient. That was right before all the trouble started."

"I heard you," Ann said. "It took a little time to register, but I know exactly what you said." She leaned forward putting her face in her hands. "Oh God, then I really did see him?"

"I think so. It's too much of a coincidence."

"And it was no accident that the IV came apart?"

"It's possible, I suppose, but I always had trouble believing it. It never made much sense, that way. And then there were some other things the nurse found near the IV, that someone else had to put there. I don't think you can ignore all this. Besides, he talked to me about you after the surgery, just that morning, as a matter of fact."

"What did he say?"

"The truth? He wanted to know how you were doing. He wanted to know if you were going to pull through."

All the while Phil spoke, Ann kept fidgeting, but now she sat upright. "That settles it. It's all the more reason, Phil. I'll admit this had me shocked. I wouldn't have expected this, not even of him, but I've already reached a decision. This confirms it. I already made up my mind. You can have whoever you want bring charges against him, and I'll testify. I wanted to tell you now and not wait, if time is going to be a factor."

Phil did not answer.

"I know this is something you've thought about. I know you don't want to see me hurt, but let's face it, we both know what's going to happen to me. This is the only way we can stop him, and it has to be done. I really don't count any more. The only ones I have to talk to are my girls, and I think I can make them understand, and if I don't now, then maybe they will later. I let him do this to me and I've gotten what I deserve, but it should never happen again to anyone else."

Phil was still speechless.

Ann leaned over and grasped his arm. "You know I'm right."

Finally, he said, "You don't have to do this. We can find another way."

"There is no other way, Phil. Look what he's done to me. None of this would have happened to me if it weren't for him. Look what he's done to the others. How often have we talked about it and how he just refuses to stop? We have to do this now. We don't have very long, Phil."

"It's asking a lot of you, Ann. The time will come when it's going to be very hard for you."

"Well, then that's the way it will just have to be. You're the one who has to see to it that I keep going. At least I won't have to listen to people's opinions of me for very long."

Phil had to look away. "I don't know what to say."

"Don't say anything. Just think what has to be done and get me better."

"If that's what you want." Ann could barely hear his voice. "I'll take care of it. I know what to do." He got up and moved his chair back. "I also ordered a private duty nurse for you at night. I didn't want to forget to tell you. You don't have to worry about falling asleep now."

Ann then realized. "Of course. I didn't even have time to think about that. That certainly would have been a big worry later on. I'm so glad you think of all these things."

"That's OK. You just get a good night's rest. I'll try to be back this evening. Otherwise, I'll see you in the morning."

Ann settled back in her chair as Phil left the room. He looked at his watch. There was still time to call Gordon Mulcahey's office but he didn't want to do this from the hospital. He thought how long he had waited for this; how uncertain he had been that this would ever happen. If he had any reservations what this would mean to himself or to Ann, they were quickly set aside. He rushed through rounds and got to his office a little before four p.m. Gordon was usually back from court by now and this always seemed to be the best time to reach him. Assured of his privacy, Phil placed the call.

Gordon was not in. His secretary said he had just returned from vacation and was not scheduled to begin work until next week. He had been to the office earlier and did say he might be back, but he wasn't definite. She suggested leaving a message or calling back again before five. She'd have Gordon return the call if he came in before then. Phil wasn't interested in all this. He just wanted to reach Gordon. He left his number.

He read through some articles and looked over lab reports and several insurance forms that needed his signature. At five p.m., his secretary walked back to say she was leaving and would be signing out to the answering service. Phil waited a little while longer himself before deciding to leave. He didn't make the second call. He assumed Gordon would have called by now if he had gotten his message. Just as he was about to turn off the lights and close the office door, the telephone rang. He couldn't leave now. In a moment or so answering service would reach him through his beeper with some sort of problem and someone's phone number. Then he would have to call that person and listen to however many complaints there were and give the appropriate advice. He took his beeper off his belt and waited for the signal. As soon as it began, he switched on the message screen. Hallelujah! It wasn't a patient. It was Gordon returning his call. He reached for the nearest phone and quickly punched in the number on the screen.

"Hello?"

"Hello, Gordon. It's Phil Berger?"

"Hey, Doc. Your service works pretty fast. How've you been?"

"Not bad. They told me you were just on vacation. I'll bet you have a pretty good tan."

"Nope, windburn. I went sailing. Terrific exercise but everything still hurts. Anything happening with you?"

"A lot, Gordon. That's why I called. I have to see you."

"Where are you calling from? Can you tell me anything now?"

"I'm in my office. I don't want to say too much over the phone, but that person is willing to testify."

"Really? You mean the wife? How'd you manage that?"

"A lot has happened, Gordon. I'd like to tell you all about it when I see you."

"Tomorrow's Saturday. You pick a time."

"Later in the morning is good. It'll give me time to finish rounds. Is eleven OK?"

"Fine. My office is closed. We can still use it or I can meet you at yours. Did you speak with Mel?"

"No, I called you first. We can use my office. No one will be here. You know where it is?"

"I have the address. That's great. It sounds like we may finally start making some progress. Do you remember when I said all you had to do was be patient, something always comes up in cases like this? Well, this is probably it. You're going to have to tell me how you did it. I guess I'll get all that tomorrow."

"Yes, Gordon, there's a lot and you'll hear it all tomorrow. I'll see you at eleven."

"Eleven o'clock it is. See you then."

Phil put down the phone. He would try not to think about this anymore until Saturday. A little later he got some help when his beeper went off again. He called from his car. This time it was one of the local family practitioners who had a patient in the emergency room with intestinal obstruction. Phil had started for home but hadn't gotten very far and simply turned around and went back to the hospital. A quick evaluation of the patient and a white blood cell count of 18,000 made it very clear he'd be there for a while. He called Maralyn to tell her not to expect him and spent the next hour preparing for surgery and getting the appropriate consent from the patient and at least six different family members. The patient had a gangrenous segment of bowel from adhesions and even with Gary's help, the surgery took more than two hours. Talking with the family afterwards, writing the post-op orders and stabilizing the patient was almost as time-consuming and Phil didn't get home until well after midnight. He slept well, however.

Phil made no mention of the meeting to Ann when he saw her on rounds Saturday morning. He advanced her diet and told her he would change her central line to a permanent venous access on Monday under local anesthesia. He promised she would have very little discomfort during the procedure. The other patients were seen in rapid order and Phil was able to be in his office by ten thirty. Gordon arrived precisely at eleven, looking very robust and fresh.

"Nice place you have here, Phil." He looked closely at the plaques and wall decorations. "Much nicer than a lot of the offices I've seen."

Phil locked the door and motioned for Gordon to follow. They went into the consultation room and sat down.

"This has been quite a week, Gordon. Are you ready to hear about it?"

"That's why I came over."

"I'll try to make it very brief but I'm sure you'll have many questions. I operated on this woman earlier this week. She has cancer and it's not curable. I don't have to tell you what goes on in people's minds. She thinks Dr. Stallings is responsible for this, and she doesn't want him to do this to anyone else. On top of all this, Stallings knows she's in the hospital and I think he tried to kill her a few days ago."

It was a lot for anyone to accept. Gordon listened. He avoided any reaction.

"I know what you're thinking," Phil said, "but I saw what was done. He was on her floor very late at night. This was right after her surgery, and she was very heavily medicated. Someone disconnected her IV and arranged plastic pads and towels around her bed, so she'd bleed right into them and never be aware of it. Her nurse spotted it just in time or else I think we would have lost her. I'm sure it wasn't an accident, and he was the one who did it."

"She knows about this?"

"Yes. I explained it to her. She even thinks she saw him standing beside her bed just before it happened."

"And she's willing to testify against him?"

"She is now."

Gordon rubbed his face. "Man, I was hoping for a break, but this is hard to believe. You mean this really happened?"

"Just as I told you."

Gordon was still skeptical. "You've known her all this time and you didn't know she was sick?"

"Gordon, to tell the truth, I was completely shocked. She was actually operated on somewhere else six months ago and kept it completely secret. That was when she was supposed to be on vacation. I learned about it last week when she developed complications and I was called in to see her. I had to operate this week and I found that her original tumor had spread. Now she doesn't always say it in so many words, but she thinks this is her punishment for what happened to her husband. She thinks she's gotten what she deserves but Stallings should be punished, too. She was very emphatic about arranging a meeting with you."

"So that's how all this came about. I wondered about that." Gordon became quiet and seemed lost in thought. "I'm not going to question her reasoning. I'm going along with you on that. Obviously, I'm not very good at making predictions about her." He looked again at Phil. "How's she doing now?"

"She had a very rough week. She's doing well now but I will have to start her on chemotherapy. I don't know how long that's going to give us."

Gordon reacted with a grimace. "That's not good, Phil. This is going to take a lot of time. I think we can start moving on this right away, but we have to have some idea of a time frame. What's your best guess?"

"A year, I hope. It's hard to say. It could be more. It all depends on how she responds to the chemotherapy."

"I should talk to her very soon, then. When I do that, I really should have a stenographer with me, and she should have her own legal counsel. I'd be willing to do that while she's still in the hospital but that's liable to raise a lot of questions. I don't want to tip our hand. I'm very conscious of the time factor but we can still make maximum use of it and see her after she gets out of the hospital. What she has to do right now, though, is speak with her own attorney and let him set something up with me. That will give him time to familiarize himself with this matter. This way her rights will be completely protected. If she doesn't have someone, I'm sure Mel can recommend someone who's good. He can even give him a lot of the background he'll need to understand what's going on. That would be the proper way to do this. Is she in good enough shape for this right now?"

"I'll find out. I think so. I'll tell her what you said."

"And then get back to me. I want to discuss this with Mel, and I want to know what she says, particularly about an attorney for herself. That's going to be very important because a lot of this will be self-incriminating."

"You think something can happen to her even though she's terminally ill?"

"No, but let's do it right. We'll try to play that down as much as we can and there are some angles we can use. I'm sure the court would be lenient and there's all sorts of immunity that can be offered for her testimony, but let's make sure she has all the protection she's entitled to."

"That's good," Phil said. "I'm sure she'll appreciate that. I'll go back over to see her this afternoon and I'll get started on this. Anything else you want to know?"

"Yeah. Tell me what else this Stallings has been up to and let's go back over this other thing a little bit more. Give me some more details. I've gotten a good feel for this thing, but I want to hear what it sounds like one more time."

They talked for another forty minutes and this time Gordon took notes, in particular when Phil mentioned that Dr. Stallings had asked if Ann was going to pull through just after her surgery. He watched him underline that entry several times. When they were finished, Gordon seemed even more satisfied. They agreed to speak again on Monday and to leave separately.

Returning to the hospital now would have meant a second trip later in the afternoon for rounds, so Phil drove home for lunch and a couple of hours of relaxation. He alternately browsed through the newspaper and caught some of the action of a baseball game on TV. After his beeper had interrupted him for the third time with yet another message, he decided he might just as well go back for rounds now. The first patient he saw when he got back to the hospital, was the one he had operated on the night before. The patient was doing reasonably well but the nurses were still very concerned and there was the usual plethora of questions. He answered each very patiently and then saw the rest of his patients. Ann was the last one and was having her best day thus far. Her only unpleasant moments were the few times she saw Dr. Stallings pass by her door. He never looked in and Ann thought he was acting as though he didn't know who was in the room. Phil reassured her. He reminded her she was much stronger now and much less vulnerable than earlier in the week, and she still had the private duty nurse at night. He didn't think she had any cause to worry. He then went on to tell her about Gordon Mulcahey, who he is and how he had been introduced to him by Mel Silverstone. He admitted he had talked with him before and had followed some of his advice. Ann questioned this but appeared to take it in her stride and did not seem upset. Phil was completely truthful and told her everything they had discussed earlier in the day. It was particularly important that she have her own legal counsel. She would be implicating herself by her own testimony and her attorney would want to consider very carefully how this was being presented. Ann understood and even though troubled by this was also fully resigned to it. She couldn't think of a lawyer at this time other than Mel Silverstone and Phil suggested that he could probably recommend someone else if he didn't feel he should handle the matter himself. Once that was settled, the district attorney had said he would move quickly towards bringing an indictment. Somewhat reluctantly, Phil emphasized the sense of urgency with which they were treating the matter. Ann was no less realistic and said she had hoped they would. She thanked him and then asked if she was still being discharged as planned the following Tuesday. Phil said he would put in the venous access on Monday, take out the skin staples from her wound and she should be all set to go the next day. Ann said if he kept his word, he could expect a big hug and kiss on Tuesday. For the first time in a long while, Phil left feeling very optimistic.

Sunday was spent with the family and little of consequence occurred except that Ann had reported Dr. Stallings walking back and forth past her room an inordinate number of times. She was very apprehensive, and Phil suggested calling her night nurse who agreed to come in earlier. That eased both their concerns.

Monday was much busier. There were a great many arrangements that had to be made. A series of telephone calls took place throughout the day between Phil, Gordon and Mel Silverstone. Phil was to turn over to Gordon all the information he had on Dr. Stallings, in particular the names of all the patients whose deaths he was thought to have caused and the circumstances regarding each one. In all likelihood Ann would be represented by Peter Futterman, a highly regarded young attorney specializing in criminal law who had worked in the district attorney's office for six years before entering private practice. Mel had recommended him and somewhere in the course of the many telephone calls, he had been contacted and expressed interest. Interviews were to be arranged, first with Phil and then with Ann, so that he would have sufficient background information before Ann gave her statement. Gordon wanted to set that up in Ann's home as soon as he could after her discharge, with Phil's approval, of course. Before that, Phil wanted her seen by Dr. Seymour Breiling, an oncologist, while she was still in the hospital. He wanted him to discuss chemotherapy with her even though it wouldn't start until there was further recuperation. In addition, Ann had the venous access inserted that afternoon using the previous central line site. That made it much easier, and she had absolutely no discomfort during the procedure. The skin staples were also removed and at this point, a fine line remained the length of the wound. Ann couldn't have been more pleased.

Dr. Breiling wanted additional tests done and this could have delayed Ann's discharge but Phil managed to have them completed by Tuesday morning. He asked if Ann was worried about being home alone and suggested she have an aid at least for the first week. Ann told him she had a cleaning lady that came in five days a week. If he was also concerned that she might have an unwelcome visitor, she reminded him that Jack's business was security systems, and her house had the best that money could buy. There were also two pistols in the house and Jack in his total commitment to home security had made sure Ann knew how to use them. Phil's final question was to ask who was taking her home. Two employees, her secretary and bookkeeper, were coming for her. Ann then asked if Phil knew what was coming next. She had him bend down and gave him the big hug and kiss she had promised. She also told him how grateful she was and that he hadn't disappointed her. She always knew he would take the very best care of her. Phil tried not to show it but he was very deeply moved.

XIII

Phil had difficulty keeping to his regular work schedule over the next few days. First, there was the meeting with Peter Futterman. He found him to be very professional in his demeanor although he wondered if his somewhat youthful appearance might be a disadvantage. Over the course of their discussion, however, it was evident he was very intelligent, articulate and understanding. Phil was very hopeful he'd agree to represent Ann. Next, he arranged a meeting at Ann's home and drove Peter there to introduce them and lend whatever assistance he could. It also gave him an opportunity to observe Ann's progress. The first few days had been very discouraging. Even the slightest physical effort had left her totally exhausted but now she felt herself getting stronger and her spirits were much better. She spoke very candidly with Peter Futterman and was equally impressed with him. Peter recognized the unique nature of the case and complimented Phil on helping him understand what was involved. He would be very happy to represent Ann and felt her interests could be very well served. This was agreed and Phil spoke privately with Ann for a few minutes before he and Peter left. On the way back, Peter could only remark on how incredible all this was and how it was certain to get enormous media attention. Phil started to wonder about his priorities but then Peter asked if he thought Ann would be able to manage physically.

Phil said he hoped she would, but they would just have to wait and see.

He had to make other calls as soon as they arrived back at his office. Peter had left his car there and excused himself after Phil agreed to keep him fully informed. He left a message with Gordon Mulcahey's office and then called Dr. Breiling. The oncologist wanted Ann to start chemotherapy, but Phil was afraid this would make her very sick at the same time she was to meet Gordon. He told Dr. Breiling he had just seen Ann and he thought the treatment should be delayed. He said he would call him as soon as he thought she was ready. The delay would be minimal, and he knew it would not really make a difference in her management.

A little later Gordon returned his call. He was very pleased that Ann now had an attorney and of course, he knew Peter Futterman very well and thought very highly of him. This meant he could plan to take Ann's statement and he would call tomorrow to set this up. Phil was more than welcome to be there, and he'd let him know the time. He thanked Phil for his help and said he'd see him at the deposition. Phil let out a big sigh of relief as he hung up the phone. Everything seemed to have fallen in place but there were still patients to see and no time for further reflection.

Even with the most careful planning, Phil almost missed the meeting. On the day they were all to convene at Ann's house, one of his hospital patients abruptly began vomiting blood. All the usual measures were employed to control the bleeding but after the fifth unit of blood had been given and gastroscopy confirmed continued bleeding from a large duodenal ulcer, he took the patient to surgery for a subtotal gastrectomy. By the time he completed the procedure and was certain the patient's condition was satisfactory, the meeting was well under way. He arrived at Ann's home to find her secluded in another room with Gordon Mulcahey, a stenographer and Peter Futterman. Donna Moreland was the only other person present and had remained in the living room. Gordon had been taking Ann's testimony for almost forty-five minutes and Donna did not think they should be disturbed. She didn't know how much longer they'd be so Phil tried to make himself comfortable as Donna filled him in with some of the earlier details. Twenty minutes later, Gordon emerged with the others.

"Phil! We were wondering when you were going to show. Isn't that just like a doctor? You never can get one when you want one."

There was subdued laughter and greetings and Ann put her arm in Phil's and leaned against him.

"How did it go?" he asked.

"Fine. They're all very nice."

"Tired?"

"A little."

"She was very good," Gordon said, "and I told her she's given us just what we need to get after this guy. She's our key and she's gonna be just great." He walked over to her and gently put an arm around her waist. "You must do some pretty good work, Phil. If I hadn't already known, I never would have guessed this lady just had an operation."

Ann looked up and smiled. She seemed more fragile and helpless than at any time before. Gordon led her to a sofa and had her sit down.

"I'll have Donna make you some coffee or tea. I want you to rest."

He took Phil by the arm and directed him to the room where the stenographer was packing up her equipment.

"I wanted to talk to you alone," he said quietly. "I agree with you. I don't think there's a problem with her mind. She comes across very well. She's really got it in for this guy and wants a conviction no matter what. Frankly, I'd be willing just to settle for an indictment right now, but I think we can get that. I have one question, though. How's she doing? How well is she going to hold up? She says she's going to start taking chemotherapy. Doesn't that make them very sick?"

"It probably will, but we won't know just how much until she actually starts taking the medications. If we have to, we can adjust the dosages or treat the side effects. On the other hand, it may not be that much of a problem."

Gordon's expression was grim. "You have to understand what my concerns are. I have to move quickly and get her before a grand jury. Once I do, things are going to get very hot and heavy. I've got to know that won't be too much for her. Then I have to know how much time I have before this case is put on the calendar. Stallings' lawyer will need time to prepare. If he wants to, he can get enough delays to see to it Mrs. Hartway never makes it to the stand. I don't think he will because that will make it look very bad for his client and I'm sure Dr. Stallings wants his patients to keep coming back to him. My guess is they won't stall, and they'll let this come to trial while Mrs. Hartway can still testify and just try to discredit her. My question is what kind of shape will she be in when that time comes? What kind of time frame are we talking about? Maybe you can't answer me."

Phil replied promptly. "I can. You have at least three months without any problems of any kind and if she has any response to the chemotherapy, it could be six months. If she gets a good response, it could be for a year or more. Based on what I found at surgery, I think this is a very reasonable assumption."

"OK, so I've got three months for sure, probably six, and maybe if we're lucky, twelve. That's not the best news I've ever had, but it's not the worst, either. We're just going to have to work very fast. I have that list of people you gave me and once we get the indictment, I'm going to have to start working on them. I also have to subpoena the hospital records and I may start doing that this week. There's a lot to do and I only hope to God she's able to hang in there. You know, you can say what you want about her complicity in this thing. You can condemn her or make excuses for her. I don't think that's important anymore. I think she's one hell of a courageous woman and she's very determined to get this guy. Right or wrong, we've got to make our case against him and let the jury decide."

Phil looked puzzled. "What do you mean, right or wrong?" Gordon did not answer right away.

"Oh, it's just something I keep thinking about. Has all this happened the way we're seeing it? Has there been outright intent each and every time or is this some illusion that she's compounded by a bunch of remarkable coincidences? You're probably thinking to yourself, what the hell is he saying that for now. Well, don't get me wrong. I just spent an hour with her, and I know everything you've told me, and I believe both of you. It's just that this is a very unusual and perplexing situation and when we get down to the nitty-gritty, I don't think anyone will be able to make it less perplexing." He raised his hand to emphasize the point. "They may not want to, but we'll try. I don't know who'll benefit from it. That's something I have to think about and that's why I say let the jury decide." He wrinkled his face as he looked at Phil. "You as confused as I am right now?"

"No. I guess that's all we can really do," Phil said.

"Basically. Don't forget, I want to take this guy down as much as you do. One way or another, I think we can do it. What we have to do, is prepare the best case possible. If it doesn't look like the jury is going to go for it when it gets to that point, well, maybe we'll have to think of something else. Just don't ask me now, what that might be. I may find that I'm really going to have to play with this one. Anyway, let's go back out to the others. Donna and I really have to get back to the office."

Phil lagged behind as Gordon walked back into the living room. He watched him talk briefly with Ann as the others stood nearby and then made their way to the door. Peter Futterman also had a few last words to say to Ann. It was obvious Phil was staying longer and they called out their goodbyes as they left. He was about to sit opposite her, but she made room on the sofa and he sat down next to her. They looked at each other and Ann smiled, but it was a wistful smile and she seemed distant.

"What are you thinking?" Phil asked.

"Oh, maybe a thousand things," she said, "or nothing. I can't be sure."

"Are you going to be ready for all this?"

"Do you mean the grand jury and all that sort of thing? Of course. Actually, I was thinking more about the chemotherapy. You know I have my appointment with Dr. Breiling tomorrow. He's going to start the medication. When he does, I feel that's when I'll actually begin to die."

Phil was startled by the reply. "Nonsense! There are people alive today only because of chemotherapy."

"But not in my case," Ann said, "and you know it. Look don't be short with me. It's my illness and I have to deal with it as I see it, not the way you see it or Dr. Breiling sees it. I wouldn't have to take it if my condition wasn't bad, so that tells me one thing, and it works by killing some of my tissues, so that tells me something else. One way or another, it tells me I'm dying."

"That's not the way to look at it." Phil was insistent. "Many times it's given, just to ensure the success of an operation."

"But again, it's my case we're talking about, not some hypothetical patient that has a chance. It doesn't apply. Look! Indulge me a little. Maybe if I get all this out now, I'll feel better tomorrow and later too, when I have to speak to my girls."

"You still haven't told them anything?"

"No. I've spoken with them since the operation, but they know absolutely nothing. Gordon says I can tell them I really didn't know what Dr. Stallings meant to do, that he acted mistakenly. In court, I'm to say it was his idea, he took the initiative, he exploited my feelings. Since I didn't discourage him, he thought we were acting in collusion. That's supposed to give us a much stronger case. Actually, he wants me to be very specific. He pretty much wants me to say Dr. Stallings came right out and said Jack would be dead after the surgery. He says that if I'm positive that's what he meant, that's how I must make it sound to the jury. I don't care. If that's what I have to say, I will."

"But that sounds just like the way it happened. That's what you told me. I don't think it's anything different."

"That's what I think," Ann said, "but sometimes just one word can change the whole meaning. Maybe I'm just making this sound a lot more difficult than it really is. I've never had this experience before. I just hope I can convince the girls. Gordon said he would talk to them and explain what will be said at the trial is what he would call courtroom strategy. They're so young. I have no idea what they're going to think, and it terrifies me. And then, of course, there's my illness. I don't know which is going to be a greater shock."

Ann closed her eyes. She had an anguished look.

"How long did I really have after Jack died? A few months, maybe a little longer, that's all. Do you remember the time you saw me and asked how I was, and I said fine? That was probably the last time I really felt that way. That's when the worry started and then it was guilt and now this. Can you imagine, for just those few months I brought all this upon myself. So many wonderful things were going to happen to me and look how it turned out." She turned to Phil again. "Do you think Jack can see everything that's happened? Do you think there's an afterlife? God, what if I wind up in the same place he's in, and we're together again? I'm not trying to be funny. I'm very serious."

Phil remained silent and Ann slowly rose to her feet and walked to where his jacket was lying on a chair and brought it back to him.

"Then there were all the thoughts I had about us. I saved a joke for you after the surgery but with everything that happened, there never seemed to be a good time for it. I can tell you now. One of the times when you were changing my dressing I was going to look down at the wound and say that I always hoped you would get into me one day but that was not what I really had in mind. I would have liked you to take me seriously, but there's no reason to have those thoughts anymore, so I don't. I can't even imagine a man putting himself inside me now. Who would want to? Besides, I couldn't even let anyone, not with what I know is in there." She put her hand on her abdomen. "You can't really disagree with that, can you, Phil?"

She kept looking at him, her eyes luminous and searching. Suddenly he went to her, drawing her to him and holding her very tightly. He felt a deep warmth rush over him and then the smooth texture of her cheek against his. Their bodies seemed to blend and for all that time he was lost in a heady swirl of unexpected emotion. Very slowly Ann took her arms from him and pulled away never taking her eyes from his face. His hands reached for her, but she gently moved them aside and then began to cry. Phil started towards her, but she turned away.

"I think it's best you go now, Phil."

Troubled and confused, Phil stood motionless. "I don't think I can leave you like this. "

"I'll be fine," Ann said. "I probably just needed this so I can start feeling better. One good cry and I'll be a totally different person. Don't you worry. I really think I'm going to be fine."

"I'd feel a lot better if you weren't so upset. There's no problem for me to stay a little while longer."

"No, please, Phil, it's better if you go now. I'm really going to be all right." She smiled, as if to give assurance, and led him to the door.

Phil stepped quietly outside and stood for a moment after the door was closed. He started down the walk but stopped abruptly when he heard Ann crying again. It left him feeling helpless but then he continued on. He had done all he could, and Ann would somehow work out the rest for herself.

The balance of the day went reasonably well, and he was able to spend the entire evening at home without interruption. Maralyn asked about Ann as she had on occasion before, and Phil did say he made a house call earlier. He then quickly mentioned she'd be starting her chemotherapy tomorrow to emphasize the reason for the visit. Maralyn hoped she'd do all right but otherwise had little else to say. The following morning, Ann left a message with service that she was feeling better and would be keeping her appointment with Dr. Breiling. That gave Phil a bit of a lift and he felt even better later in the day when Dr. Breiling called to say Ann had been in for the first course of treatment and all had gone well. She had seemed to be in good spirits and even joked a bit, showing Dr. Breiling the wig she had bought to conceal the eventual hair loss. Phil thanked him for the call and felt much more at ease.

It remained quiet the rest of the week until Friday when Phil was given a message to page Malcolm Mueller after he finished his last case that morning. He did so and was asked to come to the Chief of Surgery's office to discuss an apparent problem that had just arisen. Dr. Mueller was alone and motioned to Phil to sit down as he closed the door behind them. His expression was unusually solemn.

"I asked you here, Phil, because I think you may be able to help with a situation that's just come up. It has a lot of us concerned. I'll come right to the point. This morning we received notice that a number of our hospital records are being subpoenaed by the district attorney's office. Now I want you to notice I said district attorney, not county attorney. We get a lot of requests from that office for comp cases and things like that, but this apparently is a very different type of situation. What makes it even more difficult to understand is that all the charts belong to just one person, Stan Stallings. Naturally, since this involves a person in the surgery department, I was the first staff member to be made aware of this. I couldn't give any explanation and I didn't mention anything else, but you don't get along very well with him. It's been a lot more obvious this past year or so. I just want to ask you, do you know anything about this?"

"I can't say that I do."

Dr. Mueller got up from his chair and began pacing behind his desk. He kept his eyes on the floor.

"I see. Well, I don't think it was unreasonable of me to ask the question. Anyway, this matter is of major concern to me and to the administration. We feel it cannot simply be left to take its own course, whatever that may be. Some other inquiries were made this morning. Our attorneys are friendly with many of their colleagues elsewhere, including the district attorney's office. They've made some phone calls for us. They weren't able to get much information, but the one name mentioned was yours. Are you sure there isn't something you can tell me?"

Phil was surprised and he suddenly felt very uncomfortable, but he just shook his head.

"No. I'm sorry, there's really nothing I can say."

Malcolm Mueller sat down again and swung his chair so they were facing each other.

"I'll be more specific with you, Phil, and very candid. Our source is someone who works in the district attorney's office. He couldn't tell us what this is about, but he did say he overheard your name mentioned. Now, I don't know what any of this means, but if you do, you should think very carefully about your position in all this. If this is something that is going to adversely affect the hospital and you are in any way involved or responsible, you're going to have a very uncertain future here, at best. You have that on my authority, and I'm sure I can speak for administration, as well."

Phil suddenly leaned forward in his seat. "Your authority? You're threatening me with your authority? Where the hell was your authority when you saw all the things that go on around here and did nothing about them? Where was the authority when cases were taken to the OR that never should have been done and we had to listen to all that bullshit afterwards telling us, yes, that was the right decision? Where was the authority then, Mal, that was supposed to stop that sort of thing? What were you doing, saving it until you could use it against someone like me?"

"So, it was you who went to the district attorney?"

"No, Mal, it wasn't me. It was you. If you'd only done your fucking job, there never would have been a problem and there never would have been a district attorney. *You* brought him here."

Malcolm Mueller's face was ashen and he was trembling. "You son of a bitch. God damn you! You think all I had to do was snap my fingers and every surgeon in this department would fall in line and do things just the way Phil Berger says they should be done." His voice was choked. "Phil Berger's always right, isn't he? If you don't do it Phil Berger's way, you're not doing it the right way. Forget about someone else's judgment, it's just Phil Berger's that counts. Forget that these other people also went to medical school, took surgical training programs, have the clinical experience, and sometimes more experience than Phil Berger has. That doesn't count. Only what Phil Berger says counts." Teeth clenched, Malcolm Mueller struggled to control himself.

"That's not it, and you know it," Phil said. "If you'd only stopped worrying about your own cases and your own practice so much, you'd have seen what I'm talking about. I'm not talking about cases where there's an honest difference of opinion. Stop trying to cover up. I'm talking about two or three guys, and really one in particular, who'll operate any time they have the least little excuse. That's not reasonable surgery or judgment. That's just greed and deceit."

Dr. Mueller's voice was barely audible. "You can't do anything about it." Phil stared at him, his face strained. He wasn't sure he had heard him correctly. "What did you just say? Did you say you can't do anything about it?"

"Yes," Dr. Mueller said. "You can't."

"I'll be damned! You *do* admit it. You *do* know that it goes on. And all the time you were making out like I was the one that was making a big issue out of nothing. Why you're nothing more than a goddamned fraud." He sank back in his chair.

"Careful, Phil. I know what I am but the liberty to express your opinions of me still has some limits. Be careful. It's just too bad you don't realize how many limits there really are. You think it's so easy to control everyone's actions in this department, to see that everything is done just so and according to all the proper standards. Well, I've got news for you. You can't. You can't watch each and every person in this department each and every minute. You can just hope everyone has enough ethics and moral sense to act accordingly. Even with that, I think we do a pretty good job. You don't see anyone going around killing his patients one after another, do you?"

Phil would have answered, but this certainly was not the time.

"You don't think I do very much. Let me tell you something, I've talked plenty with some of these surgeons, including your friend, Stanley. They're smart. They know just how much they can get away with and that's it. They're full of excuses and promises they'll be more careful the next time. What am I supposed to do, restrict their privileges? What grounds do I have for that? I'm sure to wind up in court and I don't even know what I'm trying to prove. Want me to get the state involved?

I can do that if we have someone who's incompetent. I don't think we have anyone like that and I sure as hell don't want them trying to decide if we do. You've heard some of the stories about their decisions. Come on, Phil. We can still try to work out our problems ourselves. We don't have to try to hurt each other."

"There are some people who may not feel that way," Phil said.

"Then I hope they know what they're getting themselves into. I don't know what this is about and for the life of me I don't know why the district attorney's office is being brought into this. If it means someone thinks something criminal has occurred, I can't see that as happening or I would have heard about it. I'm still chief of this department and regardless of what you may think, if all this does is make the hospital look bad, then whoever is responsible better start looking elsewhere. I think I can safely say, if that person is a doctor, they won't be able to continue their practice here."

"You're directing that last remark to me?"

"Only if it applies."

"Then I take it there's nothing else you have to say to me?"

"No, except that even though you can be irritating at times, you are a strong asset to this department. I would hope you're not making a mistake."

"I don't think so," Phil said, and got up and left.

Phil was incensed, partly because of the encounter he just had but much more by what he thought was carelessness and a betrayal by Gordon Mulcahey's staff. He hurried to a phone booth to call his office. He found Gordon just back from lunch.

"Hi Doc, what can I do for you?"

"I've run into a problem, Gordon, and it has me pretty upset."

"Go ahead and tell me what it is. Mrs. Hartway's OK, isn't she?"

"Yes, she's OK It has nothing to do with her. I'm the one with the problem, Gordon. Someone in your office was overheard mentioning my name regarding the investigation and this was passed on to the hospital's attorneys. They apparently began making inquiries in your office right after the hospital records were subpoenaed. I just spent a very unpleasant fifteen minutes or so with the Chief of Surgery who is trying to find out if anyone in the hospital is involved. He has me very high on his list of suspects and getting my name from someone in your office hasn't helped me convince him he's wrong. I'd hate to tell you how he's threatened me. I will say he had a very strong opinion about whether or not I should renew my office lease. I really don't need this right now, Gordon."

"I'm awfully sorry, Phil. If that did come from here, there's no excuse, but this isn't a secret organization and people can overhear things. Still, that information shouldn't be given out. I just wonder if he wasn't doing a little fishing and was just trying to draw you out. I hope you didn't say anything."

"No, I didn't. We did a little shouting, but that was about it."

"Good. Keep it that way and try to stay cool. If you think they're getting a little upset now, just wait until we get the indictment. Then you'll see the real fireworks. That's going to make the news media and what you went through today is nothing compared to what'll happen then."

"Oh, hell! You really think so? Peter Futterman said the same thing. I just thought we'd go into court and present all this evidence and try to get a jury to convict him. It never dawned on me there might be a lot of publicity. I guess I was hoping it would be very quiet and most people around here might not even hear about it."

"Are you kidding?" Gordon said. "This'll probably be front-page news all across the country and anyplace else where people can read, and someone has a printing press. Mark my words, Phil. This is going to be very big."

Suddenly Phil had another concern.

"That isn't the reason you're going after this case, is it, Gordon?"

"Come on, Phil, I think you should know me better by now. The only thing this case is liable to do for me is show the world how big an asshole I can really be. I'm sure I've told you I hate to lose cases or look like a fool in the courtroom, but this just may be the one where I really fall on my face. It's not going to be easy and maybe after it's over somebody's going to say it's my lease that shouldn't be renewed. When it comes to publicity, Phil, I've got to worry about some very bad personal publicity coming from this, not that it's going to be my ticket to some big, plush practice somewhere."

"I'm sorry," Phil said. "I'm completely new at this. Sometimes I really don't know what I should think. You don't sound so positive now."

"I go up and down. Sometimes I'm more of a realist than at others."

"And you think the hospital is going to look pretty bad in all this?"

"It's not going to look like some great citadel for the relief of the suffering."

"Maybe I haven't given that enough thought."

"I'm afraid it's a little too late for that, Phil, and besides, maybe the hospital deserves some bad press. After all, it did let these things happen. With something like this I think there's a price everyone should pay."

"A lot of good people are going to be hurt."

"You mean other doctors and the nurses who work at the hospital? If they're so good, why couldn't they see what was going on and do something about it? Why did it have to come down to this? Sorry, I don't buy it, Phil. This thing is gonna go where it wants to go and I don't have any sympathy for anyone it turns up who should've done something different. I don't think you should, either."

"But I have to work with these people."

"Then you have something else to consider, but I wouldn't make it too complicated. Our objective is to get a conviction and I wouldn't start worrying about other things that may interfere with that. Putting him away is too important. You agree with that, don't you?"

"Yes, but I thought it would be done very quietly. I didn't think this was the type of thing either side would want to publicize. Now you have me thinking of possibilities that never occurred to me and ones that I know I wouldn't like to see happen. It's not going to be easy to disregard any of this."

"Then I don't think you should," Gordon said, "as long as we can all remain resolved to bring about a conviction. I don't know what else to advise you, Phil."

"I understand. I don't think you really have to worry about me. My feelings about this whole thing aren't about to change."

"Good. Then I guess we're all set. I'm going before the Grand Jury just as soon as I can, possibly in two weeks, and things should really begin to roll after that. Call me about the middle of the week and I'll let you know where we stand. And Phil, I'm sorry about your name being mentioned. I know that can make problems for you. I just wish there was some way I could have prevented it."

"That's OK I'm sure I can survive that and a lot worse. I'll call you next week."

Phil had a lot more to worry about now. The hospital and its staff were certain to receive a great deal of adverse publicity and unfavorable public opinion and Phil did not agree with Gordon that this was entirely deserved. At a time when any hospital's image was becoming a very important consideration within the community it served, Middle Valley would unquestionably suffer very substantial damage. It disturbed him that so many would be stigmatized when only a relative few deserved that. Regarding his own susceptibility, he was much less apprehensive. He saw nothing in the attitude of his colleagues that suggested they either knew of the investigation at this point or of his possible complicity. Apparently, the hospital's administrators had not been able to obtain any further information and were simply awaiting the next development. Stanley Stallings certainly must have known that some sort of probe was in progress, but his actions did not indicate this. They frequently saw each other in the course of their routine activities and as always, he was most cordial. Finally, even if many of his colleagues eventually became very resentful, Phil felt the close relationship he had with so many of his patients and his outstanding reputation would sustain him and his practice.

Then there was Ann's current state of mind. Phil kept in touch with her almost daily by telephone to lend support and encouragement. As the date for the Grand Jury proceedings drew near, the strain upon her became much more obvious. She had brought her daughters home to explain what was about to happen, but they were too upset when they learned of her illness, and never really understood. Everyone was in a prolonged state of depression, and it took the combined efforts of Phil, Gordon and Donna Moreland over several days to help weather the emotional shock. Finally, the proceedings were held, and Gordon managed to obtain the indictment, but not without considerable difficulty. What seemed to influence the decision most was the apparent attack on Ann's life when the IV was disconnected, moments after Dr.

Stallings was seen on the floor. Gordon was satisfied but said it proved a much tougher fight lay ahead.

There had been enough warning so that Stanley Stallings could not have been unduly surprised that some action would be taken although he probably never thought it would be a criminal indictment. It was quite likely, however, that he was surprised by the number and presumed accuracy of the allegations. At his arraignment he naturally professed complete ignorance and it was obvious from his attorney's remarks that his defense would rely heavily on their contention that the charges were the result of the deluded imagination of an irrational, terminally ill cancer patient. Ann had been warned to expect this but still found it upsetting to have her condition described in this manner and her emotional stability called into question. Offsetting this to a considerable degree was the support she received from her immediate family, which comprised mostly Jack's relatives. They remembered how insistent Jack was to have the bypass and then adamantly refused the amputation that would have saved his life. It was inconceivable to them that his wife could have played any role in determining the course of those events. Like some others, they thought she was guilt-ridden and delusional and with two young girls who would soon lose their only parent, they were very sympathetic to her. As for Dr. Stallings, he had clearly botched Jack's surgery and if the authorities now felt a criminal act had occurred, then so be it. They would be there to help Ann as much as possible and see justice done.

The media was very cautious in its initial coverage and tried to take an even-handed approach to all this although it was frequently mentioned that Ann's illness had to cast some doubt on her reliability. The medical community, as would be expected, had a much stronger opinion. There was widespread anger and disbelief that charges of this sort could be brought against a seemingly reputable surgeon. Phil could not be sure how his role was being regarded and looked for tell-tale signs as he went about the hospital. Some physicians, knowing that Phil had been one of the last to treat Ann, sought him out to ask if he thought she was mentally competent and if there was any evidence the cancer had traveled to her brain. Others were very clearly distant and reserved. Initially he thought paranoia, for which there was ample reason, might be causing him to misjudge them but when several of his colleagues overtly ignored him, he realized they had to feel he was somehow involved. Stanley Stallings, of course, had changed. No longer imperturbably affable, the few times they chanced upon each other there were brief stares and then Dr. Stallings would look away and busy himself, completely disregarding Phil's presence. He welcomed other doctors, however, many of whom came up to him to voice their support. Phil could only observe and let the matter take its own course.

At home there was yet another problem. Phil had made certain to tell Maralyn of the indictment just after it was handed down. He didn't want her to hear about it secondhand and felt he owed her a lengthy explanation. He described everything, how Ann had come to him in the first place, her conversations with Dr. Stallings, other procedures he had performed and the patients who died, the attempt on Ann's life a few weeks ago. Maralyn was astounded. Phil hoped she understood now why he had to be so secretive. He patiently answered question after question as Maralyn tried to fathom everything he said. She was very concerned with the repercussions this might bring. She reminded him he had a wife and two daughters, a comfortable home, a respected place in the community and a good practice he had worked hard to build. He could be jeopardizing all this. Phil said he was fully aware of this, but once Ann Hartway had spoken to him, he no longer had a choice. Regardless of the outcome, he still didn't think he'd be hurt. Maralyn simply reiterated that it was fine for him to be so moral and idealistic but what of the price he might have to pay. All Phil could do was reassure her it would all work out. One thing was agreed. No one else must know of his involvement. Afterwards they would have this same conversation time and time again and always with the same conclusion. It placed a strain on both of them.

The strain was even greater on Ann Hartway. Gordon and Phil spoke frequently to discuss her condition and progress. It was felt her emotional state would improve as she gained strength, but she continued to tire very easily. The ongoing question was how much improvement would there be and for how long? Phil remained optimistic and for the present this seemed to satisfy Gordon, but Ann required constant encouragement. Present circumstances had made her virtually a recluse, venturing out only for her medical treatments and this had to have an adverse effect. No one had a better suggestion, however.

In the midst of all this Phil was paid a visit by Gary Barlow. He had called while Phil was in his office and wanted to stop by for a few minutes if Phil wasn't busy. He was told to come over whenever he could and about twenty minutes later, he was ushered into the office. He fidgeted a bit after he sat down and seemed uncomfortable. There was the usual small talk at first.

"Have you been to the hospital very much the past few days?" Gary finally asked.

"A little. It's been quiet," Phil said.

"I didn't think I'd seen you much. Talk to any of the guys?"

"Not really. One or two, maybe."

"Run into Malcolm Mueller at all, while you were there?"

"No. I can't remember that I saw him."

"You know what's been going on, though, don't you?" Phil nodded.

"You probably don't hear the same things I do, though. Some people are saying that you might have started this whole thing. I'm not sure where they're getting their information. They may just be guessing but Malcolm Mueller seems to think he knows a little more than anyone else and I've been told he's had some pretty nasty things to say about you."

"What has he been saying?"

"I don't know. I haven't spoken to him directly. It's just what I hear from the others. I guess he knows we're very friendly and he just won't say anything to me. It's not just him, though. A lot of people are mad and most of them think you're working with Mrs. Hartway. You did operate on her and you're still taking care of her. Everyone remembers how critical you've been of Stanley and the way he manages his patients. Some of them are talking about taking some sort of action against you. I don't know what they think they can do but frankly, I'm getting very concerned, and I think you should be, too. I don't want to see you get hurt."

"Isn't this just a little bit premature?" Phil asked. "I haven't admitted anything; Stanley hasn't, and neither of us has been convicted yet."

Gary scowled. "It's not a joke, Phil. Everyone agrees someone on the surgical staff has to be helping the DA's office. A few of the guys have said it's unfair to think it's you just because you're taking care of her but a lot of the others say it has to be you. Look how many times you used to ask me about him. I'm even afraid to tell you what I think. And don't forget, the chief of the department is putting the word out and who knows how many people he's talked to."

Phil shrugged. He was totally noncommittal.

"Look. Please understand why I'm here. I don't know if you are involved or to what extent. If you are, you have only my respect and gratitude. It's something that I unfortunately just wouldn't be able to do, even though you know how I feel about that prick. If he's really done the things we're hearing about now, then it's much worse than I ever thought and I'm just thankful someone has finally begun to put a stop to it. It's something we all should have done, and I feel very badly that I didn't do more but I'm not like you. I don't let myself get into these things the way you do. I'm not into peer review and quality assurance and all those things that you always get involved with. I don't think it means I care any less for my profession than you do. I just can't handle that stuff. It's aggravation. I have to tell you something I've never told anyone else. You know how I am. Most people know I'm a good surgeon but most of the time I give the impression of being a clown. I almost gave all this up once, no, actually twice. I was in my residency, and we had a cystic hygroma of the neck to do in an eight-year-old kid. I was the assistant resident on pediatric surgery, and I had to help the senior resident do the case. You remember how it was in your training. There wasn't anything you didn't know about the patient. You prepared for everything so you wouldn't screw up and have some attending come down on you and tear you apart. We were operating and everything seemed to be going fine. I remember it was a very big lobulated cyst. All of a sudden, we notice a bare hand in the wound. We were so absorbed in what we were doing we didn't know where it came from or what it was doing. Next thing we realize it's the anesthesiologist and he's feeling for the carotid pulse. Somehow the kid got away from him and arrested. I don't know if it was the anesthesia or hyperthermia or what. I know his temperature was 106. He was on a respirator for a couple of days and then he died. I didn't come in for a few days after that. I figured even if you broke your ass and gave your patient the very best care possible and then someone else drops the ball and this sort of thing happens, maybe I'd better look for some other kind of work. Then I decided that wasn't the way to deal with that, so I went back. Right after I get back, the kid's father shows up on the floor with a big sack filled with his son's toys and says he knows his son would have wanted the other kids on the floor to have them. So right back out again I went, this time for a week. When I came back it was decided, and not just by me, that I was going to have to change my whole attitude if I was going to make it. Even now I still can't handle really sick kids."

Gary's eyes glistened.

"You remember Billy Hickman? I felt I had to go to the wake. After all, I knew the family and he had been my patient for so long. I watched his brothers and sisters kissing and hugging him, brushing his hair, and stuffing his pockets with all his favorite toys. They even put his old beat-up sneakers in the casket with him. I just made it out into the parking lot before I cried like a baby. Thank God it was at night, and no one could see me. That's the only time that's happened to me since I've been in practice. I learned way back if I continued to take everything like that, I'd wind up a basket case. I loosened up. I never gave the patients any less. They always got as good care as they would get anywhere, and they still do. I don't think you'll disagree with that. But I had to make it easier for myself and I just started looking for some relief and that's when the clowning began. It's my way. I start looking for something to joke about the minute I walk in the hospital each morning. It got me through Vietnam, and it gets me through here. You don't seem to need anything and maybe you don't, but I'm convinced most guys do. Did you ever notice how it was in your residency when an attending had to give some bad news to a family? These guys were always so abrupt and matter-of-fact. I could never understand it back then. I always wanted to grab them and tell them those were real people and you just told them someone had cancer or died and that was a loved one and couldn't you show some compassion or sympathy, but that was their way. They knew they couldn't let themselves show or feel anything more. I couldn't be like that, so I let it all hang out but then I'm always looking for a little humor to get me back on track. I started doing it back then and I do it now. Christ, how else could anyone have expected us to get through Vietnam?

Every day guys would go out and then later they would come back in, some with their feet blown off, some without their legs. And most of the time they never even saw the enemy. It was all booby traps. We'd finish the amputations and close the holes in the gut and repair the arteries and veins and this would go on day after day. You know how we pronounced guys over there? You'd get called up to Graves. I never had to go much since I was a surgeon but every so often, I'd get called. A medic would bend over and look the other way while he unzipped the bag. You'd stand back as far as you could and then sort of just peek into the bag. You never knew what you were going to see. Almost everything was gunshot wound to the chest. There might not be any chest, but the cause of death was still gunshot wound, chest. Once I remember there wasn't anything in the bag but big clumps of dirt. The medic said there really was something in there but that's all they could find. I think with that one we finally had to draw the line. Gunshot wound, chest, no matter how we stretched it before, just wasn't going to make it. That one became extensive shrapnel wounds chest, abdomen, and extremities. Of course, there wasn't any chest, abdomen or extremities. There wasn't even any shrapnel. Tell me. How were we supposed to handle that?"

Phil had been listening very carefully.

"I don't know," he said.

"And I don't know either," Gary said, "and I don't know what all this has meant, and I don't know what's really going on at the hospital and I don't know if you're involved and I guess I really don't know much of anything. I really just wanted to tell you in case those things I'm hearing at the hospital are true, you better think of some way to cover your ass. And if they are true, I think you're doing a tremendous thing and I'm truly embarrassed that I'm not doing more to help you, but I have to admit I just couldn't hack it. I just hope you don't go down the tubes for this. I may be a little selfish, too. There's no one else over here I prefer to scrub with."

Phil managed to smile. "I appreciate what you said, Gary, and I understand. I'm also grateful for the information. I didn't realize there was that much animosity towards me. There's really not much more I can say. I don't want the hospital hurt by this thing, and I don't want to see anyone on staff hurt, including myself, except for the one person who deserves it. I'm really not the one responsible for this and I think the others should hold off in their accusations. In the meantime, there's really not much else I can do except make rounds, take care of my patients and more than ever before, try not to screw up."

Gary stood up, smiled, and extended his hand. "Take care," he said.

As he left, Phil called after him. "If you hear anything else, don't forget to let me know. What's a little more grief?"

Once he was alone, he became very worried that much of what Gary said could be true. He never doubted that he might bring some resentment to himself but now it seemed much more than he expected. For a while he had been thinking of speaking with Brandon McAleer, his former chief of surgery at University Hospital, and asking his advice. This seemed a most appropriate time. It certainly made sense to look into obtaining surgical privileges at another institution if he was going to be harassed It was a troubling decision and he felt he should discuss it with Maralyn even though he knew it would upset her. He mentioned it to her that evening after dinner and as expected, she did not take it well. She wanted to be supportive but could not understand how he could take such risk with their future. At one point she asked if he really thought Ann Hartway was worth all this. Phil reminded her the more serious issue was not with Ann, but with Dr. Stallings and that effective action had to be taken. Maralyn wanted to know why he felt it was his responsibility and Phil said he was the only one who knew the situation well enough to believe the charges. And if he was wrong? Well, he was quite sure he wasn't and anyway, this was now for a jury to decide. He admitted he was worried, but he was satisfied it had to be this way. Maralyn still had very grave misgivings and felt he was being unrealistic. She remained very apprehensive and bitter, and nothing further was resolved. Phil had planned to make his call the following afternoon but just before that, he was contacted by Gordon Mulcahey. Gordon was in need of some information and thought Phil would be able to get it for him. He gave him three names, one a patient and the other two probably relatives of patients who had been at Middle Valley. He wanted Phil to find out whatever he could about these patients and let him know what he thought. He preferred not to give any other information until Phil reviewed the charts and called him with his impressions. As a result, Phil never got to speak with Brandon McAleer and returned to the hospital late that afternoon.

The accounting office was able to provide the two names he needed and a short time later he was seated in a cubicle in the record room with all three charts in front of him. Each of the three had been patients of Stanley Stallings, which was not entirely unexpected. The first, Ida Tedesco, was seventy-four years old when she was operated upon three years earlier for persistent abdominal pain and a mass in the body of the pancreas of indeterminate histological type. Multiple needle biopsies had been inconclusive and Dr. Stallings had pushed for surgery although the patient still had severe asthma attacks. Medical clearance was eventually obtained, and the patient died on the sixth post-operative day of respiratory failure. No tumor was found. The second patient, George Dulcimer, was operated on six years earlier at the age of seventy-seven for a suspected leaking abdominal aortic aneurysm. He had been known to have a small aneurysm and multiple previous episodes of renal colic. He arrived in the emergency room one morning with severe flank pain and an ileus. For whatever reason, this time there was much greater concern about the aneurysm, and he was quickly taken to surgery and explored. The aneurysm was intact, but it was elected to resect it. The patient died of renal failure ten days later, a small stone still lodged in the right ureter, which remained partially obstructed. The third patient, Cecil Armbruster, was a forty-seven-year-old cirrhotic with so-called chronic relapsing pancreatitis who underwent a partial pancreatectomy five years earlier and barely made it off the operating table. Phil vaguely remembered the case. The patient died of massive hemorrhage shortly after arriving in the recovery room. Phil wondered how Gordon knew about these patients. All three fit the same pattern as the others who were now being investigated. Each had questionable indications for surgery, additional serious medical problems, and the same end result. Phil had not been overly critical of these cases at the time but now someone who was not even a physician was calling his attention to them. He remained completely mystified until he reached Gordon in his home later that evening.

"You have to tell me, Gordon. How did you know to have me look up these three cases?"

"Why? Did I hit paydirt?"

"Don't you know?"

"No. I'm waiting for you to tell me."

"I think you may have three more cases like Jack Hartway and Frank Spalding and the others." Phil went on to describe and compare them at length. Gordon said nothing until Phil was finished.

"I must admit that's what I suspected," he finally answered. "It wasn't really clairvoyance or any great detective work. Keep this just between the two of us: I've had all his phone lines tapped ever since the indictment. He's had all sorts of phone calls but the families of these three patients never stopped calling and he's never returned the calls unless he's done it from the outside. I think one of them called over twenty times. What do you make of that now that you know what happened to their relatives?"

"I'll be damned. You mean it's been going on that much?"

"I can't say at this point, but it would certainly seem that way. We keep thinking we see the iceberg but maybe it's just the tip. Whichever it is, something keeps getting bigger. I'll have to get some people working on this right away to see how much it's going to help us. I certainly need more proof. At this point it's just a lot more innuendo and I already have more of that than I really need. We still have a long way to go before we're ready to walk into court and time is not on our side. I really can't imagine any case being more difficult."

"You are making progress though, aren't you?"

"Oh, yes, but we're also drawing a lot of blanks and I don't know if we'll have enough hard evidence when it comes time to present our case. I'll have to do that while Ann can still be a good witness and that means I'll probably have to ask to have the trial date moved up. I'll need a note from you for that. That means we'll have less time to prepare. I also don't know what the other attorney will do. He may not go along with that and claim he needs more time for his defense. If Ann can't make it all the way through — and from what you've been telling me, she hasn't shown that much improvement — we may not have any case at all. I don't think that will happen, though. We've been given a very decent judge and I'm pretty sure he would move the case up after I've explained the situation to him. I also think Stallings' attorney would want to see this go to trial.

It would look bad for his client otherwise and I'm sure he feels he can win this thing hands down. At this point I'm not so sure I would disagree. Have you noticed, I haven't said a thing about psychiatrists, emotional disorders, or Mellaril?"

"They don't have to know that, do they?"

"Well, I'm sure as hell not going to tell them. Let them find that out. That's their job."

"You're worried about that?"

"Not as long as they don't know. We know what it was all about, but can you imagine what it would sound like to a jury? Ann has to be discredited. I'm sure you realize what his attorney would try to do with that."

Phil suddenly turned very pale. "I just remembered! That's probably in her hospital record."

"Really? You think so?"

"Yes! Patients are always asked what medications they're on when they come into the hospital." He fidgeted in his seat. "Maybe she decided not to tell them. I don't know."

Gordon remained placid and noncommittal. "You don't seem to be bothered by this."

"There's really nothing I can do about it."

Phil slumped against the back of his chair. "You're not exactly making me feel very confident about this."

"No, I'm not, but I will promise you we'll give it one hell of a shot. If I haven't told you already, there are just two things I detest. One is to lose a case and the other is to look like a fool in court. I can't always control the first but if I enter a courtroom, you can be damned sure I ain't ever going to look like a fool. That much I'll guarantee you. However, it might be a good idea for you to play it safe and have some other options, if things don't go well. Are they still giving you a rough time at the hospital?"

"It's hard to tell. I don't notice it that much but it's common knowledge someone has to be working with your group and a lot of people think it's me. That leak from your office was probably the most damaging thing but there's nothing I can do about that now. I guess I can say I get a cold shoulder from a fair number of people these days. Certainly, no one's patted me on the back."

"How about Dr. Stallings? His behavior towards you change any?"

"He hasn't really said anything to me. I guess he's ignoring me, too."

"No vindictiveness or hostility that you've been able to notice?"

"No, not really."

Well, in a sense, that's really too bad. He seems like a remarkably self-controlled individual and I guess that's just what you'd expect. Just in case he does come after you, say with a pistol or a scalpel or tries to run you over, I would like you to let me know. That's the sort of thing we could really use."

"Gee, thanks a lot!"

"Especially if you had witnesses."

"Come on, Gordon."

"Hey, what's a little joke between friends? Anyway, I will need a note from you. Just something that says Ann's condition is not good and in your medical opinion the trial should be held at an earlier date. That should let us stretch things safely and still get into court while she's in reasonable shape. Does that sound OK to you?"

"Yes, but I do have a question. What did you mean before when you said I might want to have some options?"

"When was that?"

"When you were talking about how the case might go, when you said you don't like to lose cases or look like a fool."

"Oh, that. Well, I just thought if the decision goes against us, it could get pretty rough for you at the hospital. You might want to think of another affiliation until things settle down. I don't know how it works in your profession, but I imagine you're still going to have to earn a living. I know there has to be some concern in that area."

"More so with my wife than with me, and exactly for the reason you mentioned. I will be looking into something else though, just to be safe."

"Does your wife know much?"

"It's a long story. I told her everything right after the indictment."

"Does she think you've done the right thing?"

"She's having a hard time. She's very worried."

"Then you've got it at home as well as the hospital."

"You could say that."

"God bless you, Phil. I just hope to hell when it's over we're all going to feel it's been worth it. It's one thing when someone is feeding you to the lions and you don't have a choice, but when you're doing it to yourself, you really have to wonder. You agree?"

"You want to start discussing ethics and morality now, Gordon?"

"No, anything but that, Phil." Gordon laughed. It was the first time anyone had laughed during the entire conversation.

"I think it's best if we just hang up now. Listen, thanks for that information. We'll stay in touch, OK?"

"Sure, Gordon. So long."

It was more difficult now to maintain a positive outlook. Phil remained hopeful but he began to wonder how much longer he would be able to cope with all this. Surgery and patient care, no matter how complicated the problem, was a welcome respite, unquestionably the easier of the two. Most nights he would lay awake, thinking about this and that night was no exception. Nor was it any better for Maralyn. Very often she could not sleep and the two of them lying side by side, awake, only added to the strain. The mornings offered little relief.

XIV

Phil looked forward to the meeting with Dr. McAleer with mixed feelings. He needed the support of someone in his position but wasn't sure how McAleer would accept his explanation of his current problems. Phil wasn't certain if anything he could say would sound convincing. He was very uneasy during the drive to Dr. McAleer's office and kept mulling over a myriad thoughts. The added distance had its drawbacks. If he did become more active at University Hospital, much greater time would be needed for travel, leaving that much less time to be spent at home. Even though they weren't getting along so well right now, he was certain that would annoy Maralyn even more. This hadn't been a pleasant trip and now, as he drew closer to the hospital, the congestion of the city streets made it a lot worse. He eventually found a parking garage that still had vacancies and walked the remaining three blocks to the hospital. Many of the sights remained familiar and filled him with nostalgia. He was early and would have liked to walk through several of the floors and recall some of his past experiences but was afraid someone might recognize him. He wanted to avoid having to explain why he was there.

The appointment had been made a just a few days earlier for two p.m. and Phil thought he would have to wait when he arrived in the office. Dr. McAleer was already there, however, and immediately came out to greet him. Now in his early sixties, he was still robust with the broad smile Phil remembered so well.

"Phil! You look terrific."

"You look very well too, sir. I want to thank you for seeing me."

Dr. McAleer ushered Phil into his private office and motioned to him to sit down.

"No thanks necessary, Phil. I just wish more of you fellows would stop by to let me know how things are going. Do you ever get in touch with any of the other people from your group?"

"No sir, I don't."

"Well, I suppose we all get a little too busy for that sort of thing. I guess they're pretty well spread out around the country. You're not too far away, though. Close enough for me to get reports about you from time to time. I've heard a lot of good things about you, Phil, and I can't say that I was ever surprised. You were a very fine surgeon while you were here."

"Thank you, sir."

"That's your hometown where you're practicing now, isn't it?"

"Yes, it is."

"It's gotten a few headlines recently, hasn't it?"

"Yes, sir. That's why I'm here."

Dr. McAleer nodded as he sat back in his chair.

"I have to admit I thought of that. The situation you have out at your place has been quite a topic of conversation around here. I certainly don't know what to think. I've listened to the television reports and read everything the newspapers have to say, which really hasn't been much. I assume there's a lot more that isn't being said or else somebody has definitely gone off the deep end. Would I be out of line if I asked if you're involved in some way?"

Phil took a deep breath. "Whether or not I am, there's an awful lot of people who think so. That may eventually cause some very serious problems for me."

"Good lord, I see what you mean. But if this story is true, they might as well close up that whole hospital. You won't be the only person hurt." He thought for a moment. "I remember you in your residency. You were always so honest, a stickler for even the smallest detail. I can see you getting involved in something like this, but there has to be some reason why they think you are. I'm not trying to play detective, but you must have some idea what that is."

"I'd rather not say. I did operate on the woman who's the primary witness and I'm still taking care of her. I guess it may be guilt by association."

"She's very sick according to the news reports."

"She is."

Dr. McAleer shook his head.

"You know, I've held this position over fifteen years, and I've been practicing surgery for more than thirty years, but I've never heard of anything like this. I can't even imagine anyone in our profession thinking of something like this. What's the explanation? If this turns out to be true, it's going to be devastating for all of us. There are so many challenges facing us. This is the last thing that we need now."

He looked at Phil but did not get any response.

"You know what frightens me? Let's say this surgeon did whatever he's accused of. Then how do you explain it? Is he an aberration or could there be others? Think about this. Why would he do it? I wonder if it has anything to do with the kind of medicine we practice today.

"Look at the changes we're seeing. They're tremendous, more than ever before. Besides health reform and managed care, look at all the technological advances, organ transplantation, joint replacement, CT, the MRI. The future will be even more amazing. Look at the work in genetics and intrauterine surgery. No one could possibly disagree that medicine is vastly superior today and yet our problems are so much greater and so complex. We rely so heavily on technology and now we have to worry if we're using it properly. We used to spend much more time with the patient but that was because we didn't have as much to offer. The history and physical exam meant a great deal more. You got to know the patient a lot better, and the patient got to know you."

He leaned back in his chair and sighed.

"You think we could practice that kind of medicine today? With reimbursements the way they are, you'd go broke in no time and there's no way any amount of time at the bedside can equal what a CT scan will show. If a patient complains of right upper quadrant pain and fatty food intolerance, how much more history do you need before you order an ultrasound to get your diagnosis? If the patient's very sick, how much time will you spend each day examining him compared to the time you'll spend reviewing his chemistries, EKGs, x-rays, scans, blood gases, monitors? What do you rely on more to tell you how the patient is doing? His parameters, not him. Even when you know they're going out on you, you don't try to comfort or reassure. You're too busy intubating or pushing dopamine or defibrillating. You're battling numbers and conditions and who's to say that isn't the way it should be but look how impersonal it's made us with our patients."

Suddenly, he leaned forward. "Here we're talking away and I've really forgotten myself. Can I get you something, Phil? Coffee, a cold drink?"

"No, thank you. I'm fine."

"It's no trouble. I just have to flash my secretary."

"No, thanks. I'm really OK."

"Well, just speak up if you change your mind." He leaned back.

"Anyway, I can't help thinking about this. That thing at your hospital has been on my mind so damned much. Now that I have you here, I'd like to know more. Somehow, we have to understand what's happened, if there's any truth to it." He paused and looked at Phil. "Is there?"

"Is there what, sir?"

"You're not being coy with me, are you, Phil? Is there any truth to these reports?"

"I'm not the jury, Dr. McAleer."

"You don't have an opinion?"

"I'd rather not say. It wouldn't mean anything."

"It would to me, but never mind. That's OK." He reached over and riffled through a thick stack of papers on his desk. "You see these? Know what they are? They're denials and rejections of length of stays from HMOs and PPOs. I'm afraid we've become very defenseless. That's what we have with managed care. If you're not allowed into a particular plan and it's offered to some of your patients, you're not going to see them again. Even with those you can who belong to HMOs and PPOs, you have to send them right back to their primary physicians after you've treated them. You can't follow them for anything else unless they send them back to you. How does this allow you to have a strong doctor-patient relationship? It takes a lot of the satisfaction away from the practice of medicine. Everyone admits it's not as enjoyable anymore. This doesn't affect me so much since I'm full-time, but it must be a terrible problem for people like yourself in private practice. I wonder how many of us would have still gone into medicine, if we knew this was going to happen? You would, wouldn't you?"

"Yes."

"Of course. Anyway, it also makes you wonder what our medical societies are doing about this. They claim the AMA has one of the most powerful lobbies in Washington. I don't see it."

He motioned towards his desk again.

"Those papers I showed you, the denials, we get them anytime a patient is kept in for three days. Know why? It's because the reimbursement from the HMOs goes up significantly after the first two days. No matter what, they never approve a third day. That's part of their cost control. If it's more than three days, fine, but never that one extra day. I'd like to spend more time out on the floors working with the residents. Instead, I have to deal with this. How is a practitioner supposed to feel if he knows neither he nor the hospital will be reimbursed no matter how sound his judgment? This surgeon at your hospital, can anyone say he really cares for his patients? If the charges are true, of course not, but how the hell did he get this way? Did the medicine we practice today make him that way?"

"I wouldn't want to think so," Phil said. "I think it has to be the individual."

"You're probably right, but what kind of message are we sending with all these changes and all this technology? This surgeon operated on people he shouldn't have, right? Did he forget what they were? Did he stop caring about them? Or did he think our technology and his efforts would overcome their problems? Did he become unrealistic? Has technological improvement changed some of our attitudes and altered our judgment?"

"It shouldn't, Dr. McAleer, if I understand you correctly. I don't think that's any excuse for what he's done."

Dr. McAleer shook his head. "I'm not trying to make excuses for him. I'm trying to understand him. You know, we all have a responsibility to our profession. Mine is probably greater because I'm the head of a department and I supervise a large training program. I always have to be thinking of the message we're sending to the young surgeons and sometimes I come up with the damnedest notions. Were you here when we made the switch from the cloth gowns and drapes in the operating room to the disposables?"

"Yes, I remember."

"Well, I never liked disposables even though they've become a fact of life. I used to think of some of the big names who probably used the same gowns and drapes we were given. Today you put on a gown and just before that, it was on some tree in a forest somewhere. You'd be amazed how much I fought and resisted at board meetings, and they'd keep showing me the figures on how much more economical they were. Of course, I finally had to give in. It wasn't that the cloth gowns felt better, and instruments were less likely to slide off cloth drapes. I just felt we were losing more and more of our tradition. To me those cloth drapes and gowns represented something. You're probably going to think this sounds ridiculous, but I thought if all these things are used only once and then thrown away, couldn't we eventually begin to regard patients in the same way?"

He paused, as if expecting Phil to reply.

"Pretty crazy thought, huh, but the fact is all this technology could undermine a lot of our traditional thinking and values. Maybe to some people the patient is less important than the technology." He pointed to a CT scan hanging from an x-ray view box. "Look at the sophisticated studies being done on eighty- and ninety-year-old senile patients. I suppose the malpractice situation has a lot to do with that, but still, these patients warrant that kind of attention? Maybe that's what happened with your surgeon. Maybe he's gotten the wrong message. Today there aren't many situations where you just have to throw up your hands and admit you can't do anything more. You just have to have the good judgment or sense of ethics to say when you shouldn't. Maybe this surgeon can't do that. Maybe to him the primary thing is the technology, and the patient is secondary, like the disposables I told you about. He's got to keep using that technology. There's a lot of people like that in the profession, but I'll admit he sounds like the worst." He paused and then gave Phil a perplexed look. "How'd we get on this subject anyway?"

"I was telling you about the problems I'm having at my hospital."

"I know," Dr. McAleer said. "I was just joking. I'll bet you never expected me to go off like that."

"I am surprised at some of the things you said. I guess I had no idea how someone like you might view our profession. You apparently give it a lot of thought."

"Well, don't forget, Phil, I run a pretty big department with lots of different people and personalities doing things lots of different ways. Sometimes you have to try to tie everything together. That's when I usually get these ideas. I don't think they're profound. They're just useful for trying to see the big picture, if there is such a thing."

Phil smiled. The conversation had been interesting but thus far had only touched on the reason for his visit.

"I started to say before, Dr. McAleer, that I may be in for a fairly rough time for a while at my hospital. It's occurred to me that it might be wise to start seeing patients elsewhere, at least until I see what the situation will be at Middle Valley. Frankly, I was wondering if there might be an opportunity of that sort here, either part-time or in a clinic, something to keep me going in case they really try to freeze me out."

Dr. McAleer frowned. "Do you think it could really come to that?"

"I hope I'm overreacting, but it could happen. I see a lot of patients by word of mouth, but I still need referrals from other physicians."

Dr. McAleer shifted in his chair and smiled. "I'm sure something could be worked out. You know I always thought of you as one of our best. I'd certainly love to have you back with us again. We could probably start off letting you take some emergency room calls. Sometimes the patients have pretty decent insurance. We should have some applications on hand but if we don't, we'll send you one and you'll send it back with your curriculum vitae."

"Thank you."

"Don't be silly. I'm very happy to do this. It would still have to go before our board of directors but there shouldn't be any problem. I think I still have some influence in this institution. Normally we require a letter of recommendation from the head of your department. Do you think there'll be a problem with that?"

"Probably not, although I don't know how far he can go. I've had a very good record."

"Well, we'll take that into consideration. One other question. What will happen if your situation doesn't change, and you remain as busy as you are now? I know you have a pretty decent drive to get here."

"About twenty-five miles. I guess if I couldn't give you enough time, then I would give up the position."

"Fair enough. I don't think we would like to give privileges and then have them resigned, but it's an understandable situation. I would be happy with whatever is best for you, Phil."

"Thank you very much, sir. You've given me a lot more reassurance. I'm very grateful."

Phil stood as Dr. McAleer came around his desk. They shook hands.

"Talking to you today did me a lot of good too, Phil. I got a lot off my chest, which I wouldn't have otherwise. Don't feel I'm doing this only for you. University Hospital stands to gain quite a bit from this, too."

Phil managed a somewhat embarrassed smile. He hadn't expected quite this response. Dr. McAleer walked him to the door.

"How's your family? I meant to ask earlier."

"They're fine, sir. One will be in high school soon."

"How many children?"

"Two girls."

"And your wife? I remember you introduced us at a dinner. That was after you left here and if I recall correctly, you had just gotten married."

"Your memory's excellent, Dr. McAleer. That was quite a while ago. That was Maralyn. She's very well, thank you."

Dr. McAleer placed a hand on Phil's shoulder.

"You've done well. Don't forget to ask Eleanor if she has any forms. You'll keep in touch with me, and I'll try to expedite your application. I also want to wish you good luck with that situation at your hospital. As you can see, it worries me, and quite a few others, too. I guess that's because none of us can understand it and we're all afraid it's going to hurt our profession. I just hope it can be resolved fairly. I'm sure you've been in court before. That can easily become one great big crapshoot and you know how much the lawyers just love to give us a bad name. I don't see anything good coming out of this except that we might be getting rid of a real bad apple. You know, I still have to think some of the people in your department had to know some of this was going on. There must be internal procedures to ferret out things like this. Your place is accredited just like this one and I don't see how it could ever happen here."

Phil looked at him quietly and Dr. McAleer sensed what he was thinking.

"You're trying to tell me something. Well, I don't have all the details you have and maybe I'm naive. One of these days I guess that's something we'll all find out." He held the door open. "I'm glad to have you with us."

Phil left the office feeling relieved and certainly more encouraged. The secretary did not have any applications. One would be sent to him and then his appointment would merely require the formality of approval by the board of directors. Traffic was light during the drive home and he carefully clocked the time. It took forty-two minutes to reach Middle Valley Hospital and he did not feel his speed was excessive. That made him feel even better.

There was less anxiety now and Maralyn even found some consolation in Dr. McAleer's very gracious response. Tension at home had diminished and Phil was much less aware of rebuffs and the like in the hospital. It was as if a substantial degree of normalcy had returned to his life. More than a week went by uneventfully.

A brief interruption came in the form of a surprise visit by Gordon Mulcahey. He appeared unannounced one afternoon just before Phil was about to start office hours. The secretary brought him to the consultation room where Phil had been working on insurance forms. Neither spoke until the secretary had left and Gordon closed the door behind her.

"Surprised? A little bit of cloak-and-dagger. You never can be sure when or where one of us will turn up."

Phil smiled and looked befuddled. "I spoke to you just a few days ago."

"Yes, but when things happen, they happen." He sat down. "I wanted to speak to you in person. First of all, I thought we almost had the clincher yesterday. You pay attention to this."

"We had Mrs. Tedesco's family in yesterday, just informally to get some background information. We were up front and told them we were just inquiring into Dr. Stallings' activities and checking on some of the surgery he had performed. No one was making any accusations or had any suspicions. All of a sudden, the daughter-in-law gets very flustered and starts saying that it was a mistake, that they didn't understand Dr. Stallings and he was wrong when he thought they agreed. Her husband then shut her up and wouldn't let her say anything more. He wouldn't make any more statements without a lawyer, and we had to let them go. It wouldn't have done any good anyway. We couldn't have used anything they said without a lawyer being present. Neither of the other two would come down without a lawyer so we told them we'd let them know. Pretty interesting, wouldn't you say?"

"Yes!"

"Number two, I've spoken with the judge whom I happen to know very well. It's Charlie Perrine. I don't think we could have gotten anyone else who would be more reasonable or fair. He's very sympathetic to our problem and will put the case on any time we want. Furthermore, and this is really key, he's going to let us use all the evidence we've gathered, even when it doesn't specifically pertain to Jack Hartway, per se. There's a very strong legal issue here that I was very much afraid of, but Stallings' lawyer has agreed to let us use anything without challenging it and the judge has agreed to go along with that. I think his attorney feels there's no way we can make our case so the more we throw at them, the more he can make a shambles of our arguments. One thing he certainly has to do at the trial is make Dr. Stallings appear as lily-white and unjustly accused as he possibly can and his best way to do that is to let us use everything we can and just beat us down each and every time. If you like to watch football, that's what this trial is going to be like. He's going to let us take the ball wherever we want to go and he's confident he can stop us whether we run or pass, go long or short. It's a good strategy. I just hope ours works better. One thing I'm not telling them about until the trial is the tape. That's touchy but it might make him change his whole tune right now so I'm going to save that for a surprise later on. We're in as good position now as we could ever hope to be. What I do need, though, is more time. I could use at least another couple of months. I know you've seen Ann recently. I'd like to know if I have that time."

Phil winced and shook his head. "That's always a tough question. There could be a problem at any time. I'd have to see her again and talk to her. I think we'll be OK but it's always going to be a gamble."

"I know that. Just see what you think and get back to me. I have to get it on the calendar. I'd like all the time I can get but I still want to put her on the stand while she's in reasonably good shape."

"I'll see her tomorrow."

"Good, and then you'll get back to me?"

"Yes, right after I see her."

"Fine." Gordon stood up and whirled his coat around him squinting over the top. "And now I'm off to my next secret assignment."

Phil watched as he left and then prepared for office hours.

Ann did not come to the door when Phil arrived the following afternoon. It had been left unlocked and he let himself in. He found her resting in the den and it appeared she might have spent the night there. Several large pillows and a light blanket were to one side of the sofa while she remained at the other end and waved to him as he entered the room. She smiled as he approached and greeted her with a light kiss on the cheek. She took his hand and then slowly shifted her position to make room beside her. He studied her face for a brief moment. It had lost much of its fullness, and this only seemed to accentuate her features and make them even sharper and more striking. There was still a sensual quality about her, even being as ill as she was.

"How are you doing?"

"About the same. Still can't seem to get my strength and my appetite isn't any great shakes, either."

"You are eating, though?"

"I'm trying, but you wouldn't know it by looking at me." She held up her arm and pushed back the sleeve of her robe. There had been further soft tissue loss and her arm was disturbingly thin.

"I know some of this is from lack of exercise, but I just wish I had the urge or energy to do something. I just can't seem to get going."

"I know it's not easy," Phil said. "You haven't been getting any pain in your abdomen, or cramps, have you?"

"No, that's been all right, and I don't think any of that fluid has come back. I check that every day. God, that was awful. I really guess I'm not doing badly, but I just wish I could feel stronger or put on a little weight."

"Gordon wanted me to give him some idea when I thought we could go to trial. He needs time to prepare but he also wants to be sure you'll be OK."

"He's called quite a few times recently. I guess he's checking up on me. I certainly wouldn't know what to tell him. This is my first time with this type of problem, you know." She laughed. "You're the one with the experience. What do you think?"

"I can't be sure either. I think you're doing pretty well but these things are difficult to predict. I could talk with Dr. Breiling. Has he said very much?"

Ann suddenly leaned forward. The mention of Dr. Breiling's name seemed to disturb her.

"That's another thing. I'm glad you mentioned him. He's really had very little to say lately. He seems awfully distant, as though he really isn't interested in treating me. I knew there was something I wanted to tell you."

Phil looked surprised. "That doesn't sound like him. I could believe that of some other people on staff but not Dr. Breiling. I wouldn't expect that."

"Well, maybe I'm wrong. It's hard to be sure of anything at this point. All I know is that I must be all right for that trial. That much has to be done for me and I don't care how the two of you do it. Even if I do begin to feel better, I know it's only temporary. I'm not sure I really care that much; I just want to be able to testify when the time comes so if you have any doubts about my condition, hold the trial as soon as you have to. That's my only concern."

"I understand and I'm just as concerned as you are, but I have to be guided by Gordon's wishes. If he says he needs the time, I haven't much of an argument at this point. I certainly want him to have the strongest possible case when we go to trial."

"So do I! Look, I'm even going to testify that Dr. Stallings told me Jack would not survive the surgery, that he would see to it that he didn't. I'm going to be very specific even though it may not be quite what he said. That's how much I want this case to go well. Anyway, I know that's what he meant, and Gordon has told me I can say that. He's given me a great deal of latitude with my recollection of those conversations. We even decided I'll be performing a service by simplifying the jury's work."

Phil shook his head and smiled at the same time. "I guess that's how it works. Well, that's between you and Gordon but I have no objection. I have absolutely no experience with this sort of thing. I'm just trying to do what is best medically for you."

Ann took his hand. "I know you are. I wouldn't be here now if it weren't for you. I know how sick I was and how difficult the surgery had to be. No one else could have done this for me. There are plenty of problems I could have had by now, and I haven't, and that's only because of you." She studied his hand, and then her own. "Do you think there could have been something between us?" she asked without looking up. Then as an afterthought, "If I hadn't gotten sick?"

"Yes."

Before today Phil would have groped awkwardly for a reply. This time he answered convincingly and without hesitation. It could've been that he was still not entirely sure of his feelings or in some way was acceding to her condition and her wishes, but nonetheless, this was the answer he wanted to give.

Ann surmised everything. She lifted Phil's hand and pressed it to her lips.

"I don't care why you said it, Phil. The reasons may not be the ones I'd like to hear. I believe you anyway, and that is what is most important to me." Her eyes were very sad. "I wouldn't let anything happen between us now, not with the way I am. This is not what I wanted you to have. You deserve what I was then, and I could never give you anything less. I really think I get much more satisfaction thinking how it would have been, and I think about it often. It's one of the few consolations I have left. I know it would have happened and you just made me that much more certain of it. I know how wonderful it would have been." Tears began to fall slowly down her cheeks. "You'll never know how much you've really done for me, Phil, or how much I've cared for you."

Phil sat motionless for a while, not knowing how to respond. He wasn't sure if a more overt expression of his feelings was expected now, or if he was even capable of that. When he finally looked over at her, he thought she might give some indication, but Ann had regained her composure and seemed much more tranquil now. She smiled affectionately at him. Both knew there was nothing more to say. Phil reached over and squeezed her hand. Then he got up and slowly walked to the door.

Now more than ever, he did not want to fail her. The ride back to his office was a torment. He never thought he could have feelings for a patient beyond the usual concern and compassion that was expected of him. He would never have thought it befitting nor would he ever have admitted it to himself. But that was before Ann Hartway had begun their relationship, and now he was inextricably drawn to her. He was still confused by all this but he did feel greater responsibility for her than anyone else and he knew it would only be for a little while longer. That saddened him very deeply. He dreaded how it would end.

As soon as he reached his office, Phil called Dr. Breiling. He had just finished a treatment and came to the phone after a short delay.

"Hello, Phil. What can I help you with?"

"Are you very busy right now, Seymour? I need a few minutes to ask you something."

"Go ahead. I'm in between patients at the moment."

"It's about Ann Hartway. I've just come from seeing her and I wanted to get your impression as to how she's doing. I've been put in a position where I'm supposed to tell how long she'll be in reasonably good shape. I don't want to just guess. I called to find out what you thought."

"I don't know anything more than you, Phil. You know how hard it is to judge these things. She's doing pretty well right now, but I don't expect that to last very long. Three months, maybe six months. Once she starts developing problems, she'll probably go downhill very quickly."

"That's pretty much what I thought," Phil said.

"Sure. The way you described your operative findings, she could get into trouble at any time. These tumors are not that responsive. Three months might even be too long."

Although not unexpected, hearing this was disheartening. "Anything new in the way of treatment?"

"You mean chemotherapy? Not anything worthwhile, as far as I know." Dr. Breiling hesitated briefly. "Look, as long as we're talking like this, maybe you'd like her to see some other oncologists? There are plenty in the area and one of them might be familiar with another protocol. That wouldn't bother me."

Phil thought that was gracious but unnecessary. "I don't think so, Seymour. You always seem to know just how to handle these problems. I don't think Ann will want to go chasing after other opinions."

There was another momentary pause.

"I think I can be very frank with you, Phil. It's hard for me to say this, but I have a big problem taking care of Mrs. Hartway. I'm starting to get some very disturbing comments from some of the other people on staff. I'm sure I don't have to tell you. I depend on their referrals. Some of them have told me not to expect to see their patients while she's under my care. I have a lot of respect for you, Phil, and if you want me to keep seeing her, I will. But I prefer to work something else out. There are plenty of good oncologists nearby who are on staff at other hospitals. They can do just as well for her."

"I see." Phil hadn't expected this, and it upset him. "I'm sorry you feel this way."

"I am too, Phil. I never thought I'd have to say this to anyone. Maybe it's not a lot of guys who made comments to me, but believe me, it's enough. I'm sure you have very good reasons for what you're doing but personally, I'd rather not be hurt by this thing if I can avoid it."

Phil realized he had no choice but to acquiesce to Dr. Breiling's wishes. "I understand. I'll discuss it with her and see where we go from here. Would you give me some names and once we decide, send your records to that office?"

"Sure. I'm not abandoning her, Phil. I'm just turning her over to someone else and I'll even set it up, if you like. I knew you'd understand. I just wish there was some way you could protect yourself. Some of the things I hear at the hospital aren't very nice. I've never paid much attention to what goes on in your department but right now there seems to be an awful lot of bad feelings towards you. I know if it was me, I'd be having a great deal of trouble sleeping at night."

"I'm sleeping pretty well, Seymour. I don't think anyone at the hospital really knows what all this is about. When they do, I wonder just what opinions they'll have then. In the meantime, I'm taking things as they come and I'm getting my sleep. I appreciate your honesty, Seymour. I'll get back to you to let you know what we're doing."

It took several more phone calls, first to Ann and then back and forth to Dr. Breiling to resolve this particular impasse. Ann was surprised and hurt by his decision. More than that, she was concerned this might mean an interruption in her treatment and was assured it would not.

Other arrangements were made very quickly. Gordon was also made aware of this and the best estimates of the time element. In spite of Phil's concerns, he was very adamant about putting off the date of trial for at least four months and later when the actual date was set, it turned out to be more than five months away. At first, he insisted Dr. Stallings' attorney asked for that amount of time to prepare his defense and threatened delaying tactics if Gordon didn't agree. When the attorney, Donald Spangler, stated in a subsequent interview that he and his client were ready to face his accusers and go to trial at any time, Gordon admitted that it was he who had asked for the later date. He pointed out to Phil that Ann was the only person to come forward so far to accuse Dr. Stallings and that there would certainly be considerable questions on whether he actually caused Jack Hartway's death. After all, Jack Hartway probably would still be alive today if he had agreed to an amputation. To lend credibility, Gordon felt he had to establish a pattern and that was taking a lot of time. He had Phil's evaluation of the three cases most recently uncovered, and these certainly fit that pattern. There was still, however, a great number of details that had to be worked out. It was generally accepted that greed was the motive and Dr. Stallings' finances were being extensively investigated. He had been cautious enough not to make any incriminating bank deposits, but Gordon had already uncovered records of sizeable purchases of traveler's checks around the time of each of these cases. Gordon felt the investigation was taking shape and he was moving as quickly as he could. He agreed that the extra time this required was a risk, but it was one he had to take.

Phil understood but at the same time did not find this reassuring. As much as he wanted Gordon to develop the strongest possible case, he was even more concerned with the progress of Ann's disease and her eventual effectiveness as a witness. He would mention this to Gordon repeatedly in their frequent telephone conversations, and as he noted further deterioration, his pleas took on a sense of urgency. Gordon, however, still insisted the trial could not begin any earlier. Even after he had been told Ann had begun to exhibit periods of mental confusion and had become much weaker, he still would not agree to any change in the trial date. Phil actually found he had little regard for his concerns and that he himself really had little influence on the pre-trial strategy. He frequently made his displeasure very obvious, and in an effort to ameliorate those feelings, Gordon took great pains to keep Phil fully informed of the progress being made and the manner in which he planned to conduct the trial. His opening remarks would cover the entire breadth of Dr. Stallings' mismanagement of his patients. He wanted everything laid out in the most precise detail at that time before he called any witnesses. He wanted the jury and the public to know the complete character of this man at the very outset. Then he would call Ann Hartway to the stand to begin substantiation of the charges. He was going to implicate Dr. Stallings in the bleeding episode from the disconnected IV and would probably call Phil to describe his conversation with Dr. Stallings earlier that day. He hoped Phil wouldn't have any objection and they would discuss what he would say later on. After that, he planned to question each of the family members of the different patients. A number of them had already been to his office and he intended to get to the rest well before the trial. Each had been advised to have legal counsel with them and Gordon used the meetings to explain just what criminal acts had taken place and how each was believed to be involved. Most reacted with indignation and denial but there were a few who began to offer explanations and then were cut short by their attorneys. Gordon found this very encouraging. He emphasized that cooperation with his office at this time could be very helpful to those involved in contrast to what would happen if it was revealed later during the trial. Another reason for wanting the delay was to give them more time to think about this. He was sure some might be intimidated and agree to provide testimony. It hadn't happened thus far, but he felt there was still time.

    Phil repeatedly had to weigh this with his increasing anxiety over Ann's worsening condition. She had very little strength and tired much more quickly after the mildest exertion. Of greater concern were the occasional lapses of memory and confused responses that Phil had begun to notice. At one point he considered ordering a CT scan of the head to determine if cerebral metastases were present but then decided that if they were, it was better to leave them undetected and undocumented. He tried to give Ann all the support he could but clearly the optimal time for her to have taken the witness stand had already passed. He made mention of this to Gordon time and again but was always gently but firmly rebuffed. Regardless of her condition, Gordon continued to insist he could lead her through her testimony. There might be some problem with the cross-examination but here too, Gordon would look out for her. He repeatedly urged Phil not to worry but as the day of the trial drew near, there was more a feeling of trepidation than relief.

XV

Anger and resentment had been growing at Middle Valley. At first, the media had been given limited access to the hospital and the staff. The administration did not wish to give the appearance that it felt the hospital had anything to hide. At the same time, it did not want any interruptions in its routine daily activities.

A policy had been agreed upon by the various parties and initially there had been reasonable compliance by both sides.

The media was free to move about the main lobby and had been given a conference room for a work area and storage of equipment. The hospital staff was told to be polite but very careful with any comments they might be asked to make. They were discouraged from giving interviews. These were usually impromptu, brief and carried out whenever someone was willing to spare a moment or two. Any response was always in defense of the hospital and its fine professional staff.

This made for an increasing amount of frustration among the reporters and other media personnel. Physicians were sought out in their offices and Phil was no exception. At this point, they were unaware of the role he played; this in spite of the added attention he received as Ann Hartway's surgeon. Like many others, he declined any comment. The ones who did, spoke out with great animosity towards those responsible for this travesty. A great injustice was being done, although no one seemed to know much more than that.

The news people gradually became more intrusive in their efforts. No one was spared, even visitors. A number complained they had been harassed. One question, in particular, seemed to be a favorite. Are you uneasy having someone in a hospital where several patients may have been intentionally killed? When a representative apologized for this and promised greater discretion, the decision to bar the media from all hospital property was reinstated.

Phil usually kept to the patients' floors and the operating room. One morning he ran in quickly to check his hospital mail. Several physicians were standing near the doctors' lounge talking with a young man Phil guessed was a reporter. Val Rogoff was among them. He was one of the few who had called Phil several times to offer support. This time he motioned him to stay back.

"It's a whole load of horseshit," Arnie Brice said. Then he noticed Phil. "Speaking of horseshit, why don't you ask that guy what this is all about?" He motioned in Phil's direction. "Nice going, Phil. Why don't you tell him what a real good guy you are? Tell him how you treat your friends."

The reporter immediately approached Phil. "Excuse me, sir, but can I speak with you?"

"I'm going in here," Phil said.

"I just need a moment, sir. Could I have your name please?" He turned the page on his notepad. "What did that other doctor just mean?"

The others kept watching Phil. His face became flushed. The reporter positioned himself between Phil and the door to the lounge.

"You're a physician here, sir? Could you give me your name? Do you have an opinion about the charges that were made?" He was no more than a foot away from Phil, poised, ready to begin taking notes. Rogie quickly came up behind him.

"You'll have to excuse us. I have to talk to this doctor." He reached around and took Phil by the arm. "C'mon. We'll go in here."

"Hey, Doc. Gimme a break. I'm trying to do my job."

Rogie held the door open for Phil. "I'm sorry. This is the doctors' lounge. You're not allowed in here. As a matter of fact, it's my understanding you're not allowed back here at all. What's your name? Shouldn't you be wearing some identification?"

There was a smirk on the young man's face as he retreated. "You weren't so concerned where we were when I was talking with your friends. What's the big concern now, Doc? This doctor knows something?" He stared at Phil.

Rogie pulled Phil into the lounge, leaving the reporter in the hall. No one else was there.

"Forget what you just heard. Arnie Brice is an asshole. What fuckin' internist knows what goes on in surgery, anyway?"

"Thanks. That's the first time that's happened."

"You've been pretty lucky, then. I knew it was bound to happen. You OK? You don't look so good."

"I'm all right. I just wish it would all be over."

"You think that will happen?" Rogie whistled. "I don't think things will ever be the same around here again. There's an awful lot of very pissed off people. Some of them are not going to change, no matter what."

Phil's color faded. He looked pale.

"You'd think there would've been some other way. Believe me, I wish there was. I never expected any of this."

Rogie looked at him. "I can only guess what you're saying, Phil. I never asked you anything before, and I won't now. I have the utmost respect for you. I don't know what else anyone can say. It makes me nervous, but we'll survive. We have to."

Another doctor came into the lounge and barely seemed aware of their presence.

"I guess you and Gary are the only ones." Phil looked down. "Thanks, Rogie. I really appreciate what you did. I better check my mail and get going. Just a little while longer, but then it's likely to get even worse." He shook his head.

Rogie watched him as he left.

"Don't let it get you down, Phil. Don't let it do anything to you."

Phil sat in his car for quite a long time. Then he drove back to his office. This incident left him quite shaken and from then on, he was seen even less frequently in the hospital.

As Phil had learned, waiting all this time clearly had its disadvantages. One that was beyond anyone's control was the weather. Winter had arrived with its gray, overcast skies and chill, damp air. On this particular day, with the trial about to begin, Phil would soon find out how many others there were, as well. As he drove towards the courthouse, no matter where he looked, it all seemed so bleak. There had already been some snowfall but what there was had quickly become covered with a thick layer of grime and soot. Shards of dirty gray-black ice and hard-packed snow jutted out along the roadside adding to the dreary mood. All one could see in the sky were dark, foreboding clouds. A few times it looked as though the sun might be trying to break through and that led to some uncertainty how the day would turn out. Phil had the same exact feeling about everything else that was about to happen. It made him nervous but at this point, he was resigned to whatever the outcome would be. He just hoped for the best.

He pulled into the parking lot a little before nine a.m. The appearance of a number of large vans and trailers in front of the courthouse initially took him by surprise. He couldn't believe he had momentarily forgotten about the media. This was the one day when they would most certainly be out in full force. He recognized the call letters of the major television networks as well as some of the smaller local ones. Parking spaces were still available but only at a considerable distance from the courthouse. As he walked from the car, he noticed how still and quiet it was. It remained that way until he approached the building and saw the activity that was going on both outside and within. No one would have doubted that this was a major news event.

He took care to sidestep the heavy cables that ran across the entrance floor, and it was a simple matter to follow them to the appropriate courtroom. A large crowd was milling about in the corridor and once Phil was able to work his way to the door, the ebb and flow carried him into the courtroom. A seat was supposedly being held for him near the front of the room by Mel Silverstone and Phil immediately began looking for him. Both men spied each other at the same instant and a moment later Phil was squeezed rather uncomfortably beside Mel in the third row. He recognized Peter Futterman sitting a little to their right in the first row and just ahead of him, standing with his back to them at a long table, Gordon Mulcahey. Phil tried to absorb everything at once, the expanses of wood paneling, the high ceilings, the imposing oak bench from which the judge would conduct the trial. He was impressed and more than a little awed.

"It's finally happening, isn't it?"

"That it is," Mel said, "and not a moment too soon from what Gordon says you've been telling him. When did you see Ann last?"

"Yesterday. I stopped over in the evening. Donna Moreland stayed with her."

"How's she doing?"

"Not that well. I'm really concerned how well she's going to hold up. I don't think Gordon should have waited this long."

"I know, but it had to be this way. Gordon needed the time. How about yourself? How are you doing?"

"I'm very nervous."

"Not like your buddy over there." Mel motioned to the front of the room on the left. "Doesn't look like it's bothering him one bit."

Phil immediately saw Stanley Stallings. His face was visible only when he turned to the right and whenever he did, he was either smiling or laughing. Phil was amazed at his attitude but thinking back, he usually reacted this way no matter what the situation was. He had always found it very irritating then, and it was even more so now.

There were only two other people Phil recognized in the courtroom. Both were members of the hospital's administrative staff. He was certain two others with whom they frequently spoke were attorneys for the hospital.

"Where is Ann now?" Phil asked.

"Oh, she wouldn't be here. If she has arrived, she'd be in another room. They'll call her when they're ready. She still has plenty of time."

Phil took a deep breath and rubbed his hands. "I wish this thing would get started."

A little before nine thirty, they were asked to rise, and the judge made his appearance and the jury filed in. Judge Perrine was a short, stocky, balding man who seemed as intent in looking over the courtroom as everyone else was in looking at him. He then made some initial remarks, but Phil was too busy studying him to pay attention to what they were. There was complete quiet after that, and Phil began to think someone might have forgotten what they were supposed to do next. Finally, Gordon rose from his seat, put down some papers he had been reading, and walked to the front of the courtroom.

"Your Honor, ladies and gentlemen of the jury, if you had asked me a year ago if I'd be standing before you today, about to tell you what you are now going to hear, I would never have believed it. Just like me, in the beginning, you may find you're also having this difficulty. I expect that and so should you. I will also tell you, in the end, believe it you will. Of that, I have no doubt. A crime can take many forms. Sometimes it is very clear what the crime is, who committed it and what the punishment should be. At other times it strains our senses to recognize that a crime has been committed. That is particularly true when a crime is unusual or unique, or in the most extreme, when it has never been heard of before. Then we really find ourselves taken to the limits of our ability to learn the truth. This is a very difficult task but not an impossible one."

Gordon approached the jury, looking at one, then another.

"I'm really no different to any of you. It takes a great deal to convince me that a crime has been committed and that someone is guilty of that crime. I will tell you right now, I will not enter a courtroom in this capacity unless I am convinced of this. Do you know why? Again, I will tell you. It is because there is nothing more serious than to accuse someone of a capital offense and then prove that person's guilt. The consequence of that, ladies, and gentlemen, has no parallel. This knowledge never leaves my mind for an instant. I want you to know this about me, ladies and gentlemen, because in a moment I will begin to convince you completely that these crimes had indeed taken place and were carried out by the person who is the defendant in this courtroom today."

Gordon returned to his desk and briefly looked down at a sheet of paper he had previously placed apart from the others. He then turned back to the jury. Phil tried to get some sort of indication from Mel on what he thought of Gordon's remarks thus far, but he was completely noncommittal.

"About one and one-half years ago, Dr. Stallings operated on Jack Hartway for a clogged blood vessel in his leg. Mr. Hartway had previously been rejected for surgery by another surgeon because of the opinion that Mr. Hartway did not need the operation. The surgery did not go well and there were complications and Mr. Hartway eventually died. On the surface this did not seem too unusual although Mr. Hartway was young and in reasonably good health and should have come through the surgery with a good result. Bad results do occur in surgery, even when not expected. But in this case, there was another factor. Mr. and Mrs. Hartway did not have a very happy marriage. In fact, as you will soon learn from Mrs. Hartway, she was very unhappy and when she accidentally and unintentionally conveyed these feelings to Dr. Stallings, he made it clear that he could eliminate the source of Mrs. Hartway's unhappiness. Taking advantage of her duress at the time, Dr. Stallings purposely mishandled Jack Hartway's surgery causing complications he knew would inevitably result in the patient's death. For this Ann Hartway paid him thirty thousand dollars. And this is where it all might have ended except that in time Ann Hartway began to have second thoughts about what had happened, particularly when she began to realize through conversations with others, that this was not the only time Dr. Stallings had done this. When this information was first brought to the attention of my office, we, of course, were very skeptical but were nonetheless obliged to carry out an investigation. In time we were able to accumulate very convincing evidence to support these allegations, evidence that you will hear in very careful detail. You will hear from operating room personnel who witnessed the operations performed on Mr. Hartway and were so appalled by the poor quality of the surgical technique that they couldn't explain it. Remember, this is supposed to be a very competent surgeon. You will be told how Dr. Stallings tried to hide the very considerable fee he received from Mrs. Hartway. We have records of this. You will also be shown a pattern of similar treatment of other patients, all with the same result and all with enormous fees paid to Dr. Stallings and very substantial immediate benefit to the next of kin."

"Let me tell you of another patient. We learned that well before Jack Hartway, Dr. Stallings had performed surgery on a seventy-four-year-old male who was a very poor medical risk. The operation was a hiatus hernia repair and the patient expired after the surgery. Our medical experts have reviewed this patient's hospital record, which is supposed to accurately depict the patient's general state of health. They have concluded this patient should not have undergone the surgery, first, because the alleged condition did not require it, and secondly, because it was a virtual certainty he would not survive. His offspring received a very sizeable inheritance."

Gordon paused momentarily for a glass of water and then resumed.

"Although we found this very suspicious, it was also very speculative. Another case that was brought to our attention was that of an extremely obese individual who underwent a weight-reduction operation by Dr. Stallings that carried a very high risk. Here again was a case of a very unhappy spouse but in this situation, the patient was very reluctant to have the surgery and very fearful of the operation. The spouse quite literally forced him into the surgery, and he subsequently died. She promptly remarried a very short time later."

Gordon walked back to the jury.

"By this time, you must be wondering just what kind of a case we've put together here. Sounds like a lot of conjecture, a lot of unfounded suspicion, doesn't it? Then let me tell you what happened next. Of course, you must realize that we are now looking into the cases Dr. Stallings is treating in the hospital at this time. We want to see what he is doing now, today. These are people who have not yet had their surgery. Suddenly we learn from one of our sources that an elderly gentleman with very severe emphysema is about to have a large hernia repaired. Our informant has expressed concern that the patient's breathing will become even worse when the herniated organs are placed back in the abdomen causing greater pressure on the diaphragm. The informant feels this pressure could be so great as to jeopardize the patient's survival. Oddly enough, however, the one test that would show the patient is too poor a risk for the surgery comes back as normal. Anyone with knowledge of medicine would realize this particular patient could not have produced a normal test result, but Dr. Stallings prepares to go ahead with the surgery anyway. Fortunately, the anesthesiologist recognizes the discrepancy and orders the test repeated. It shows a very low value, and the surgery is cancelled. Do you know how the first value was obtained? By having the patient's nephew, who is completely healthy, present himself to the laboratory as the patient and then by having his blood taken for the test. Only then could the operation have taken place and who would the benefactor have been? The nephew who had accumulated very substantial gambling debts and would now have inherited the patient's very lucrative business enterprises. How do we know this? The technician who drew the blood sample in question has identified the nephew as being the person from whom the blood was drawn, and you will hear him testify to this very fact just as you will hear corroboration of each and every statement that I have made. You will hear a very careful description of this sordid scheme wherein both the surgeon and the patient's nephew collaborated to bring about the patient's demise through a totally inadvisable operative procedure for the financial gain of both. That is how these crimes were committed, ladies and gentlemen, by operating where no one else would because of the inherently high risk these patients presented and by purposely carrying out technical errors that were not recognized as willful acts at the time but nonetheless caused complications that were fatal. When testimony is completed, ladies and gentlemen, you will see these acts as having been crimes, and crimes committed by that man, Dr. Stanley Stallings."

Gordon stood for a moment looking directly at Dr. Stallings who stared back, expressionless, unmoving. It was a test of wills, some might think, and on Dr. Stallings' part, defiance. That might not have been to the jury's liking and Donald Spangler nudged him, breaking the impasse. Gordon continued.

"There are other cases, which in time I will cite with appropriate detail. There was a seventy-four-year-old woman with asthma, a seventy-seven-year-old man with a kidney stone, a forty-seven-year-old man with inflamed pancreas. All were very high-risk patients who underwent surgery with great reservation by their consultants and all expired. The surgeon in each instance was Dr. Stallings. All matters pertinent to each of these cases will be brought before this jury so they might decide how appropriate the surgeon's actions were and what his prime considerations might have been. And to aid the jury in this task, I will also submit the testimony of two of my investigators who visited Dr. Stallings' office with an elderly patient whom we had recruited. The patient had a relatively harmless surgical condition and had also been provided with medical records showing that she had a rather serious heart attack only months before. That sort of history would normally preclude any elective surgery. The family—that is, the two investigators, made it clear that the patient was a great burden, and they were tired of caring for her. They also made it very clear they would benefit considerably from the patient's will. Dr. Stallings agreed to perform the surgery for a fee of thirty thousand dollars and eliminate their burden. His only stipulation was that no mention should be made of the recent heart attack." He started to walk away from the jury but then abruptly turned to face them. "Oh yes, there's one other thing I should tell you about that visit. One of the people there was wearing a recording device. That visit was recorded in its entirety on tape and will be heard by you pending the court's decision regarding its admissibility."

Several gasps were heard throughout the courtroom. Gordon said nothing more for the moment, his actions very carefully calculated for maximum effect. Phil strained to see Stanley Stallings' reaction. For once, all did not seem as calm at his table. There were hurried conversations and in one brief glimpse, he looked noticeably concerned. He certainly wasn't smiling any longer. Gordon, for all this, remained completely composed and after another glass of water, slowly returned to his place in front of the jury.

"Mr. Spangler can, of course, review its contents any time he wishes."

There was a further pause. Judge Perrine sat forward upon hearing all this and looked over at Stallings' table. He didn't say anything but took a very deep breath that was audible to most of the courtroom. Then he settled back.

"Why then," Gordon asked, "did all this happen? You can't have a crime without a motive. What was the motive for all these horrendous deeds? The motive, ladies and gentlemen, was greed, greed on the part of those who stood to benefit monetarily or otherwise from the patients' deaths and greed on the part of the surgeon who performed these operations for an exorbitant fee. And how do we know this? We know this from financial records, the admission of relatives who dealt with Dr. Stallings and his own statement, which is heard on the audiotape that was made in his office. As you hear the evidence, I have no doubt you will clearly recognize this.

"And finally, ladies and gentlemen of the jury, what is it that you must decide after you have heard all the arguments, all the evidence, all the witnesses? What is the one most important question you have to consider? What is the crime that Dr. Stanley Stallings is being charged with today? You must remember he is being accused of one, and only one, very specific criminal act. He is accused of having purposely and willfully brought about the death of Jack Hartway through errors and mistakes in surgical judgment and technique that he purposely and willfully made before and during two operations on this patient so as to produce complications he knew the patient would not survive. He did this while taking advantage of the faults and weaknesses of others solely for his own monetary gain. Although other similar instances will be presented to you in detail, it is his guilt or innocence in just this one case that you must decide. I ask that you listen carefully to all the evidence submitted and weigh with even greater care how it relates to this one charge. I ask you to be fair and open-minded in your judgments. I know my esteemed colleague will make much of the unique and unexpected nature of this crime. I'm sure he'll call it inconceivable and beyond belief. I'm sure he'll tell you that it's unthinkable for someone who has taken a solemn oath to save lives to commit such an act. But again, I will ask you to listen carefully to all the evidence and then ask yourself if what you hear describes a man sworn to save lives. I'm sure my esteemed colleague will also tell you that it is impossible for the crime of murder to be carried out as I have described. Again, I ask you to listen to the evidence that I will present. Tell me if it is any less a crime to operate on someone you know will not survive the operative procedure and who could very well live without it than it is to put a gun to that person's head and pull the trigger. Yes, ladies and gentlemen, this is a very extraordinary crime, an unheard-of crime, possibly even the perfect crime, except that one of those involved could not bear this any longer and decided to come forward. She did not want this to happen anymore. If not for that, we probably never would have learned of these heinous deeds, and I say heinous because in the commission of this crime, this doctor violated the most sacred of trusts, a trust and privilege we give only to doctors so that they may enter into the very depths of our bodies to make us well when we are sick. We trust them. We depend on them. No one else has this gift, this trust, this right. And this man betrayed all of this. I am sure my adversary will tell you that no physician or surgeon can always guarantee success, that no matter how competent or conscientious, every doctor has his failures. I am sure the cases that I will describe will be characterized as just that, those inevitable failures all doctors must have. Again, I ask you to listen carefully and weigh everything fairly. Ask yourselves if these, sound like unavoidable failures. Tell me if consultants strongly caution against surgery and lab results do not support the need, that these deaths need to have happened.

Please, ladies, and gentlemen of the jury, listen very carefully to the evidence and let that determine your decision."

Gordon placed his hands on the railing in front of the jury and leaned forward, his head bowed. Phil thought he had finished speaking. Then he slowly raised his head and looked at each of the jurors.

"I'm sorry, but bear with me for another moment, if you will. I didn't think I would have anything more to say at this point, but I can't help feeling I have to leave you with another thought. I want you to follow me very carefully because I think you'll find this very important and it shouldn't be overlooked. You know your responsibility here today is to decide if a crime has been committed. If a crime has been committed and someone else knows of it, I want you to think what the greatest fear must be for the person who committed that crime? Would anyone argue that would be the fear of getting caught, of having someone else reveal the crime and who was involved? In this case, we know someone was capable of doing that. That person is here today, and you will hear her testimony very shortly. She's Ann Hartway, Jack Hartway's wife. So now I can also imagine the guilty person doing something very desperate, to avoid having those crimes revealed. That leaves me with just one last unanswered question and maybe you'll be able to answer it for me. Ask yourselves, if a crime wasn't committed here why was an attempt made on Mrs. Hartway's life six months ago?"

There was considerable reaction throughout the courtroom, but it subsided quickly. Gordon waited until it became absolutely quiet again.

"This is not a fantasy or an attempt to bring drama into these proceedings, ladies and gentlemen. You have to look no further than the records of Middle Valley General Hospital to see that this did indeed happen. Six months ago, Mrs. Hartway underwent major surgery. On the second night after her surgery, while she was heavily medicated, during the early morning hours, someone placed a plastic pad on the side of her bed and towels on the floor just below that. Then they disconnected her IV, which had been attached to a large tube in the major vein in her chest. Now there was nothing to prevent Ann Hartway's blood from flowing onto the plastic pad and then the towels on the floor. Nothing could be heard; she could not be aware, and she almost bled to death. A nurse walked into her room just in time. It was two a.m. It's quiet then and normally there's just two nurses and an aid on the floor. But that same nurse will testify she did see another person on the floor just before she went in to Ann Hartway and found her bleeding, a person she really didn't expect to see, a person normally not expected to be there at that time. She will confirm the identity of that person and I will tell you who he is right now. He is seated in this courtroom. He is Dr. Stanley Stallings."

Many of the spectators reacted with consternation and shock and it caused enough of a clamor for the judge to strike his gavel repeatedly to restore order. Gordon stood erect and surveyed the jury one last time. "Ladies and gentlemen, remember the question I asked you just a moment ago. Would this have happened if someone had not been trying to cover up a crime?" He looked at each one and tried to gauge the individual reactions. Finally, he said, "You have been very patient, and I thank you very much for your attention." He smiled confidently and walked back to his seat.

Phil couldn't have been more elated or impressed. He thought Gordon's opening statement was nothing short of masterful. He was just about to extol his rhetoric when Mel abruptly silenced him. He had not noticed that Donald Spangler, Dr. Stallings' attorney, had taken his position before the jury and was about to begin his opening remarks.

"Your Honor, ladies and gentlemen of the jury, I will keep my remarks very brief. As a matter of fact, when I first became Dr. Stallings' attorney and read the charges against him, I seriously questioned whether there should be any response from the defense at all. My concern, ladies, and gentlemen, was the impression I might give if I did answer any of these charges, that it might be construed that I thought these charges were worthy of such concern, that I thought some of you might believe what you just heard, that there could be any credibility to any of this whatsoever. The fact is, ladie,s and gentlemen, I can't believe any of this even in my wildest imaginings, and I can't believe anyone else could, either. And I want this understood before I say another word. I have a responsibility to my client, and that is to provide the best possible defense for him, particularly since this is a most serious charge. All that aside, and with all due respect for this court, I have to be honest and tell you that I feel I'm taking part in a travesty and that very reluctantly, I am assuming this role in what I feel is a completely unfounded fantasy. That a case such as this can come before as respected a court as this might be thought by some as a tribute to our system of jurisprudence, but to me it is a miscarriage that is unsurpassed in my memory. I have no doubt as to what the outcome will be. The only question and concern for which I don't have an answer, is whether or not my client will be able to withstand the toll this terrible ordeal has placed upon him.

"Now, having told you why I have reluctantly prepared a defense, you should know what the substance of this defense will be. You must be wondering about this just as I did at first. After all, how does one argue against the absurd? Actually, it's not difficult at all. I will simply point out to you, certain things about which I am sure you are unaware, as I was at first, and then you may decide if Dr. Stallings could be guilty as the prosecution has charged.

"I would first like you to know Dr. Stallings has been in practice in the Middle Valley area for twenty years. His practice has continuously grown during that time and he has built up a following through his skill and dedication that is as loyal to him as he is to them. My biggest difficulty was deciding which of them would testify on his behalf as to his qualities as a physician and a surgeon. Everyone I interviewed insisted on doing so and those that weren't chosen did not accept that decision graciously. Each and every one of them felt they had an obligation to stand up for him. This same feeling is echoed by his colleagues at Middle Valley Hospital, and you will hear testimony from many of them as to Dr. Stallings' skill as a diagnostician and surgeon. You will be able to compare Dr. Stallings' statistics regarding operations performed, complications, deaths, infections and so on with the rest of the surgical department and you will see how impressively he has performed under very demanding conditions. Along with this I want to emphasize right now that Dr. Stallings has never been brought before any hospital committee for any of these alleged acts or any other impropriety whatsoever. Do you realize what that means? Here you have perhaps the most scrutinized profession in the world and one of its members has been charged with the most outrageous of crimes and not once did his peers ever find him responsible for even the slightest infraction. That means not once did the peer review committee, the hospital ethics committee, the tissue committee, not one of these, ever cited Dr. Stallings for any sort of violation of medical practice or procedure and yet today, he finds himself on trial accused of murdering a patient with the clear implication that there were also many others. Tell me, ladies and gentlemen of the jury, with his every activity being watched so carefully, how is this possible? If he is indeed the demon that the prosecution is trying to portray, don't you think sometime in these past twenty years he would have been found out? Don't you think there would have been talk? Don't you think his would have been the type of practice that would have faltered and not grown and prospered as it has done? No, ladies and gentlemen of the jury, when you hear all the testimony, it will not be the description of a man who is so deranged as to be able to cast aside the solemn oath he has taken to protect and save lives and instead, commit murder. No, what you will hear is the very essence of a very dedicated and caring human being who is there at all hours of the day and night, regardless of what the conditions might be, regardless of whether the patient is wealthy or impoverished.

"I have to tell you something that I did. I decided I wanted to learn whatever I could about this person I was going to defend. I spent several weekends with him day and night. I was with him at four in the morning when he sewed back the face of some indigent vagrant with the same painstaking care he had used earlier on the wounds of the son of a member of the hospital's Board of Trustees. I was with him early on a Sunday morning when he worked feverishly for several hours to stabilize an elderly woman who was in shock and who would later have most of her intestine removed because of gangrene.

"That patient, by the way, survived. But it is precisely that type of patient that the prosecution would have you believe my client would dispatch without a moment's hesitation. And yet, all I saw were valiant, unceasing efforts to save those as well as many others." He turned to look in Gordon's direction with just the slightest sarcasm in his voice. "Might I also add, this too can be found in the hospital's records."

He went back to addressing the jury directly. "It's ironic. Here we are today about to weigh testimony on a charge of murder when everything I ever learned about this man would make sainthood a much more fitting consideration. Many people today feel they owe their lives to this man. Now do you think he could have attained this stature or reached this position in his profession if he had been offering a sort of extermination or elimination to the families of his patients rather than the salvage and cure of these patients? How many people can there be out there who would like to see their family members eliminated in this way? Certainly, if there are any, it can't be this number. It has to be a very rare individual who goes to a doctor's office who does not want to be helped. I'm sure you won't disagree with that. I believe you will find even in the case you are deciding here today, both the patient and his wife went to Dr. Stallings in good faith to get help for the patient's condition. How does the doctor make the determination who has come to his office for what purpose? He can't just come out and ask them and why would he? We've already said with the rarest possible exception, everyone who goes there does so for the purpose of being helped. Just on the basis of percentages, if he flat out asks each one, he's going to be wrong time and time again. Besides offending an awful lot of people, I'm sure you'll agree he's not going to have much of a practice. If you think about it, that really doesn't seem to describe Dr. Stallings, does it? I will not say anything more at this point, ladies and gentlemen, except to ask you to use reason and good sense when you listen to the testimony. You are going to have to decide, each and every one of you, just what it is you find most believable, the District Attorney's contention that Dr. Stallings purposely caused his patient's death by a series of precise intentional technical flaws in the surgery or that he died as a result of complications that are hardly unusual for a case of this sort regardless who performed the surgery. By the way, you will also hear testimony from experts in the field who seriously question whether an operation can be so performed that a precise series of complications can be reasonably expected leading to the patient's death. In other words, surgery is hardly the reliable instrument of murder as, say, a loaded gun is. However, that may be getting ahead of ourselves. Good luck, ladies and gentlemen. You have a tremendous responsibility, but I know you will be equal to the task. Please remember to use your common sense and thank you for your attention."

Phil slouched backward in his seat, barely hearing the judge declare a ten-minute recess.

"I don't think I liked any of that."

"What did you think," Mel said, "that his attorney was just going to roll over and play dead? He knows how hard it's going to be for Gordon to convince this jury. You'd better not get your hopes too high. This is a case the defense shouldn't lose."

"But Gordon sounded like we had a pretty good chance."

Mel nodded, but it was not to give assurance. "Just remember what I said."

Phil was extremely confused at this point and sat through the remainder of the recess in silence. It seemed much less than ten minutes when the judge returned, and the courtroom once again became quiet. The court was called to order and the prosecution was asked if it was ready to proceed. Gordon answered affirmatively and called the first witness, Ann Hartway.

Most everyone turned in Ann's direction when she entered. Phil waited until she passed by before he looked up. She was accompanied by a court officer who was ready to lend assistance, but Ann managed well enough by herself. She had done all she could to make herself look well but so much time had passed. Her clothing hid many of the signs, but her face was gaunt and her hands and fingers, bony and thin. Only her eyes still had that luminescent glow. Regardless of everything else however, all must have known she had once been a very beautiful woman.

This made Phil very sad. He never wanted any of this to happen to Ann. He knew why it had to be, but it was just so terribly unfair, all of it. He listened and watched as she took the oath. She must not have seen him yet and he wondered if she would look for him. Her eyes were now on Gordon Mulcahey as he approached the witness stand.

The testimony she gave was essentially that which Phil had heard so many times before. What differed this time was the clear observation that Ann was no longer in complete control. Gordon had to lead her through the questions, patiently rephrasing them when her answers were not what he specifically wanted. Her responses at times were only partly relevant and when this happened, Gordon would bring her back to the matter under consideration and eventually extract the answer he sought. Even to someone like Phil, unschooled as he was in courtroom procedure, this seemed like a considerable breech of courtroom protocol, but Donald

Spangler seemed content to let it continue. He objected on just two occasions and perhaps then only to be certain the jury clearly understood the questionable tactics Gordon had been forced to use. He must have thought this would be more damaging if allowed to proceed unchallenged. Ann's voice wavered considerably, and a microphone was provided but rarely used. Only when she was asked if Stanley Stallings had assured her of her husband's death did her voice become emphatic. Then her answer was very explicit and clearly heard. Yes, he had, and she had acquiesced to each and every one of his demands. That brought the only audible reaction from the spectators and from then on, the rest of the questions were anticlimactic. Gordon could not even make anything of the near-fatal hemorrhage since Ann had been so heavily medicated and didn't have any recollection. He concluded his examination very quickly and was then called to the bench by Judge Perrine. It was impossible to overhear what was being said but the judge spoke to him at length and Gordon never replied. The judge did not look pleased and when he finished speaking, Gordon simply walked back to his seat without any expression whatsoever. Donald Spangler then stepped to the witness stand and introduced himself.

"Good morning, Mrs. Hartway. I'm Donald Spangler, Dr. Stallings' attorney. I'm sorry you haven't been feeling well. I'll try to be as brief as possible." He smiled as he spoke, but Ann would not look up. He stepped back and although still speaking to Ann, faced the jury.

"I listened very carefully to the answers you gave Mr. Mulcahey and I must admit some of the things you said trouble me. Perhaps you would be good enough to clarify a few things for me. Your husband saw Dr. Stallings after he had already been to see another surgeon, isn't that correct?"

"Yes."

"And that was to obtain another opinion, correct?"

"Yes."

"And I assume you went to see Dr. Stallings on someone else's recommendation?"

"My husband did. I went with him."

"Yes, of course. That was to see if his circulatory problem could be improved, wasn't it?"

"Yes."

"Was there anything you had heard or knew about specifically regarding Dr. Stallings at that point? In other words, should I assume that someone had told your husband Dr. Stallings was a specialist who might be able to help him with his problem?"

"Yes."

"So, you and your husband went to see Dr. Stallings expecting that he would recommend whatever measures he felt could benefit your husband's condition, if there were any. At that time, you hadn't heard any of these horrendous things that are now being said about Dr. Stallings, had you?"

"No."

"Up to that time, then, would I be correct in saying that both you and your husband thought of Dr. Stallings as being a competent and proficient surgeon who would recommend a course of treatment to improve or correct that condition?"

Ann did not answer and looked about helplessly, apparently unable to follow the question. Donald Spangler sensed the difficulty.

"Let me rephrase the question for you, Mrs. Hartway. When you and your husband first saw Dr. Stallings, you both thought he was competent and would try to help your husband?"

"Yes."

"And then, would it not be fair to say, that this is what Dr. Stallings would have had to assume was the intent of both you and your husband when you walked into his office?"

Gordon Mulcahey rose from his chair. "I object, Your Honor. There is no way Mrs. Hartway can be expected to know what someone else's thinking might be—"

"Your Honor," Donald Spangler interrupted, "I believe that is a very fair supposition to ask the witness to make. She and her husband went to see Dr. Stallings and I'm sure they both must have had some expectation as to how the doctor would regard them. I just want to know if it is reasonable to assume that Dr. Stallings had to think they both wanted help for Mr. Hartway's condition when they first walked into his office. That's all. I think it's very simple. The witness certainly must know what kind of impression they first gave my client."

Judge Perrine responded promptly.

"Objection overruled. The witness will answer the question."

Once again, Ann looked hopelessly confused. "I don't remember the question."

"Will you please ask the question again, Mr. Spangler?" the judge said.

"Mrs. Hartway, may we assume Dr. Stallings thought you and your husband wanted his help to improve your husband's condition when you first went to his office?"

Ann hesitated and then answered faintly. "Yes."

Donald Spangler stepped back and smiled. "Thank you, Mrs. Hartway." He looked at the jury and then continued.

"Would you agree with me, Mrs. Hartway, that not all surgical operations turn out well? I know neither of us are physicians, but it does seem to be common knowledge that some operations result in complications and death. Is that not so?"

"Yes."

"And is it not so, that when your husband suffered complications after his initial surgery, Dr. Stallings strongly recommended an operative procedure, an amputation to be exact, that would have saved his life, and your husband refused?"

"Yes, but he purposely caused the—"

Donald Spangler lurched forward cutting her short. He raised his right hand in admonition.

"No, Mrs. Hartway, please just answer the questions. I'm sure Mr. Mulcahey will give you every opportunity to make any comments you wish later on, but right now I must insist that you only answer the question, yes or no."

"But I am trying to answer the question. You won't let me."

Judge Perrine leaned forward. "I know you're trying to be helpful, Mrs. Hartway, but the court requires that you answer only what is precisely being asked. Please avoid details unless you're specifically asked for them. Mr. Mulcahey will allow you to clarify anything you want later on but you can't do that now unless Mr. Spangler asks you to. These are very strict rules, and all witnesses must abide by them."

Judge Perrine was clearly being overly solicitous and protective towards Ann, but it was unlikely she could appreciate this. Her composure had been reasonably well-maintained up to this point but now she trembled as the strain began to take its toll. All seemed aware how precarious her condition was, and Donald Spangler appeared concerned he might not be able to finish questioning her before all the allegations had been answered. He looked as though he was reassessing his approach and his tone softened.

"Mrs. Hartway, I just want you to try to remember if it is true that your husband refused to let Dr. Stallings amputate his leg?"

Ann was crying now. Judge Perrine leaned down and asked if she would like a brief recess, but Ann did not answer. He then called for a fifteen-minute recess and Ann was led into his chambers.

Phil was becoming very anxious. Ann had testified for the prosecution as well as could be expected and now he would have liked Gordon to move on to other evidence. Court procedure of course, would not allow that and Donald Spangler was proving himself more than just a temporary annoyance. Whatever confidence there might have been earlier was now waning. At precisely fifteen minutes after the start of the recess, Ann re-entered the courtroom and as soon as the session was called to order, Donald Spangler once again asked the question.

The brief respite seemed to have been of some benefit. Ann now answered clearly in the affirmative. Donald Spangler rephrased the question.

"You're saying, Mrs. Hartway, that Dr. Stallings did offer your husband an operation at the time when he had gangrene of his leg, which would have saved his life, and your husband refused to let the surgery, an amputation, be done?"

"Yes."

Donald Spangler shook his head. His expression was one of doubt and confusion.

He approached the witness stand.

"Mrs. Hartway, I'm going to try to sum up what's been said so far. See if you agree with me. You've told Mr. Mulcahey that Dr. Stallings intended to kill your husband for a certain sum of money and did, in fact, cause that to happen by improperly operating on him in a purposeful and willful manner. You've told me prior to this, both you and your husband went to see Dr. Stallings to obtain his help in making him better and this was the intention that was conveyed to, and recognized by, Dr. Stallings. Later, when his life was at stake, Dr. Stallings recommended surgery that would have saved his life. You've admitted that. Now that doesn't make sense. What you've told Mr. Mulcahey and what you've told me clearly contradict one another. You allege that one man has purposely taken another man's life but what you describe is one man trying to save another man's life. If you think back to everything you've just said, isn't that what you would think too?"

Gordon quickly rose to his feet. "Objection, Your Honor! Mrs. Hartway has already answered that question several times. She's made it quite clear just what she understood Dr. Stallings intended to do. I don't think the question has to be asked again."

"Objection sustained." Judge Perrine's gaze shifted to the defense table. "However, I will allow this line of questioning to continue, gentlemen, as long as I feel it has relevance. You may continue, Mr. Spangler."

"Mrs. Hartway, your husband had gotten another opinion about the problem with his leg before he saw Dr. Stallings, didn't he?"

"Yes."

"And didn't Dr. Stallings agree with that opinion at first, that surgery wasn't really necessary?"

"Yes, in the beginning."

"Wasn't it only after your husband insisted his circulatory problem was interfering with his physical activities that Dr. Stallings finally agreed to operate?"

Ann's voice was weaker and her response more hesitant. "Yes."

"Wasn't he so unhappy with the limitations his condition had caused that both of you felt he should have the surgery, since that was the only way the condition could be improved?"

"He really didn't have to."

Donald Spangler looked confused and glanced at the judge.

"I'm sorry, Mrs. Hartway. I'm not sure I heard what you said."

This time the microphone amplified her response.

"He didn't have to." "Who didn't have to, Dr. Stallings?"

"He didn't have to. It wasn't that bad."

Donald Spangler shook his head in frustration.

"Please, Mrs. Hartway. I must know who you're talking about. Is it Dr. Stallings?"

Ann's head drooped and she seemed to be looking at her hands, which she continuously folded and unfolded in her lap. "It only bothered him when he played tennis. How important was that?" Once again, her voice was barely heard in what was now absolute quiet.

Donald Spangler threw his arms up and then brought his hands together as if in prayer. He leaned forward in Ann's direction.

"Are you talking about your husband, Mrs. Hartway?"

Ann did not answer and to some it seemed she might not even have heard the question.

Donald Spangler turned to the judge.

"Your Honor, I feel I must continue but this is extremely difficult. I really do need the witness's attention. This is a very serious charge and I owe it to my client to properly question this witness."

"I know, Mr. Spangler. We are all learning patience, and I am afraid we will all have to continue to do so, if justice is to be served. Please continue." Judge Perrine leaned towards Ann. "Please try to pay careful attention to Mr. Spangler's remarks, Mrs. Hartway, and answer his questions as best you can."

Ann lifted her head but remained silent. Donald Spangler stared at her very briefly and then walked back to his seat. He picked up a notepad that had been lying on the table and looked very pensive as he glanced through the first few pages. He pursed his lips several times as he continued to read but remained expressionless and finally put down the notepad and returned to the witness stand.

"Mrs. Hartway, I am going to ask you to allow me to preface my next question. I'm sure we would all agree the jury is being asked today if it believes in a series of events as you and Mr. Mulcahey have described them or instead, in some other manner in which these same events could have occurred but without the complicity of my client. I think everyone would also agree, unless there is absolute proof of any allegation, that the jury is going to believe whatever makes the most sense, in other words, whatever is most plausible. I suppose another way to put it is that the jury is less inclined to believe whatever it perceives as the more unlikely explanation, and as that becomes even more absurd and preposterous, so does the jury's acceptance of that become less and less. That brings me to my next question, Mrs. Hartway. You say you indicated to Dr. Stallings you were very unhappy in your marriage. That is correct, isn't it?"

Ann did not answer and gave no indication she either heard or understood the question. It was asked again, this time very slowly and much more deliberately.

"Mrs. Hartway, did you tell Dr. Stallings you had a very unhappy marriage?"

Ann finally answered, "Yes."

"Mrs. Hartway, well over fifty percent of marriages in this country end in divorce. Wouldn't that suggest most marriages are unhappy? Please answer the question."

"Yes, I suppose so."

That response pleased Donald Spangler.

"Well, thank you, Mrs. Hartway," he said and smiled. "So your unhappy marriage shouldn't have surprised Dr. Stallings. Then let me ask you this. Haven't you heard other people make comments, even jokes, about their marriages, both good marriages and bad ones?"

"I have."

"It is a very popular topic with a lot of people. Many comedians have done very well with that subject. You don't have to answer. I'm just elaborating. Then it's quite possible Dr. Stallings had very good reason not to take you seriously when you said that. Could you agree with that?"

"No, that's not true."

"OK That's your answer. Well then, let's talk about divorce. That's a very common occurrence today. Wouldn't you agree that's the standard way to get out of an unhappy marriage today?"

"I suppose so."

"Very good. You never considered that for yourself though, did you?"

Ann was again very slow to respond.

"I thought about it. I just knew it wouldn't be good."

"What wouldn't be good, Mrs. Hartway?"

"I don't know. Everything, I think. What did you ask?"

Phil was becoming very upset. He nudged Mel.

"I don't think she can go on like this."

"Let's just see what happens," Mel said.

Donald Spangler again looked up at the judge and then at Gordon. His frustration was very evident. He let out a deep breath.

"Mrs. Hartway, are you saying a divorce wouldn't have been good?"

"A divorce? There wasn't any divorce."

Donald Spangler shook his head.

"I know, Mrs. Hartway. I know there wasn't any divorce. You went instead to a surgeon to get help with your marital problem." His face quickly tightened. "I'm sorry. Please strike that last sentence from the record."

The judge nodded to the stenographer.

"Mrs. Hartway, please try to answer one simple question for me. You did not think a divorce would be good for you, correct?"

Ann's eyes were closed, but she did answer. "Yes."

"So, if I understand you correctly, Mrs. Hartway, you did not choose to do what everyone else does. You never even explored the possibility of a divorce. All of a sudden, while you're in Dr. Stallings' office, you get this idea that he can help you with your marital problems and remarkably enough, at the very same time, Dr. Stallings is able to sense just what you have in mind and, bingo, the plot is hatched. That's just great. That's what you want the jury to believe?"

He waited for a reply, but it was obvious Ann had not been following him. "That's OK, Mrs. Hartway, you don't have to answer." He stepped back and looked over at the jury. "Let's see if we can't go on to something else. You knew of these alleged activities of Dr. Stallings for a while, but you didn't report him right away, did you?"

"I told someone, not right away".

"But you didn't tell the authorities until after your second operation, did you?"

"I think that's right."

"I don't mean to be indelicate or disrespectful, Mrs. Hartway, but weren't you rather ill at the time and isn't that when you began chemotherapy?"

Once again Ann seemed to falter. Her voice could hardly be heard. An attendant moved the microphone closer. "If you say so. Yes. I think you're right."

"Could we say then, Mrs. Hartway, as a result of your illness or the medications you've been receiving, there may be times when you become confused?"

Ann looked about helplessly. She did not respond.

Donald Spangler studied her carefully.

"I'd like you to answer the question, Mrs. Hartway. Do you ever get confused?"

He waited, but Ann still didn't reply, and he began to walk back to his table. He did not notice that she had begun to cry. His next remarks were delivered while he faced the jury.

"In a moment, Mrs. Hartway, I'm going to ask you just how your husband reacted when he was told he'd have to have an amputation in order to save his life. But first, have you ever been told by a psychiatrist to take Mellaril?"

Just then several gasps were heard from the spectators, and he turned quickly to see Ann slumped forward. Even before an attendant could reach her, she had begun to slowly lift her head.

"Mrs. Hartway, are you all right?"

Her head bobbed up and down. She seemed no longer to have the strength or control to hold herself erect. Two officers gently leaned her back in her chair. She did not appear to be in distress but neither did she appear to be aware of her surroundings. Her breathing was regular, but it was shallow and frequently interrupted by deep breaths and sobs. Gordon rose from his chair and raised his hand.

"Your Honor, may I approach the bench?"

Judge Perrine motioned him forward and a brief conference followed which included Donald Spangler. The judge's gavel signaled the end of the discussion.

"There will be a fifteen-minute recess," he called out and then withdrew to his chambers followed by both attorneys. The jury was led away, and Ann was taken to another room, presumably to rest and possibly to see if she required any medical attention.

Phil remained spellbound by all this. Only after Ann had left the courtroom, was he able to detach himself just enough to try to understand what happened.

"What's going on, Mel? I knew we waited too long. There's no way she's going to be able to continue. Do you think I should go to her?"

"Just stay here."

"Damn! We should have gone earlier, even if it meant we didn't have as good a case."

"The case is going just the way it's supposed to."

"What do you mean?" Phil tried to get Mel to look at him. "Do you know what's going on here?"

"Why don't we wait until Gordon comes back. Then we'll know exactly what's happening."

"Why are you making this so mysterious now? Why can't you tell me what this is all about? Everything just seems to be falling apart."

"I'm not saying anything more, Phil. Let's just wait for Gordon."

Phil was very agitated and could not sit quietly. He knew it would do no good to press Mel further. His mood swung back and forth between bitter disappointment and rage over a feeling of betrayal. Moments later the door to the judge's chamber opened and Gordon walked out into the courtroom and straight to his desk. He looked up only once, precisely at the place where Phil and Mel were sitting. His expression remained completely impassive, except for one brief second when both eyebrows arched and then he looked down and began putting papers into his briefcase.

"That's it," Mel said. "Let's go. It's a mistrial. It's over."

Phil was stunned. "What do you mean? What's over? This session?"

"No. The case is over. Finished. *Finito.* That was it, the whole thing, beginning and end."

Phil could still not fully comprehend what was being said. He made out only bits and pieces of the commotion going on in the courtroom, Donald Spangler crossing to Gordon's table, his face livid, glaring at Gordon, a voice, seemingly disembodied, calling out from the front of the courtroom that the court was adjourned, news people stumbling about, firing questions, recording answers, conjecturing among themselves. He became aware of Mel pulling at his arm.

"Let's get out of here. You'll follow me to my office. Gordon is going to try to meet us there as soon as he can get away. You'll have everything fully explained to you."

Phil stood firm. "What about the rest of the case? What about our witnesses? What about Ann?"

Mel stopped and came right up to his face. "There aren't any witnesses. There never were any. We never did have a case. This was as far as we wanted to go. This was as far as we could go. Now will you please follow me. You can see Ann later. Donna is with her now."

Phil could not remember how he found his car and if he followed Mel or had been able to find the way to his office himself. His thoughts were just too chaotic. He arrived in front of the building just as Mel was getting out of his car. Mel motioned to him to come along and together they made their way to the second floor. Once inside Mel instructed his secretary to have Gordon join them as soon as he arrived but otherwise, they were not to be disturbed.

"I don't know if you can use a real stiff drink now, Phil, or you just look like you can. I know I'm going to have one. Care to join me?"

"No, thanks."

He poured himself a straight scotch and took a healthy slug. The bottle was left on his desk.

"We'll leave that for Gordon." He looked at Phil. "I suppose what you really want is an explanation and you're certainly entitled to one. That's why Gordon wants to be here in spite of all the other explaining he's going to have to do today. He really went out on a limb for you. You, of course, don't realize it but we've always known we didn't have a case, or rather, we didn't have a case we could prove in court. We tried but there was never any way we could get the hard evidence we would've needed for a conviction. I don't think that was anyone's fault. It was just a very, very unique type of crime. We needed Ann just to get through Gordon's examination. After that we wanted her to fall apart as quickly as she could so we could get a mistrial declared. We figured she'd break down under Spangler's cross-examination. It really worked out very well. That's why we had to wait until she was in pretty bad shape. I'm sorry but that was really the only way."

Phil shook his head. "I can't believe what you're saying. All that work. Is that really what happened?"

"Think about it," Mel said. "What would it have sounded like if all the witnesses we called just kept denying one charge after another? Did you really expect any of them to admit to something that would incriminate them? You think their lawyers would have allowed that? And then, after all the character witnesses Spangler would have called—and I might add, many of them would have been your colleagues, how do you think all that would have looked to the jury? Do you think any of those doctors wanted to believe this? Don't forget, whatever Stallings has done reflects on each and every one of those guys. We really couldn't let it get that far."

"And you knew about this the whole time?"

"Yes, I have to say I did. Gordon and I have worked together quite a bit in the past and we respect each other.

"Since I knew you pretty well, he wanted my opinion on this whole thing. It was really the two of us who decided how this thing should be handled. It was very risky, Phil. I don't know if you can appreciate that. The important thing is that both of us believed you and we believed Ann Hartway and we felt we had to take the chance."

Phil sat with his eyes closed, shaking his head from time to time. "Where does this leave us now?"

"In pretty good shape, I think. We made some pretty strong charges in court and never gave Spangler the chance to completely refute them. I don't think the hospital can afford to leave it like that. There's got to be some sort of additional investigation, probably by some high-powered committee and I'll bet it'll be a good one. I don't think they would chance a whitewash. This will finally make them take a hard look at this man's record and take some pretty strong and effective action against him. I can't see it going any other way."

Phil sat quietly a little longer. "I wish I could see it your way but after what you've just told me, I guess I should be glad to settle for that. I honestly thought we had a good chance for a conviction. I really thought this was going to be a real tough, close case."

"I know you did."

"I never really understood this whole thing from the start."

"Oh yes you did, but as a doctor, not as a lawyer."

"I guess so." Phil looked around the room. "Do you think Gordon will still show up?"

"He should. He said he'd stop here on the way to the office. I imagine the news people have him tied up a bit unless the judge is still tearing into him."

"Why is that?"

"Well, he just might think Gordon knew he didn't have much of a case and set all this up. Of course, I have no idea why he'd think that."

"Do you think I should wait?"

"Well, he really did want to speak with you. He was very concerned how you would feel after all this. He didn't want you to think he had let you down."

"I'll wait then. Do you have something to do? I can wait outside."

"No, not really. Let me check with my secretary. I'll be back."

Phil was left longer than he expected. It gave him time to think but there were still many more unsettling questions than answers. He could just imagine how the other doctors were going to react once the news spread. Then there was the explanation he would have to give Maralyn. He dreaded her reaction and it would probably be worse later on with Ann. This had not gone the way he would have liked.

"Went to the bathroom," Mel explained when he finally returned. They sat together for a few more minutes before the door opened again.

"Well, I made it," Gordon said, as he tossed his coat aside and sat down heavily in the nearest chair.

"You want some of this?" Mel asked, pointing to the bottle of scotch.

"I could really use it, but I better not. I still have a number of people to talk to. I'll have enough trouble trying to convince them that I haven't lost my mind, much less that I'm not an alcoholic to boot." He looked at Phil. "How're you doing, Phil? OK?" Before Phil could answer, Gordon turned back to Mel. "Christ, I've never had to do so much fast-talking in all my life. Did you see Spangler? Did you see how red he got? If he had a gun, I swear he would have shot me. Could you hear him while we were in the judge's chambers? Christ, can he yell. By the way, what's a hatchet job?" Gordon winked. "He kept using that expression. Any idea what he was talking about?"

Both men laughed. Phil, as an outsider, did not, but at least now he could understand what they found amusing. Gordon motioned in his direction.

"Did you tell him?"

"Some. I was really waiting for you."

"We really did the best we could, Phil. I know this is not what you expected, and I don't know how much Mel's told you, but we really never did have a chance for a conviction. I knew that the first minute I heard your story. What I didn't know was if I could ever believe it. Well, you convinced me all right. What I had to figure out then was how we could realistically stop this guy. Mel and I went over every conceivable possibility. Of course, we didn't even know we'd get to court until Ann Hartway decided to testify. It was still up in the air until she started looking pretty bad. Then we got this idea. We did interview all those people but we knew they would only do us a lot of harm in court. I guess we both hit on the idea of going for a mistrial about the same time. This way we would get our charges out into the open and not give the very competent Mr. Spangler the opportunity to tear them apart. And he would have, I assure you. Did you hear him today? He's pretty smart. He knew just where to attack our case and he was just getting started. You heard him bring up the Mellaril. By the time I would have gotten a bunch of denials from the witnesses I would have called, and he finished with all his character witnesses, not one single person would have believed us. Not only that, he would have made our defendant look so good we all would have thought we were watching the second coming. The last thing I wanted to do was give this guy the opportunity of coming out of this looking like the next prince of princes. You said it yourself, he's awfully good with words. If he had gotten on the stand, I'm sure he could've made up something that was very convincing and very self-serving. Do you understand what I'm saying?"

"Yes, I think so. Mel has already explained a lot of this."

"Good. I should have figured that. You were taking it too well." Gordon laughed but he quickly became very serious again. "One other thing. If you feel I deceived you, I did so for a very good reason. First of all, I wanted you to keep thinking we had a case so you'd keep digging. Everything you came up with only served to reinforce our belief in this case, and believe me, a lot of us really needed that. There was a lot of skepticism, on everyone's part, and we needed a lot of convincing, which you definitely supplied. We also wanted you to believe we had a case, because we wanted you to act that way. Do you remember how upset you were when you found out someone had leaked your name in connection with this investigation? That was done on purpose."

Phil recoiled in his seat.

"I gave them your name. I guess that surprised you. Look, we needed everything we could get and frankly, once you were known to be involved, I thought he might try to do something to you. Didn't you ever notice the same people at a lot of the places where you'd be? Didn't any of them ever start looking familiar?"

"No. What are you talking about?"

"We had you under surveillance twenty-four hours a day for more than two weeks. I thought if he did that thing to Ann Hartway in the hospital, he might very well try something with you. Who knows? He still might."

Phil looked surprised. "You really mean that? I would never have thought he'd try anything like that."

"Don't be so sure. If I read him right, he's a very calculating individual. I'll bet he thinks of himself as above the system and above everyone else. This was a big put-down for him today. I don't think he's going to try anything with any patients for a long time, but I'll bet he may try to get back at someone else. I think he's that type of person."

"You think I should be worried?"

"Not worried, just aware. Look, I'm sorry we put you in this position, but at the time we thought it was worth taking the risk. The idea was to catch him if he did try something and keep you from getting hurt at the same time. That would have been all we needed. As it turned out, we should have saved the money. The overtime really put a dent in our budget."

Mel caught Gordon's attention. "Do you want to tell Phil about the list of choices we had?"

"Oh, that. No, you tell him. He probably wants to kill me already, as it is."

"Our first choice was a couple of shots fired at you and Gordon's people grabbing Dr. Stallings with the smoking gun in his hand. Second was a knife and third, I believe, was a length of clothesline. After that, we left it up to his ingenuity. We thought we'd let him surprise us."

"You're making it sound pretty funny now, aren't you?" Phil said.

Gordon rubbed his face and yawned. He looked tired. "Yeah, I suppose we are. After a day like today maybe that's just what we should do." He turned towards Phil. "And maybe you should know just exactly what kind of a day I had today. Don't take this personally because I have the utmost respect for you but remember, all this came about because you guys couldn't clean up your own mess. I didn't ask for this. My reputation means everything to me and I didn't have to put it on the line. I didn't have to stand before a judge today who is a really decent person and for whom I have the greatest respect and put up with a tongue-lashing he thought I deserved. I tried to do what I thought was the right thing and this is how it turned out. I know how much this means to you and how you must feel but I also want you to know what it's meant to me, too."

Phil nodded his head. "I know that Gordon. It's been very difficult for all of us. I know how hard you've worked, and I appreciate it. I guess each of us has had to pay a price. I accept it."

"I still want to know how it went with the judge?" Mel asked. "I'd like to know what he really said. Do you think he caught on?"

A smirk came over Gordon's face. "Maybe, in the beginning, until I got him to listen to the tape. I still have to go back but at least he's beginning to see what I was dealing with and he's becoming more sympathetic. He just wants to be sure I really did have a case and I wasn't just bullshitting everyone. I may have to bring Reggie Green down there just to give a little more credence. He was even talking about some sort of reprimand or censure because of my so-called conduct of this case but I think he's gotten off that. It started out very badly, to say the least. He really tore into me about the rules of disclosure. That's all I heard for the first ten minutes."

"Well, we knew that was going to happen. Did he want to know about the other witnesses?" Mel asked.

"I didn't let it get to that. I just told him that Ann Hartway had obviously lost her credibility as a witness and that she was the pivotal point of my case no matter who else I was going to call. So, we really had no choice. He was pretty pissed, but at least he didn't go berserk, like Spangler. I'll bet he must be in some emergency room somewhere. I thought he was going to explode. I purposely didn't look at him when I mentioned the tape. Did either of you see his reaction?"

"We couldn't see that well from where we were sitting," Mel said. "His back was to us the whole time, but it did seem to stir them up a bit."

Gordon looked pleased. "He wasn't going to make an issue of it, not then, anyway. There was no way he was going to let that jury think his client had anything to worry about. I knew I had that one figured right." He pumped a fist in the air.

"What if Ann had surprised you and gotten through today's testimony, then what would you have done?" Phil asked. "You would have had to go on, wouldn't you?"

"Nope," Gordon said. "That's where you would have come in. We would have had to tell you what we were really doing and that evening, you as Ann's doctor would have decided she could no longer continue because of her poor condition. You might even have decided to hospitalize her then. You follow?"

"You didn't miss a thing, did you?"

"Couldn't afford to. I told you, I never like to lose, and I never like to look like an ass. With a mistrial I figure my record is still intact and besides, I really think we got what we went after. I'm sure the hospital will carry out its own investigation of the charges now. It really has to, and once they get a clear look at that man's record his privileges should be pretty severely curtailed, if not revoked. I can't think they'd cover for each other so much that all this would be swept under the table."

"I hope not," Phil said.

"Well, you know them better than I do, but I'd bet on it. They say the wheels of justice turn slowly in our society. Let's see now. Let's say this whole thing took about three hours today. Tried, convicted, and sentenced in just that short amount of time. I'd say that's pretty good, wouldn't you, Mel?"

"The only thing better would have been to find a tree, buy a rope and rent a horse."

"I hate to keep bringing up these things but I'm not as sure about this as you are." Phil said. "What if the hospital doesn't have an investigation? What if it decides it isn't necessary?"

"Well, in that case, I'm sure they'd be ignoring public reaction. If they decide that, I'm certain there will be plenty of letters to the newspapers from concerned individuals who will want these charges looked into before they go to that hospital again. Just so happens I have plenty of friends in the newspaper business who just love to print those kinds of letters. Speaking of those letters, Mel, do you have any of them ready, so I can show Phil, just in case?"

"Damn!" Phil shook his head and laughed.

Gordon stood up smiling. "Still trying to catch me, Phil? Still think there might be something I haven't thought of? Mel, are all your relatives like this? What more do we have to do to prove ourselves to this guy?"

"Nothing as far as I'm concerned," Mel said. "We didn't miss a thing?"

"Where's Ann now?" Phil asked.

"He doesn't stop." Gordon smirked. "Just kidding. She should be home with her nurse, and I also told Donna to stay with her for a little while. I spoke with her before I left but she was very shaky. I don't know how much she understood. I'm really very sorry, Phil, to see what's happened to her. That didn't make it any easier for me, either. I'll try to get to see her again later on, but I know her place will be swarming with news people." He put on his coat. "The three of us should have a drink when this whole thing is over. Right now, there's still a few more people I have to explain things to, particularly my boss. That should be fun, trying to con him." He moved closer to the door. "Are you going to be all right, Phil? I may be able to handle the flak I'm going to get better than you. Do you think you'll have that much trouble at the hospital?"

"I really don't know. I hope not. I know I can forget about some referrals for the time being, but as long as my patients know I've done nothing wrong, they'll keep coming back. I guess I'm something like you. I've had my own rules. I always do everything I can for my patients, and they know that. I should be OK until this blows over."

"Let's hope so," Gordon said. "I'll talk with you guys again soon."

Gordon left and Mel looked over at Phil.

"Are you pretty well squared away with all this?"

"I guess so."

"What are you going to do now?"

"I don't have anything scheduled. I left the rest of the week open because I thought we'd be in court. I guess I'll stop by Ann's and then I'll probably go home and tell Maralyn just what happened. That should be very interesting. She was never in favor of any of this."

Mel got up and walked over to Phil. He put his hand on his shoulder.

"I'm sure she knows you did the right thing. You accomplished a lot today." He escorted Phil from the office. "I'm sure it'll all work out."

The stop at Ann's home was very brief. The TV and news people did not know who he was and the answer that he was a family friend allowed him to get to the front door without being bombarded with questions. Ann had been brought home with her private nurse after it had been determined she was suffering nothing more than exhaustion. She was then given medication prescribed for her by her current oncologist and Phil could see her sleeping soundly in her room. He spoke with the nurse who felt she was doing much better and just needed some rest. He asked her to tell Ann that he had stopped by and would be back again in the morning. She was to call him if she needed him.

Maralyn had been home for several hours when Phil arrived. She had heard about the mistrial on the local TV station, which had interrupted its usual broadcasting. She was clearly very upset.

"It didn't go very well, did it? They said on TV the star witness for the prosecution got sick and that ended the trial. That was it?"

"There's quite a bit more to it than that. A lot of things happened. Now everyone knows about Stanley and what he's been doing to his patients. I know it wasn't proven in court but the important thing is that it will put a stop to it. It wasn't perfect but it accomplished what we wanted."

"You think this was worth it? All the aggravation you always complain about, and now the problems that this will cause? I don't understand you. He's free."

"No, he's not, Maralyn. The hospital has to take some action against him now. They can't leave it like this. This was the only way and you'll see it's going to work. I know how you feel now but give it time. It'll be OK."

Maralyn began to cry, and Phil started towards her but she moved away.

"I can't believe you put us through all this and for what? Look what it did to me when I thought you were having an affair with her. Now it's the worry over what this will do to your practice."

She dabbed at her eyes with a tissue.

"I don't understand you, Phil. Haven't you been saying less money will be coming in because insurance payments are lower now? You told me not to worry because you might be able to make that up with a bigger volume but what's going to happen if you don't get referrals? Isn't that just going to make the problem worse? And you think today makes it worth all that? They've done nothing to him. You had this big trial that you wanted and it's over today before it even started. What did it really do for us, Phil, you, me, the kids? You really thought about us? I don't think so and you can't say you got anything good out of this. Those TV cameras were all over Stanley when he walked out of the courthouse, and I've never seen anyone smile so much."

Phil wasn't going to argue any more. "OK, Maralyn, I can't convince you you're wrong. Let's just see what happens." Maralyn reached for her handbag and took out her car keys. "I have to pick up the girls at the library and we'll probably have something to eat while we're out. There's food in the refrigerator if you're hungry." As she walked towards the door, she asked, "Did you ever do anything about Dr. McAleer and the position at University Hospital?"

"Not yet. I'm waiting to see what happens. It's definitely there if I want it." He heard the door close while he was still speaking.

XVI

Phil had little reason to be seen at the hospital over the next few days. He hadn't scheduled any surgery and most of his patients had been discharged. Sentiment there was running very much in Dr. Stallings' favor. Phil had seen some interviews on TV and read others in the newspapers. No one gave any credence to the charges. Stallings and his lawyer railed at the outcome. In no way could they be pleased. The district attorney had been deceitful and had used very questionable tactics depriving them of the complete vindication they knew was a certainty. All those interviewed after the trial were in agreement.

Gordon was very terse in his comments to the press. He was also very disappointed, more so than anyone else. His case rested on one person's testimony and unfortunately that person could not continue. He took responsibility but didn't think he should be faulted for that. The charges had merit. Only the administration refused comment. The entire matter was under review.

Phil had more time to spend with Ann. Gordon had tried to explain what happened before they left the courthouse and Donna tried again later at home, but Ann was just too exhausted. It wasn't until the following day when she was more rested and alert that she understood there had been a mistrial. Even though it was repeatedly explained why everyone was satisfied with the outcome, Ann was disconsolate. She had clearly come to believe Stanley Stallings would be convicted. Anything less could not be accepted and no matter what was said to her, she remained very dejected. Phil considered tranquilizers or mood elevators but in her weakened condition he did not want to medicate her any further. She also decided not to have the private duty nurse any longer in spite of everyone's misgivings.

Phil knew he would have to get back to the hospital soon. He was extremely concerned about the attitude of the staff. Anticipating their reaction had become much more difficult for him than he had expected.

He had his office schedule an admission late in the week. Just by chance, the first person he saw was Gary Barlow.

"You still work around here, fella?"

"Hi, Gary. You can still say that. I've just been keeping a low profile."

"I would say so. This is the first time I've seen you."

"I haven't been in. This turned out to be a pretty light week."

"Yeah, sure. When are we going to cut the bullshit and start talking seriously? I just heard something I'm sure you'll be very interested in."

"Yes? What's that?"

"Your good friend, Stanley Stallings, is about to have his privileges suspended. He doesn't know it yet. Buddy Humboldt was just in administration throwing his weight around. As hospital president and chairman of the board of directors, he put it on the line. Any questions about our Stanley have to be cleared up once and for all. He was very serious and since he's the leading contributor to this hospital, I guess he's got everyone else serious too. He wants an impartial panel of outside surgeons to come in here and review each and every case Stanley's ever done in this hospital. He says the hospital's reputation is at stake and with his name plastered all over it, so is his. He says Stanley should not be allowed to operate until the panel makes its report."

"Where did you hear this?"

"In administration. I had to pick something up there and I had to wait while they were getting it together. That kind of pissed me off, but then I heard this whole thing. You know Buddy. He doesn't care who's around when he wants to make a point. He'd even take a crap in the middle of Main Street if that's where he got the urge. But he probably owns that too, so that wouldn't really surprise anyone."

Phil slowly began to smile.

"You're serious?"

"Damn right. I heard it no more than fifteen minutes ago."

"I've been thinking just the opposite. I thought Stanley was doing OK Everyone seemed to be for him."

"No. That's just us. I think administration and the board have been hearing other things. It sounded like they were going to do that anyway, even before Buddy came barging in. Maybe they just wanted him to think that. Who knows? I knew you'd be interested. You've been trying for this for a long time now, haven't you? I don't know how much you figure in all this, especially that trial, but somehow, I have the feeling you deserve congratulations." He reached out and shook Phil's hand.

"Could you imagine having my old chief and your chief on that panel? Stanley wouldn't stand a chance. I don't think he'd ever touch a knife again." Gary thought for a moment. "Maybe you'd better not say anything to anyone about this until the word gets around a little more. Let somebody else pass the word."

Phil laughed. "Who am I going to tell?"

"You're right. That wouldn't exactly be a good public relations move for you right now. But that'll blow over. Whatever you did was the right thing. They'll realize it. Just give them time."

"Thanks, Gary. I appreciate this very much."

"No sweat. Just let me know when you're ready to give me a hand again. See you."

Phil was very pleased. In spite of Gordon and Mel's optimism, he had begun to think Dr. Stallings might emerge unscathed. To many, he was a much maligned and much more sympathetic figure. It could even have meant a sanction of all he had done.

His first thought was to call Ann Hartway but then he decided he'd wait until later. He had several errands and additional office work that would take most of the afternoon, and he planned to stop at her house before going home. There didn't seem to be any problems with his patient, and he decided not to make afternoon rounds. It even looked as though he'd finish ahead of schedule when a call came from the emergency room to see two of his patients who had been in a motor vehicle accident. Although neither was seriously hurt and they were later allowed to return home, it wasn't until seven p.m. that he finished everything else and was ready to leave for Ann's house. Then he received a call to please check his patient, Mrs. Tillinghast, on 3 Main. The nurse didn't think it was terribly urgent, but the patient didn't seem to look as well as she had earlier. Maybe he'd like to see her now rather than be called later. The hospital wasn't that much out of his way, so Phil was back there a short time later. He was changing into his lab coat in the doctor's lounge when he heard his name called.

"Hello, Phil. You're right on time."

Phil looked across the lounge. Very few of the lights had been left on. He hadn't noticed anyone else when he first walked in and the voice took him by surprise.

"I didn't see you sitting there."

"I didn't think you had. You really don't have to rush to see your patient. I can assure you she's actually quite all right."

"What are you talking about, Stan? I have to go upstairs."

"Yes, I know. I had the nurse place the call to you. I wanted to speak with you, and I thought this was the best way to get you here."

"You had me called?"

"That's what I just said. I told the nurse your patient might be having a problem and that it probably would be a good idea to call the woman's doctor. That's Mrs. Tillinghast you've come to see, right? I know you're not going to believe me, so see for yourself. I can wait."

The light was dim in that corner and Phil could not make out his expression.

"What are you trying to pull, Stan? I don't think any of this is very funny."

"It's not meant to be funny."

"Then I really don't know what you're waiting for. There's nothing we have to discuss."

"If you give that a little thought, Phil, I'm sure you'll realize you don't really mean that. Why don't you see your patient, so you'll have a clear mind. I'll wait for you right here."

"Suit yourself." Phil started for the door. "I don't know what you think this is going to accomplish. I think this is pretty stupid."

"I'm sure that's what you're going to think. See your patient, Phil. I'm trying to help both of us."

"I'll bet you are."

He left to see his patient and it was just as Dr. Stallings had said. She was perfectly fine and yes, it was he who had suggested to the nurse that she make the call. Phil really didn't know what he should do next. He returned to the lounge and found Dr. Stallings still seated on the couch.

"So, what now?"

"Well, wasn't it just like I told you? She's fine, isn't she? Now if I was really the type of person some people think, wouldn't you have expected me to do something drastic to get you back here, something with her IV perhaps?"

"I don't find that very funny, Stan."

"Forgive me, Phil. You're right. That's not anything to joke about. I just wanted to show you how you can be wrong about me. I've gone through a lot of trouble to get you here, so I would like a little of your time now. I'd like us to go someplace where we can speak privately. I think it's very important and I'm sure you will, too. You won't be disappointed, I promise you." There weren't any smiles now and he seemed very sincere.

"I still don't see the point in any of this."

Dr. Stallings moved to the edge of his seat.

"There's been a tremendous misunderstanding here. This is really going to hurt the two of us and for no good reason."

"That's not the way I see it."

"Maybe if you listened to me, you might see it another way."

Phil stood silently for a moment. "I don't want to have any discussions with you, Stan. What's going to happen now is up to the others, not me. Anything you have to say to me is going to be a waste of time. If that's why you got me here, forget it." He was very brusque as he stood up. "I'm late and I really have to leave."

Dr. Stallings frowned. "I'm sorry you feel that way, Phil. I really hoped you'd be more reasonable. I think you would have wanted to hear what I have to say."

He still hadn't moved from his chair. He leaned back and wasn't even looking in Phil's direction now.

"Maybe I know some things about Ann Hartway that you don't." Phil stopped abruptly.

"What are you saying?"

"Nothing that I care to discuss here. It's just that you may not know everything you should. Maybe this will surprise you but it really shouldn't. You know we weren't exactly strangers. We got to know each other pretty well when I was taking care of her husband."

Phil stared at him angrily.

"What are you suggesting now, Stan? What kind of crap is it this time?"

"Calm down, Phil. I told you, you don't know everything but I'm not going to talk about it here. If you want to continue this conversation, what I am suggesting is that we go back to my office." He leaned forward again but didn't attempt to get up, waiting instead for Phil's answer.

"I don't trust you, Stan. As far as I'm concerned, you're always trying to pull something. What kind of garbage are you trying to feed me now?"

"Well, you're not going to find out this way, are you, Phil? All you have to do is come back to the office with me and then you'll have all your answers. You'll see. I'm not playing any games with you. This is too important for the both of us. I also have something to show you, something Ann left with me, but that's it. I'm not talking about it here any more."

Phil glared at him. "Ann? Now it's Ann?" There wasn't any answer.

"How long is this going to take?"

"Not very long," Dr. Stallings said as he stood up. "I know this is going to change everything you've been thinking. Are you coming to my office?"

This was the last thing Phil wanted to do, but it was just a short ride to his office.

After all he had said, he felt he could no longer refuse.

"Against my better judgment. Yes, I'll go to your office."

Dr. Stallings finally smiled. "Great! You won't be sorry." Then his expression changed. "I have just one more favor to ask of you. I need a lift. I left my car at the office and walked here for the exercise, but I forgot I have to bring this back." He reached down beside his chair and lifted a rather large instrument case. "It's not that heavy but it's a pain to carry all the way back to my office. It's my colonoscope. The focusing mechanism is off and I have to send it out to be repaired. You don't mind, do you?" His smile returned. "We are going to the same place."

"What if I did, Stan? Would it make any difference? Come on. I'm right outside." Dr. Stallings slipped the instrument case behind the front seat and then got into Phil's car. It was no more than a five-minute ride and Phil stopped in front of the building. All the lights were off and it appeared no one was still there.

"Where do you want me to park?"

"Why not around the back, next to my car."

Phil swung around the building. At first, the parking lot looked completely empty.

"Where's your car?"

Dr. Stallings pointed to a darkened area under some trees at the other end and Phil pulled into the adjoining space.

"Perfect," Dr. Stallings said. "We can come out through that door, but we have to go in through the entrance over there." He motioned to their left, towards the middle of the building. Phil grimaced and followed him inside.

The only light was from the exit signs and Phil had to be careful as he climbed the stairs behind Dr. Stallings. He felt better when the lights in the hall were turned on and they were in his office. Phil looked around. It was many years since the last time he was here but there didn't seem to be any changes as he remembered it. Dr. Stallings very graciously directed him into the consultation room and asked him to wait while he went into another room. Phil was about to sit down when he noticed a syringe lying on the floor near Dr. Stallings' desk and carefully picked it up.

"Are you in the habit of leaving syringes around, Stan?"

"You found that thing? Where was it? I'll have to tell you about that." He appeared in the doorway. "Let me take that from you and get rid of it now."

He took the syringe, avoiding the needle, and went back into the other room. A moment later he called out again. "I know you want to get started, Phil, but you have to give me another couple of minutes. I meant to bring some papers up from my car and you know what else?" He was back in the doorway again. "We forgot my colonoscope in your car. Let me have your keys for a second and I'll be right back up."

Phil made little effort to hide his impatience and disgust and reached into his pocket and tossed the keys over to him.

"Thanks. You wait right here. It's pointless for the two of us to go downstairs." With that, he was gone, and Phil took a long, deep breath and sat down to wait. Moments later Dr. Stallings was back, slightly winded, but with colonoscope and papers in hand.

"See. That wasn't so bad." He put down the papers and instrument case and handed back the keys. Then he settled into his chair. "I had to bring those papers up now. My secretary would have killed me if I had forgotten them one more time. Anyway, I apologize. That's all taken care of and now we have some very important matters to discuss."

He rested an arm on his desk and smiled. He seemed very relaxed now.

"I really came here to listen to what you have to say about Ann Hartway," Phil said. "I'm not really interested in anything else, and you said this wouldn't take long."

"I'll get to that. Are you in that much of a rush? I want you to hear something else first. I'm sure it'll make you understand this whole thing a lot differently." He slowly revolved a slight turn in his chair.

"Please try to bear with me. I'll tell you right now I know you were working with the district attorney. I know you were helping him while he was trying to build this case against me. So does everyone else."

He looked at Phil.

"At least you're not trying to deny that now. I appreciate that. Besides whatever I might have been told, I'll tell you how else I know. Only a doctor, a surgeon, could have come up with all this. It might also surprise you that I don't really hold you responsible and I'm not really angry with you. I know how you got involved, and once you did, anyone who knows you could have expected this. I'll admit there are times though, when I think I should be trying to find a way to hurt you just like you've hurt me. But that's not my nature. Actually, that was a damned good analysis of those cases, if that's what someone had in mind." He studied Phil very closely for a brief moment. "You don't think that was part of a confession, do you? I was watching your expression. At least I see I'm not boring you.

"Frankly, how anyone could have expected to prove that is something I'll never understand."

He paused momentarily and shook his head.

"Anyway, I want to go back to when you first came out here to practice. I want you to know at the time I was very impressed, so much so that I said to myself, if anyone was going to be real competition, it wasn't going to be the others who were already here. It was going to be you. Let's face it. You came out of a very good program, you had the ability, you were very personable, good appearance, you had all the qualities. And that's not to say you haven't done well. But after a while I began to see something else and that something else made me wonder just how successful you really would be. You're going to think I sound foolish but I'm talking about your sense of ethics, your moral righteousness that affects everything you do and the way you look at whatever anyone else does. You always try to be so terribly precise. You may think that's a wonderful quality but how many doctors do you think want to work with someone who watches every decision they make, waiting to see if some self-conceived set of scruples is being violated? It's too much. Either you never learned that, or it doesn't make any difference to you."

Phil had listened to every word.

"I can't buy that, Stan. I think that's quite an exaggeration."

"Not to me and I assure you, not to a lot of others, too. I feel very certain that's had an awful lot to do with all these charges that were made against me. I'll admit I'm partly to blame and I'll get to that in just a minute, but why didn't anyone else come up with these cases? Come on, Phil. I know you did. No one else thinks the way you do."

A smirk crept across Phil's face.

"So now *I'm* to blame? I'm the one who caused all this?"

"No, I didn't say that. I just said I'm partly to blame. I never realized how all this could look to someone else. There's no question. I did make a lot of mistakes. I thought I could help all these people. I really did. I don't like to give up. I honestly thought their conditions deserved some sort of attempt. I see now that it looks pretty bad charging what I did but let me tell you something. These people were all high risk. They came to me and that's what I thought it should be worth to them. You've seen what's happened to reimbursements. Medicare payments are way down, and you can't even bill the full balance even if they have good secondary coverage. People are joining HMOs left and right and they're paying peanuts. How about your expenses? Have they gone down? Aren't you having trouble keeping up? Everyone else I talk to says they're having problems. Try collecting money these days. If these people are willing to pay, I say that's just fine. What I charged them is what we should be getting."

He watched Phil's reaction.

"This isn't a problem for you?" He shook his head. "Man, you really are holier-than-thou, aren't you?"

He kept looking at Phil a little while longer.

"How about all the trauma cases that we treat? We bust our tails night and day to pull those patients through and we only get what some fee schedule allows, a few dollars here, a few dollars there. Some lawyer comes along and settles the case by shuffling a few papers and making a few court appearances and he takes a third of the award. What's that sometimes, a few hundred thousand, a million? For the same case, we wind up with one or two thousand, and that's if we get paid. Some system, huh? OK, I guess I'm not going to be the one to change it. It was my mistake but it's not the way the district attorney made it look. That's what we should be getting for the work we do, but we're just too damned humble."

"You really want me to believe this, don't you, Stan? That's fine, but I remember listening to your ideas about health care and controlling costs. At the time, you said something about how you'd treat patients, too."

"What are you talking about?"

"That time in the surgical lounge, when Gary was joking about culling the population."

"Oh, that. I remember. What did you think, you heard some terrible admission?" He was smiling now. "I've wondered what someone might make of that. You can't be serious. That was just a meaningless discussion. If it was so important, how come the district attorney didn't use it at the trial?" He laughed. "Don't you have any idea how ridiculous you sound?"

"I also remember when you asked me how Ann was doing after her surgery and that night she almost bled to death when someone disconnected her IV. I suppose you still want me to say I'm being unfair if I think you did that, even though you were seen on the floor right before it happened, at two in the morning. Not one other doctor is around at that hour, but you are. I know. It's just some more of that innuendo stuff. Can't be anything to it, right?"

"You know what happened and you know damn well I got that call to go to the emergency room. My lawyer checked that out. The answering service has a record of the call. You know I didn't make that up. Haven't you ever gotten calls like that and the patient never showed up?"

"A man called and that could have been you."

Dr. Stallings threw his hands up.

"You're going to keep twisting this around no matter what explanation I give. You're not giving me any chance at all. You just don't want to believe me, do you?"

"Stanley, you were seen on the floor just before it happened! You know what those connections are like. It didn't disconnect itself."

Dr. Stallings spoke very deliberately.

"You know why I was up there. I went to see patients while I was waiting for this other person to show up in the emergency room. That's not unreasonable. It's also not unreasonable to think of some other way the line could have come apart. Maybe it wasn't put together properly. Don't you think that's more likely than someone trying to kill your patient? I'll bet that's what the jury would have thought if the trial had gotten that far."

His expression changed now. He gritted his teeth.

"That was a pretty lousy trick, by the way. My lawyer told me what you tried to do, sorry, what the district attorney tried to do. You and your friends really tried to screw me, Phil. I hope you realize that. I should be very bitter. How could you have possibly thought you could prove those charges?"

"That was the district attorney. He must have thought he could."

"My lawyer doesn't think so. He thinks it was a set-up. He says he was very lucky to get away with it this time."

"Isn't that what you'd expect him to say?"

"Yes, I most certainly would, because that's exactly what you tried to do."

"Why do you say it's what I tried to do?"

Stallings remained silent for a moment and then bent forward. He put his face in his hands, then took them away and stared at the floor. After a little while, he lifted his head. Phil watched his every movement.

"This isn't getting us anywhere. I really hoped you might see things a little differently, but I can see your mind's made up. I was going to make a suggestion, Phil, but I doubt very much you want to hear it. I was going to say no matter how either of us feels about this situation, one thing is very clear. Both of us are going to be hurt, probably a lot more than we have already. I know my reputation has been very badly damaged and you have an awful lot of your colleagues very angry with you.

"We can still help each other and we're both going to need that. I think if we're seen having a little more to do with each other at the hospital, it'll mean something to all the others. They'll probably realize we've agreed it was just a very unfortunate mistake. It doesn't have to be a big change at the start. I think if we just help each other with an occasional case and then let it build from there, they'll see we're trying to put this whole thing behind us. That could be a tremendous benefit for us. No one is going to hold it against you if you show them that you were just misled by your patient. I can even help by saying that I probably should have handled some of these cases a little differently. I've already admitted that to you. Don't you understand what I'm trying to say?"

"I'd rather wait to see what happens," Phil said. "I understand what you're saying, but it's not up to me to change what the others are going to think."

Dr. Stallings tone was more frantic.

"But don't you see what this is going to do? These charges are ridiculous. It just shows you that anything can be made to sound any which way you want. This woman is going to wind up destroying us. She isn't even well. This is a sick, deluded mind that's made all this up. She was even seeing a psychiatrist and taking Mellaril, for God's sake! She's probably feeling all sorts of guilt, and this is what's come of it. It would never have been proven if they had been able to finish the trial. Everyone knows that. Why should I come out of this being treated as if I'm guilty?"

Phil was losing his patience.

"Stanley, you know the answer to that just as well as I do. You're just going to have to do the same as me, wait and see what happens. Remember, no matter what you're telling me now, you brought this on yourself. I don't have to say any more than that. You know what I'm talking about."

Dr. Stallings did not reply but just sat motionless, eyes downward, staring blankly.

"Stan, you said you had something to tell me about Ann Hartway. Are you going to get to that, or should I just leave?"

He slowly straightened. There seemed to be a need to clear his head. He shook it several times.

"You're not going to like the way this is going to end. It's going to hurt you."

"You're not threatening me, are you?"

"No. I would never do that."

He opened his desk drawer.

"You didn't believe me when I told you this woman could hurt us. I meant it. She was here today."

Phil's eyes widened.

"Poor thing, she was so weak she could barely walk in here. I couldn't understand half the things she was trying to say. She kept trying to get something out of her purse. I finally went over and helped her. Do you know anything about these things?" He took a small silver-colored pistol from inside his desk drawer and held it between two fingers. "I don't."

"Oh, my God," Phil said.

"See what I mean. Who knows what else she's capable of with her mind the way it is. She could even turn on you and I bet she wouldn't even know she was doing it."

"Where is she now?"

Stallings didn't answer. He looked for a place for the pistol but then put it in his jacket pocket.

"Where did she go? And what are you doing with that?"

"Taking it with me when we leave. I can't keep it here. I'll get rid of it someplace." He saw Phil's expression.

"What do you want me to do? Put it back in the drawer? Do you want to hold it?"

Phil shook his head.

"You're worried about Ann?"

"Yes."

"She's OK A little agitated, but that's understandable. I know what she's been through. I think she was even feeling a little better when she left."

"Do you know where she went?"

He leaned back and sighed.

"I can't convince you. You're still worried about her. One of these days I think you'll realize, Phil, I'm probably the most harmless person you'll ever know."

"OK Just tell me. Where is she now?"

"I don't know. I guess she's home. I offered to call a taxi for her but either someone was waiting for her, or she had something else arranged. She made it very clear she didn't want my help."

"When was this?"

"Just before I was ready to leave. Everyone else was gone and she just caught me. Then I thought I'd better get in touch with you right after she left. I think you can see, Phil, I don't want to make things any worse. I could really make trouble for her now, but there's been enough of that. I hope that tells you something."

Phil was barely listening now. "How was she when she left?"

"I just told you. She was better. I gave her some valium. I think that probably helped."

"You did what?"

"I gave her some valium. What are you getting so excited about? It was i.m., just 5 milligrams. It'll hardly touch her."

Phil remembered the syringe.

"She's too weak! You gave her that and then let her leave?"

"What did you expect me to do, keep her here? She wanted to shoot me. That valium probably kept her from going off the deep end again."

Phil quickly rose to his feet. "I've got to get over to her. I had no idea this was what you were going to tell me."

Dr. Stallings shrugged. "Well, I don't know what else you might have thought. What other impression did you think I was trying to give you? She certainly has never had a very high regard for me."

Then he got up too and began to come from behind his desk. At the same time one of the outer doors of the office could be heard to open and close.

"Are you expecting someone?"

There was a blank look on Dr. Stallings' face.

"I don't think so." Both men stood fast. Someone knocked softly on the door. Dr. Stallings looked at Phil before calling out to the person to enter.

Phil took several steps back but stopped immediately when he saw it was a middle-aged woman.

"Oh, Helen, it's you." Dr. Stallings suddenly struck his forehead with his hand. "For God's sake, you know I totally forgot. I have to apologize, Helen. You know my secretary, don't you, Phil?"

The woman looked puzzled and barely acknowledged Phil. "You just spoke with me no more than a half-hour ago, Dr. Stallings. You said you had those papers and wanted to go over them with me. You mean you really forgot?"

Dr. Stallings looked embarrassed.

"I really did, Helen. I'm sorry. Dr. Berger and I were talking, and I've had so many other things on my mind."

The woman looked at him with disbelief. She was crushed. "You don't know what I went through to get here. I left George in the middle of dinner and told him to help himself. He's going to be furious when I get home."

"What else can I say, Helen? I really can't go through this now. Dr. Berger and I were just leaving. Put yourself down for whatever time you want and apologize to George for me. I'm really very sorry. There's just no way I can do any work now."

He ushered everyone into the reception area.

"You'll come down with us now. Where did you park your car?"

"Near yours," she said with some annoyance. "Why did you pick the darkest spot behind the building? I've never seen you park there before."

"I guess I wasn't thinking. There's a door right there, but I must have forgotten for the moment. You can't get in that way, anyway."

Phil couldn't listen to this any longer. "I really must be leaving now," he said.

"Yes, of course."

Dr. Stallings directed them to the door. A moment later they filed through the rear exit and walked to their cars, which were directly ahead. Phil wasted no time and was about to pull away when he heard tapping on his side window. He saw Dr. Stallings leaning down.

"Wait a minute, Phil. You left your trunk open. I'll close it for you."

Phil couldn't remember having done that. He looked back to see Dr. Stallings lift the trunk to slam it shut, but it stayed open.

"My God, what is this?" he heard him yell. "Phil!"

Phil had already begun to get out of his car.

"Helen, do you see this? I think there's a body in the trunk. Look, there's a syringe. My God, it looks like it's Ann Hartway! Phil, this is horrible!"

The words rang in his ears as Phil approached the rear of the car. He looked into the trunk and saw the dark, motionless form. Slowly, sickeningly, the realization took hold. He could still hear Stanley Stallings speaking but the words were meaningless. He could do nothing else but continue staring into the trunk. He could not look up. He knew whatever his expression was, Stanley Stallings was smiling.

CPSIA information can be obtained
at www.ICGtesting.com
Printed in the USA
BVHW042255120623
665865BV00004B/29

9 781800 164741